RJ BAILEY

SAFE FROM HARM

SIMON & SCHUSTER

London · New York · Sydney · Toronto · New Delhi

A CBS COMPANY

First published in Great Britain by Simon & Schuster UK Ltd, 2017
A CBS COMPANY

Copyright © RJ Bailey 2017

3 5 7 9 10 8 6 4 2

Simon & Schuster UK Ltd
1st Floor
222 Gray's Inn Road
London WC1X 8HB

www.simonandschuster.co.uk

Simon & Schuster Australia, Sydney
Simon & Schuster India, New Delhi

A CIP catalogue record for this book
is available from the British Library

PB ISBN: 978-1-4711-5716-5
eBook ISBN: 978-1-4711-5718-9
TPB ISBN: 978-1-4711-5717-2

Typeset in Sabon by M Rules
Printed and bound by CPI Group (UK) Ltd, Croydon, CR0 4YY

Simon & Schuster UK Ltd are committed to sourcing paper
that is made from wood grown in sustainable forests and support the Forest
Stewardship Council, the leading international forest certification organisation.
Our books displaying the FSC logo are printed on FSC certified paper.

For Lisa Baldwin,
PPO extraordinaire,
and 'Maddy'

We are looking for an experienced Female CPO/PPO/Driver OR an experienced Driver with a knowledge of security for our clients in North London. (The candidate gender restriction is due to cultural reasons.)

You will be driving the new Rolls-Royce Ghost and MUST have previous experience driving luxury cars.

- SIA accreditation essential.
- You will be driving a young mother with one child who is schooled in London, with occasional duties for the father.
- Your contracted hours are Monday–Friday 0730–1800 during school term times, with alternate weekends (flexibility essential).
- 2–5 days at a time during the summer may be spent in Monte Carlo with possible short trips in the winter months to St Moritz.
- To apply for this role you must have a London base and be flexible to adapt to the family and their needs.

Advertisement in *Personal Security* magazine

PART ONE

ONE

There is a man coming to hurt us. Probably more than one man. Two or three, perhaps. Not four. They won't need four to deal with us. After all, we are trapped down here. There is no way out from this cold, concrete shell. We are crouched in the dark, dozens of feet below ground. The power to this level has been cut. There is no phone signal. Which is mostly irrelevant because my phone is almost out of battery. What I do have is two broken fingers on my left hand. The pain is making me sweat.

I slide my good hand into my T-shirt and find the knife wound I have picked up. It is long and shallow and oozing along its length. Lucky there was some Kevlar fabric under there to deflect the full force of the blade. Otherwise it would have been game over. As it is, the wound is a couple of points to the opposition.

It can't be long now. I reach out with my right arm and stroke her warm skin, trying to reassure, but she recoils at my touch. She blames me for all this. She's right. It's my fault we ended up down here. What had I been thinking?

In the army they told me about controlling the battle space. That firefights had to be undertaken on your own terms, not the enemy's. I had to admit, I'd lost control of the battle space. I'd lost control of everything.

SIT-REP, as we used to say, AGTOS. Situation Report: All Gone TO Shit.

Someone once tried to explain to me why football is so endlessly fascinating to its fans. It was all to do with unpredictability and consequences, he said. If you studied any match closely, you could trace how one bad pass, a missed tackle, a fluffed corner, a reckless clearance or an untrapped ball could, after seven, ten, fifteen further moves, be responsible for a crucial goal. It was, I suppose, a version of that old trope about a butterfly flapping its wings and causing a hurricane, albeit somewhat more prosaic. But I got the drift: the most insignificant event can have momentous consequences down the line.

It had some relevance to the way the dominoes had fallen in my life. At least, I have come to think of them as toppling dominoes, when in fact it was a pile-up of unrelated events that only in hindsight appeared to display some sort of logic. It was an attack of cystitis, of all things, that got me my dream assignment. That sent me on my way to America. Far from home. It was everyday female biology that brought my daughter back from her friend's house that day.

And it was a can of baked beans that killed my husband.

Ocean Spray giveth, Heinz taketh away. That was the beginning of the sequence of events that led us here, to a crepuscular, subterranean garage. It's not fair. But neither, so they tell me, is football.

I can hear voices now, echoing down the enormous lift shaft that will bring the men to us. Then the whoosh of air, the ding of a bell, a muffled warning ('Doors Closing'), the soft whirr of very expensive, very well-maintained machinery, with its own power supply, as the industrial-sized lift descends. They are coming.

TWO

Twenty months earlier

Like most people on The Circuit – the ad-hoc and often fractious fellowship of Personal Protection Officers worldwide – I am very good at packing. I take a modular approach, with the commonest essentials already encased in plastic sleeves in my wardrobe to be laid into the suitcase in the appropriate order. And there is always a Ready To Go pack, too, filled with the tools of my trade – spare batteries, travel plug, solar charger, camera, lightweight jacket, wash kit, broad-spectrum antibiotics, a supply of various currencies, tampons and a first-aid kit with haemostatic packs. This time, though, the packing seemed to be getting away from me.

When I had first tossed the Tumi suitcase on the bed and unzipped it, the inside had seemed cavernous. Now, after placing in the jeans, day and evening dresses and the one-piece Chloe jumpsuit (what Paul called my *Mission Impossible To Get Into* outfit), it seemed to be imploding like something out of Stephen Hawking's imagination. The black hole of the interior was definitely shrinking.

'I'm going to need a bigger suitcase,' I shouted, looking at the pile of clothes still on the bed. I don't usually bother with hold luggage when I'm flying and working, but at least two of the travelling party were putting suitcases in the belly of the beast and that removed any advantage of carry-on.

'What have you got?'

I turned to look at Paul, my husband, who was pulling on a waxed cotton jacket over a shirt and jeans.

'What's this? Dress-down Tuesday?' I asked.

He shrugged and smiled, his eyes crinkling. On me, those lines just looked like age. On him, they looked cute. He was more than ten years older than me – he could see the forces of fifty massing on the hills for an attack and his hair was now evenly balanced between dark and grey – but I couldn't help feeling that, by some freak of nature, I was busy catching up with him.

'How much have you got on?' he repeated.

'One reception, one lunch, two dinners,' I recited. 'Two cocktail parties and a fundraiser. Plus two TV shows and a radio. Dressy was the word that came down from on high.'

'I hear they have shops in America,' he said, snaking his arms around my waist.

'I hear that too,' I said, unwrapping his hands. 'It's

7

time I won't have.' I gave a sigh, thinking about the next five days and the plans that had crumbled to dust before our very eyes when the work call came for me. 'I can't believe we managed to lose Jess for a whole week and Elena for five days of those and here I am packing for the States.'

Elena was our au pair, who was heading home to Estonia to see her family. Paul turned me, stepped in close and gave me a quick darting kiss on the cheek before leaning back. I caught a hint of the Tom Ford I had bought him for Christmas. 'We could always ...'

I knew that look. Paul was no different from every other man.

'Let's be clear, dear,' I said quickly. 'There's no chance of one last fuck in case my plane goes down so you can always remember me that way. Have a wank on me.' That didn't come out quite like I intended, so I put a finger to his lips.

Those eyes crinkled again. 'Shields up already?'

He was referring to my psychological barriers, which come down to block out all extraneous emotions when I'm working. Nothing, apart from the job in hand, gets through to me. I'm hardly alone in that. How can a nurse work with dying people all day long and still function? How do firemen face the next day after carrying an asphyxiated child from a house? What about the cops who have to trawl through some depraved bastard's computer looking at ...

We all have shields. And Paul was right. Mine were already clicking into place.

'Yup.'

I disentangled myself with a slight reluctance and looked at the case again.

'Do you really need three pairs of shoes?' he offered.

'Trainers and two flats.' I'm lucky to be tall enough to get away with flats, even at the formal dinners. I have colleagues on The Circuit who swear by heels with scored soles for grip. Not me. If I have to run, I want something on my feet that won't snap and that sticks to the floor like octopus suckers. It's why I tend to favour floor-length clothes for formal events, just in case someone wonders why I'm not in needle-heeled Louboutins like everyone else. 'And if that's the best you've got, I'll figure this out myself. Get going.' I looked him up and down. 'Where you off to anyway?'

He wouldn't be wearing such a casual outfit if he were heading for the Civil Nuclear Constabulary HQ near Oxford. He'd be in either a dark suit and tie or full CNC uniform, depending on the occasion.

'A few house calls to make. And I've got to pop in at St John's Wood on the way.'

He said it matter-of-factly, but I knew what St John's Wood meant. A weapon was to be drawn. It was my turn to step in close. 'Is there trouble?'

Paul shook his head. 'Just routine, ma'am. Then I'm off for the rest of the week, remember? All on my lonesome.' He gave me a kiss on the forehead – I might be tall but he was taller still. It was one of the things I liked about him straight away – no more hunched shoulders and cricked necks stooping down to be at the same level as men of average height.

'Look, I'll call you, let you know I got there safely, eh?'

'WhatsApp me. It's free.' Paul was always bang on the pulse of technology, whereas I definitely dragged behind the beat.

'Of course. You'll be all right?' I asked, feeling a wave of affection for him crash over the shields and take me by surprise.

'It will be a feast of China Garden and the Tiffin Hut.' Paul was a good cook, but he drew the line at preparing meals for one when both Jess and I were away. When I returned there would be a forest's-worth of takeaway leaflets on the fridge, neat circles around the numbers of his favourites. 'And I'll be here when Jess gets back from her sleep-over, for sure,' he added. 'So don't worry.'

'I won't. Love you,' I said, hoping he knew I meant it, despite my next comment. 'Now fuck off and leave me alone.'

I pretended to fuss over my packing until I heard the sound of Paul's car starting and then let out a long, slow breath. In truth, part of me didn't like travelling, didn't enjoy leaving home, hated those bloody barriers

I had to put between us. But I knew it was the wrench of closing the door behind me that was the hardest part. Once I was in that car on the way to Heathrow, I began looking only forward, to doing my job and doing it well, the shields locked solid.

But there was a craving to hear Jess's voice before I put her aside for a few days. I punched in her number but it came up busy. Of course it would be. Chatting shit, as Paul put it. I'd already had to have words about the size of her bill. Her response? Well, apparently all her friends have unlimited-minutes contracts. *What cruel, cruel parents we are*, I thought. But I smiled inwardly at those big imploring eyes of hers and the round, as-yet-unformed face, due to change as womanhood began to exert its influence. It had started already. The rocky shores of adolescence were ahead, the treacherous shoals of Hormonal Bay. I hoped we wouldn't get wrecked on them. I tried her one more time, sent a text, and let the shields click fully into place.

I pulled out the trouser suit and put it to one side. I could always double up on one of the outfits. After all, it was unlikely I'd end up in *Mail Online* with a split picture: 'Unknown Woman Wears Same Outfit Twice'. And besides, Paul was right. They did have shops over there.

Then my mobile rang. It was Jess, panic and shame laced through her voice.

It had begun.

11

THREE

Most people think the Concorde Lounge is the *ne plus ultra* of Terminal 5 hospitality, but they are wrong. There is a level above it, one where 'by invitation only' really means just that. If you have to ask, you won't get in. My Principal – as the main client is always known on The Circuit – doesn't have to ask.

It is decorated like a gentlemen's club in St James's, all leather and polished wood, spacious and uncrowded to offer a degree of privacy. No windows look out onto the tarmac. The kind of people who use this particular lounge don't like windows. If they can see out then there is always the chance that people can see in. When T5 was built, there was a huge piece of bulletproof plate glass put in. Even that left some of the V-VIPS feeling exposed to the elements. And to other people. The sort with telescopic sights or long-lens cameras. It is now a large square of panelled walnut.

It is ingrained in me that clients shouldn't travel with members of the general public. Taxis, limos, private jets, yes. Transport where any Tom, Dick or Ali could buy a ticket – not if you can help it. But if we had to go out with the great unwashed (or the armed and dangerous) then this lounge wasn't a bad place to start.

I did the usual scan of the space, moving my eyes from right to left, the opposite to how you might read a screen or a book. The cognitive theory is that the visual cortex, forced out of routine, is more likely to pick up anomalies or potential threats if made to move out of its comfort zone. It's part of our 'What's Wrong With This Picture?' training.

There were four in our party including me and the other three were spread across two Chesterfields with a glass coffee table between them. It was a small number for the occasion, but Gemma, the Principal, liked to travel with minimal entourage. Gemma had one of the sofas to herself, glass of champagne in her hand. Opposite her was Martyn, her Parliamentary Private Secretary, and Emily, her P.A. They, too, had started on the fizz.

I gave the lounge another scan. I was probably at Yellow, that is the minimum level of alertness. The threat potential in the lounge was low. Even so, it paid to stay in Yellow. Slipping back to White – the state you are in when reading a magazine or watching TV or just daydreaming about friends and family – was not an option. For the time being, I didn't have any friends or family. It would stay that way while I was on duty.

There was one other cluster of people in the lounge, six men – boys, really – all remarkably young, which suggested someone else was footing the bill for their travels. They were on Jack and Coke – and I had thought it was a little early for champagne– and sliding into a mix of raucousness and suppressed giggles. One of them sneered at me with a curled lip when he caught my eye. They probably thought I was being disapproving. All I was thinking was: *mostly harmless*.

Gemma raised a hand, as if I hadn't spotted her. I'd suggested we start together from her home, but her husband's PPO had driven her to the airport. His name was Bruce, and he was good, very old school – ten years in The Regiment – so I had been happy to comply. 'There you are,' she said, as if I was a lost stray.

I parked my Ready To Go bag and sat along from Gemma, nodding at Martyn and Emily as I did so.

'Champagne?' Gemma asked, holding up her glass, then, after a beat, she smiled. 'Only joking.'

We all knew I had five days without a drink ahead of me. 'Green tea.'

Emily organised this with one of the white-jacketed waiters. 'Everything all right? You look flushed.'

'Yes ... no ... just a minor hiccup with my daughter. All sorted.' It didn't do to admit to your Principal that your private life had breached the shields. Like I said, as far as they were concerned, you didn't have anything to worry about other than their protection. It kept the contract simple.

'Good.' Gemma had got to know a little about Jess – and the travails of puberty in the instant communications age – in the past eighteen months since I had been working for her. But not too much. She was my Principal, not my confidante.

Gemma took another sip of her drink. She looked well, although she had changed since our first meeting. Close to sixty, her hair was thick and shiny and her skin enviably taut. Maybe it was the HRT regime that she had become so evangelical about. She had lost weight, too, although not enough to make her look gaunt. She was dressed in a two-piece in a shade of red that suggested she was TV-ready. But then, she was always TV-ready these days. It was rumoured her husband, Grant, had coached her in becoming media-savvy, right down to choosing her working wardrobe.

Grant had made a fortune in telecomms. He was one of those millionaires – maybe billionaires – with enough liberal guilt to try to give much of it away. His wife became passionate about foreign aid and its failings. Which is how, fifteen years after hubby cashed in his share options, she came to be flying out to a conference on 'The Challenges of Immigration in the Developed World' as a representative of the British government.

'Emily was just telling us about some slight changes to the schedule.'

I nodded at Emily. She was twenty-eight, Oxford-educated, with a penchant for flowery vintage-style dresses and riding a sit-up-and-beg bicycle through London traffic. Today, though, she had opted for an update of the classic Chanel suit and her dark hair was pulled back and bunched to show she was in full business mode.

I pulled out my phone, ready to alter the relevant pages. I would go through the Tactical Aide Memoirs for the trip on the plane and insert any fresh protocols as required.

'I just emailed you a new PDF,' said Emily in the husky forty-fags-a-day Lauren Bacall-ish voice she affected, even though she was a non-smoker. She had once told me that she had heard on Radio 4 that men found deep voices both sexy and authoritative. The problem was, after a couple of drinks she forgot all about it and slipped back up a few octaves. She was trying too hard. The real, bike-riding, Biba-wearing her was just fine. 'Should've come through by now.'

My phone pinged. And there it was. I scanned the document. There was a meeting with the head of the US Border Force that wasn't on the previous version. 'Randall Nesso,' I said. 'Not a popular man with some people.'

'Which is why,' Martyn said, 'we have Secret Service

protection for that afternoon. With pistols and ear-pieces and everything.' His eyes sparkled as he said it. He was teasing me. *What good is a bodyguard without a gun?* was one of the first taunts he had made when we met. I'm not a bodyguard, I had explained, nor a bullet-stopper. My job was to make sure things never got to the 'taking one for the team' stage.

Instead of being annoyed by Martyn, I had pulled his personnel file, just to see if there was anything in there that might explain his waspishness. There were spaces between the lines you could bathe a hippo in. One of the jobs of a PPO is to know the nature of the people who surround the Principal. Any weakness could be used as leverage by a hostile party. Full disclosure was the guiding rule.

It turned out that Martyn lived something of a double life. At weekends he was known by various names – Martha, Lauren, Chantelle – as if he was trying them on for size. What he was definitely trying on were women's clothes and shoes. He was also spending a fortune on electrolysis for his beard. Most of this transitioning took place at weekends in Brighton, but a quick search of his desk had thrown up receipts from Maxine's, a club in King's Cross catering to the gender-flexible.

Of course, all this was no concern of mine. Until it was. Over a brew one evening I told him what I knew, which I suspected was barely scratching the surface of his favourite foundation. The ultimatum was simple: tell Gemma or I will. He chose to break the good news to her himself and now they swapped make-up tips. Meanwhile, I knew he couldn't be blackmailed. Well, not about that at least.

My next conundrum was whether that disclosure rule applied to Emily. She was having an affair with a married man. Not only married, but someone in the Opposition, tipped for a shadow cabinet post in the near future. He is in his thirties, a former RAF Tornado pilot, who lost his first wife to a drunk-driver and remarried one of his interns. He wouldn't be close to the seat of power in this parliament, too inexperienced, but maybe two cycles' time. Nevertheless, despite the young bride, he was a notorious womaniser. I had to admit it was unlikely he was taking Emily to the Premier Inn – he didn't even stump up for the Marriott, the cheapskate – to try to pump her for information about Gemma's proposed budget increase in overseas aid. That wasn't the sort of pumping that was going on. So I'd let that run for a while. My instinct was it would sort itself out when he got bored and moved on.

Still, that was in the future. I had to stay in the here-and-now. 'The Secret Service will have their own way of doing things,' I warned them. I didn't mention that they sneered down from very lofty heights on all private contractors.

'I'm looking forward to it. It'll be just like *The West Wing*.' Martyn put a finger in his ear and drawled, 'POTUS has left the building.'

Emily, clearly less excited by the thought of the Secret Service, leaned over to me. 'Have you seen who's in the corner? Behind you?'

I nodded. 'Six drunks. All about twelve years old. I'm thinking of calling their parents.'

She shook her head at my ignorance and named a band that I had heard Jess mention. Emily's eyes were bright as she listed the various members. There were only four of them. The other two must be management and protection. I turned and identified the PPO. He wasn't much older than them. And he shouldn't be letting them drink that much, so quickly, so early. And he certainly shouldn't have joined in. But it wasn't my gig and I turned back.

'Cute, huh?' Emily asked, and shrugged when she didn't get an answer.

The band was probably in the V-VIP lounge for its own protection. If a grown woman – more or less, anyway – like Emily could exude such lust when just saying their names, I couldn't bear to think what a group of hormonal teenagers might inflict on its members. The airport authorities would have decided it was safer for all concerned to sequester the band away from their adoring public.

The lounge manager, an elegant Eurasian woman

dressed in a midnight-blue uniform that she managed to make look like a million Hong Kong dollars, approached us, casting a surreptitious glance at the pop stars. 'Excuse me, your flight is now ready for boarding. If you'll just follow me.'

When I thought about it later, I wondered whether, if I had not got on that flight, if I had pleaded family problems, then maybe things would have turned out differently. But PPOs don't have family problems. Except when they do.

FOUR

I don't normally like First Class. Controversial, I know, but these days First Class on a decent airline means cocoons – not so much seats as mini-cabins, complete with doors. Some even have double beds. The occupant is cut off from other passengers. They don't even have to look at their fellow travellers. Which means, if my client is in that little upmarket shack, I can't see them either. That makes me uncomfortable. EOP – Eyes on the Principal – is the watchword. Which is why I prefer Business. So I was perfectly happy to stow my Ready To Go bag above Seat 16a in the lesser cabin and watch Gemma settle into a nearby seat.

That day, someone else also preferred Business – the band, who took up position at the rear of the cabin and began a sustained bout of braying about all the extras they were getting. A pair of socks from the amenity kit came spinning down the aisle. I could sense Gemma, who was sitting parallel with me, bristling, even though she was apparently reading a briefing document.

Then the singing began. Even I recognised their hit, with its irritatingly anthemic chorus and greeting card lyrics. I stole a glance at Emily. She was smiling at this personal little performance. I gave her my best scowl. *Don't even think about joining in.*

I found the purser – a no-nonsense woman in her forties who exuded a quiet air of competence – and showed her my House of Commons pass. It was the closest I had to official documentation, apart from my Security Industry Association accreditation, but that looked a little like an IKEA loyalty card. The portcullis on the HoC laminate was much more impressive.

I explained who Gemma was and that she was on important government business and, against my normal instincts, the purser agreed to move her up to First Class, which had only two other passengers, and me to the front of Business where I could at least watch her door. That kept me in control. I also suggested, as politely as I could, that they didn't serve the four musketeers and their two chums any more drinks for a while. She gave a tight smile and said that such an action had already been noted. They'd be allowed one more with their meal and that was it.

Gemma made a half-hearted protest about shifting up a grade then did as she was told. I moved my RTG bag up the cabin with me. I settled in. Now I was between Gemma and most of the passengers and she only had the pilots, the two moneybags who could shell out First-Class cash (or, more likely, their shareholders could) and some of the crew in front of her. It was what Ben, my former boss, called a KISS situation. Keep It Simple, Stupid.

Still, I consciously stepped up a gear as the engines powered into a whine. Colour? Yellow, shading into Orange. No in-flight movie for me. But then, that was what Gemma paid me a 70k-a-year retainer plus expenses out of her own pocket for – so I didn't complain about not catching up on *The Avengers* franchise or the latest instalment of *Frozen*. It's why I always pre-ordered a vegetarian meal – less chance of food poisoning – and why I carried two passports – one for the stamps and visas of places such as Israel that might cause trouble down the line, the other relatively pristine with little evidence of where I might have been. Civilians aren't meant to have such things, but there are so many ex-spooks from MI5 and MI6 on The Circuit, it wasn't difficult to call on their expertise to organise duplicate passports. All it takes is money.

I waited until the last moment to fasten my seatbelt and took out the in-flight magazine as the 777 pushed back. I'd be flicking without reading, but it gave my hands something to do. Gemma leaned out of her doorway and held up the eyeshade from her amenity kit, which, at the front of the bus, probably included a whole branch's-worth of Jo Malone or Kiehl's. It was a signal that she was going to sleep. Fine by me. At least I'd know where she'd be for the next ten hours or so.

I'd met Gemma two years previously. She had been a keynote speaker at a conference at the Hilton, Manchester, on the particular problems facing female migrants. It was that summer when the news was filled with tales of drowning refugees, trying to cross the Med in leaky boats. But then every summer since then has been like that. The survivors all had extraordinary stories and those of the women were often particularly harrowing, from the FGM they had suffered as young women, the sexual price some of the smugglers extorted from them when the money ran out, to the makeshift brothels in some of the camps across the Channel.

Gemma was in opposition back then, but was making a name for herself in the media as an advocate for the policy of every country in Europe, including Britain, taking their fair share of the dispossessed. It was not a universally popular view, especially in the wake of the mass sexual assaults by asylum seekers in Cologne. But she had put her money where her mouth was and she and her husband had funded medical centres and refuges for women on the Italian island of Lampedusa, and Kos and Lesbos in Greece, three very over-stretched arrival points for the diaspora. That was the theme of her speech that afternoon. That women, as victims many times over, needed particular care and attention.

I wasn't there with Gemma. I'd been hired by the organisers as a GS – General Security – because of the high percentage of female attendees. If they needed someone frisked or quizzed, they had to have a woman on hand, and the RST, the Resident Security Team, was – as usual – predominantly male. This lot were pretty good, but it only needs a woman to say she is going into the Ladies and a gap in the protection opens up. I have had whole jobs where I was employed solely to chaperone visits to the toilet by the Principal. Plus that day in Manchester they required additional SIA-qualified hands because there was talk of some anti-immigration groups causing trouble, although so far none had materialised.

I was at the side of the stage, listening to a proud, beautiful woman with an eye-patch tell the story of her trek from Eritrea to Libya. She had lost the eye to bandits who preyed on the migrants heading north, the result of the beating they meted out when they refused to believe the few measly dollars she gave them was her entire stash. It was very hard not to feel anger, and there were tears in the eyes of the people in the auditorium at some points, but I couldn't afford to lose focus. Shields were up. I stayed at Orange.

I was aware of a disturbance and raised voices that were coming from beyond the curtain behind me.

Some of the front row glanced my way, as if I were responsible for the distraction. I stepped backstage to see if I could defuse the situation.

I recognised Julia, one of the organisers, who looked as if she had been trying to pull her own hair out. She tugged at the short, dark crop once again and when she spoke I realised she was close to crossing from strident to hysterical. She was speaking in a vitriolic whisper to an equally harassed young man, who was blushing deeply.

'Look, Craig, you go up there and tell Mrs Kerr she is due on stage in an hour.'

'I'm sorry, she says she can't,' he said, loosening his tie and pulling it away from his reddening neck.

'And I am expected to rearrange the whole afternoon's running order, am I?'

'Till she feels better.'

'What's wrong with her?' I interrupted.

They both turned to look at me. Craig blushed deeper.

'What's wrong with Mrs Kerr?' I repeated.

'Women's trouble, apparently,' said Julia, in a voice that sounded as though she was chewing nettles.

I tried to picture Mrs Kerr. In her late fifties. Probably not a bad period, then. 'What room is she in?'

'Five-ten,' said Craig. 'But she doesn't want to see anyone.'

'Tell her I'll be along in five minutes.'

26

'Who are you?' Craig asked, looking down at the laminate swinging around my neck.

'A woman,' I said slowly, as if he were a particularly dumb ten-year-old. 'Five minutes.'

I went up to my room and grabbed the first-aid kit from my RTG, hoping I had something in there that might help.

Gemma Kerr was lying on the bed, shoes off, trousers loosened at the waist and pulled down to show the top of her knickers, which were lacy and a surprisingly racy scarlet colour.

'Look, I just need to bloody well rest!' she shouted as I walked in the door. 'Will you all just fuck off and die.'

'Wait outside,' I ordered Craig, who had got there ahead of me.

He happily did as he was told and I crossed over to the bed. 'Mrs Kerr, I'm a security operative here for the conference. I'm not a doctor, but I do have medical training.' I put the case on the chair and unzipped it. 'Tell me your symptoms.'

She did so.

I let my shields slide down somewhat. This wasn't a job for a PPO. 'And you've never had this before?'

'No.'

I shook my head in disbelief. 'Not even on honeymoon?'

'I spent my honeymoon in Hong Kong, sightseeing

between my husband's meetings with Chinese tele-comms companies.'

'You've been through the menopause?'

'What's that got to do with anything?' she snapped irritably.

'It's a danger time for this sort of thing,' I said calmly.

She gave a curt nod. 'Yes.'

'OK, let's see what we can do.' I went back to the corridor and sent Craig off for some bicarbonate of soda and cranberry juice. I ran a deep, hot bath and told Mrs Kerr to get in it. Before she went into the bathroom, I placed all four bottles of water from the mini-bar at one end of the tub. 'Drink all that and pee. A lot. And take some of these.'

She had managed to slide off the bed and was walking stiffly, as if over broken glass. I handed her two strips of tablets.

'What are they?'

'Trimethoprim. Antibiotics. But once you start make sure you take the full course. Three days.' I pulled out another blister pack from the first-aid kit and broke out two codeine. 'For the pain. Once Craig is back I'll mix some bicarb. Then I'll get some sodium citrate sachets from the chemist.'

She dragged herself into the bathroom and half-closed the door. I heard her undress and test the water temperature in the bath.

'Don't put any bubbles or salts in,' I warned her.

There came tentative splashes of entry. After a few moments she admitted a sigh of what sounded like relief. How could a woman her age not have suffered cystitis before? I used to get it about every six months. And I certainly did on my honeymoon with Paul, which we spent in Jamaica. Although admittedly we didn't talk telecomms much.

'Drink. Piss,' I reminded her. 'That's two separate instructions, by the way, with a full stop between them.'

She gave a little laugh. 'What's your name?'

I have a lot of names to choose from. I gave her the one I was born with.

'And you do what again?'

'Today, general security. But also PPO, although mostly the soft kind.'

'PPO?'

'Personal Protection Officer.'

'A bodyguard?' she asked.

'Technically. But you'd be surprised how often you end up giving advice on how to stop a cystitis attack or ameliorate a hangover or helping buy underwear for the wife. Or the mistress. Or sometimes both.'

Craig came back and I asked Gemma's permission to come into the bathroom and mix up a bicarb drink for her. 'It will alleviate the symptoms, but it's not a cure,' I warned her. 'You still need to take the antibiotics.'

I handed over the glass of alkaline solution and also one of the cranberry juices. She had placed a flannel over her breasts to cover them, although it wasn't quite up to the job. But I'd seen clients in every state of undress and distress and I'd learned not to stare.

'Who do you work for?' she asked after she'd taken a slug of bicarb and pulled a face. 'The hotel?'

'No, an outfit called Creative Security Resolutions. Based in London.'

'Full time?'

'Contract by contract.'

'Married?'

'Yes.'

'Children?'

'One. Girl. Jessica. Jess.' It was good to say her name after spending the day with a metaphorical stick up my arse. I relaxed a little and regretted it. I suddenly felt like a drink and my day wasn't done yet. I made the effort to refocus.

'Which is why you do contract by contract?'

I nodded. She wasn't my Principal, so the rule about over-sharing did not apply. 'Up to now. She's getting big enough not to need her mum all the time.'

'Who looks after her when you are doing something like this?'

'We manage.' I didn't want to go into the pros and cons of au pairs.

She switched to drinking the cranberry. 'On my bed

there is a letter. It was pushed under the door. Could you read it for me?'

I went back out into the bedroom, where Craig was busy staring at his watch as if he could will time to stop. 'How is she?'

'We'll see. How long till she's on?' I asked him.

Another look at his wrist. 'Twenty minutes.'

'Tell Julia she'll be down in thirty. And tell her to fill if she has to. Maybe she knows some jokes.'

His face squashed like a rubber ball. 'I doubt that.'

'Well, maybe she can juggle. But Mrs Kerr will be there in half an hour,' I repeated, just in case there was any doubt.

After he had left I extracted a pair of latex-free gloves from my first-aid kit, pulled them on and picked up the single sheet of paper. It wasn't written in green ink, but it might as well have been for all the bile in there. The guy didn't like Mrs Kerr or her black – although that wasn't the word he used – friends or the Muslim terrorists she encouraged to come to this country and destroy our way of ... blah de blah. It finished with a warning not to walk down any dark alleys while in Manchester.

'Have you read it?' she shouted.

'Are you drinking and weeing?'

'Not at the same time. What do you make of it?'

I scanned it again. 'Unpleasant, to say the least. But probably harmless.'

31

'Probably?'

Yes, probably. But how did the guy – a guess, but the odds were I was right – know which door to push it under? A hotel employee was the most obvious answer. I decided I'd tell the head of the RST my suspicion, just in case. But there was no need to worry the shadow minister unduly, not while I was there. 'You can never say for sure, not from one letter.'

'If you were my PPI what would you do?'

'PPO. I'd take us to Orange status while you were in the city. Make a strict plan of what you are doing, where you are doing it, with whom you are doing it and stick to it. I'd make sure you had a PPO at all times and I'd change whatever method you are planning to go back to London by – preferably switching to a car, rather than train or plane. Public transport is never good.'

My more colourful colleagues on The Circuit call going out in public 'wading through cunt soup'. I'm not that misanthropic. Not yet.

'And I'd also show this to the police. And I'd take the advice and avoid any tours of dark alleys. And I'd switch hotels if you're staying over.'

'God, I feel better. What a relief. You're a genius.' I'd heard that tone a million times, nearly always when I have used nothing but common sense.

'Good.' I pulled out my phone. 'I'd better tell my supervisor where I am.' I walked to the window and looked out. It was one of those that only opens about four inches. There was no balcony, no fire escape, no way of entry into the room. The letter-writer wouldn't be coming in there. 'I'll be in the corridor outside if you need me.'

'I was just wondering ...'

'Yes, ma'am?'

'Would you like a job?'

FIVE

Colour: Yellow. The cabins of the plane had slipped into the soporific routine of a long-haul flight. A meal had been served, champagne, G&Ts and wine consumed, the in-flight entertainment service had begun and the young men to the rear of me were suffering the effects of the early-morning booze. They'd be dehydrated by now, exacerbated by the altitude, and doubtless their mouths were feeling like they'd been sucking up sand and some cracking headaches were beginning their preliminary drumrolls. By the time we landed, they would feel like shit. I can't say that upset me too much.

I was re-reading the arrival protocols – Gemma and the rest of us would be met by limo airside, which was reassuring – when I heard a slight commotion from behind me. A call signal bonged and the purser walked back from First Class. I undid my seatbelt and stepped to the curtain that separated the pampered from the merely privileged and checked on Gemma in her pod. She still had the mask in place and was asleep. Only then did I look down the aisle to see what was happening.

Most of it was taking place at the second curtained intersection, between Business and Economy, and on the far side of it at that, so all I could see were ripples in the blue drape. But I could hear the voices, some strained.

I looked down at Martyn, who mouthed: 'What's going on?'

I pointed over my shoulder, back towards First. 'Tell the attendant to ask the captain to put on the fasten seatbelt signs.'

That would have the effect of winnowing out those who instinctively obeyed rules.

'Tell him there might be a disturbance.'

'What kind of disturbance?'

If I knew that, I'd have had a better idea of what to take out of my RTG bag. As it was, I went for the MLA fast-strap restraints. 'Now, please.'

Emily the P.A. had headphones on – her own, expensive, noise-cancelling ones, I noted – and was blissfully immersed in some movie. She didn't so much as glance up as I passed.

There was a band member standing in the aisle and I gently moved him aside. There was another electronic bong. At that moment the stewardess came over the address system. 'Ladies and gentlemen, as you can see the captain has switched on . . .'

I took a deep breath, pulled the curtain aside and stepped through into Economy.

There were two of them and I wasn't going to wonder how the staff had allowed them to get so drunk. My guess would be they smuggled their own alcohol – in bottles of 100ml or less – on board to supplement what the airline was serving. I gave myself a bird's-eye view of the area in my brain, as if plotting all this out on paper, which we PPOs do a lot. Scribble on paper, I mean. Those who know such things claim it is like football coaches writing out potential match-plays – except instead of players, it's car here, Principal there, bad guy here, PPO there. It keeps you sharp.

I had moved to Red, even though there was no direct threat to my Principal. But, given that you shouldn't be wielding a selfie stick like a rapier, there was a more general concern about safety on board. This came under Hostile Environment Assessment.

Cramped into the space next to the galley was the pair causing the disturbance, both well into their thirties, their faces flushed from the booze. The one with the selfie stick was the taller: thickset, face folded into a hateful scowl.

Her partner in insobriety had no weapon, but I clocked her nails. They explained the stripes down the face of the male steward, who was to my right, his eyes wide with shock. Blood was seeping into his collar.

Another attendant was in the aisle, gripping the seat backs, holding in check a couple of passengers who had either come to assist or gawp. She was doing the right thing. This confined space did not need any more bodies in it. Or blood.

The purser was slightly to the left of me, and she swayed back as the stick arced in front of her face. Finally, I had the band's PPO standing directly in front of me. His contribution was to tell the two women to fuck off. Repeatedly.

There are lots of good guys on The Circuit, ex-military, police, the various security services, but I suspected this wasn't one of them. He had the feel of a lad who had been doing doors six months ago and got lucky.

I grasped his shoulders and swivelled him to encourage a return to Business. He struggled a bit so I kneed him in the back of the thigh. Hard. He crumpled to one side and then he was gone. I turned back to the fracas.

'We only wanted a fuckin' photograph with the lads,' said Ms Selfie Stick. 'Just a photo.'

She held up a Samsung in her left hand to make the point. 'And that twat –' I assumed she meant the numb-legged PPO '– he assaulted us. I'm going to sue his fuckin' arse. I'll get one of those lawyers off the telly. No free, no win.'

Close, I thought, *but no cigar.*

'We just want a quick selfie,' echoed the smaller of the two, as if this were still on the cards. She had a rodent-like face with nicotine-stained teeth and was wearing a pink velour tracksuit. But I could ignore her as long as I stayed away from the nails. She was a tail-gater. Her chum was the more dangerous of the pair.

I returned to watching the end of the stick pendulum back and forth in front of the purser. 'If you will just return to your seats, we'll see what we can do,' she said.

The duo simply gave a torrent of highly imaginative abuse back. I moved to take a position behind the purser.

'Just fuckin' let us take the pictures and then we'll go back to our seats.'

'When I say the word,' I said softly in the purser's ear, 'I want you to duck. Go straight down, as if crouching. OK?'

A nod.

I could feel bodies pressing against my back through the curtain. Either the PPO or his charges. Neither would improve the situation.

'Now.'

The purser dropped and I used my height to lean over her. I grabbed the selfie stick and pulled. The woman lost her balance. I yanked her to one side and down and, as subtly as I could manage, with the purser's body blocking most people's view, I hit her with a short, sharp jab to the temple. Not hard, but accurately. Enough to traumatise one of the arteries to the brain. It can be dangerous, and it can lead to all sorts of lawsuits from the no-win, no-fee bottom-feeders she was so keen on, but sometimes you take that chance. Sometimes, you enjoy taking that chance. I let her go and she crumpled to the floor.

Her friend screamed loud enough to bruise eardrums and, as if there really were an option to flee off a plane at 38,000 feet, began scrambling down the aisle, lashing out with her nails and spittle whenever anyone blocked her path.

I barged past the attendant and the passengers. I managed to grab the woman's right arm, get it up her back, then snagged the left – the screaming was really hurting my ears now – and wrapped the fast-straps around her wrists. They were thick and a lot less damaging than the thin plastic ties some use. When you are a civilian PPO, bruises and abrasions from restraints are never a good idea. Lawyers love them, mind.

I had her pinned to the carpet when I became aware of the applause around me and, worse than that, the flash of phone cameras. I had a feeling that was going to be all over Instagram, Vine, Tumblr, Twitter and Snapchat. Which is not where any PPO wants to be.

I stood and indicated that one of the stewardesses should take over. My job was done. And for about thirty seconds it was. Then the woman on the floor, the one with my straps around her wrists, went into cardiac arrest.

I listened at the intercom while the captain called MediLink, the outfit that advises on airborne crises. As instructed, he asked if there was a doctor on board. There wasn't. The MediLink specialist, somewhere in Toronto, recommended an immediate divert. I could almost hear the pilot's brain computing his options. It isn't something you do lightly; diverting a 777 can cost up to half a million dollars. The airlines are never best pleased. But then the captain declared a medical emergency to air traffic control and requested an alternate destination airport with an ambulance on the tarmac. I felt the pressure change almost immediately. We were going down.

For the most part, you only end up at Gander International Airport if something has gone wrong. Badly wrong. Once, most transatlantic flights stopped at this Canadian boondocks to refuel, and it was a base for hunting U-boats in the Second World War, but these days the little town of 10,000 people doesn't see much action. Apart from the aftermath of 9/11, of course, when thirty-eight flights landed in a matter of hours as the skies over North America were cleared. It was the biggest day in Gander for forty years.

There was no such fuss when we arrived. The

captain's medical emergency was one of the two main reasons planes land at Gander, the other being something going 'tech' on board. Like an engine catching fire. The Canadians took off the cardiac-arrested passenger – a Mrs Tanya Carlton – and her friend, Miss Sharon Allerton, for hospital treatment. Between us we had made both of them comfortable on board and Sharon, shocked into sobriety and remorse, had confessed they had been doing cocaine in the lavatories. Hence, probably, the little pink rodent's heart attack.

I gave a statement to the local police, as did the purser and cabin crew, and all backed up my story. As did the phone footage. No excessive force (not on the second one anyway) and a release of the restraints once I realised she was in trouble. Prompt, correct and smooth medical treatment for the cardiac episode had been available from both crew and myself.

Nobody mentioned – or had caught on film – my surreptitious punch to Sharon's temple, which was just as well. It's not like in the movies. Incapacitating someone isn't easy and it always has risks. I knew of one PPO who ruptured the aorta of one hostile with a punch to the solar plexus. No matter that the man had a congenital condition, it was manslaughter. All my girl got was a bad headache, which, I was fairly certain, she would have trouble telling apart from the damage caused by her cocktail of drink and drugs.

I asked Gemma if she wanted me to get a VistaJet for

the rest of the journey, but as we would probably be on our way before that could be expedited, she deemed it not worth the expense.

The purser told me there were local journalists out on the tarmac, but that the captain had denied them permission to board. The official line was: medical emergency caused diversion. The rest, he said, could wait until we were all back home.

I was beginning to tell myself that I had been very lucky and the captain had just announced we were ready to take off once more, when my phone rang. I took the call. As I listened I felt a numbness course through my veins, as if I had been injected with anaesthetic. The words didn't make any kind of sense. And then, three of them did, with a shocking clarity. The shields didn't just come down, they shattered like glass under a tack hammer.

Paul was dead. My husband was dead.

SIX

Imagine a scream that goes on and on, building and building, until you think your brain might explode. Except nobody else can hear it. The sound is in your head and your head alone. And you only get a respite, and then just for a few seconds, a minute at most, when you wake up and you've forgotten all that went before, or imagine it wasn't real. And then it kicks in, your constant companion until – maybe helped along by a bottle of wine and a glass of scotch – you silence it with sleep.

I don't really remember the immediate aftermath of Paul's death. Bits of it come to me, the memories like fragments of a shipwreck thrown onto a beach, forlorn and bleached by the sun. At Gander there was a strange – to me, at least – role reversal, where I became the Principal and Gemma and Emily and Martyn looked after me. There was a VistaJet booked all right, but it was to take me home, back across the Atlantic. Gemma and Grant picked up the tab.

The media frenzy was intense but short-lived. 'Heartbreak of Have-A-Go Air Hero' sums up most of the headlines. They were there till the funeral – which, thanks to my old boss Ben and Paul's colleagues, had security to rival a G-20 summit – but after that the interest tailed off. Gemma kept in touch, sporadically, but politics doesn't favour those left behind.

Gemma had said, during our last conversation, that she had never figured me for one of those who would crack. She thought I'd shrug it off and come back to work. It was, she said, the best tonic. I couldn't explain about the shattered shields, about how I couldn't operate when my personal life mixed into my professional one. They should be like acid and oil, two separate layers. Not one swirl of intermingled colours, like petrol spilled on water.

Which left Jess and me. After a while we settled into a routine of lots of hugs and long nights watching TV in pyjamas while she drank hot chocolate and I demolished a bottle of red. After Jess went to bed I would play some David Sylvian from Paul's collection, and wallow in his seductive melancholia. And some more wine.

I only really argued with Jess when I decided we had to move house. I had lived in Chiswick with Paul for almost a decade and everything was marked with his name. His favourite restaurant, La Trompette, our pub, The Hole in The Wall, High Road House, where we'd had his fortieth . . . the butcher, the baker, and the bloody candlestick maker. They all shouted one thing: Paul was here, and he's not any longer. He'd gone into that Long Dark where, let's face it, there is no light at the end of the tunnel.

After the rows, I promised Jess I'd give it a little longer, to see if the ghosts faded, but I knew we'd have to go eventually. Every trip out of the house was like being pricked with a thousand pins. I was slowly falling to pieces and I knew moving would be a step in the right direction to preventing a total collapse.

Meanwhile, after several months, some of Paul's friends came calling. Most, really, the vast majority, were genuinely concerned. They brought flowers and memories. Duncan, his immediate boss, brought a detailed account of what happened that day, why the last few minutes of a routine SIG – the Strategic Intelligence Group – operation had killed my husband.

But a few clearly brought other intentions. I had heard it said that young widows give off some sort of pheromone that triggers the protective instinct in males. I think it triggered something else, because I found myself turning down dinner, holidays, the opera, Wimbledon centre court. I bought myself a vibrator instead. Jimmyjane. Bronze. Almost a hundred quid. But worth it for me to stay away from concerned old chums with hard-ons. I'll take my orgasms alone for the time being, thanks.

And we did move house. To not far from where Paul and I had lived before Jess, although the streets were unrecognisable now. I bought a flat in a converted industrial building on the canal near Islington, close to the Angel, which meant Jess had an easy commute to school – easier than from Chiswick – which partly helped mitigate the trauma she felt at leaving familiar ground. Also, she loved ballet and dance and I showed her Sadler's Wells and promised we'd become members.

And me? I had no real job to resign from; I had some money from Paul's investments and a surprisingly small pension from his employer but I'd cleared the mortgage and had some cash in the bank left over from the move, which I placed with my dead husband's financial advisor to give me an income. On paper, I was sitting pretty. Except I wasn't. I was sitting feeling fat and ugly and drinking too much and thinking about dominoes. And somehow, I managed to do that for close to two years, letting my thoughts unspool over the ruins of the shields that had once held me in check.

The whining of the lift has stopped. I hear a distant, disembodied woman say that the doors are opening. But it isn't on our floor. There is an intermediate one, a full-size car wash. More voices echo down the shaft, male. A laugh. Not a very nice laugh, either, more one of disbelief at how easy this was going to be for them. And how hard it would go with me.

I check my wound again. The blade cut through the outer fabric and has almost severed my bra. I think that was the idea. Tits out for the boys. I give it a tug. The remaining nylon and Kevlar webbing seems to be holding. It should do, it's a ProTex, standard issue for female Secret Service agents in the US who also don't want their tits falling out at inconvenient times. They cost a small fortune. Right now, it feels like money well spent.

'Are they going to kill us?' she asks from the darkness, a crack in her voice.

'Not if I have anything to do with it.'

That, apparently, is not too reassuring, because she begins to sob, great heart-breaking catches in the throat. I pull her close. 'It'll be OK. They're only angry with me.'

I step away into the blackness.

'Don't go.' Brittle and afraid.

'I have to.'

'Where are you going?'

'To get something to fight with.'

It sounds as pathetic as it felt. My left arm is burning up now, as if someone had held a lighted candle to the fingertips and was playing it up over my forearm. It hurts enough to make my breathing dangerously shallow. I make the effort to fill my lungs, wincing as it stretches the knife wound open. I check it again. There is more blood than last time. I need the SwiftKlot in my RTG bag. It will have to wait.

A bell pings.

'I won't be a second.'

The machinery whirrs, the cables take up the slack. They are coming down. With reinforcements.

Colour: beyond Red.

SEVEN

Most days, it wasn't unusual for me to wake up full of self-loathing. It normally involved a pledge to stop drinking in the morning and then a bottle or two of wine that night. I had been out for a drink with Freddie, an old army friend, and we'd progressed far past the two-bottle mark. Always did with Freddie, because it was easy to slip back to the days when we could smell nothing but shit, sand and dead soldier. To the old, comforting stories. She'd been a CMT, a Combat Medical Technician, like me, and had spent some time on The Circuit before doing a Kevin Costner and marrying a client. It didn't last. She was a girl from an estate in Plymouth. He was Californian and if not gay, 80 per cent of the way there. Freddie didn't reckon that 20 per cent of a husband was what she had in mind, no matter how many Manolos, Mercedes, manicures and massages she could have. She never went back on The Circuit, though. Which was a shame, because she was good at it.

So we drank to remember the times we had together before that little car crash of a marriage. Before *both* our car crashes of marriages. It nearly always came back to the day I had walked in on her and a Rupert – an officer – putting a novel spin on stocktaking. But, no matter how hard we hit the vodka and the ill-advised grappas, normally I managed to get up to make Jess breakfast before she went to school. But now my bleary eyes told me it was gone ten by the radio-alarm. And I could hear voices. Jess was still home.

I pulled my hair into something presentable, went to the bathroom, splashed water on my face and cleaned my teeth. Twice. I put deodorant on over last night's sweat, just as a temporary measure, I told myself. I did some mild stretching, careful not to pull anything. I had a pain in my kidneys, a dull throb. Not a good sign.

Back in the bedroom I climbed into some fresh clothes and walked along the corridor to the living room. There were three of them in the kitchen, making toasties, and clearly the conversation had switched as soon as they had heard me coming. One of the friends I recognised from a previous visit, the athletic Aileen. I introduced myself to the second of our guests, a short, intense-looking girl with long dark hair and flawless skin. Her name was Saanvi.

'What are you doing home?' I asked as I fiddled with the coffee machine.

'Teacher training,' offered Saanvi.

'Inset day,' added Aileen.

'Can I get anyone a drink?' I asked.

'We're fine,' said Jess. 'We're just going to my room.'

'You don't have to ...'

But the three had already scooped up their half-eaten sandwiches and were trooping off along the corridor. 'Don't get crumbs on the bed,' I shouted after them. The only response was a whisper, a fit of giggling and a snort from Jess. The door slammed and I heard the sound of tinny music from a phone or laptop. I knew from experience it would become as annoying as a trapped fly, so I switched on Radio London. It was out of habit that I listened to the station. It always had the best traffic reports for the capital, useful if you had a client to drive. *When I used to have clients to drive.*

I poured the coffee black and sat down on the sofa, feet on a coffee table I'd picked up at a shop on Upper Street. It was a nice 1960s shape – G Plan or Ercol or similar – but too far-gone to worry about putting cups or feet on it. One of these days I'd polish it up, maybe.

I hadn't decorated when I moved in. The walls were plain and clean and that suited me just fine. I didn't have much to put on them. A Modigliani-type nude that Paul had bought and a Pollock-lite mass of lines from an art student who had been a neighbour the last time we lived in north London. Then there were photos of Jess, from a close-up of her face covered in bubbles during bath time, through the ones of her on various beaches, including my favourite of her facing down the waves on the south coast of Jamaica, when we had returned to the island for the first time since our honeymoon.

Then there she was growing rapidly, from a red-coated princess running amok in Disneyland Paris (which Paul always claimed reminded him too much of *Don't Look Now* for comfort), through a whole series of dance lessons: tap, ballet, modern, jazz. There were images of picnics in Richmond Park, school discos, or whatever they called them now, a bevy of over-made-up girls going off to their first grown-up gig at the O2. Nothing for the past few years, though. Nothing since Paul died. There were still photos of Jess being taken, I'd seen them on Facebook before she unfriended me, but they were passing into the NSP – Not Suitable for Parents – stage. There were boys in them and drinks other than Ribena and Tropicana.

I heard Jess's bedroom door open and she appeared in front of me. She'd changed into jeans and a long-sleeved T-shirt that was cut just beneath her bra to show an expanse of midriff. I bit my lip.

'Mum, there's this trip I want to go on.'

'Today?'

'Noooooo,' she drew it out so it was almost a sneer, then cut it short when she realised she actually needed me to agree to something.

'When is it?'

'Next year. It's to Indonesia. Everyone's going. We'll learn to dive. It's an important part of the biology curriculum. Plus we'll be helping the local communities. And the planet.'

'Indonesia?' I asked. Colour: Yellow, bleeding into Orange.

'Yes.'

'So it's basically a field trip.'

Jess considered this for potential traps. 'I s'pose.'

'What's wrong with the Jurassic Coast? That's where we went.' Although as I said it I knew that these days nothing short of Jurassic World would do.

'Mum,' she said. 'This is more than looking at cliffs and old fossils. Dead things. This is about life. What's happening now. We'll be staying in remote villages. Mapping coral reefs.'

Colour: Red.

'I'll think about it,' I said. When I can actually think.

That clearly wasn't good enough. Jess was in an Action This Day frame of mind. 'Every other parent said yes straight away.'

'Including Saanvi's?'

'Why do you say that?'

'Because she's here,' I said. 'And I can ask her.'

Jess flushed and put her hands on her hips. 'That's just racist.'

'What is?'

'Assuming her parents are more strict because of the colour of her skin.'

I might have spluttered at that point, but my phone rang. I looked at the caller ID. Ben Harris. *Ben Harris*? I clicked it off.

Jess turned to go.

'You haven't told me how much,' I said to her back.

She stopped and mumbled something, which I hoped I hadn't heard right.

'How much?'

She repeated the figure. I'd heard right.

'Jesus. Are you travelling by private jet?'

'Muuuum. I knew you'd be like this.'

Then she was gone. A moment later the trio left, faces set in selfie-suitable pouts. They were certainly ready for their close-ups. I allowed myself a moment to relish the entire flat, breathing a sigh of relief at their departure.

Five thousand pounds? I wondered if it was one of those 'scientific' and 'ecological' trips where privileged Western students get to build the same village latrines over and over or the identical rhino gets darted and tagged every fortnight. Maybe every trumpet coral and basslet on this Indonesian reef had already been counted, dozens of times.

I heard Jess in my head. *'Muuum, you're so cynical.'*

Five K.

I walked out onto the balcony and looked down at

the canal. It was too early for a drink, but I already felt that little knot of anticipation in my stomach. I wanted a cigarette but had sworn not to light up at home, even when Jess wasn't around. Several of her friends were already puffing away. I didn't want to give her the chance to accuse me of hypocrisy whenever I warned her not to start down the nicotine road.

Below me, one of the old, vanishing narrow boats was chugging by. The sort that looked like a scrapyard had been emptied onto the top, with all sorts of junk it was impossible to imagine would ever be of any use to anyone ever again. It was like the world's worst boot sale. At the tiller was a gnarled man in his sixties or seventies, roll-up cigarette in his mouth. He appeared to be mumbling to himself. Probably cursing the newer boats that had appeared on the canals, some of which looked like they'd floated off the pages of *Elle Deco*. With London house prices still climbing beyond ridic-ulous, some young couples had taken to canal living, but decorated their boat as if it were a flat in Chelsea. The waterways were now a 'lifestyle' choice according to the Sunday supplements. I guessed the old boy down below would agree. Except his particular lifestyle was dying out.

Jess'd love me forever if I paid for Indonesia. Or at least she would until the gap year rolled around and she needed flights and hostels and four months away in Cambodia and Laos.

I felt that stab of pain once more, the one that tells you that for the moment you probably can't tell your daughter how much you love her without something being thrown back in your face. Maybe, for now, it was enough that *I* knew it. The phone rang again. Ben Harris. This time I took it.

Later, I would spend a long time wondering if I should have just let it ring out, for all our sakes.

EIGHT

It wasn't just my pocket of Islington that had come up in the world over the last few years. Ben Harris had moved on from Creative Security Resolutions and graduated from Park Royal to Knightsbridge, in a building next door to Il Convivio, an old-school Italian with ultra-modern prices. His company was called Hippolyte and the offices were decorated in tasteful neutral tones, with what looked like expensive art on the walls and very fancy light fittings, which might have been art too. The Ben I knew had gone in for displaying whiteboards and Sharpies rather than Wilmotts and Slaters.

He had been short and to the point on the phone. Come and see me, he'd said. I had spent the best part of two hours trying to erase the damage of the previous night until I realised that I wasn't going to win that battle. Or the war. I scrubbed up, but not as well as I would have liked.

I was shown through by Jovanka, a pencil-slim,

well-groomed young woman in a sharp black dress, whose hips moved enough to register on seismic sensors. I felt like a sack of King Edwards next to her.

Ben was behind a desk reclaimed from an industrial site, thick and steel. He, too, had undergone something of a makeover. He looked younger, superficially at least, neater and smoother than I recalled. Really, he looked like he was trying to channel Don Draper, with his short hair and Hardy Amies suit. The shirt was gleaming white, the tie Richard James (I knew that because I had bought Paul a similar one) and I would guess he had ironed his underwear. Or, more likely, someone had pressed it for him.

He leapt up as I crossed the floor and came from behind his desk, grabbing both my biceps with an iron grip and planting kisses on my cheekbones with pinpoint accuracy.

Still holding tight, he put his head to one side, took a half-step back and examined me. 'How are you?'

'You know ...' I said. 'I'll be fine when I get some circulation back in my arms.'

'Sorry, sorry. It's just so good to see you. Sit, sit. You want something—?'

'I'm fine.'

'And how's Jess?'

Where to start? I ducked it. 'She's good, too. Great place,' I said, spinning my chair back and forth to take in the room. The inspiration was Memphis Italian, I supposed. Normally the clients had that kind of furniture, not the PPO providers. Ben was clearly doing well. 'How long have you been here?'

'Fourteen months now.'

'And Hippolyte?'

'You didn't hear about us?' He looked surprised or perhaps a little offended that I didn't know of the company. Like an actor who doesn't want to be recognised, but is not best pleased when he isn't.

'I let my subscription to *Security Industry News* lapse.'

I'd never had a subscription to *SIN* but Ben frowned as if I had broken a cardinal rule. 'Well if you hadn't . . . and if you'd been paying attention, you'd know that the industry has had one massive growth spurt.'

That happened. The Circuit expanded and contracted, like lungs. It swelled to bursting in the wake of the invasions of Iraq and Afghanistan, when a lot of work that should have been done by the army was put out to tender to civilian security outfits. It was when the cowboys came along in droves. It shrank again when the situation over there became too dangerous and people started asking questions about how many private contractors had been killed. 'Domestic or foreign?' I asked.

'Domestic, mostly. London especially.'

I waved my arm around to indicate the opulence of the room. 'Hence this.'

Ben slightly missed the point I was trying to make about his extravagant fittings. 'Yes. Hence Hippolyte. But, the expansion has only been in one area. Can you guess?'

'Not really.'

Ben looked disappointed that I wouldn't play his game. 'The big boom in this city is in female PPOs.'

He sat back and let me think on that for a moment. My cogs were slow. Well lubricated for sure, but with the wrong kind of lubricant. It took a while for them to rotate into place.

'Ben, did you call to offer me my old job back?'

'You must have guessed.'

'You asked me three months after Paul died. I think I told you to go fuck yourself.'

'Grief,' he said, sitting back behind his desk. 'It makes us say things we don't mean.'

'Not always,' I said. 'The offer was insensitive. I think you said, "I know Paul's dead and what-not but I need a woman to travel to Moscow with a client, right now." I said I wasn't ready and you said I had to get back on the horse. And then I told you to fuck off and die.'

He nodded, as close to an apology as I was going to get. 'But why else would I call you now? You must have realised that's what I'd do. I don't have time for social calls.'

'I was curious.' And thinking about five-grand field trips.

Ben played with a pencil for a few moments. 'Well, are you ready to come back?'

'Honestly? I don't know.'

'You have to sometime. Look, shit happens, we both know that. What happened to Paul was ...'

'Inconvenient?' I offered.

'Don't put words in my mouth. But you aren't the first woman to lose her husband.'

'Mine was a little different,' I said softly. Two men in balaclavas don't step out of an alley and put four bullets in a husband's face every day, mangling his features so that I barely recognised him when I had to identify his poor body. At least other wives know how and why their husbands died for the most part. But because he was part of an 'ongoing intelligence operation', the precise details were sketchy. Two men shot him shortly after his shift ended. Arrests were made, to no avail. And the killers were still at large.

'Did you ever get therapy?' he asked.

'Every therapist I ever met needs more therapy than their patients.'

'My man was very good. Helped me get over the death of Robert.'

Robert was a springer spaniel. A dead dog wasn't quite in the same league as a murdered husband, but it was a waste of breath pointing that out. I stood. 'I think we're finished here. I appreciate your concern—'

'There is no concern,' he said flatly. 'You know me

better than that. I didn't call you in because I thought you needed cheering up. Or because I was worrying about your state of mind. Or because you've obviously let yourself go. Charity has never been my strong suit.' He made a show of tidying some papers on his desk. 'I asked you here because I need an operative, just like last time, but I thought by now you might have ... calmed down a little.'

For some reason I stood my ground, which he took as a signal to continue. 'Look, all over London there are Ultras with wives they don't want to leave alone with a man, certainly not a young, well-built guy who works out and looks after himself. Maybe it's a cultural thing. Sometimes it's jealous Russians with a beautiful wife who they know didn't marry them for their good looks and the size of their dicks. Sometimes it's a Saudi prince who doesn't want any man with his wife and daughters. Maybe it's someone who appreciates there are situations where a woman is worth two men. And there are even some male clients who prefer women PPOs. You tend to be much less conspicuous than some bull-necked thug. Frankly, I don't care what the reason is. Right now female PPOs are a licence to print money. What was that politician paying you?'

'Gemma? Seventy,' I said, still rooted to the spot.

'Well, you'd get a hundred now, easily. When you are back to being fully match fit.'

An Ultra was an Ultra High Net Worth Individual, as

opposed to mere 'Hunnees' or 'Honeys', regular poverty-stricken High Net Worth Individuals. A hundred grand a year was probably an Ultra's florist bill, too. In that world everything went up in multiples of 100K.

I sat down once more. 'I might not want to get match fit. Honestly, it doesn't seem all that important now. You know, what happens to an Ultra or two.'

'I understand,' said Ben. 'We all burn out on that. I had some Ukrainian in here whingeing about his wife's handbag collection and how she had asked Hermès to line the shelves of her handbag closet in leather. And just for a second I heard a voice in my head going: *handbag closet*? But you've got to ignore that voice. They are not like us, the rich, that's all you need to know.'

I thought of that old joke: *The rich are different from us. They have a shitload of money.* But I know that wasn't what Ben meant. They live in a different country, an archipelago scattered across the globe: London, New York, Monaco, Moscow, Singapore, a yacht on the Med, a villa in Morocco ... And all the money that fuels this fragmented country of the rich acts like a huge gravitational field, distorting reality. And when you're very close to huge piles of it – as happens when you are a PPO to billionaires – you can't see how life is bending out of shape.

'But a hundred grand plus expenses. Who knows ...?' He let that dangle.

'One day I, too, could have leather-lined shelves?' I suggested.

'Or Jess could,' he said.

My mouth did its twisty over-my-dead-body thing of its own accord. *Leave my daughter out of this*, I thought. But I couldn't help thinking what the money would do for her.

'What else are you going to do with your life? Go back into the army? Too old. What else are you good for? And think on this – in a couple of years you'll be waving Jess off to university. Then that's it. Empty house. But unless you want her to come out with a small nation's debt like every other kid, you've got to fund her. Look, you're a top PPO. Well, you were a top PPO. It's a waste you just sitting in Dalston—'

'Islington.'

A wave of the hand dismissed everything outside an SW postcode as unimportant. He suddenly looked serious. 'There are colleges all over the city offering security courses. Some good, most average, some fraudulent. The quality of candidates I'm getting is pretty low. I have families asking for a female PPO and I'm having to send them along to my rivals. Someone like you, who could brush up nicely in a couple of weeks.'

'Thanks.'

'You're welcome. As I said, I'm not a charity. I wouldn't ask if I wasn't ...'

'Desperate?'

'. . . certain you could pick up where you left off.'

A silence thickened over the desk between us.

'I don't know.'

'Yes, you do. You do know. But right now, you're just afraid to admit it to me or to yourself. It would mean stepping up. And you aren't sure if you have the wherewithal. Fine. Go away. Think about it. Call me when a hundred K sounds good.'

I muttered something that might have been thank you – although I wasn't sure what I had to thank him for, apart from a fistful of insults – and was on my way out when he called my name. I turned back, still gripping the door handle.

'And don't forget. Next time I see you . . .' Ben ran his hand up and down, a few inches from his face and then down over his body. The message was clear: do something about *this*.

NINE

Back home, I started running another bath, my second of the day, sprinkling in the salts that Jess had given me for Christmas. The year she claimed I had been too drunk to carve the turkey properly. Mind you, it had ended up looking like I had used a fragmentation grenade rather than a knife. I'd hit the sherry a mite too soon.

While the bath ran I walked through to the bedroom and stripped off my clothes. I wasn't looking forward to this, so I kept my bra and knickers on while I stood in front of the mirror. Mismatched underwear, I noted. Black top, almost-white-with-lace bottoms. Time was I would never have done that. I closed my eyes for a second and felt the room sway. Already I could taste that first drink of the evening. Something gentle, just to take the edge off. A beer, perhaps. I never drank beer until recently. *All those empty carbs,* a voice would say. But the voice never explained about the visceral pleasures of the first mouthfuls of a cold beer on a warm day. Or vice versa.

OK, let's go. I opened my eyes. I'd gone up a bra size a while back, but hadn't actually bothered buying new underwear. How else could I explain those little crescents of fat poking over the side, looking like a pair of uncooked gyoza dumplings trying to escape from my B-cups. Chances were my ProTex bras wouldn't fit either – they were unforgiving at the best of times. And they were more than a hundred quid a pop.

My upper arms weren't quite into bingo wings, but they could be bingo winglets. Anyway, the taut dome of muscle that stretched the skin when I bent my arm had disappeared and my stomach ... the only word I could think of was slack. I didn't like the way the knickers cut into the flesh either. On the plus side, my ankles still looked great.

My finger hovered over the scar, about the size of a ten-pence piece, just above my hip bone. It was fleshier now than when the bullet went in. Even just touching it gave me an electric tingle and a flash of heat, dust, shit and blood. So I pulled my finger away without making contact.

I stepped away from the mirror, pulled off and discarded the underwear and went back to the bathroom, grabbing a phone on the way.

I slid into the water, so hot it reddened my skin, and looked down at a body mostly hidden by a protecting veil of foam. Although he hadn't actually voiced the thought, I imagined I could hear Ben's cold, hard tones telling me to do something about *that*. I scooped the phone off the edge of the bath and hesitated. Nina or Freddie? In the end, Nina got the gig. After all, she owed me.

TEN

We met at the outside tables of the café at Kings Place, the shiny tower on the canal that housed the *Guardian* newspaper and several concert halls. It was convenient for her, because it was where she worked, but as I had no such constraints as a job, it was fine by me, too. I didn't like the place much, though. It always felt soulless and ersatz to me, especially with a knifing wind blowing over the canal and swirling around the pillars. But we were outside because Nina wanted to smoke. I didn't. It made me feel good to refuse her offer, even though part of me was in turmoil as I shook my head.

I hadn't seen Nina for a few months and expected to be blasted for my lack of contact, but she was late and flustered.

'Everything OK?' I asked. 'We can do this some other time if you want.'

'Everything's fine. Or it would be if you could kill my editor. Or, better, maim. Didn't you used to be able to castrate a man with a pair of nail clippers?'

'I think that was in *The Girl with the Dragon Tattoo*,' I said. 'We never learned to do that. Or if we did, I was away that day.'

'Pity.'

Nina was Scottish, a smidgen past forty, with, if you were being reductive, a hooked nose, beady eyes and narrow lips, which made her look, in certain lights, like a bird of prey. It was more attractive than it sounded. Nina had been a reporter for years, starting on what she called the 'soft' side, mainly in the arts pages, before moving over to hard news. It suited her. She had the raptor-look of someone perpetually on the trail of a cheating politician or tax-dodging oligarch.

She took out a cigarette and lit up, blowing smoke from the corner of her mouth that the wind caught and swirled in my face. I moved my chair slightly.

'What's up, then, stranger?' she asked, with a slight emphasis on the last word.

'I'm sorry I haven't called.'

'I know, things to do, empires to build, people to see. Oh, no, that's me . . .'

'I've been distracted.'

'Sitting by Jacob's Creek, so I hear.'

I stared at her questioningly. How did she know about the bottle of last resort when only the 24-hour Afghan shop was open? 'I've spoken to Jess once or twice on the phone. I'm her godmother, remember?'

How could I forget the weeks of Nina's existentialist

struggle with her conscience about whether it was moral to be a godparent when you doubted the very existence of the deity? It'd be hypocrisy, she'd said. I reminded her that she worked for a national newspaper and had stood in for Polly Toynbee on occasion when her own politics were SNP. That seemed to swing it.

'I'm thinking of going back to work,' I said quickly, as if it was something I had to get off my chest.

Nina raised her eyebrows but said nothing for a moment. Just a slight tightening around the mouth that was hard to read. 'Bastard hours, as you said yourself.'

'I know.'

She stubbed out her cigarette and lit another. I always felt inferior to Nina. She was Paul's friend from university originally. Paul had backpacked around Asia for a few years before he finally went to college, which is why he was a little older than her. Although he had subsequently dropped out to join the army, he had kept in contact with a handful of fellow students, including Nina.

Confrontational was the best way to describe her social style. Even from the start, she would always throw out challenges – favourite Dostoevsky short story? Bruce Springsteen or Bob Dylan? Spit or swallow? Best Ridley Scott movie? (I can still hear Paul's groan when I said *Aliens* ... how was I to know he didn't do the sequel?). Nina was far more cultured than me – she worshipped theatre whereas I only saw adults being paid to raid the dressing-up box – and I couldn't tell which Pieter Bruegel was which.

Yet I knew from all the calls and cards after Paul's death that she was a loyal friend with a far softer side than the brittle carapace she showed the world. And she knew from the way I sorted out her last boyfriend-but-one that I'd step up for her if need be.

'How would Jess feel about that?' she asked eventually. 'You'd need help with her. There'd be another stranger looking after her, I suppose?'

'As it's all to fund her trip to Indonesia, I don't think she'd mind. Besides, she doesn't need much looking after.'

'Indonesia?'

I was pleased someone else sounded surprised. 'I know, some mums have kids with special needs. I have one with special wants. It's what passes for a field trip these days. It's going to cost money.'

Nina blew some more smoke. 'Is that the only reason for going back?'

It was a good question. I looked out over the canal. The mobile scrapyard was gliding by once more, heading back away from the centre of town, the engine making a soft putt-putt. The old silver-bearded man at the rear raised a hand, as if he recognised me. I waved back.

'Maybe not.' Like when you are emerging from an illness that has put you in bed and have those bright flashes of normality, the indication that you might, after all, live, I had been getting these echoes of the old job. The tightening in the stomach. The ramping up of the senses. I hadn't really appreciated then what they were. Or maybe I had. Maybe that's why I picked up the call from Ben. 'Thing is, I don't know where to start.'

'With what?'

'With me.' I pushed my chair back and prodded my stomach. 'Look at me.'

She pulled a very unsisterly face. 'What do you expect me to do?' She pulled on the cigarette, burning it to the filter, and softened her voice. 'Sorry, I mean, what can I do to help?'

'I need someone to take me in hand. Someone to play sergeant major. You're good at that.'

She looked at me through the curtain of smoke she had generated, as if seeing me for the first time that day. 'And you do look a fright.' She thought for a minute. 'It'll cost you, though. Trainer three times a week. Spas. Exfoliants. Your skin is shit, I hope you don't mind me saying. And waxing.' Her eyes rolled down, just in case there was any doubt about where she wanted me waxed.

'Waxing? Why waxing?'

'I bet you've let yourself go down there, too.'

'What's that got to do with anything?' I asked.

'Tidy muff, tidy mind,' she said with a straight face. 'How long have we got?'

'Don't know. Two, three weeks,' I said. Ben's offer wouldn't be on the table forever. 'A month at the outside.'

She pulled out her phone and began to tap on the screen.

'What are you doing?'

'Making appointments for you. I'll send you the diet I use.'

'You have a diet?'

'I have a dietician, luvvie. How do you think I stay so svelte?' she asked.

'I thought it was the cigarettes.'

'Fuck off.' But she smiled when she said it.

My phone rang and I saw it was Jess. Probably calling to apologise for being so snitty. 'Hello, darling.'

'Mum.' That one word told me she wasn't calling to say she was sorry. It was tremulous and worried.

'What is it, sweetie?'

'Dad's back.'

ELEVEN

The darkness in the garage is total. I'd had a few minutes for my eyes to adjust but all I can see is patterns generated by retinas struggling to cope with the lack of stimulation. Dark whorls on a darker background. Little random flashes of light. I try to recall the layout of the boxy room, but the picture is incomplete. There are cars, stacked in a cartridge-style rotating storage system. Designed for those people who have ... well, too many cars. Motorbikes. Carbon-fibre racing bicycles, gathering dust. Workbenches ...

Hold on: workbenches? I force myself to picture them. Wooden tables. Red metal boxes, Snap-on Tools. Would there be a weapon in there? Something to save us? I couldn't see me taking on four, five or six men with a gammy arm and a ratchet socket wrench.

I would have laughed but for the sound of sobbing coming from a few yards away.

I stand still for half a second, trying to catch my

breath, to calm the thumping in my chest. I think of Paul and the very last time I saw him alive. The day I went to America.

I had pretended to fuss over my packing until I heard Paul leave and then let out a long, slow breath. In truth, part of me didn't like travelling, didn't enjoy leaving home. But I knew it was the wrench of closing the door behind me that was the hardest part. Once I was in that car on the way to Heathrow, I began looking only forward, to doing my job and doing it well. *You wanted this*, I reminded myself.

I pulled out the trouser suit and put it to one side. Paul was right, damn it. They did have shops over there.

Then my mobile rang.

It was Jess.

'Mum, I want to come home.'

It's all about timing, I thought. 'Well, I'm not going to be here. You know that. I have to go away. You'll be OK at Becca's.'

'No, I won't.'

'Why, what's happened?' Becca was her best friend at school and I knew the parents, vaguely. It had been their idea for Jess to spend half-term over there.

'I've had an accident.'

I tried to keep the surge of panic I felt from my voice. 'Are you OK? Anyone hurt?'

'Not that kind of accident. My period started. I didn't know ... it was so embarrassing, Mum.'

I could hear tears, a catch in the throat. I decided not to press for details. 'I'm sure they don't mind ...'

'I feel terrible as well. I just want to lie on the sofa with a hot-water bottle in my own home.'

'But I won't be here, darling. And Elena won't be back until Thursday.' Although Paul would be home that evening. And he had booked time off, I reminded myself.

'I know that. I'm nearly thirteen, Mum. I can look after myself. I'll have cheesy beans on toast till you get back. Please? I've got keys and Becca's mum will drop me off.'

There's hardly anything in the fridge or the cupboard, was all I could think.

'Mum?'

'OK, baby. I'll get your dad to buy some supplies. That all right?'

'Thanks, Mum. Have a good trip.'

'And apologise to Becca's parents,' I added hurriedly. But she had gone.

I clicked off, trying to remember how excruciating life could be at that age. Worse now, of course, because Becca could easily double or treble Jess's embarrassment with a few entries on social media if she so wished. But I was fairly sure Becca wasn't that kind of girl.

I looked at the time. Twenty minutes until pick-up. I dialled Paul. And that phone call started the mundane, quotidian, prosaic process that would kill him.

Clunk. Lift stopped. The little bong. The horrible, patronising voice. I am back in the present, back in the garage.

'*Doors opening.*'

TWELVE

He looked good for a man I thought was dead. He was deeply tanned, his blond hair streaked by the sun, those blue eyes still sparkling, even though their setting was a little more careworn than I recalled. He was sitting in the armchair in my living room, one of my beers in his hand, a big shit-eating grin on his face as if nothing had happened. Jess had made herself scarce; I could hear music coming from her room. It was getting towards late afternoon, the sun sliding behind the apartment blocks opposite and the sight of that beer made me long for a big glass of red.

He was dressed in a black suit with an open-necked shirt and a loosened tie. It looked as if he had just come from a funeral and was kicking back. Maybe he had. I didn't much care.

'Hello, Matt,' I said, trying to make my tone freezer-cold. 'Make yourself at home.'

He held up the beer. 'Jess said you wouldn't mind.'

'Jess isn't always right. How did you find me?' We'd

hardly kept in touch since he went AWOL from our marriage.

A shrug. 'It's never hard to find anyone these days. I would've come when I read about Paul—'

'But?'

'But I didn't. I was still in Ibiza.' He gave me that lazy smile of his, which looked good all those years ago and might still look good to some people. It made my flesh crawl.

'Excuse me,' I said. I walked down the corridor, knocked on Jess's door and put my head in. 'You OK?'

She was sitting cross-legged on the bed, her laptop next to her, the screen angled, as usual, so that I couldn't see, but she was playing with her phone. 'Yes, I'm just installing this game Dad showed me.' I didn't like her calling him Dad. It had taken a while for Paul to earn that title. To me he had never given it up. Matt, on the other hand, had abdicated that particular throne.

'Matt, you mean.'

She looked at me pityingly. 'You can have two dads, you know. Niamh has two mums.'

'What game did he show you?' I tried to sound neutral. I was thinking *Grand Theft Auto: The Amphetamine Connection*.

'*Super Smash Bros in Las Vegas*. It's like *Super Smash Bros . . .*'

'But set in Las Vegas.'

'Exactly!' She beamed. 'Alisha has it. It's very cool.'

'Dad', I saw, had gone up in her estimation. How come there wasn't universal excitement when I finally put *Candy Crush* on my phone?

'I'll be out in a minute,' she said, dismissing me.

I went back into the living room, in no mood to beat about any bush. 'What do you want, Matt?'

'My father died. Funeral was this morning.' That flapping sound was the wind leaving my sails. Me and my lucky guesses.

'I'm sorry to hear that,' I said, and meant it. 'Why aren't you at the after-party?'

'After-party?' A little bit of my old PPO world creeping back in. There were always 'after-parties' at every event to be screened, even if most of the job was media blocking – keeping the press outside where we wanted them. But you didn't call them that at funerals.

'Wake, then. Reception. Whatever. I liked your dad. He was a good guy.'

He finished the thought for me. 'Unlike me?'

There were those who saw me marrying Matt as a major character flaw on my part. *How could you?* But they would be judging me on the Matt of the last five or ten years. The first incarnation of Matt, the one I hooked up with, was smart, funny, charming, caring, considerate, selfless, handsome and had money in the bank. The latter versions of Matt were only some of those things. Then again, he also gave me Jess, which stacked up well in the 'plus' column.

'It's just that . . . you know, a death makes you think about things. The bigger picture. Choices you've made. Like us.'

Sod it, I thought, *I do need a drink.* Training could wait twelve hours. I went to the fridge behind the breakfast bar that separated the living and cooking areas and found two inches of Albarino in the door compartment. I tossed them into a glass. Matt had got up and was now leaning on the counter, still droning his fortune-cookie wisdom.

'. . . all those years not seeing Jess. What a waste.'

'And some child support might have been nice.'

Matt looked pained. 'You were earning more than me. Besides, I thought you liked being a minder.'

I hate that word. Being called a minder was like being called a bouncer – we were light years away from that shaven-headed, dark-glasses-wearing world. 'PPO. And it's a living, true. But the hours can be shit. Meanwhile I had a husband who went on a stag weekend to Ibiza and never came back.'

'I did come back.'

I tapped the side of my head. 'Not in here.'

It was why I thought he might be dead. He had gone on one long drugs binge and I honestly thought he'd never come out of it alive.

'I came back and found you shacked up with Paul.'

'Talk about rewriting history. You came back, went back, came back. Told me having a kid and being chained to the marital bed was a mistake ... no, hold on, you said only fucking one woman for the rest of your life was inconceivable. You were sorry. You asked for a divorce. Then you dived headfirst into a pile of Class As. Then you found the only way to support your habit was to start selling the shit. That's the truth, no matter how you spin it.'

He took a mouthful of beer and swilled it around like it was mouthwash. 'Look, I've given all that up. The Class As. Young man's game.'

'Took you long enough to find out. You're way past young man.'

Matt looked me up and down like I was horseflesh. 'Pot and kettle.' He nodded at my glass of wine. 'That won't help anything. Not in the long run. I'm almost totally sober. Oh, I think a beer on the day I put my old man in a furnace is allowable. But most of the time ...' He gave a little whistle. 'Clean. Look, I know I did some stupid things. And a postcard wouldn't have gone amiss, I suppose. But what was I going to say?'

I felt a mean little worm raise its head. 'Wish you were here. The gear is A-1 and there's always some Swedish girl who'll suck my cock.'

'Don't be nasty. It's unbecoming.'

'What about Christmas and birthdays? It was a long

time before Jess accepted that nothing, not even a card, was arriving from Daddy.'

'Well, I'd like to do something about that.'

'What, you've got a sack of the cards you never sent? Wheel 'em in.' He winced. I tried a little touch of the conciliatory. 'Come on, Matt, we went different ways, that's all. I admit, I did blame you for a while. I mean, it was your decision to split, not mine. But that feeling faded. And now we aren't the same people.'

'Don't say that. That's why I am here. To start again. I just want you to tell me this.' He reached over and let his hand rest on my arm. 'How can I get you and Jess back into my life for good?'

That's when I hit him.

THIRTEEN

A hammer. A hammer and a long screwdriver. That is the sum total of what I have managed to find to defend myself in the seconds it took for the lift to descend to our level. I put the hammer in my right hand and weigh it. It is light. I struggle to lift the screwdriver with my left. Trying to make a fist, even with the good fingers, causes me to gasp. Fire shoots up my arm. And when I lift the screwdriver, it seems to me it weighs more than the hammer, such is the effort of raising the limb. I have to face it: I am single-handed in every sense of the word.

I opt for the hammer and take the eight paces to be back at her side. She grips my waistband and I run the back of my left hand over her hair as gently as I can. Even the softest touch sends needles of pain up my arm.

Not long to wait now.

I have been here before. Not here, exactly, but in situations like this, waiting for some insurgents to break through a door or a window, feeling that mix of fear and excitement. But back then, I had four or five good men with me, lads from the bottom rung of society, who by some odd alchemy had been turned into a fighting force, albeit a particularly foul-mouthed and often misogynistic one.

'So a woman turns up to work on a building site and the boss says no women allowed. But she picks up a bit of wood, saws it into pieces, then builds a bench before his very eyes. He sits on it. Tasty. OK, then, he says, you're on, but we work by hand signals. If I do this – he mimes twisting a screw in – it means I want a screwdriver. If I do this – he demonstrates banging a nail in – a hammer. So she goes off to work and things are going well until the afternoon, when the boss makes the screwdriver sign to her across the building site. She tries to shout something but he can't hear. So she fondles her tits, rubs her belly and then feels her crotch. What? he asks. So she does it again – breasts, belly, crotch. Eventually he walks over and she does it again. Tits: "It's in your top pocket". Belly: "You fat". Crotch: "Cunt".'

Gerry's favourite joke. What I wouldn't give for him by my side. And his SA-80.

Clunk. Lift down. A heartbeat of silence. 'Doors opening.' Loud now.

I put the hammer in my armpit and look at the useless phone one more time, praying for it to work. Nothing.

I step forward as the doors part to bleed out a vertical bar of white-hot light. Within a second, the whole garage is flooded with it, and I see the blurred outline of the men within, stepping out from the glow like aliens emerging from a spaceship in a sci-fi movie. And another, unmistakable, noise.

That of a round being chambered into the barrel of a gun.

FOURTEEN

'You're ready to go then?' Ben asked over his shoulder as he lowered the blinds in his office.

He had given me the eyes-up-and-down of a suspicious border control officer when I walked in. I was in a dark linen dress with a jacket with three-quarter sleeves over it, black shoes with low heels, and was carrying a leather document bag-cum-briefcase. My hair was freshly cut, my make-up minimal but effective, my lower areas trimmed to perfection. And I was wearing matching underwear, Myla, no less. I felt good and didn't care who knew it.

Outside, the sun was shining, flaring off the building opposite. Ben had lowered the blinds enough to kill the glare and he turned up the air conditioning a notch.

'Pretty much,' I said. I was enjoying the twin feelings in my stomach. One was of muscles that had tightened up over the past four weeks, the other the little frisson of getting back to work. Like a little drip-feed of adrenaline, just enough to cause a pleasant buzz.

Some – like Nina – would say the job is boring. That nothing ever happens. But that's only true if you do the job right. We don't want excitement. Excitement equals failure. Some say it is like the army, where 95 per cent of the time boredom is the real enemy. But in the army you – or, you hope, someone higher up – have a good idea where the next attack might come from. As a PPO you have no forewarning. So boredom isn't an option.

Ben returned to behind his desk, sat, shot cuffs adorned with fat gold cufflinks so heavy they must have constituted a daily workout whenever he lifted a cup of coffee, and fixed me with his tell-the-truth stare. 'And childcare?'

'A live-out au pair.' It sounded so easy when I said it. But the interview process had been tortuous. I had started thinking of au pairs like Elena, but with only two bedrooms in the flat, a live-in was impossible. Eventually I had found Laura, in her mid-twenties, with a degree in media from Bournemouth, living at home and saving for travel in a year's time. She was smart, fashionable and near enough to Jess's age for my daughter to engage with. Jess had given her a thumbs-up, the references checked out, so I gave Laura the job.

Now it was my turn to audition.

'You've not done the cyber-security diploma, have you?'

I didn't know there was a cyber-security diploma. 'No. Is that a problem?'

'Not for what I am about to offer you. Could be in the future. Some clients demand computer skills.'

'Never my strong suit,' I admitted.

'Not to worry. Something to look at later, perhaps.' Ben pushed two folders across the top of his desk towards me. 'I've kept you north for now. Is that OK?'

'Yes.'

'Although you won't be surprised to know we are getting a lot of requests from Holland Park and Knightsbridge, so if these don't work out, we'll reconsider the geography.'

'Islington is on a tube line, you know.'

He looked doubtful about that. 'So, this is what we have that springs to mind. One Russian national. One Pakistani national. Request for female PPO, in the first case to keep away unwanted media attention from the wife and in the second, fear of kidnap.'

'Of the Principal?'

'Or child. Daughter, age twelve. There was an older son, too, but he died.'

'How?'

He frowned as he studied his computer screen. 'The earthquake in Nepal. He was on a trekking holiday. Nothing suspicious.'

'What is the kidnap risk assessment?'

'Low. A family member was taken in Islamabad two years ago, but it was an express K&E.'

An express kidnapping and extortion was when

someone is held just long enough to clean out their bank accounts with whatever cards are in the victim's wallet or handbag or using whichever online passwords could be bullied or tortured out of them. K&R was kidnap and ransom, when someone else was expected to pony up the cash. You worried more about K&R because the motive might not always be money. And they were the cases that usually ended with a body.

I reached over for the files. He placed his right hand on them, fingers spread. The gold cufflink sat there like a paperweight. 'I want you to go for both of them.'

'Why?'

'Things have changed since you were last in the game. You need the practice. By the way, as you might expect, the family here –' he tapped the green folder '– are Muslim. Will that be a problem?'

I shook my head. I knew what he was referring to. Not any innate prejudice on my part – PPOs don't have prejudices, they get in the way – but the fact that it was considered very likely that Paul had been killed by one of the cell he had been watching. Word had reached the Civil Nuclear Authority of a threat by members of an organisation called BOI – Blade of Islam. The day he died he had spent a shift in a van watching a café and phone shop where BOI were believed to have some sort of information exchange or letter drop. On his way home, as I had asked him to, Paul had stopped to buy some dinner for Jess. Just popped into a corner shop for comfort food.

Bread, beans, bacon, eggs, ice cream. And when he came out, they were waiting for him. Bang. Bang. To the face.

The day of the murder Paul had gone to St John's Wood – the facility there was not only a huge electricity sub-station for London, but since the 2012 Olympics it had held the Civil Nuclear Constabulary Metropolitan armoury. There he had drawn a standard-issue Glock 17 and an ASP telescopic baton and travelled by Ford S-Max to the stakeout location, where he transferred to a surveillance Transit. The regular police believed the surveillance was compromised and that he was murdered by a BOI hit team. Various Muslim groups certainly claimed the 'execution' on their websites over the following days. I didn't tar all of Islam with the same blood-soaked brush. I knew better than that. But I did sometimes dream about finding myself in a room full of BOI and a handful of weaponry. Who wouldn't?

'There's rather a basic Principal profile in each one. Could do with fleshing out. And there is an equally crude Risk Assessment Report and PVC.' Potential Vulnerability Considerations. Dear God, The Circuit loves its acronyms. 'Maybe you can beef them up too. First meeting is with the Russian tomorrow at two in the afternoon. The next is the day after, at midday. Addresses are in the file. Plus the phone number of the primary residential security officer.'

His hand finally lifted and I took the files and slid them into my document bag. It wouldn't leave my side now. Any file detailing protection measures could easily be turned to become an offensive blueprint. It was why I had recently had a key and combination safe installed in the flat.

'I'll report back,' I said, stood and smoothed down my skirt.

'Good.' He leaned back in his chair as I turned to leave. 'By the way . . .' I looked back over my shoulder. 'Looking good.'

'Thanks.'

'Make sure this –' he tapped his head '– is as fit as the outside.'

When I got home I asked Laura to stay on for an extra two hours, which she was happy to do. She and Jess were creating a vlog. Jess had decided she would become an internet celebrity. The fact she had very little to say was not a hindrance to this ambition. Their first one was going to involve visiting Rosemary Gardens and filming on Jess's phone all the dogs they could find (with, I suggested, the owners' permission) and having a virtual canine beauty contest online, with sardonic *Come Dine With Me*-style voiceover.

'You've done your homework?' I asked.

'She has,' Laura confirmed. 'I stood over her while she did it. We'll be about forty-five minutes and I'll make her something to eat before I go.'

I felt a rush of gratitude towards this young woman in

her tight jeans, Doc Martens and 'Beckham for DKNY' T-shirt. With no make-up and her dark hair plaited, she hardly looked older than Jess. Apart from the nose stud. I wondered how long before Jess would start feeling her life was incomplete without a similar adornment. Well, it would be two years or more before Mum said yes to that.

When they had gone I took out the files and laid them on the new desk I had bought myself (a KLUNK or something similar from IKEA – Heal's kind of money wouldn't start flowing for a while) and opened the laptop. I did a Google search on my prospective employers, starting with the Russian, Andrei Asparov. Sexist, I know, when the job will be PPO to the wife, but in my experience the husbands tend to leave the bigger footprint all over the net. And, of course, it is usually them paying your salary. The wife only comes into focus gradually, and sometimes remains a ghostly figure. But there was surprisingly little on Mr Asparov. I wondered if he had hired an ICC – an internet cleaning company – an outfit paid to make sure his profile stayed low.

One item, though, made several appearances, particularly in the *Evening Standard* and the *Mail*. Mr Asparov had been in a planning dispute with his neighbours in Holland Park over his mega-basement. It had been an acrimonious row by all accounts between Asparov and a member of a 90s rock band who had invested his money in a quiet street and didn't fancy two years of excavation to build a subterranean city.

In the end, Mr Asparov had decamped to The Bishops Avenue and bought somewhere that already had an underground domain. He also disappeared from view. There were pictures of his wife, however, who looked dramatically different in each photo, until I realised he was on wife number three. The latest one was a real beauty, although that didn't extend to her eyes, which looked like black holes. I was reminded of a shark.

I called Nina and left a message, asking if she had any information on him. Somewhere in the *Guardian* there would be a briefing file on him that all journalists could access, if only to list subjects that might generate letters from m'learned friends. Most billionaires have something they would prefer to keep out of the newspapers.

I went to YouTube and put the wife's name in. A couple of videos came up, one of them expensively directed by Vaughan Arnell – and even I knew he didn't come at a discount – with Mrs Asparov riding a horse along a beach, pursued by a horde of barbarians. It ended with her singing from the balcony of a lighthouse.

Well, I say singing, it was that melismatic scale climbing that has escaped from TV talent shows and started breeding in the wild. Anyway, I wasn't sure whether Katya Asparov had talent, because the voice was relentlessly Pro-Tooled and auto-tuned. That, I realised, was Paul speaking. I had no idea what those things did. But Paul spent an inordinate amount of time raging about 'modern music'. Before he died he had switched back to vinyl, so he could enjoy the crackles on his old Neil Young LPs. I would then sing 'Old Man' at him in Mr Young's whiny cat-in-a-mangle voice.

It took a second to pull me back. I knew that I could spend hours replaying such moments with my dead husband, like watching family videos. I did worry that if I didn't re-run them then, like old film stock, the colours would bleach and the gelatine scratch and Paul would fade from view. But the alternative was to stay trapped in the past with Paul and Neil Young and I couldn't do that to Jess.

I glanced at the 'requirements' page where the client laid out what they needed in a PPO. Someone, I wondered if it was the husband, had said: 'Must like shopping'. I don't know how, but those words managed to carry an undertow of wearied resignation. There was also a hand-scribbled addition. 'Must bring gym wear to interview'. Strange. Maybe that was what Ben had meant when he said the game had changed.

I started on the second client, Malik Sharif, who made his money from importing luxury cars into Pakistan, textiles, property and banking. A significant percentage of the cheap clothes on the high street came from his factories but, I was pleased to see, he was a vocal supporter of workers' rights and factory safety. His massive mill in Karachi was held up as a model of compassionate capitalism for the whole subcontinent. As I suspected, the wife – there appeared to only be one this time – was barely mentioned. As with Asparov, she was younger than him, but the gap was not so significant, about twelve or so years from what I could make out. I checked the paper files and I was out by two years, but close enough.

The requirements page was a little more fulsome for the Sharifs.

We are looking for an experienced Female CPO/PPO/Driver OR an experienced Driver with a knowledge of security. (The candidate gender restriction is due to cultural reasons.)

- The successful applicant will be driving the new Rolls-Royce Ghost and MUST have previous experience driving luxury cars.
- SIA accreditation essential.
- They will be driving a young girl who is schooled in London and her mother.
- The contracted hours are Monday–Friday 0730–1800 during school term times, with some weekends (flexibility essential).
- There is the possibility during the summer of several weekends in Monte Carlo with possible short trips in the winter months to St Moritz.
- Applicant must have a London base and be flexible to adapt to the family and their needs.

Well, the weekends away might throw up some problems with Jess, but it was par for the course. It isn't a 9–5 job. Although this was close to it. I suspected with the daughter and wife there wouldn't be too many late nights. But the Rolls-Royce Ghost? I didn't like that. Not the car, just its high visibility. As Paul used to put it so succinctly, it's like driving with your bollocks hanging out. People'll notice. I hoped they hadn't gilded that particular lily with a personalised number plate. Don't much like those, either. People with them always think: smart, witty. Most observers seeing them think: tosser. And they are always easy for someone to remember.

My mobile rang. Nina. I had seen her a couple of times since our initial meeting at Kings Place and we had even trained together. Her tone was bright and breezy. 'How's it going?' she asked.

'Good. You got my message?'

'I did. Your Russian friend has the usual backstory. Local politician. He traded votes for Yeltsin in return for mining interests, which he got for a song. He's a non-dom. Has shares in Arsenal Football Club and a box there. On wife number three.'

'I saw. She's a looker.'

'Well, almost right. Just change one letter and you'd be there. She's a pop star of sorts.'

'What sorts?'

'The sort that used to hang around Circus or Blast

in Moscow, hoping to snare a metals magnate. Andrei pays for the best American, British or Swedish producers to come over and make the album and then probably buys or downloads every copy himself.'

'So no media blocking needed here?'

'In her dreams. She's also a nail ambassador.'

'For who? B&Q?' I had this image of an airbrushed supermodel with a comic Russian accent explaining the difference between rounds and ovals to DIY customers.

'Ha-ha. Poppy Gunn. It's a top Russian manicure brand.'

'How's Mr Asparov's relationship with the Russian government? I don't want to come home glowing with polonium.'

'Good. That is, the regime likes him. Or at least, it doesn't hate him, which is just as important. But I don't know why you'd bother with the Russians. Sharif, well, he seems to be an honest-to-God businessman.'

'Honest to Allah,' I corrected.

'Right. Wouldn't they prefer a female Muslim bodyguard?'

'They're pretty rare, Nina. In this country, at least.' Although rumour had it that at least one hairy-arsed ex-SAS bodyguard on The Circuit enjoyed operating beneath a burka. He claimed you could get away with murder under there. Which we all knew meant he could carry a concealed weapon. 'Given that most of us are ex-forces or police.'

'I suppose so. Anyway, no skeletons rattling away in cupboards for the Sharifs that I can find. She's big in a couple of charities back home. Let me see ... Sightsavers, CARE, Sadohari Foundation, ORBIS. He's big in CatSlam.'

'Cat what?' It sounded like either a medical procedure or a form of feline torture. 'Is that a charity?'

'CatSlam? It's more a business concept. Catwalk to Islam. If Olivier Rousteing puts feathers on his autumn-winter collection for Balmain, within a week Sharif's people are offering H&M a salwar kameez trimmed with feathers. Stella McCartney goes all Op-Art, then bingo, they have headscarves and shawls with very similar motifs. There's even a market for burkas, with the latest patterns embossed black-on-black on the fabric, so they still look like plain sacks from a distance. But the wearer knows they have a designer sack on. The Muslim fashion industry is worth billions.'

'Who knew?'

'The *Financial Times*, last week. Double-page spread. Apparently some of the big fashion houses are talking about copyright and plagiarism issues. Which means they have realised they're missing out on a slice of that action. That's about it, though. Good luck.'

'I appreciate it, Nina. Thanks. I owe you a drink.' I jumped in before she could say anything about my training regime. 'And I'll have the peppermint tea.'

We said our goodbyes and I was glad she hadn't asked about cigarettes. I was down to two a day, but couldn't slough off that last pair, one first thing in the morning, the other late in the evening. I finished up and put the folders in the safe in the bedroom. Even thinking about smoking made my throat tighten as my body anticipated the pleasure of the first nicotine hit.

Jess and Laura came back and set about making pasta and pesto. I had an 'Eat Yourself Thin' salad to look forward to and the *CIA World Factbook on Russia and Pakistan* to read.

I had just pulled it from the shelf when Jess came over and handed me a brown envelope. 'Mum, I meant to say, this came for you while you were out. Laura had to sign.'

'Sorry,' mouthed Laura. 'I should have said.'

'That's OK,' I said.

But, as I soon discovered, it wasn't OK. It was a long way from OK.

FIFTEEN

Seething is not a good look for an interview, so the next day I buried my anger as deep as I wanted to bury an axe in my ex-husband's skull. I took a cab to The Bishops Avenue, on Ben's tab. I was carrying the gym gear as requested. I have never got my head around the appeal of The Bishops Avenue. I had worked there before. It had none of the glamour, shopping or restaurants of West London, just rows of overblown, tasteless mansions, many of them left to fall into disrepair. What it did have was space and relaxed planning permission. As Asparov had discovered, in places like Holland Park and Chelsea you had neighbours whose daily reading was the planning application noticeboard. In The Bishops Avenue you could build Disneyland and no neighbour would complain. Mainly because, for large swathes of it, there were no neighbours. The properties were simply bricks-and-mortar safety deposit boxes, unlived in and unloved.

The Asparov house was in the section near Hampstead Heath, which at least had some life to it, with a far higher percentage of occupancy than the more northerly section. It was also more modest than I expected. True, it had high fences and gates, razor wire and cornets of spikes and CCTV cameras. But this wasn't one of the bloated monstrosities the area attracted. With its simple pillars either side of a black shiny door, it looked like the kind of place I could live in. If I had a spare two hundred mil and a copper mine in Russia.

I pressed the intercom next to the gate and announced myself. There was a crackle that might have also been a word. I waited for the snick that would let me in. None came. I tried again. 'Wait!' was clearly audible now. Wait for what?

I was aware of a buzzing from the grounds of the house, growing louder. It sounded like a fifty-pound bee, and when it burst into view, I wasn't far off. It hovered above me, maybe twenty feet off the ground, the little props frantically whirring to keep the drone aloft. It described a circle and even above the racket of the little engines I thought I could hear the camera lens zooming in and out. I turned so it got my full face. Once it was satisfied, it darted away and I heard the buzzing fade. The door gave its snick. Well, Ben had said the game had changed. Entryphone cameras and CCTV were clearly no longer enough. The up-to-date oligarch had to have a fleet of drones. And the people to operate them. I stepped into the grounds.

There was a car parked on my right, one of the big Audis. As I passed it, the rear door opened. 'Welcome. Get in, please.' The engine purred softly into life.

The voice had a rotund English accent, but with an oddly metallic edge. I crouched down and peered in. There was no driver.

'It is quite safe,' said the dashboard.

I glanced up at the house. It was about a hundred metres, if that.

'Thanks, but I need the exercise,' I said. With a mosquito-like whine the door closed again with a sulky clunk. *Boys and their toys*, I thought. Rich boys, that is.

I walked up a gravel path and did a quick recce of the garden. There was a second, wider path that led to the rear of the detached house. Judging by the aperture at the fence end, this was where the cars came and went from the property. There was only one other, apart from the Audi, in sight, a Range Rover with blacked-out windows to one side of the mansion, sitting in front of a low garage that probably accessed the subterranean levels where the cars were stored and serviced. More cameras slowly tracked me as I approached the house, some on stalks emerging from well-kept bushes, and others attached to the walls of the house. I could see small protrusions from the lawn that looked like sprinklers. I would bet at least some of them were motion sensors.

I didn't have to knock, the door was opened by a butler, gussied up as if he had stepped out of a TV drama. He had a well-fed look, his cheeks reddened as if he had been at the port already, and when he spoke it took me a moment to place the voice. 'Do come in. You are expected.'

It was the voice from the Audi dashboard.

'Thank you. Sorry about refusing the lift. My mother told me never to get in cars with disembodied men.'

A flashbulb of a smile went off. 'Quite right, miss. It's just one of the newer services we offer. It takes some getting used to.' I couldn't be sure, but I sensed there was a whiff of disapproval in there.

There came the click of heels on polished wood as a young woman marched towards me. She was a bleached blonde with a hefty fringe and cheekbones so sharp, she looked as if all the air had been sucked out of her mouth to get the effect. She was dressed in a cream two-piece suit and the sort of steep, vertiginous, spike-heeled shoes that can give you a nosebleed. She looked down at her clipboard, said my name with a Slavic accent and waited for my confirmation.

'That's me.'

'Can I see some ID?'

Not bad, I thought. Some non-electronic security in place already. I handed over my clean passport. She checked the photo, frowned at it – it was about as flattering as every other passport pic I had ever seen – and offered it back.

'Come.' She turned and led me down a hallway decorated primarily in red and green, with a big splash of polished walnut from the staircase, and into a side room, where a man in his forties with two wings of greying hair over his temples was sitting behind a desk. The simple modesty of the outside of the house had been left behind here. Picture frames were gilt and ornate and held voluptuous naked women, the fireplace was black marble, veined with gold, with several levels, supported by pillars. It looked as if it was modelled on a wedding cake and you could roast an ox in the hearth. I suspected it wasn't original to the house, the scale was all wrong. An ormolu clock was on the mantelpiece and if it had been a peacock it would be strutting about, pleased-as-punch with itself. The chairs were thickly padded and looked like Louis XIV reproductions, although I assumed they might not be reproductions, and the intricate cabinets lining the walls were inlaid with ebony and tortoiseshell. Above me the ceiling was freshly gilded rococo, the gold finish still bright and shiny.

Three televisions showing financial channels were mounted on the walls, and there were two computers on the desk, flanking my interviewer. He motioned for me to sit down. I examined his square face, the eyes set just a little too close together, the well-muscled neck, the elegant hands with a better manicure than mine. This wasn't Andrei Asparov.

'I was expecting to see Mr or Mrs Asparov.'

'Sit down, please.' His English was lightly accented and when he smiled the face lost its slightly forbidding aspect. 'Mr and Mrs Asparov had to go to Moscow. Mrs Asparov was offered a slot on *Good Morning Russia*, to perform her new single.'

'Too good an opportunity to miss,' I said, my voice idling in neutral.

'Indeed.' He held out a hand and I took it. Firm did not do the grip that clamped over my hand justice. 'I am Gregor Mitval. I am head of the residential security team. You would be reporting to me anyway. Please, sit,' he repeated.

I did so and put the gym bag to one side. 'Reporting how?' I asked.

'Just the usual. If you get the position, then I like to see all your pre-deployment tactical notes for every day and then a detailed de-brief document at the end of the day.'

'So you need to know where Mrs Asparov is going and where she has been.' The job was PPO-cum-spy, then. The phrase 'conflict of loyalties' popped into my head and I parked it in a prominent position.

'Precisely. There will be times when we need to send a team with you as back-up.'

'Such as?'

'Film premieres, launch parties, fashion shows, personal appearances.'

There came a whirring noise and I thought, for one moment, that the drone had entered the room. But I turned to see all the artworks disappear from their frames. I had heard of security devices that remove valuable paintings from the walls if the house alarm is triggered, sliding them into a metal safe hidden in the cavity. But this wasn't that. A fresh set of paintings, these more twentieth century and abstract, appeared in place of the Ruben-esque nudes. 'The afternoon art collection ...' he offered, as if it were entirely normal for all the paintings in a house to be electronically rotated and replaced.

'How many changes are there?'

'Only three. Morning, afternoon, evening.' I looked as a very average Picasso – so probably only worth a hundred million – slotted into place. I'd almost forgotten that in this world, art and money had a commensal relationship, intertwined like two voracious creepers and as impossible to tease apart.

He pointed to an empty cup on the desk. 'Coffee?'

'No thanks.'

'Are you sure? It's Sumatran Kopi Luwak. Three hundred pounds a cup.'

I'd come across it before. *I'd rather have the cash*, I thought. 'The one where the civets eat the beans and the farmers collect them?'

'It's delicious.'

It's also bollocks. There is more fake and adulterated Kopi Luwak out there than there are Louis Vuitton bags. It was just another way of demonstrating to the normal world you had too much money.

'I'll pass.'

He shrugged, disappointed. Maybe it would have been his excuse to have another three hundred quid cup himself.

'Now, I have your CV here,' Mitval continued. He put on a pair of black-framed glasses and peered at one of the computer screens. 'Army trained, I see. That's good. Combat experience. Medical training, also very good.' He held up his iPhone. 'Technical. Not so fine. You know about RSCA for the cars?'

I nodded, not having a clue what he was talking about. This was no time for weakness. I hazarded a guess. 'That's how the Audi is controlled?'

'Indeed. We are just bedding the system in. You tried it?'

I shook my head. 'I still prefer a human behind the wheel.'

'Me too. But this is the future. All this is very good. Very impressive CV.' He indicated the paperwork. 'You trained with the Colonel himself?'

I nodded. Everyone on The Circuit knew Colonel d'Arcy. He was based in Geneva, but twice a year ran PPO courses in the UK, which he modestly dubbed masterclasses. He was in his seventies, but you still wouldn't fancy your chances in a fight or a car race against the wily old fox. His masterclasses were twice the price of any other training scheme, but worth it.

'One thing worries me.' Mitval took off the glasses.

'What's that?' I asked.

'The gap.'

'Gap?'

'This twenty-month break you took. A long time in this business.'

'Not really,' I said as evenly as I could. 'A few bits and pieces change. The job is what it has always been – protect the Principal.'

He nodded approvingly. 'That is true. But I don't know if you have seen photographs of Mrs Asparov.'

'I have.'

'Then you will know she is a very fit woman. Very fit.' I examined his words for any hint of a double meaning, but there was none. 'She does Bikram yoga twice a week and has a personal trainer in the gym –' he pointed to the floor, indicating the subterranean world beneath our feet '– every day except Sunday. She runs half-marathons. Swims for an hour every afternoon.'

God, I thought, *all that singing must really take it*

out of you. That and perhaps knowing that, as you tick through your twenties, wife number four might well be revving up on the start line.

'And, without being rude in any way ...' Now the smile positively dazzled. 'She is somewhat younger than you.'

Ouch. 'I think I'm meant to look after her, not race her to the next lamppost. Or run half-marathons with her.'

The grin wattage lowered a little bit. 'True. But believe me, she does take some keeping up with. She's like a whirlwind. So, just to be on the safe side, we would like to check your fitness levels. Nothing too strenuous. The gym is empty right now.'

'It's not exactly standard procedure.'

'Perhaps it should be. I bet half the thugs who work as bodyguards in London would not be able to manage a hundred metres without bursting a blood vessel. Bags of muscle, that's all. Not you, of course. But, as I said, it has been a long lay-off. OK?'

Still not my idea of a day at the beach. 'OK.'

Back to full power on the smile. 'Excellent!'

If the space he had planned for Holland Park was anything like the one lurking beneath The Bishops Avenue, it was little wonder objections were raised to Asparov's basement over there. The first floor down was the obligatory cinema plus an in-house recording studio for Katya Asparov to torture innocent songs to death. It was large enough to fit the London Symphony Orchestra in. Minus two held the swimming pool, sauna, steam room and gym. Below that was the garage level. The garage apparently routed cars via a large vehicle elevator to a car wash facility then up to ground level.

My New Best Friend showed me to a changing room that could have housed both sides at an FA Cup final. It felt lonely and echoey as I stripped off and put on a new sports bra, T-shirt, sweatshirt, leggings and Under Armour cross-trainers. I stretched a little and wondered why I had agreed to do this. But Ben wanted a full report, whether I got the job or not. I knew why – if they rejected me, he would want to be able to send a more suitable candidate along next time, tailored to what I had told him. He didn't like to miss out on commission. Besides, maybe it was part of the new norm.

I poked my head through the door marked 'Pool'. It wasn't, as I had half-expected, Olympic-sized, but you could still have loaned it out to Sea World for dolphin shows. There was no smell of chlorine, so I suspected it was ozone or UV treated. Along the opposite wall from me was a large mosaic of Mr Asparov dressed as Neptune and Mrs Asparov not dressed at all, her modesty protected only by Neptune's beard and trident. I wondered if her head was a single panel, one that could be prised off and replaced in a jiffy when the next Mrs Asparov came along.

There was a small plaque on the wall. I peered at it. 'Conceived, Designed and Built by London Underground Ltd.' Not, presumably, the guys who ran the tube, but one of the many companies creating a whole underworld for rich Londoners to frolic in. There was a web address, too, but I didn't bother memorising it. The chances of me needing a ten-car garage were slight.

I stepped back into the dressing room and took the other door that led to the gym. Mitval was in the middle of the room, still wearing his navy-blue suit, but with a pair of trainers on his feet. It was hard to gauge the size of the installation to begin with, because two of the walls were mirrored, but it was large enough to have four of every type of fitness machine and still leave a large square of foam matting in the centre for floor exercises. Maybe, on top of everything else, Mrs Asparov was a gymnast, too.

'There you are,' he said. From his pocket he produced a wristband. 'If you'll put this on, the telematics feed through to the computer over there for analysis.' There was indeed an Apple MacBook open on a small table, next to the water fountain. Above it, four black-and-white CCTV screens showed various views of the outside of the house. I put it on, walking over to take a cup of water as I did so.

'Music?' he asked.

'No,' I said. I had a feeling I knew exactly what was on the playlist in that gym. 'Thank you.'

'Shall we start on the treadmill?'

We did, with me running while he adjusted the speed slowly upward. As he did so he kept up a stream of information about the set-up at the house. There was an RST of six, all male. The garage below had nine cars, including two Porsches and two Ferraris. They were for the Asparovs' use only. If I took the job I'd be expected to toggle between a Range Rover and a Mercedes S Class, which were kept in a conventional above-ground garage.

He asked me about which courses I had done: defensive driving, tactical driving, emergency evacuations from a scene, hostage negotiations, pistol certification – which I had done in Slovakia – ambush situations and extraction scenarios. As the speed crept up and the incline came into play, I kept the answers short. I was doing OK, but I knew that four weeks had not been long enough to put me back at my best. But my breath was coming easy and I settled into a long loping stride. After ten minutes he slowed the belt and lowered it. I was breathing hard but not ragged. I emptied the cup of water then wiped my forehead. There was just a small film of sweat.

'Very good. What can you bench-press?'

I didn't lie. 'I used to be able to do my body weight

and then some. That was a while ago, mind, and it's not quite back up there yet. But it's coming along.'

He grunted as if he didn't quite believe me. 'Let's do the rower.'

He stood over me while I did five very fast minutes, actually enjoying the burn in my arms and thighs towards the end. The machines were top-of-the-line commercial gym quality and a pleasure to use. Even the rack of free weights looked reassuringly expensive.

'And chin-ups.' He indicated the rubber-coated parallel bars jutting out from the wall. I could reach them easily, and so had to cross my legs at the ankles and raise my knees to clear the ground before I began the pull-ups. At ten he was happy enough to tell me to take a break.

I helped myself to some more water, trying to hide the little shake in my right arm, and took in as much oxygen as I could.

'Warmed up?' Mitval asked.

I drew a second cup of water. 'You could say that.'

As I turned I became aware that a third person had entered the room. I was annoyed at myself for not hearing him, but he moved on the balls of his feet with an easy, feline grace that belied his stocky build. He was shaven-headed and both the arms that poked out of his vest top were covered in lurid tattoos. A bag of muscle, as Mitval had put it.

'OK, on to the next test. Imagine I am the Principal.

You have to come and save me. For that, you have to get past our friend Bojan.'

Our friend Bojan gave a formal bow and then began to walk around the perimeter of the mat, staring at me side on like a matador might appraise a bull.

'Don't be ridiculous,' I said. 'Checking my fitness is one thing but I'm not fighting.'

'I just want to see how you handle yourself,' said Mitval evenly, as if this were an everyday request.

'No.'

Mitval gave an expansive, arm-waving shrug. 'Well, it's immaterial. The door to the changing room is there. The lift out of here, just around the corner. But Bojan is also between you and them. He will stop you leaving.'

'He can try.'

They both thought that was hilarious.

I took several paces towards him. 'Bojan—'

I didn't even see the blow coming. Didn't sense his weight shift or the foot connect. I was simultaneously aware of two things, his right leg going back into position and a small nexus of pain in my right rib, just below my breast. I took a step back. The first thing one is inclined to do when one has been hurt is to grab the wound. Just like soldiers automatically duck when they come under fire. But grabbing the affected area is a bad move. One, it isn't going to help alleviate the pain. Two, it leaves all your defences down.

'Come on, I don't want the job this badly. There's always Primark,' I said. That was the problem with army training. It incubates a way of coping with danger by the application of black humour. I could tell from his expression that this particular quip hadn't travelled well.

Bojan stepped in, feinted with the same leg, then snapped it back and brought his left around in a swinging arc. I was fast enough to block this one, but the impact jarred my arm up to the shoulder. I shook it to keep it loose. Now I was on the balls of my feet as well. Whether this was part of the job interview or if they just wanted to play with or even humiliate me, it didn't matter now. It was clear they weren't about to let the afternoon's entertainment slip away.

I am trained in unarmed combat, but not the balletic sort. No fancy drop kicks for me. In most cases, a PPO is fighting in confined spaces, in the back of a car, a hallway, even, as I recalled, an aeroplane. Kickboxing moves won't work there, you need something up close. The army taught me to fight in a way not much changed from the days when Sykes and Fairbairn instructed the Commandos and Special Forces in English country houses appropriated for the duration. When I took my PPO course I was tutored by someone who had served in 14 Intelligence Company in Northern Ireland, also known as The Det or Int & Squint. Charged with infiltrating the IRA and the loyalist paramilitaries, they had developed a fast, dirty form of self-defence, perfect for a crowded pub or a back alley. Add to that Colonel d'Arcy and his espousal of Krav Maga, a Hungarian self-defence system favoured by the Israelis, and on paper I was pretty well equipped.

What I needed was to find some anger. I was pissed off with these boys, but not enough to fuel a fight. I found it in Matt, in the letter that had arrived from a solicitor's office, saying that he wanted free access to his daughter. And suggesting if it wasn't provided, then he would press charges for assault. Apparently there was photographic evidence of the 'beating' I had given him. One slap across the face does not, in my book, a beating make.

I felt a burst of indignation and, yes, hatred flare up inside. As it did so, I rode the wave of disgust that followed and moved in. I got one short, sharp punch in and suddenly I felt pain explode in several places at once. I retreated. Bojan was smiling. His feet were making the quick, shuffling movements of a boxer.

'Bojan is Serbian,' explained Mitval, as if he was narrating a wildlife documentary on BBC2. 'A lot of Russian kidnappers use Serbian hard men. You might have to face a man like this for real.'

I stole a glance at Mitval. There was a sickly light in his eyes. He was obviously enjoying this. If I did by some miracle get past Bojan I would make sure he regretted this charade.

I didn't say anything, just swallowed on a dry throat and did a quick check to make sure nothing was broken. No. Not yet. But he'd caught me on the wrist and my hand was full of pins and needles. I worked the fingers to restore life into them. I'd discovered one thing. He was fast. Frighteningly fast. And I wasn't.

As if reading my mind he came at me in a blur of limbs. He was like a belligerent octopus. I ducked and twisted away and a shovel-like hand caught me a glancing blow on the head. A second one followed up, and the side of my face became fire.

Again I managed to pull back. He had the strength and he had the weight advantage. I had height and reach, but I would imagine he was a difficult man to hurt. I recognised some of the moves he had made from my training in Krav Maga, the 'art of going home alive', which was developed by Hungarian boxer and wrestler Emrich Lichtenfeld in the 1930s. If he was an adept student of that, or even worse, the more advanced and brutal KAPAP system, as used by various elite forces, I was probably fucked. I just wasn't match fit.

He beckoned me forward, inviting me to come back at him.

I should have settled for counters rather than attacks. As I lunged in I saw the right arm coming towards me, the hand angled to hit me with the edge. It would be like a blow from the blunt side of a sabre.

I grabbed the wrist, pulled him towards me and went back. He lost his balance and I planted a foot firmly in his stomach. As I hit the mat I felt the air blast from my lungs, but at the same time I flipped him over. Old school.

I whipped around in time to see him convert the throw into a perfect roll, landing on his feet and turning. Before I had managed to get up, his foot caught me under the chin, sending me sprawling back. I could taste the tang of iron. But it was no time to check my dental condition. I scrambled to my feet, awkwardly, and it took me three or four precious seconds to get my balance back. That was when I knew they were playing with me. He could have taken me in that small window, and there was nothing I could have done about it. Bojan was breathing hard, not from exertion but excitement. He wanted to prolong this pleasure.

I now had only Mitval between me and the exit, but that would do me little good. If I turned to run, even if I managed to palm aside Mitval, Bojan would be on me within two or three paces. And I really didn't want to turn my back on him.

I was sweating and I reached down to take off my top. As I did so I grabbed the T-shirt underneath and in one movement took them both off. I only had my sports bra on now. The cool air on my sticky skin felt good.

Bojan couldn't help but stare. The Colonel once told

me that a woman taking her top off could paralyse a man for half of a second. But that was widely thought to involve flashing your tits. Getting the bra off was too much to ask, but I reckoned even the underwear might get me a third or a quarter of a second. Not much, so I knew I had to move immediately, with my clothes still wrapped around one arm. I moved in close, fended off the kick with the sweatshirt and T-shirt and got a forearm to his nose. A grunt, of what I hoped was pain.

Then I hammered a fist over his ear, just to set it ringing, and with my left poked a finger deep into his eye socket.

That gave me a proper, satisfying scream. The retaliatory blow set my own ears humming and I staggered, but I went into him, rather than away. My right kidney bore the brunt of a vicious hooked swing, but I kneed him hard in the balls, keeping my knee there for a long second and grinding patella against scrotum. One eye was glaring hate at me, the other was half-closed, red and weeping. I went between them for a docker's kiss: a head butt on his already damaged nose.

Then I flipped his legs from under him and he went down. Already I could see him compartmentalising the pain, readying for another attack, so I stamped down on his ribs. He got my ankle on the second one, but by then I knew from the sweat beading on his forehead I had damaged something in his chest. I broke his grip, which was noticeably weak, and twisted away. I went back in and let my full weight drop onto his chest, landing on my knees, knocking the wind out of him, which came with a satisfying roar of pain. He clutched at me but again I broke free, rolling away from him and coming up in front of Mitval. He gave a slow round of applause.

'Brava. I think the job is yours.'

I pulled myself up to my full, aching height. His eyes flicked down to my breasts. They didn't have to flick far because I was towering over him. 'Fuck off,' I said, and rarely had those two words sounded so satisfying. I pulled my arm back and he flinched. But I let it drop. Point made.

In the changing room, I pulled on the T-shirt and sweatshirt with some difficulty. Overused muscles were stiffening. I pushed my regular clothes into the holdall without bothering to change into them and got into the lift. Nobody tried to stop me.

In the hallway, the butler watched me leave, his face impassive as he inclined his head in farewell. Didn't get the door for me, though.

Once I was out in the street I called Ben. I didn't engage in conversation. I just said: 'One thing. No more fucking Russians.' Then I hung up.

SIXTEEN

'Man down! Man down!'

The scared voice screaming in my ear is so loud I don't think the lad needed comms.

I ask him his location. How many of them. Two pax comes the answer. Only one of the pair hit.

Underneath the flag. Ground floor.

I raise my head over the bonnet of the Land Rover. It takes me a few moments to spot a tattered standard hanging limply from a flagpole that has been tied to a balustrade. It wasn't more than 200 metres away. A few rounds ping into the rear box of the 'Snatch' Land Rover, to remind me what lies between me and the doorway, beyond which a wounded man might be bleeding out.

I hear the pops and smacks of small-arms fire and the odd whine of a ricochet from nearby streets. Somewhere around the next bend C Company was under hostile fire. Our shitty, shitty Land Rover had taken a couple of hefty DShK rounds through the engine. Then the driver had taken one of the 12.7mms through his Alpha helmet. I didn't bother trying to give him any aid. Man down and staying down. We got out of the vehicle as the sides began to bulge and distort with every hit. Soon the metal box at the back would resemble a colander.

The Snatch is a disgrace. The Americans have vehicles that could withstand RPGs. The Snatch, which was designed for operations in Northern Ireland, could be taken with a tin opener.

I glance up at Gerry, a lad from Leeds who has been trying very hard to grow some manly stubble. His eyes are red from the dust and his lips cracked. He is scanning the ruined houses behind us, with particular attention paid to windows, open-air galleries and rooftops, watching our backs. Good lad.

I tell him where we have to get to and he nods, as if I'd just said we were popping out for a pint of milk. I know his insides aren't as calm as his exterior. I certainly know mine are as wriggly as a bag of snakes.

I wait until he is crouched behind me at the front wheel of the Snatch, count to five and give him the go signal. My feet scrabble on the dirt for a second until my boots find traction and I sprint at a crouch, ignoring the way the medi-pack straps bite into me. Gerry, not so encumbered, skips alongside me, spinning as he goes to cover us through 360 degrees. I hear the *chatter of his SA80 and the alarming zip of return fire slicing the air around my head.*

Dust devils dance around the doorway that is our target, as AKs stitch holes along the wall. But it's our God watching over us that day, not theirs, and we tumble inside, slamming the bullet-riddled door shut and letting the cool darkness take us.

I wait a minute, my breathing loud in my ears, my eyes adjusting from searing sunlight to a softer gloom. They are watering freely and I blink to clear away the film of water. 'OK, Gerry?'

'Nominated. Not elected.'

It would be a line from some old movie he watched with his dad during the long years the old man was dying. I'm not sure Gerry ever actually made it to school, but ask him about the films of Randolph Scott or the story arcs in Home and Away *and he is on it. He also has a good working knowledge of antiques and how to buy property in the country.*

The building is just a barren, empty shell of inter-connected rooms, many of which, judging by the smell, have been used as latrines, either by the insur-gents or us. Probably both. It reminds me my bladder is at bursting point. I'd have to find somewhere soon or piss myself. I had to stop waiting until I could no longer stand the pressure. Urinary infections are the bane of women in this place.

We find the two of them in the room farthest from

the door to the street, which I really don't like. Too easy to box us in.

Gerry reads my mind.

'I'll be out here.'

My throat is parched from grit, heat and fear. I suggest everyone has a drink and take a gulp of lukewarm water that does little to alleviate my thirst. Gerry does the same and then trots off to take up position.

It is Big Rex, a Geordie, who has been hit. With him is Charlie, a handsome mixed-race boy from Moss Side, whose good looks are spoiled by the scars from a bottling in a pub when he was sixteen. Four years ago, I remind myself. They are all still boys. But then, I'm still a girl, really. We just grow up a little faster.

I take off my helmet, unsling my pack and kneel.

'I got the bastard,' Rex says.

For the first time I notice the crumpled shape in the corner, the dark sprays of blood up the walls. I don't feel much about a dead insurgent, not when I have one of ours to tend. I pull on my latex-free gloves.

My radio comes alive. 'You OK, Buster?' It is Freddie, the senior medic, the West Country twang in her voice somehow more pronounced over the airwaves. Buster is my nickname. Because I'm always saying I need a pee. Like in Blockbusters *– 'I'll have a "p", Bob.' So I was Blockbuster for a while. Which, of course, got scrunched over time down to Buster.*

I look at Rex and lift his hands away from his

stomach. I do the quickest MARCH-P casualty assessment protocol ever. Basically it's a to-do list to remind you where and what you should be checking in the patient. 'I have an AW,' I tell Freddie. Abdominal wound. Not much I can do about that. It could be he was lucky and nothing much was hit by the AK round. Or he could be bleeding to death as I look at him. 'Cat-B. I'll need a casevac.' Casualty evacuation.

That was Freddie's call. It would mean a request to brigade HQ. 'So do I. I've got three Cat-As.' Category A means danger of death, patient requires immediate surgery. Three? Even for Freddie, that's a lot. 'There's a Chinook incoming. Five minutes.'

I get the HLZ location. The clearing two blocks away. The Chinook won't wait long. We had to be there. I hate Chinooks, big, clumsy, noisy and dangerous. But I liked the alternative even less.

'He going to be OK?' hisses Charlie.

I give him a look that tells him he shouldn't be asking. Not in earshot, but I give an optimistic reply. I clean up the wound as best I can, apply SwiftKlot to stem the bleeding – I know it isn't quite the miracle dressing the makers pretend, but there are times when it is just what the CMT ordered – and give him a ten of morphine intra-muscularly. Just enough to take the edge off, not enough to reduce him to a dead weight.

I explain we are going to have to move. I tell Charlie to look at the map and work out a route. It's partly *to distract him while I find a corner of another room, pull down my trousers and take a long, satisfying pee.*

Outside there is a lull in the fighting. It means nothing. The insurgents don't take tea breaks. They are probably regrouping.

When I return Charlie tells me there is an alley out back. If we do a right, another right, then a left, we'll be at the Helicopter Landing Zone. I pull Rex to his feet and he shrugs me off. 'I can walk.' Fit, proud young man that he is, he probably can, even with a bullet rattling about somewhere in his abdomen. He picks up his SA80, and we gather at the door to the street.

I imagine – or maybe I don't, maybe they're real – the familiar deep thwap-thwap of the Chinook's blades slicing the air. I prepare for the blast of heat that will hit us as we step outside, the temporary blindness caused by the unforgiving sun.

'OK,' says Gerry, 'let's go.'

We open the door and freeze. It seems every insurgent in Iraq is out there. All with either an AK or an RPG raised, pointing at us. Gerry makes to close the door, but it won't come. The hinges are frozen. We all try. And then the first rocket is fired, whooshing towards us . . .

I sit up, aware of how wet the sheets are. The dream, as always, is not entirely accurate. We didn't lose a Snatch driver. I usually carried my own SA80, although I can only use it under strict LOAC rules, the Law of Armed Conflict that tells soldiers who, what, why and when they can pull the trigger. Big Rex was shot at a command post. It was a head wound, not stomach. He died instantly.

But some things were true – I was always hot, sweaty, thirsty and I always needed a piss.

I padded down the corridor to the bathroom, checking on Jess en route. The sassy, manipulative teenager disappeared when she was asleep. Her features were set in a relaxed half-smile, as if her dreams were sweet indeed. She had thrown one leg out from under the covers, pinning her one-eared monkey beneath it. I wondered how long the one-eared monkey had left as a favoured sleep companion.

I went over and kissed Jess, as softly as I could, like a butterfly landing on her. She made the sort of sound you make when you are trying to get a hair out of your mouth, and rolled over. Monkey fell to the floor and I scooped him up and tucked the poor thing next to Jess. 'Love you,' I said. Neither the monkey nor Jess responded.

I went to the kitchen, poured myself a large glass of iced water and drank it in one. It was strange, I never had combat dreams when I was with Paul. All the bad things, from the army and before, were boxed and put in some cerebral attic. He was like the proverbial little boy with his thumb in the dyke, stopping them bursting through. Now he was gone, they were free to flow at will. And I sometimes felt I was drowning in them.

Or maybe it was the fight with Bojan that had triggered the dream. Technically you might say I had won the bout, but I was all too aware that I had been lucky, that my winning tactic was hardly a blow for sexual equality. In retrospect I thought maybe he hadn't been frozen by the sight of my chest. What he'd done was take a long look to show me he had the time to window-shop. It was another tactic aimed at humiliating me. I was fortunate that his timing had been off and mine, for once, had been spot-on. But the victory, if that's what it was, had come at a price. I could see that cost written on my body. Nothing was broken, but my right kidney was throbbing fit to explode and my muscles felt like I'd run a marathon. It simply wasn't used to that much adrenaline, I guess.

I looked at the clock as I gulped down a second glass of water. Four in the morning. I walked back along the corridor and, on impulse, I went back to Jess and slid in next to her. She gave a little grunt and snuggled against me. I could feel her warmth radiating through the cotton of her pyjamas and onto my damaged skin. It was like balm. I had a few precious hours before I had to put my black-and-blue body into smart clothes once more and see the Sharifs. And I wanted to spend those hours with my baby girl.

That night, while I slept with Jess tight in my arms, Ben's computer system was hacked and left with more viruses than an influenza ward. He blamed me for that. He was right.

SEVENTEEN

The blood hung in the air, a crimson arc caught by the low sun and, for a moment, I thought how beautiful it looked against the mist rising off the canal water, like a monochrome rainbow. And then the frozen second was gone, and the liquid made an ugly splatting sound onto the towpath.

I ran past for a few steps, propelled on by my momentum, and then turned back, heart thumping loudly in my ears and my breath scouring my throat. I couldn't actually speak, so I stepped on board the boat and pulled myself up onto the roof. A spray that size had to mean arterial blood.

The man who had cut himself was sitting on the top of the small, electric-blue narrow boat – the *Slim Pickens* – watching the blood pulse out of the wound with what appeared to be bemusement.

I took off the sweatshirt I had tied round my waist and quickly wrapped it around the wound. He didn't resist. I remembered my dream and I wished I had a SwiftKlot dressing.

'You OK?' I managed to gasp.

He nodded. 'It's not as bad as it looked just then. I flicked the blood off my arm. It's not an artery, if that's what you were thinking.'

I noted the cutters and the red-flecked tinplate next to him and put the scenario together. He had been installing a small array of solar panels on the roof. He'd been trying to cut a piece of metal for a housing and had slipped, the raw edge slicing into his forearm.

'Even so, that's a lot of blood. You have a first-aid kit?'

He nodded. 'But I can manage.'

'Not as well as I can.'

I stepped down into the stern and ducked inside the boat. 'Next to the fire blanket,' he shouted.

I took in a very neat and clean, but pretty old-fashioned, wooden galley – this was no *Elle Deco* boat – although much of it was taken up by a coffee machine that wouldn't have looked out of place in a Milanese café. I grabbed the green pack with the Red Cross off its hook and went back outside.

I was trying to run off the aches and bruising from the day before. I'd pounded the towpath from my flat, east to Broadway Market, and was on my return leg when I saw the accident. In truth, I was glad of the excuse to stop. It was going to take more than a run to undo Bojan's damage.

I clambered up on top once more and sat next to him and caught my breath. I hoped the smell didn't knock him out. I hadn't sweated so much since childbirth.

'Let me see.'

'Just give me a plaster.'

'Let me see,' I insisted.

'What are you, an angel of mercy?'

'Something like that. Give me your arm.'

He did so. He was wearing just a T-shirt and chinos so at least there was no clothing to cut away once I had unwrapped my by-now dark-red top. His arm was corded with sinews and streaked with blood oozing from the gash. I used one sleeve of my top to fashion a tourniquet around the top of his arm, then examined the wound. It grinned at me.

I looked it over. A voice in my head from long ago said: 'Cat-C'. No shit, Sherlock. 'It's going to need stitches.'

'No, it isn't.'

'It is.'

'Well, it isn't going to get any.'

I looked into his face. He had a week's growth of beard and grey eyes. He was probably about Paul's age, maybe a little younger, although the tanned skin, wind-coarsened by the outdoors, made it a difficult call.

'It'll leave a scar.'

He held up his other arm. There was a deep gouge running along the top. 'At least I'll have a matching pair.'

'Maybe you should give up DIY,' I said, even though I knew that second wound was probably from a bullet. 'I'll do what I can with Steri-Strips.'

'You a nurse?' he asked as I set about cleaning the cut.

'CMT.' Combat Medical Technician, but I was curious to know if he recognised the acronym.

His eyebrows went up. He recognised it all right. 'Where?'

'Iraq.' I usually didn't mention my time in Afghanistan, mainly because there wasn't that much of it. 'You?'

'What makes you think I'm army?'

I nodded at his right arm. 'I know what a bullet wound looks like. Drug dealer or army. I vote army.'

He nodded. 'Right. Once upon a time.'

There was something in those few words that didn't invite further enquiry. I let it pass. Some like to talk about it, others don't. 'You live here? On board?'

'Continuous cruiser,' he said.

'What's that mean?' I began to lay over the Steri-Strips. It wouldn't take much to dislodge them and I tutted at his stubbornness.

'Of no fixed abode. The rules say I can't stay in one place on the canals for more than fourteen days.'

'That's tough.'

'I rarely last more than three.'

'I could stitch this if you had the right gear.'

'You're doing fine ... sorry, I don't know your name.'

I told him.

'I'm Tom. Tom Buchan.' One day, some way down the line, I would find out that was a whopping lie. 'Buck to my friends.'

I released the tourniquet and began to wind a bandage over the wound, making sure it was tight enough to give the strips a hope in hell of staying in place.

The footpath was filling up with more joggers and the first of the tourists wobbling uncertainly on their chunky rental bikes. The sun had driven off the mist and it was good to feel it on my neck. I didn't recognise the next feeling at all. Someone said that being happy is all about being in the moment, which is why it is so fleeting. Like good sex, happiness is all about letting go, dropping out of time, forgetting that past or future exists. It was a long time since I had bandaged a wounded man. The last time, someone had been shooting at me. This was better.

I just need a cock in my cunt.

I felt myself redden and cleared my throat, as if he could hear that unbidden instruction, echoing down the years. 'There you go, soldier.'

'Thank you.' He did that thing of bending his arm and twisting it to make sure it still worked. Everyone does it, as if you've given them a new limb that needs to be tried out. 'I owe you a new top.'

'It'll wash out.'

I went to reach for it, but he snatched it away.

'Hey.'

'I'll get you a new one. Least I can do. That and a cup of coffee.'

While his machine clanked and hissed we sat on the bench that ran across the stern beneath the tiller.

'How do you make a living if you never stop?' I asked him.

He pointed to his dressing. 'Contrary to the evidence, I fix things. Normally without opening a vein.'

'What kind of things?'

He shrugged. 'Engines. Gearboxes. Mechanical things, not computers or shit like that.'

'Is that what you were in the army? A mechanic?'

His face tightened. He really didn't want to go there. 'No. My dad owned a garage, back when you could still fix cars with a hammer and screwdriver and didn't need something called diagnostics. I got it from him. The mechanical thing. Sugar?'

'No, thanks.'

It was black because he had no milk and that was fine because dairy was one of the many, many things I was meant to cut down on. While we drank I found myself telling him about Jess, about being a PPO and, yes, about Paul.

'Tough break,' he said.

'I always think if I hadn't called him and asked him to pick up some baked beans and shit from the shop—'

'Don't.' He shook his head vigorously to emphasise his point. 'Don't think like that. You know in the army, when you lose a guy you can always point to a dozen things, which, if done differently, might have saved his life. It's like football. You know?'

'How is it like football?' I didn't much care about the answer, but I was enjoying listening to him speak. He had a warm-butter kind of voice.

'If you study any match closely, you can follow how one bad pass, a missed tackle, a fluffed corner, a reckless clearance or an untrapped ball could, after seven, ten, fifteen further moves, be responsible for a crucial goal. It is all cause and effect. Just like life. If you dwell on how one little thing you did caused the death of someone ... well, it becomes a form of madness if you let it.'

I had a feeling he was speaking from experience.

We drank our coffees for a while. I watched a fat Dutch barge, painted matt black as if it were a stealth bomber, come huffing by. At the wheel was a heavily tattooed young woman in very tiny denim shorts and a halter-top. She raised a hand when she saw Tom.

'Where you headed, Liz?' he shouted over the thrum of her engine.

'Limehouse. You?'

Tom pointed in the opposite direction.

'Pity. See you around.' She raised a hand in farewell as the barge made its stately way east.

'Must be strange,' I said.

'What?'

'Living on the canals all the time. It's like its own little world. Own people. Own customs, I suppose.'

'That's why I like it. That's why you resent it when everyday life comes calling. Although sometimes I'm glad it does.' He indicated his wound and smiled. The Tower of Terror did its stuff in my stomach again. 'Thanks for stopping. Another coffee?'

'No, I'd best be going.'

'OK. See you around?' Somehow it sounded different than when he said it to Liz. More like a question.

My phone beeped and I ignored it. 'Sure.'

I didn't know then it would be a good few weeks before I saw him again, and when I did, it would be with news of Paul. Bad news.

Right then, though, I climbed off the barge and began a slow jog. The steps felt awkward, because I could feel those steel-grey eyes drilling into my back. Except when I glanced over my shoulder, he'd disappeared. The phone made an impatient buzz again and I looked at the message. It was from Jess. 'COME BACK AT ONCE. URGENT. THERE'S A STRANGE MAN.'

EIGHTEEN

'Can we keep it?'

I ignored Jess and stared at the open case for a good two minutes before I spoke. I had spent a quarter of an hour checking it before I had lifted the lid. The contents struck both of us dumb. Until Jess asked that inevitable question.

'Who was it delivered this?' I asked Jess.

'I told you, a man with a motorcycle helmet on. He said he couldn't wait for you and handed it over. How much is it?'

'Never you mind.' But I'd been wondering that myself. Sitting on the countertop were piles of bank-notes, a mixture of print-fresh twenties and fifties, all neatly packed in an aluminium flight case. I watched the gleam in Jess's eyes and she reached over to grab a bundle of the notes. I gently slapped her hand away as her fingers brushed the top note. 'Don't touch it. And wash your hands.'

I pulled the small envelope that was nestling between

two of the bundles and opened it. Inside was a larger version of a business card, bearing a single letter in a fancy gold font. 'A'. Well, that suggested one person. Asparov. But wasn't he out of the country?

I picked up the phone and dialled.

'Can we keep it?' repeated Jess.

I shook my head. 'Ben? It's me.'

Before I could say anything else he told me about his computer system being hacked. He was beside himself with rage, as he should be. His type of clients don't like their private details being stolen.

'Look, I've got to go,' he said, 'I've got the cyber-security guys here installing some new and very expensive defences. I reckon this is down to you upsetting those fucking Russians.'

I'd given him the full story of Bojan's little games when I had got home the previous day. He wasn't quite as outraged as I had hoped. He was now, though.

'Yeah, well, I've had a little present today from them. The Russians.' I fingered the card once more, running a thumb over the raised letter. 'Well, Asparov, anyway.'

'What kind of present? Ah, they didn't shit on your carpet, did they?'

'I don't have any carpets. No, someone delivered around eight thousand pounds. Maybe more.'

There was a silence on the line.

'Ben?'

'That's weird. You sure it was Asparov?'

'Pretty much. Listen, I need new security too. Can you ping me across the number of someone who can fit an Alpha-spec door and locks?' An 'Alpha' spec is based on an MI6 protocol for safe houses. Basically you need a battering ram to get in. Or the right keys.

'Why?'

'Too many people know where I live.' Too many Russians for one.

'OK. I'll send a list across. Let me know how you get on with the Sharifs. Hopefully you won't have to go six rounds with them.'

'That a joke?'

'Best I can manage right now.'

I hung up and redialled the number I had been given for the Asparovs. The clipped tones told me it was the butler who had picked up.

'Can I speak to Mr Asparov?'

'I am afraid Mr Asparov is in Moscow.'

'Odd, because I just got a delivery from him.'

'Ah. I see. I think it was by way of recompense.'

'Recompense?' I asked. 'Look, can you send someone back to pick it up?'

I felt him shudder at the other end of the line at the suggestion. 'I couldn't possibly do that. It would be against Mr Asparov's express wishes.'

'And what if I were to dump it in the canal?'

'I fear it is yours to do with as you will.' He couldn't

have sounded stiffer if he'd been doused with spray starch.

'Can you stop talking like that?'

'Like what?'

Like you have Sir John Gielgud up your back passage I wanted to say, but let it pass. 'When will Mr Asparov be back in the country?'

'Not for some time.'

'Then I'll wait and return it personally.'

'He will not be pleased.'

'I'm not exactly thrilled myself, friend.'

I broke the connection and fetched a carrier bag from the drawer and the latex-free gloves from my RTG holdall.

'What are you doing?' asked Jess.

'Putting this somewhere safe. Where we can't touch it.'

She stuck out her lower lip. 'But why?'

I put on the gloves and shovelled the stacks into the brown bag. The flight case was too bulky to fit in my safe, but I reckoned I could squash the notes in. 'Look, Jess, you've heard that expression: "There's no such thing as a free lunch"?'

'Of course.'

'There's no such thing as a free stack of cash either.'

'But it'd pay for—'

'Stop it, now.' I knew what she was thinking. Indonesia.

'Trust me, this has more strings attached than Kermit the Frog.'

There was a beat. 'Isn't he a glove puppet?'

'You know what I mean.'

The doorbell rang. Laura. 'Get that, will you, Jess. I'll be back in a minute.'

The safe was in the wardrobe in my bedroom, not much more useful that the average hotel safe, but better than nothing. I'd move the money to somewhere more secure as soon as I could. Not a bank, though. They'd have questions. Although not as many as I had.

I opened the safe. The only thing in there, apart from the client files Ben had given me, was a knife. Not an ordinary blade, but an Eickhorn Advanced Combat Knife, which had once belonged to Paul. It was a nasty piece of work, with a curved tip, a razor-sharp edge and a really cruel serrated section. It was perfect. I took it out, replacing it with the money. Then I slid the knife under my pillow.

Just in case.

PART TWO

NINETEEN

There are enough people in this world concerned about being shot at for BMW to make a high security version of its 7 series. The 7Li is armoured and compliant with the requirements of the class VR7 ballistic protection standard. Which means you can fire 400 7.62mm rounds at it from every angle with zero penetration. It is also blast-proofed against fragmentation and armour-piercing hand grenades. Each of the corners is reinforced for those times when you have to punch through parked vehicles or reverse your way out of trouble. Most of us PPOs have been trained to do those high-speed reverses and spins so beloved of the movies.

It's all, for the most part, a waste of time.

You'd have to go some way to find any PPO who'd ever had to ram his or her way out of trouble. If it did happen to me, I'd see it as a sign of failure – you shouldn't get yourself boxed in in the first place. And, some hostile countries excepted, you rarely get grenades tossed at you. Plus, thankfully, AK-47s are pretty rare on the streets of Knightsbridge.

Still, it's what people expect of PPOs and their vehicles, the so-called Hard Skills – fast driving, martial arts, gunplay. The Soft Skills – planning, negotiation, conflict resolution – are generally underappreciated. But that's what the job is 99.9 per cent of the time.

Three days into the PPO role for the Sharifs and I managed to get them to garage the Roller – it would be reserved for special occasions – and to use the 7Li they had gathering dust as the everyday car. It was still conspicuous to those who know what to look for, but it pulled a lot fewer stares than the Ghost. They also gave me permission to have it given the once-over by One-Eyed Jack.

Despite the name, One-Eyed Jack had perfectly good vision. Rumour had it he got the nickname from his early days doing MOTs in south-east London. If he liked you and found a minor fault, he'd say: 'I'll turn a blind eye to that for the moment, but get it fixed.'

But Jack, disproving the adage about old dogs and new tricks, had moved on from MOTs. These days he worked out of a former airfield near Leighton Buzzard. He had three big hangars, all used to customise cars. Those hideous stretch limos that were once so fashionable? Jack's work. Blinged-up Range Rovers with illegally dark windows? Same. But they were just the public face of his business. Hangar 3 was where he did the real graft, plating up cars to B6/7 blast-proof standard, increasing engine power to cope with the extra weight of the armour. He did Beemers, Audis, Mercs, Toyota Landcruisers ...

If that makes me sound like a Jeremy Clarkson-style petrolhead, the truth was that I knew about Beemers, Audis, Jags, Range Rovers and so on because they were tools of my trade. They were what I had to drive on The Circuit. The other cars that wheel-spun around the PPO world were the clients' toys – Maseratis, Lamborghinis, Ferraris. I can't tell a Ferrari F70 from a 458 – well, maybe with a gun to my head – and, even though I have a soft spot for Porsches, the variations of 911 produced over the years baffle me.

Jack came out when I pulled up on the concrete apron outside Hangar 3, wearing the Duckhams overalls that were already faded when I first met him. He was close to sixty, completely bald, his skin lined and the creases in his fingers so ingrained with oil that it would take a sea of Swarfega to clean them. Still, he had a good go with the rag he was holding and held out his hand.

'The call surprised me. I didn't know you was back in the game,' he said, showing me teeth that appeared to have shuffled apart from each other in mutual distaste. His voice was gruff, the edges rough from his old cigarillo habit.

I shook his hand. 'Just a few weeks now.'

'Who for?'

'Family in north London.'

'OK, are they?'

'Fine.' Jack wouldn't expect much more. But the Sharifs really were fine, or at least the members of the family I had seen so far. I had turned up for the interview with a headscarf on, just in case, but Mrs Sharif had told me they were none too strict about such things when in London. Mrs Sharif was, without exaggeration, one of the most beautiful women I had ever seen. Relaxed, friendly, she had made it clear she considered the whole PPO thing nonsense, at least when outside Pakistan. But Mr Sharif – who was away on business – was worried about Nuzha, the daughter. She turned out to be the kind of twelve-year-old you only read about – polite, diligent, hard-working, maybe a little too serious. Whereas Jess had had a poster of One Direction in her bedroom at that age, Nuzha had a picture of Malala Yousafzai. The young lady wanted to be a doctor. I didn't doubt she'd make it.

So, unusually, Mrs Sharif, with a little help from Ali, her residential security advisor, and a consultation with Nuzha, had hired me, without waiting for Mr Sharif's say-so. I liked that.

'What can I do you for?' Jack asked, looking over the BMW. He tapped one of the doors with a knuckle, then repeated the process on the windscreen glass. 'Is that all factory-fitted?'

'Yes.'

'Well, they make a pretty good fist of it. Unless you think your bloke's going to be attacked with an RPG, it'll do the job.'

'I don't need plate. I want you to do a number on the reversing camera.'

'Ah. OK, that's easy enough. With the hard drive, it'll be three hundred, though. Plus the VAT.'

'That's fine.' It wasn't my money. 'Just give me a receipt.'

'Take me about an hour, maybe an hour and a half. I can lend you a Range Rover if you need to leave it.'

I looked at my phone and checked the time. I had to pick Nuzha up from school in Hampstead Garden Suburb in three hours. 'I should be good. Oh, and could you check whether the driver's air bags have been done. If not, disable them and tweak the diagnostics to hide it.'

'Steering wheel and side?'

'Yes.'

The thinking behind taking out the driver's air bags was simple. If you get rammed by hostiles, a face full of giant gas envelope tends to impair your response, not to mention blocking your vision. Everyone else in the vehicle can get a free bouncy castle, but you, the driver, want to be able to see and steer out of trouble.

'That's another hundred.'

I remembered there was something I meant to ask him. 'Jack, by the way, what's RSCA? I'm a little rusty.'

He nodded at the BMW. 'This fitted with that?' There was no hiding the contempt in his voice.

'No, I heard about it on another job. Russians. Asked if I knew what it was.' Before they tried to beat the crap out of me, that is.

'It's a pile of shit, that's what it is. It controls the car.'

'Controls how?'

'Whatever you want. It's a phone app, sort of. Remote Security and Control App. You key in a code, then you can lock the car, open it, immobilise it, start it up, put the bleedin' radio on, some of them even have a "Come to Daddy" feature. Or Mummy in your case.'

'What's that do?'

'The car will drive to you. Within reason. You know, if you or your clients don't want to step out into the rain, you can pull it along the driveway. They have some sort of sensors in the bumper so you don't accidentally get run over. Still gives me the willies, though.' He sniffed his disapproval. 'And there's a "Get Me The Fuck Out Of Here" button.'

'That the technical term?'

'E-Evac. Emergency evacuation. The car comes to you a little quicker, shall we say.'

'And you don't like it because ...?' I knew the answer.

'I don't like the idea of motors that drive themselves.

Technology gone fuckin' mad. And RSCA is hackable. Very hackable. My boy Jordan reckons he can do it in under a minute. So you can be drivin' along and suddenly, it ain't you at the wheel. It's some geezer with an iPhone in the car next to you. And even if you don't have the hacking gizmo, in most cases the standard pin code is—'

'One, two, three, four?'

'No, the client's name or initials. Most people are too vain to change that to something with hashtags and exclamation marks. You don't want that on this, do you?' He indicated the BMW once again, his face aghast.

'Not after that sales pitch. One more thing – a "Disabled" sticker. A kosher one if you can.'

'Yup, no sweat. That's on the house.'

I handed him the keys to the 7Li.

'Ta.' Jack wrapped his fist round them and fixed me with his two good eyes. 'Is this just a precaution or . . .?'

'No, not just a precaution,' I said. 'I think I'm being followed.'

I didn't think anything of the kind. I *knew* I was being followed. Not all the time. Perhaps once or twice in the past week. Not always in the same car, either, but I had clocked the same driver in two different vehicles and I'd seen a classic switch manoeuvre, where one tail drops back to allow the other to move forward, thus mixing up the action so the object of attention doesn't notice. But I had noticed. Which is why Jack was working on the reversing camera. It was a device to make the camera 'live', so that you can film the cars behind you and save that to a hard drive. It could then be loaded to a USB stick and viewed at home.

It was possible that I was being paranoid, of course, and that what I thought I knew was just bullshit. Take that clocking of the driver, the one with stubble and the sort of shaved-at-the-sides haircut that made it look as if a turd had been laid on his head. I'd seen him in a Fiat 500 and an Audi A5. So what? Lots of people had two cars. Jesus, my Principal had a dozen. But I drove a different route to and from Nuzha's school and to and from home every day. I probably shouldn't be seeing the same driver twice.

The PPO mantra applied here: once is possible, two is probable, three is definite.

And I had something to be paranoid about, of course. I was the proud owner of ten grand I didn't deserve. It was tucked away in Ben Harris's rather more substantial safe. I'd had the stash checked for markers or substance imprints. It was clean, but part of me thought that the moment I spent a single note, it would blow up in my face. Maybe someone else fancied spending it, though.

But I was still hovering at 'probable' on the tail. It

was why I hadn't yet raised it with Mr or Mrs Sharif. You need to be sure before you create a sense of tension or fear in the household. Besides, even if it was a follower, there was another question. Who was being tailed? Them or me?

While Jack worked on the car, I took a walk around the airfield. It had shrunk over the years, as parcels of land around the perimeter had been sold off for housing. Jack had offered high-speed driving courses here, until the new neighbours complained about tyre-squeal and smoke.

Now he said they were complaining about the 'eyesore' of the motley collection of ruined and scavenged planes at the end of the weed-choked runway.

I walked across towards them, batting off the clouds of small flies that rose in my path. I am no expert on planes, but they were all of a vintage – an early passenger jet that had been used for fire evacuation drills, a sad, twin-engined number whose wings looked as if they had been attacked by voracious moths and a once perky little Cessna, now down on its knees – well, its collapsed undercarriage. Most of the aircraft had missing panels, wires and tubes hanging from them, as if they had been subject to sustained torture and evisceration. I could smell the pungent mix of their lifebloods – the spilled oil, grease and the kerosene – and I thought that maybe I was on the side of the neighbours. There was something very melancholy about these unloved and abandoned orphans.

This made me think about Matt and Jess. He was claiming he'd go to court unless we could work out something 'amicably' about him having access ('contact time' as he called it) to Jess. To me, it seemed unfair that he could sweep back into our lives and reclaim his stake as if picking up his winnings from the bookies. I had broached the subject with Jess and, frustratingly, she seemed quite open to the idea of having a mum and a dad again. I didn't mind the idea. Just not with that particular dad, that's all. Now maybe someone like Tom Buchan ...

I felt a once-familiar flutter build, spreading down from my chest into the pit of my stomach, and continue south.

You need a ...

Stop that. Why would some canal gypsy make a better father than a former drug dealer? Besides, the waterman had gone. When I had next passed, the mooring where Tom's boat had been was empty. I had stood and watched as another boat, a more flowery number full of canal art – decorated watering cans, milk churns and plant pots – eased its way in.

'You after Tom Buchan?'

I had turned and looked at the woman addressing me from a neighbouring vessel, the *Ragdoll*. She was in her seventies, I'd guess, with rheumy eyes, straggly grey hair and she was smoking a roll-up so skinny it must have had but a single thread of tobacco along its length.

'Just going to say hello.'

She gave a phlegmy laugh. 'What Tom's best at is goodbyes. Hold on.'

She had disappeared below and then came back up with an envelope, which she handed over to me. It had my name on it, printed in big blocky letters. I opened it. The single sheet carried a simple message: 'I.O.U. one running top'. And then a signature: Buck.

So what was I to do about Matt? The thought of sharing Jess made my stomach contract but, on the other hand, having somewhere for her to go if the Sharifs suddenly decided we needed to decamp to Monaco was attractive. I cursed myself for selfishness. It was what was right for Jess that was important. Not the convenience for my job.

But just how reliable was Matt? This was a man who had sold ecstasy, meth, cocaine . . . you tended not to hang around with nice people in that business. But he claimed he'd given that world up. Or vice versa. Yet, when I had asked him about his source of income, he had been very vague. *This and that*, as far as I knew, was not a career.

I put my head inside the Cessna. The inside was a mess, the seats slashed and torn, the controls missing so many instruments it looked like a collection of eyeless sockets. The afternoon sunlight caught the cat's cradle of spiders' webs crisscrossing the cabin. Something rustled in the stuffing of one of the seats and I backed out quickly.

I started my way back towards Hangar 3. As I did so, I came to a decision. Fighting Matt was going to be time-consuming, expensive and maybe futile. I didn't think he was going to end up on top of the Shard dressed as Batman, but I suspected he would fight hard and, if need be, dirty. What I needed to know, more than any court ever could, was how fit he was to have my daughter. So the answer was simple.

I was going to have to spy on my ex-husband.

TWENTY

There is a lot of hurry-up-and-wait in the world of PPOs. In that way, it's just like the army. A whirlwind of preparation, going to full alert ... and then nothing, stretching ahead for hours. We are used to the unexpected announcement of a last-minute trip to the cinema or the shops or a flight to Zurich or Monaco, the cars are readied, the route planned and then ... minds are changed, plans altered or cancelled altogether. Stand down.

So, like most clients' houses, the Sharifs had a room for staff to do their protracted waiting around in. Tea- and coffee-making facilities, a fridge full of soft drinks, an HD-TV, radio, a few CCTV screens showing the front and rear of the house.

I was in there nursing a brew when Ali found me. The head of security was a handsome man in a throwback kind of way. I could picture him as a Moghul conqueror, sitting astride a white stallion, cutting a swathe through enemy armies. He had a moustache that had a life of its own, a lion's mane of swept-back black hair and a chest that entered the room before he did.

'How are you doing?' he asked as he slumped down beside me on the sofa, which creaked in alarm. I wondered if they had to reinforce the furniture for him. 'Settling in?'

'Yes, fine, thanks.' He got up and helped himself to a Coke, giving the sofa another joint bashing when he sat back down.

'No questions?'

'When do I meet Mr Sharif?'

'He'll be back soon. Later this afternoon, maybe.' He looked at me in a way that could be misinterpreted, but I recognised a professional appraisal when I was subject to one. 'You have any pictures of when you were in the army?'

I shook my head. 'Not on me.' The only one I had was of me standing next to Freddie on a WMIK Land Rover during my blink-and-you'd-miss-it tour in Afghanistan. Behind us is Tom Jones, a Welsh kid (actually called Ewan Jones) who had both thumbs in the air. It was taken about two hours before he stepped on a legacy mine.

Ali took a wallet from his inside pocket and produced a creased photograph of himself in a beret, his chest heavy with medals. 'That was me. And here, in this one. Recognise the chap next to me?'

The second photograph was of Ali in plain clothes, helping a second man move through a crowd. I stared at the face. The moustache and glasses of the middle-aged man he was chaperoning rang a bell.

'President Musharraf.' I thought that impressive chest was going to split with pride.

'You were a presidential bodyguard?'

He nodded. 'And a major in the SSG.' The Special Services Group was an elite unit of the Pakistani army that, after a shaky start, had acquitted itself well in anti-terrorism operations close to the north-west frontier.

'What happened?'

'The third assassination attempt happened. My wife says, enough. One day they will get him and get you. Apparently I was on the death list of Harkat-ul Mujahideen al-Alami. You know them?'

'No.' They didn't have the kind of name that caused a warm, fuzzy feeling in your bones.

'Fanatics,' he said. 'Bloody fanatics. So we moved here. First I make a living selling cars then someone tells me about bodyguarding jobs. It's better than cars.'

'Do you miss the army?'

'Every day. Every single day. Do you?'

'Maybe if someone hadn't shot me.'

He laughed at that. But it does colour your memory somewhat.

I looked at the clock on the wall. 'I'm on. Nuzha pick-up from school.'

'Nice chatting.'

'Yes, it was.'

And I knew I had someone who would be good in a tight corner.

'Are you married?'

I glanced up into the rear-view mirror and refocused on Nuzha. Normally my attention was on the outside of the car, rather than the passenger. She was in her green school uniform and had shrugged off the hijab she wore 'because all my friends do' and her thick hair, black and shiny as a liquorice stick, lay on her shoulders. She had a round, open face and eyes that could only have come from her mother. There was every chance she would grow up to be as beautiful as Mrs Sharif.

'No,' I said. It was true, of course. And I no longer wore Paul's ring, except when totally off-duty. It always led to more questions. But if I had hoped that was the end of it, I was mistaken.

'Why?' she persisted.

'Why what?'

'Aren't you married?'

I stopped at the lights opposite Golders Hill Park. I was circling back to Highgate via Hampstead, one of a half-dozen routes I had mapped out just to mix things up. I raised a hand to tell her to wait. Next to me was an X5, a harassed woman in her thirties at the wheel, yelling at a pair of children in the rear, rendered as shadowy ghosts by the 'sun protection tinting' as they like to call the privacy glass. I managed to lip-read part of the diatribe. 'Do you know how much that school costs?'

I would imagine the kids in the back knew only too well how much the school cost to the nearest 50p, probably having been reminded with every B-grade and 'Doesn't engage in class' comment on their report.

Behind me was a UPS parcel van, to the left a solo motorcyclist, a young lad leaning over the bars, keen to be on his way judging by the incontinent bursts of revving. Behind him, a white VW Transporter.

Colour? Let's call it orange-yellow.

As I pulled away, Nuzha asked again. 'Why aren't you married? You should be by now.'

'Do you have homework?' I asked.

'Yes. "Find out why your driver isn't married".'

I turned at that and she had a wide, cheeky grin across her face.

'That's a funny old school you go to.'

'It's not like you're ugly or anything.'

'Nuzha. Please, I can't discuss such things.'

'Being ugly?'

I had to laugh. 'No. My personal life.'

'But you have a child.'

'Nuzha, please.'

'Ammi told me.' Her mother shouldn't have. The PPO file was meant to be private. 'So you had a child out of wedlock.' It wasn't judgemental, just a bald statement of fact. But it was too much.

I pulled over to the kerb, causing the UPS van to give a short, irritated hoot, and turned in my seat. There was a flicker of anger in my voice and I doused it.

'Nuzha. I will say this once. I was married. He died. I have a daughter.' OK, so it was edited highlights, but it would have to do. 'I cannot talk about politics, religion or my private life. I don't have opinions. I am here to look after you and I can't do that if we spend all the time gossiping. OK?'

If she was in any way chastened she didn't show it, simply nodded enthusiastically. 'OK.'

I reselected drive and pulled out, heading for the roundabout at Jack Straws Castle.

'Some of my friends already know who they are going to marry when they grow up.'

I simply nodded. No politics, no religion.

'But I'm glad,' she said softly, 'that you were married once.'

I caught up with the UPS parcel van and undertook him at the roundabout. I only got a glimpse of the driver, but it was enough to change everything from yellow to red. He had on the brown overalls of UPS drivers. He also had what looked like a turd on his head.

Three: definite.

Mr Sharif called me into his study after I had delivered Nuzha home. The main house was smart and modern, all sharp angles with plenty of steel and glass. The sort of home that had multiple skylights, which always made me think they must be a devil to keep clean. But people who can afford twenty-million-pound houses on Highgate Hill can probably stretch to a window cleaner or two.

His study was unlike the rest of the building, far more traditional, with no skylights but Tiffany lamps, wood-panelling, a shiny rosewood desk and carpet as opposed to parquet flooring. It felt like the office of the CEO of a large multinational. Which, of course, was what Mr Sharif was.

'Come in. Close the door.' He was somewhere in his late-forties, maybe a dozen years older than his wife. He was wiry-thin – he had played squash competitively and, so Mrs Sharif had told me with some satisfaction, was still able to whip the twenty-year-olds at his club. Like his wife he had striking eyes, but these ones were of a different order – his were hooded and challenging, as if daring you to just try and lie to him. That stare of his must have been an asset in business. But PPOs shouldn't lie to their Principal. Maybe just withhold a nugget of information or two.

Like you think you are being followed.

It might seem strange not to share that sort of suspicion, but it was not as reckless as it might seem. Firstly, every PPO thinks they are being followed as a matter of course. Or at least, acts as if they are. Secondly, you don't want to concern the Principal overmuch. They usually have enough on their minds. You start to worry them when you see the first fleck of Red in the situation. Thirdly, you don't want to appear an idiot when it transpires that plenty of young men, especially those who drive delivery vans, have that stupid haircut. No, it was Ali who would be first port of call. As resident, he would judge what was the correct response.

Mr Sharif closed the lid on a gold MacBook laptop. 'Drink?' he asked, heading for a sideboard that turned out to double as a cocktail cabinet.

'No, thank you.' No drinking on duty, no cigarettes ever, now. They can smell it on your hair and on your clothes and it doesn't project the right image. I can't pretend that giving up the final two-a-day was easy, though.

'Quite right. Please forgive me.' He poured himself a half-inch of Talisker and invited me to sit.

'I'm sorry I wasn't here when my wife interviewed you.'

'That's all right, sir.' I meant it. The rich rarely stay in one place for long, either for tax reasons or because they feel the need to bless their various habitations with visits every now and then. Most have a lot of habitations to get round.

'I wanted to know how you are getting on. Just between you and me.'

'Fine, sir.'

'You know there was another candidate for your post. A Miss Gill. You know of her?'

'There are plenty of female Personal Protection Officers in London these days, sir. I don't know them all, I'm afraid.' Only the good ones, and I'd never heard of Miss Gill.

'No matter. Nice Muslim girl. But Nuzha thought she preferred you. The Tall Lady, she called you.'

'That was quite a decision considering we only had five minutes together.'

'She has strong opinions. She knows her mind.'

'She's a remarkable little girl. You should be proud of her.' As soon as I said it I knew I had got the nuance wrong.

'Should be? I *am* proud of her.' He sat down behind the desk and appeared to gather his thoughts. It was a minute before he spoke again. 'It pains me to say it, but I am not always a popular man in my country. You know about CatSlam?'

'Catwalk to Islam.'

'Ha.' He seemed surprised and, possibly, pleased. 'It is a phenomenon. The *Financial Times* writes about it. But to some, I am a devil. An evil man.'

'Because . . .?'

'Because they see CatSlam as a way of Westernising young girls. Of demeaning Islam by introducing foreign ideas of beauty. The thin end of the wedge, you might say. Today, a scarf inspired by Milan, tomorrow our daughters will be having sex before marriage and showing their breasts in public.'

He took a drink and I wondered how I was meant to respond. I could see how someone with extreme views might interpret taking inspiration from the catwalks as an attack on their core values. But the strictly religious always disliked change, especially where fashion is concerned.

'It doesn't help, of course, that I am not one who eschews alcohol. That I only have one wife. Nor am I a man who thinks only sons have value in this world.'

I said nothing.

He held up the glass. 'You know, if you were to take a photograph of me now, you could bring all this crumbling down around my ears. Of me, drinking this.' He took a large gulp to make the point.

'How so?'

'My wife married beneath her station in life. I am a millionaire, but in the eyes of some, I will always just be a tailor who got lucky. So, to show my intentions were honourable, I created a family trust to run the business, to share the profits . . . generously. We all sup from the pot. As head of this trust, I sup a little deeper.'

He gave a crooked smile and I wondered if he was down the road on the way to drunk. 'However, fearing that my base nature will one day shine through, they have a proviso that I can be removed if I ever bring disgrace on the family.' He chortled and drank some more. 'So, cheers.'

'Your secret is safe with me,' I said.

'I know. Ali says he trusts you. As for Nuzha, rest assured, young lady, that I do love her. I know I have something special there. Of course, I would like another son, but God decides such things.' I thought his God had a position on whisky drinking, too, but again kept my mouth shut on that score. *No religion, no politics.*

'Well, thank you, sir—'

'You know today would have been his birthday. My son's. You know I had a son?'

I nodded. 'How old?'

'He would be eighteen.'

Ah. Maybe that explained the whisky. I didn't feel I could pry any further, because there were tears pooling in his eyes. 'I'm sorry. It must be difficult.'

'Difficult? I am afraid dying is something of a family trait.' He sighed. 'Do you know my background?'

'I know you built up a textile empire from a single shop.'

He fixed me with those eyes and I resisted the powerful temptation to look away. 'But do you know about

Partition? The split between India and Pakistan?' I nodded. 'My family were on the wrong side of the border in 1947. One of a handful of Muslim families in a Hindu town. My father was a tailor, and a good one, but he knew he was no longer welcome when his workshop was burned down.'

Yup, that's a community making its feelings known.

'This was before I was born, of course. They were forced to head north. But before they went, his former friends and customers used rocks to smash his hands so he could never sew again. And they raped and murdered my mother's sister. At least, we assume so. Her body was never found. But then, she was one of some fifty thousand Muslim women and girls kidnapped. Although it is now known that some of those were killed by their own families to save them from dishonour.'

I'm sure they were very grateful, I wanted to say, but didn't.

'Don't get me wrong, such things happened on the Muslim side too. We were no angels, as you say.' He paused for a second and closed his eyes. It was like Xenon headlamps being switched off. I blinked quickly in the moment before he opened them again and continued. 'The only family we had in this new Dominion of Pakistan worked in the brickfields, and that is what my mother and older brother did. But it was my mother who got the family out of there, it was my mother who opened that tiny cupboard – it was hardly a shop – in Karachi. All I did was build on her work. Muslim? Hindu? Sikh? Jain? British? A plague on all their houses. Business and family are all that matters in this world. So, you see, I do appreciate my daughter, what she might be capable of. I see my mother in her.'

'Is she still alive? Your mother?'

He shook his head. 'Nor my father or brother. A number of uncles are on the board, along with their wives and a few cousins, that is all I have as family.'

'I'm sorry to hear that, sir. But I suspect Nuzha will also go far in life, like her grandmother.' It sounded cheesy even as I said it, but I meant it.

He nodded. 'At least they had the chance to meet before she died. Nuzha's safety is paramount to me.' He seemed to snap out of his torpor a little. 'It's why you are here. Her mother, she thinks I worry too much. But as you know, people in our position are a target some-times. Blackmail, extortion. You understand that?'

'I do.'

'And we are most vulnerable through our children.'

I didn't like the way the conversation was going. I was expecting a pep talk, a debriefing of some descrip-tion, an assessment of my performance so far. This man had something on his mind other than dead sons and whisky. 'I have to ask you, sir. Is there a threat or a risk situation I should be aware of?'

He took a deeper draught of the whisky, smacking his lips with pleasure. I noticed the fingers wrapped around the glass. Long, elegant, beautifully manicured. Like the fingers of a concert pianist. 'Aren't threat and risk the same thing?' Sharif asked.

'Not quite. I can't do anything about a threat to you. But I can minimise the risk of it being carried out. So once more, if you don't mind, are you aware of any specific threat and, therefore, risk to you or your family?'

'No,' he said firmly.

And to think I was stupid enough to believe him.

Matt was waiting for me when I got home. I spotted him sitting in the car. There were cigarette butts outside the driver's window. He'd been there three cigarettes'-worth. Of course, he wasn't on The Circuit, but it is ingrained in those of us who are never to drop litter out of cars. A stray coffee cup can show someone has been watching.

I drove past my parking slot, tucked the VW into the next block's forecourt and circled back on foot so I could rap on the window and make him jump.

'Jesus!' he said as he hit the button that lowered the glass. 'You nearly gave me a heart attack.'

Shame. So near, yet so far. 'You want to see me?'

'Only if you're not going to belt me, I'd've gone up but I saw Jess arrive with some girl.'

'Woman. Laura.'

'Au pair?'

'Yes.'

'Cute.'

'Fuck off.'

He shook his head. 'Here we go again.'

I stepped back and he opened the door and got out, stretching as he did so. He was wearing a tight T-shirt and I had to admit he had kept himself in shape, even if it was a shape I no longer approved of.

'Look, I'm going to forget the assault—'

'It wasn't an assault. It was a slap. If I'd wanted to assault you, you'd still be in traction. Did you tell your solicitor that I'd attacked you?'

'Look, I don't want to go down that hostile route. It won't do anybody any good, least of all Jess. Agreed?'

The sound I made in the back of my throat was some sort of agreement, I suppose.

'Are you going to ask me up?'

'No.'

Matt heaved out a big, childish sigh. 'All I want to ask is if I make firm proposals for limited access, would you consider them?'

'What kind of proposals?'

'We have to put it in writing apparently. It involves neutral ground, what's called a Contact Centre. If I draft something, will you read it?'

'Yes,' I said. 'I'll read it. But that's all I promise.'

'That's all I ask.'

'I'm still not sure why you ... why now? Why come to see Jess after all this time?'

'Because it marks a new start for me. The thought of not seeing Jess ... It's an ache, here.' He pounded his chest with a fist. I wasn't sure whether to laugh or cry.

'Put it in writing, I'll take a look.'

'Thank you. So I'll –' he pointed at his Toyota and his eyes flicked up to the flat '– be going? Will I?'

'Yes. You will.'

'OK. I'll be in touch,' he said to my back and for once I had the horrible feeling he was telling the truth.

Not for the first time I wondered how the fuck did I get myself tangled up with him in the first place?

And then I remembered.

TWENTY-ONE

The Medical Supplies Store, or MSS, is really just a big steel container that bakes in the sun. None of us like going in. The suffocating air is toxic with hot plastic and other astringent chemicals. But when your medipack is running low, there is no choice. You have to obtain a requisition form from logistics, fill in your requirements, have it countersigned by the senior MO at the camp and then collect the key to the MSS. You could stock up on everything except morphine. The MO liked to keep that one close to his chest.

That morning I jump through all the army's bureaucratic hoops and then head across the compound, kicking up yet more yellow dust. The main activity in camp that day is cleaning the filth out of the various vehicles' engine filters. The air is alive with the hiss of high-pressure air hoses, and the resultant dislodged particles have formed into a malevolent, choking cloud. Never mind the filters, who's going to clean our lungs out once we are done here?

The MSS is tucked away close to one of the blast walls, beneath Obs Post Six, an observation tower that has been hit more times than anything else on the base, mainly because it makes for a decent ranging target from the low hills to the east of us. Those scrub-covered foothills looked smooth but, in reality, when your boots were on that sunbaked ground, they were wrinkled and creviced like a bull elephant's skin. It was great terrain for creeping up with a mortar, sighting on Obs Post Six, lobbing a few shells over and scarpering. Obs Post Six is not a popular spot on the duty roster.

I look up as an Apache helicopter sweeps overhead, its rotor wash adding a few more kilos of dust to the air, the thrum hurting my ears. It is followed by a Chinook, lumbering through the sky. The pair always remind me of a great whale plodding through the water with its smaller, more agile, attending fish zipping around. Only in this case the Apache is there to watch the vulnerable Chinook's back. Although quite what it could do about a Stinger launch I am never sure. Just take out the perps after the event.

I'm never certain how to convey what all this feels like to the people back home. Unreal, surreal, terrifying, boring, mind-numbing, exhilarating, often all within a single hour. I had tried, after a few drinks, to paint some sort of picture for the guy I met in the White Lion when I was last home. Nice guy. Despite being – how could this be? – an estate agent. An estate agent? What the fuck could they know about what it was like being in a shithole like this? But he was a good listener and, surprise, a smooth talker and he didn't wear those nasty suits or the aftershave, every bit as choking as Iraqi dust, that most of them favour.

Besides, he had said, it was only a stepping-stone. Estate agenting. What he was really interested in was property development, buying a few wrecks, getting them done up, selling them on. He honestly thought that was some kind of step up the evolutionary ladder from being an estate agent.

So after I'd voiced that opinion he'd challenged me on the morality of the British being in Iraq, when it had played no part in the events of 9/11 that had triggered the whole War on Terror frenzy. We moved on to a few pointless exchanges in which I had tried to suggest that removing Saddam Hussein was akin to taking out Hitler in 1939 and he demanded to know why we hadn't invaded Saudi Arabia instead. At the time I thought he was attacking the men and women of the army, rather than the duplicitous politicians behind the war, so I told him about the mundane realities of life on the ground. Which included a regular, long hot schlep to the MSS, just like today.

As I reach the container I can see that the door is already open. Which is odd, because there are four keys to it and all four were hanging up when I collected the one now clutched in my right hand.

I pull the door open, wrinkling my nose at the ester-ish stink of superheated polythene and the gust of hot air that wafts it over me. We've asked for a proper, air-conned storage unit and been told it is 'in the works'. But then, others had also asked for properly armoured Land Rovers. As far as saving lives went, the latter is probably a greater priority.

At first I think the noise I am hearing is a new form of helicopter, but as I step past the first row of metal shelving, I appreciate it is the unmistakable sound of energetic flesh colliding with a rhythmic, urgent intensity.

Freddie is bent over almost double, her splayed fingers grasping one of the lower shelves, her cammies around her ankles, along with her knickers. The man creating all the disturbance in the air, and sweating as if he is leaking, is a young lieutenant, a fresh- and red-faced Rupert. I am frozen in place, slack-jawed, as I watch him slide in and out of her, ridiculously pleased and relieved that he is wearing a condom and mesmerised by the oscillating movement of Freddie's breasts.

'Get the fuck out!' yells the officer in a hoarse voice. 'Can't you see we're busy?'

'And for fuck's sake shut the door behind you,' adds Freddie.

I have just reached the exit and am stepping down

when a fist catches me on the back of the head, a driving sucker punch that sends me sprawling into that hated dust.

'Look, it's very simple,' says Freddie as she pours out the teas. 'I needed a cock in my cunt. Sometimes, you do, you know. Need a cock in—'

'All right, I get the picture. Thanks.' I take the mug from her. We are in the regimental first-aid post, where she'd plucked splinters from my scalp and dressed the bigger wound at the top of my neck. Outside we could hear the low grumbles of vehicles starting up. A patrol was going out.

'Jesus, though,' she said, 'at first, I thought it was the biggest come of my life. Talk about the earth moving.'

I laugh despite myself. Just as I had stepped out of the MSS a mortar round had hit Obs Post Six. It was the blast and a few shards of timber that had knocked me to the floor. It had also put the young Rupert off his enthusiastic stride. The patrol we could hear starting up would be going out to chase the mortar team, but we all knew they'd be long gone. One fortuitous hit and the insurgents would have melted into the landscape, pleased with their efforts. It was only luck that the tower had been empty when the round detonated. 'And the look on your face when you saw us at it.'

'Now listen, Freddie. I'm not judging you. But you

know, they say women have no place on a battlefield. They'll be a distraction in wartime. No, we say. We are professional soldiers. Medics before we are women.' I let my eyebrows finish the thought.

She sighs. 'Try not to look like you are sucking sherbet all the time. You're right, it was stupid. But you do sound fuckin' judgemental. As I said, I just needed—'

'Don't say it again.' I warn her.

'I wasn't going to. But next time I'm bringing a bloody vibrator with me. A Rampant Rabbit. A whole warren of them. Anyway, I won't see him again. The Rupert. He was only here with some major and he's rotating home next week.'

'To his wife and kids?' I say, regretting the mean-spirited sharpness of the words as soon as they have left my lips.

'Oh, do fuck right off, Buster. It was just a shag. I didn't suck off Osama bin Laden. Nobody died. I didn't even come properly thanks to those bastards out there.'

'War is hell,' I suggest.

She smiles. 'It is when you need a cock up your cunt.' A giggle shakes her shoulders. 'I just love your expression when I say it. You look like . . . who's that girl in Charlie and the Chocolate Factory?'

'Veruca Salt.'

'Yes.'

'She's a spoiled rich brat.'

A *smirk spread across Freddie's face. 'I rest my case.'*

I let out a gasp of exasperation. 'I'm none of those things.'

'You, my lovely, are posh.' She amped up her burr as she said it.

'Fuck off.'

'See, you don't even swear properly. Fuck orfff.'

I know I can't win this. I am not posh, I am maybe middle class and girls like me don't normally join the army. That much I'll accept. But Freddie hardly had a Dolly Parton hand-me-down upbringing. Plymouth might be rough in places, but it isn't the Appalachians or the projects.

And so, just to show I am not a prig or a prude, I tell her about the night I picked up an estate agent in a bar and then fucked his brains out until he couldn't manage a just-one-more-time-for-the-road the next morning.

'What was his name, then, this sex machine on a stick?'

'Matt.'

'Matt what?'

'Matt ... Black.'

She explodes with laughter, launching tea across the room. 'You're fuckin' kiddin'? Matt Black? Does he have a brother called Gloss?'

I shake my head. 'No, that's not his name. It's ...' I could feel myself frowning.

'*You don't know, do you?*' Her jaw drops in surprise but her eyes show her delight at this lapse in standards. '*You didn't even ask his second name? I take it all back. You, Buster, are a fuckin' slut.*'

I grin. I feel like I've made up some ground in her estimation of me, even though I know I've done it by demeaning myself. Matt Harper had been his name. And I have an old-fashioned love letter from him to prove it.

TWENTY-TWO

At home that evening I asked Laura to stick around while I did some work. I didn't want to. For some reason I'd been thinking of that time when I had burst in on Freddie with a Rupert rogering her for all he was worth. I found the thought strangely erotic. Which was odd, because watching other people have sex – at least in the flesh – has never been one of my go-to buttons to push. Partially clothed sex – a personal favourite – yes, voyeurism, no.

But maybe that ghostly echo of Freddie's charming little catchphrase that popped into my head the other week had been right. I needed a man. Or maybe twenty minutes in the bath with my waterproof Jimmyjane.

But that would have to wait. I had with me a USB stick of footage downloaded from the hard drive One-Eyed Jack had installed in the BMW. On it was footage from the modified reversing camera. It wasn't *EastEnders* exactly, but it was going to be my evening viewing. Laura fixed fish fingers for Jess and, without asking, brought me a glass of white wine and some crisps while I fiddled about inserting the USB and opening the files.

'Do I look like I need it?' I asked as she proffered the wine.

'You looked like you've earned it,' she replied with a grin.

Such tact. 'Thank you.'

I inserted the USB and scrolled through until I found the UPS delivery van. The tail camera was not intended for surveillance work – given more time, Jack could have replaced it with something of higher quality – but it gave me enough to get the licence plate and to follow the brown van's movements. I couldn't swear to it, but I reckoned it was playing piggy in the middle – with me being the pig – with a nondescript Peugeot that popped up more than once. I noted down that number, too. I took my first sip of the wine and then I dialled Jack. He did after-hours service, too.

'I've got two numbers for you.'

'That was quick. Hold on. Oscar! Oscar! Not in the mouth!' There was a muffled noise and silence before he came back on. 'Lego. Sorry.' Jack had a new, younger wife, who came with two stepdaughters, and Oscar, a new toddler of his own. I didn't envy him the Lego-eating years, not at his age. There was the older boy, too, from his first marriage – Jordan, who worked

in the hangars, although I had never actually met him.
'Go ahead.'

I gave him the licence plates.

'Tomorrow OK?'

'Fine.' I don't know how he did it exactly, but I know
he didn't go through DVLA to ID a vehicle – too many
bootprints left all over the computers, so he said – but
an insurance database. If those cars had a UK policy,
he could get name and address. 'Can you do something
else for me? Add it to the tab?'

'Depends.' He sounded wary. Maybe something in
my voice suggested this wasn't strictly PPO business.

'If I give you a mobile number, can you get me the
registered address?'

He laughed. 'That's so easy I wouldn't have the
nerve to charge you, my love.'

'Do it anyway.'

'OK. Again, be tomorrow.'

I read out the number. 'Just email it to me whenever.
You get back to the Lego.'

He sighed. 'I think I should have bought Duplo.'

'I think you're right. Much harder to swallow.'

I hung up and switched off the computer; as I lowered the top, Laura slid a plate of grilled chicken and
broccoli over to me.

'What's this?'

'Dinner,' she said. 'I made myself some, too. I hope
you don't mind.'

'No, of course. Sit. Where's Jess?'

'She says homework. I suspect *Orange Is the New Black*.' I began to say something about the suitability of the show for a fourteen-year-old, but Laura held up her hand. 'I know. But it's fine.'

'It's got lesbians and fisting and such in it, hasn't it?'

Laura raised an eyebrow.

'That made me sound old, didn't it?'

She let me off with a shrug. 'I've seen it. It's not so bad.'

I drank some more of the wine, which had grown lukewarm. 'You OK about tomorrow?'

'Of course.'

It was a Saturday, but Mrs Sharif wanted Nuzha dropped off at a friend's place and she had a Pilates class that she wanted me to drive her to.

'You're very good at all this,' I said. 'Really. I don't think I could—'

'It's not that I'm good,' she said quickly, pulling her hair back from her face. 'It's that most people are so rubbish at it. Just be flexible. My mum was a social worker for a while. I know all about being flexible.'

'And your father?'

'Oh, this and that. He was a City trader, then opened a bar, lost everything, became a cabbie, met my mum, now he runs a minicab firm in Woking. They're not together, though.'

'And you have a boyfriend?'

She glanced down at her food. 'Sort of.'

'What does that mean?' She looked up and I could see her cheeks had coloured slightly. 'I sound old again? I thought they were still boyfriends.' Or did young men and women only have fuck buddies these days?

'No. I hooked up with someone while I was travelling.' Now that was a term I was never sure of the exact meaning of. Hooked up. It seemed to encompass a range of options. 'I'm trying to save enough money to get out to see him and for us to go travelling together.'

'Where is he now?'

'Queenstown. New Zealand. Teaching bungee jumping. Which is a worry because in some ways he is the most irresponsible person I have ever met.'

She gave a knowing smile to show she wasn't entirely serious. It made her look her years, suddenly. There were times when I looked at that flawless, unlined skin and bright eyes that I thought I'd employed someone not much older than Jess. Now, though, she felt closer to my age. Well, OK, within hailing distance. With a very big megaphone.

'Have you decided about whether Jess can go to Indonesia?' she asked.

'I'm waiting on the official letter. The one that tells me it is well organised and safe. Jess will just have to be patient.'

Her brow furrowed and she leaned forward. When

187

she spoke, her voice dropped into a basement register. 'I hope you don't mind me asking something. It's ... a bit awkward.'

'Is it about Jess?'

She nodded and I braced myself by taking a hit of the wine.

'Go ahead.'

'Have you seen her naked recently?'

She caught me just on the swallow and I choked a little. 'What?' I croaked.

'Have you seen Jess with no clothes on lately?'

'Not really. It's been a while since she started bolting the bathroom door. Why?' I asked, trying to keep the alarm I was feeling from creeping into my voice. 'What's wrong?'

'I was doing her hair the other day ... yesterday, and I noticed ...' She chopped at her upper arm with the edge of her hand, like an axe blade. 'And I think down here.' The same movement at the top of her thighs.

'What?' I asked, although the boiling acid bath in my stomach indicated I already knew before Laura spoke.

'I think Jess is self-harming.'

Jack woke me from a fitful sleep that was barely worthy of the name. I must have sounded rough because he offered to call back, but I told him to go ahead.

'OK, I have the address on that mobile. It's on the City Road. One of those shiny new developments.'

'You sure?'

'Yup. The City Towers. Apartment eighteen.'

'But that's not that far from here.' It was my way of saying too damn close. 'And don't they sell for stupid money?' Or: *How the fuck could my feckless ex-husband afford to live there?*

'I dunno,' said Jack. 'I'm not Foxtons, am I?'

'Thank God. What about the plate numbers?'

'Nothing yet, I'm afraid. Which is odd.'

'Odd how?' I asked.

'Well, my man – who is actually a woman – tells me they must be part of a group insurance scheme. Someone who owns a lot of vehicles and lumps them all in together. Don't worry, she can crack it. But it being Saturday ...'

'I understand. Thanks, Jack. I appreciate it.'

'You sure you're OK?'

'Yeah. Just had a bit of a family shock, that's all.'

Shock? It was like a punch to the solar plexus followed by a kick in the kidneys. It was all I could do not to be sick. I couldn't finish my meal, that was for sure. All I could feel was shame and the cold hand of failure on my shoulder. How could I not know?

Because you are a bad mother.

Laura had tried her best to disavow me of that, even though every avenue of thought appeared to lead to that cul-de-sac.

Laura had carefully explained about her own

problems with bulimia and her mother's baffled and horrified reaction to it. Although she hadn't realised it at the time, her illness had been a reaction to her parents' divorce. The pain and discomfort of throwing up had helped her forget the emotional ache. But what was the trigger for Jess's cutting? Was it me going back to work? The return of Matt? A delayed reaction to Paul's death?

Laura said even Jess might not know. That we had to play the long game. We should not rule out bullying, she said.

One thing she was certain about – a sudden confrontation was not the answer. Hysteria, of the kind Laura had suffered at the hands of her mother, would only drive Jess deeper into whatever sort of shell she was creating. Plus, if Laura was to retain Jess's trust, I would have to contrive another way to 'discover' the marks. If she thought Laura was a snake – apparently the current incarnation of a snitch or grass – then she would turn against her and Laura would not be in any position to do any good.

So act as if nothing is wrong?

Yes, she had said. And suppress the urge to go in and try and shake some sense into your daughter. *That transparent, eh?* I had asked. Completely see-through, apparently. Laura said if she had a chance she would look through Jess's internet history to see if she had visited any of the websites which instruct young girls in the art of subterfuge – cutting in places that parents, teachers and friends would not notice – and her text messages to see if she had any that might indicate a conflict somewhere in her social life. 'But,' Laura had said knowingly, 'you have to be aware that girls that age always have some form of conflict on the go at a low level. Jade was seen snogging Jenna's boyfriend. So Jade gets a shit-storm of trolling for a while until Jenna gives Josie's boyfriend a blowjob and they switch.'

I must have looked shocked. But she added: 'You have to understand, blowjobs aren't what they were back in your day.'

I assumed she meant in terms of taboo and mystique – I was pretty sure the mechanics hadn't changed – and that a kind of sexual inflation had made the act more workaday than when I was a teenager. It had the status of gold, frankincense and myrrh in my nice middle-class school – something to be bestowed only on very special occasions. Not quite when a star appeared in the East, maybe, but close.

So what do we do? I had asked, like I was the hapless youngster and she the wise mother.

'Knowing is half the battle,' Laura had said. 'And there is help out there. Jess is hardly alone. But for the moment, do nothing.'

Doing nothing was not in my temperament, but I knew she was right. So we all said our normal goodnights and I retreated to my bed with my laptop and the rest of the wine and did the one thing Laura warned me against – going on the internet. Trust me, you don't want to be on Mumsnet or the NSPCC at two in the morning. Or ever, really. But I did discover that more than half of all fourteen- and fifteen-year-olds had either self-harmed or knew someone who did. Main reasons? Low self-esteem, bullying, cultural isolation, bereavement. It seemed to be a close relative to various eating disorders and, most distressingly, suicide attempts.

I lay there, tossing and turning, wanting to go in and cuddle Jess and tell her whatever it was – *whatever* – I would fix it. At three in the morning, too tired and too emotional and more than a little tipsy, you are willing to kill for your child. Well, I was.

I had slipped my hand down the side of the mattress for the reassuring feel of the Eickhorn knife and it wasn't there. I began to scramble around in my panic. And then I saw the image of Jess with that wicked blade, drawing it slowly over her upper arm, relishing the pain as the blood welled thick and dark red from the split on her skin. And that was when I stabbed myself.

It was still here. The Eickhorn had just slipped further down and eased out of its sheath. I had managed to catch the tip of my index finger on the couple of centimetres of exposed edge. I hadn't cared, I had sucked at the blood, happy that it was my pain, not Jess's.

So by the time I had finished with Jack, breakfasted and dressed, I was feeling pretty bushed. The bathroom mirror confirmed this. I spent fifteen minutes putting on a false face – and a plaster on my finger – and I looked OK. Not tip-top, but I'd do.

But I couldn't stop my mind churning, that was beyond even Bobbi Brown's capabilities. I rang Nina and asked if we could have a chat that morning. She could tell something was wrong, but sensed I didn't want to talk on the phone. I said I'd come over to Stoke Newington.

I'd like to think, even to this day, that it was the distraction of my inner turmoil that enabled them to take me so easily.

TWENTY-THREE

No excuses. The shields should have been up. As soon as you leave the house you should be focused on the job. There could be a shit-storm going down in the hallway, but the moment you step over the threshold you lock it in and forget it till later. But it's hard to stay in the zone when you take your daughter breakfast in bed and clock the long-sleeved T-shirts she has taken to wearing of late without you really noticing. And the knife through the heart when she won't catch your eye. And when the job in hand is to drive a pampered woman to stretch her already perfect body ... I suppressed that thought as quickly as it popped up. PPOs can't afford to be judgemental about clients.

I was thinking it would only take me fifteen minutes or so to get over to Nina's, when the hood slipped over my head.

On a better day I might have noticed two men crouched down apparently inspecting the tyre of a Volvo estate. Or realised that I had seen the white VW

Transporter that burbled into the edge of my vision before. But this wasn't a better kind of day. My world disappeared in a rush of thick black cotton and something hard pressed behind my left ear.

I tensed, ready to push back when my bag was ripped from my shoulder. But then a retaining strap snaked round my middle body and was jerked tight, pinning my arms to my sides, like a makeshift straitjacket.

'Come quietly, yes?' the voice hissed sibilantly in my ear. 'Or we'll go inside to get your little girl. I'm not sure you'd like to watch what happens next. Think about it. Nod if you understand.'

I nodded. What I really wanted to do was shout and kick and scream. But I nodded. Then I let myself go floppy as they frogmarched me between cars heading, no doubt, for the van whose sliding side-door I heard rumble back to receive me.

There was one lecture, back when I was doing my SIA-accreditation training with Colonel d'Arcy, that baffled most of us. It was like a cross between a Brian Cox documentary and an episode of *Casualty*. It was about trauma and time, and how certain events can speed up or slow down what the lecturer called the temporal momentum of the situation (TMS, naturally). He delved into quantum physics and the way people remember car crashes – the ones that happen in slow, treacle-bound motion and those that seem to occupy a blink or a heartbeat, leaving you wondering what just happened.

The point of the exercise was to try and persuade us to keep track of real time, not to fall victim to its elastic nature. Step one: stay calm. Step two: try and find a reference point, some internal clock. Heartbeats, he warned us, were unreliable, as panic – our biggest enemy – would cause it to elevate. But if it is all you have, use it.

It was all I had.

The terror, the sheer the-lift-cable-has-snapped sense of falling into the abyss, has to be compartmentalised. Because what you are going to need are your senses, to know where you are going and how you are getting there. Listen, smell, stay alert. Don't drift off into self-pity. Or give in to lurid imaginings of what might happen to you or your loved ones. The irony was, this was all the shit that I told my Principals. Who ever heard of the PPO being snatched? Not on home turf, anyway.

They were fast. Fifteen seconds or so and I was in the VW, strapped into a seat, the door was slammed and I jerked back as the van took off. I was aware of bodies slumping down on either side of me. A hand brushed across my shoulder, down to my breast and squeezed. Hard. I tried not to flinch. He twisted until I let out an involuntary gasp. Then, even through the dense fabric of the hood, I could feel his hot breath against my ear.

'Still got those armoured titties, eh?'

I couldn't keep this particular wave of fear and panic

back. My heart rate jumped and I felt acid burn my throat. I knew who had taken me.

The fucking Russians.

As far as I could estimate it we drove for twenty minutes, through stop-start traffic. My guess was we had travelled east, but it was only that. A guess. In the movies people can reconstruct a journey by the hoot of a factory whistle, the rumble of trains or the cobbles on a road. Mostly, that is only possible in the movies. I tried hard to listen, but mainly I could hear my ventricles pumping, the breathing of the men on either side of me and a radio or CD coming from the front, playing something that sounded like a turbo-charged snake charmer who had discovered House music.

After a while I gave up trying to act as a human sat nav, as the effort was making me feel dizzy. I shut down a little, trying to conserve my energy. I was going to need it. But, for all my training, it was hard to stop little spikes of adrenaline leaking into my bloodstream.

Bad mother and now a bad PPO.

We pulled up with a sharp jab of the brakes that thrust me against the seat belt. One of the men flanking me, the one on the left, pushed me back. Of course, they weren't actually fucking Russians. Not all of them. The man who had whispered those charming words was Bojan, the Serbian I had clobbered.

And now he wanted to get even for his humiliation.

The Serbians, I recalled as my belt was unbuckled, were world-class grudge-holders. They made the Northern Irish look like masters at turning the other cheek. The Serbs were still incandescent about something that happened in the fourteenth century with the Turks. So it didn't surprise me that Bojan was pissed off. But even by Serbian standards, this abduction was an over-reaction.

As the van shuddered to a complete standstill I was pulled to my feet, thumping my head on the roof, before they pushed me down onto a pavement. 'Stairs,' Bojan said as I stumbled. They hauled me up the stone steps and I heard the creak of a door ahead.

How long before Nina gets worried that I didn't turn up? How long before someone finds the bag I had dropped in the street when they snatched me? How long before Mrs Sharif complains to Ben at the agency about his unreliable fuckwit employee? How long would I have to endure whatever they had in mind for me?

As we entered the building I was aware of the long delay of the sound of our footsteps. It was a big space. A warehouse maybe? And there was the smell of ... what? Beeswax. Sawn wood. A touch of damp and something old and musty.

I was pushed into a sitting position and let myself fall into an unforgiving high-backed seat. As the hood was removed my initial impression was of a fractured, watery world of blues and greens, until I realised I was staring at a stained-glass window and my eyes were filmed over. I blinked rapidly to clear them. I was in a church. All around me were stacks of pews, floorboards, panelling, pulpits. Obviously deconsecrated, it was now being used for architectural salvage storage.

There were three men in front of me: Bojan, the Serb; Gregor Mitval, the Russian who had invited me down to the gym; and another man in a black MA-1 flight jacket. He was fair-haired with carefully trimmed stubble, and in other circumstances I might have thought him handsome, like a tidier version of Roman Abramovich.

'What the fuck do you think you are doing?' I asked Bojan. 'Can't you take a beating like a man?'

Roman snorted at this.

'And can't you keep your big mouth shut?' Bojan replied, before hitting me.

It wasn't a hard slap. More a flick with the tips of his fingers, but it still stung for several seconds. It was also a good question. Sometimes that army-bred snarky defence mechanism of mine makes things worse. I'd have to watch that.

Mitval spoke next, calm and reasonable. 'What Bojan means is, having made your point, why did you have to go crying to Daddy?'

'I am supposed to answer that or keep my big mouth shut?' Here we go again.

Mitval smirked. 'Answer the question.'

'I don't know what the hell you're talking about.'

'So you didn't tell Mr Asparov what happened in his gym?'

I looked from one to the other. 'Why would I do that?' I had told Ben not to send anyone else to be 'interviewed', and suggested Asparov be put on The Circuit's black list, but that was all.

'To cost us our jobs, maybe?' Bojan asked.

'He sacked you?'

'Immediately,' said Mitval. 'On the spot. With no compensation.'

'But he was in Moscow,' I said.

'You can sack people by Skype these days,' said Mitval. True. And you can organise delivery of a case of money remotely, too.

'There's tribunals for that sort of thing,' I offered, like some sort of trussed Citizens Advice Bureau.

'We don't believe in tribunals,' said Bojan.

'Not those sort anyway,' added Mitval.

Roman laughed. I wasn't quite sure what Roman's grievance was in all this, but I didn't really care. I also didn't care for the way he was looking at me. If he was a dog I'd have him muzzled and chained up. In fact, it didn't seem a bad idea to do it anyway.

'Look, fellas, I'm sorry, but believe you me, it wasn't me who squealed. I won, remember?'

The tightening around Bojan's mouth suggested such reminders weren't going to help my case.

'What do you want from me?' I asked.

Roman gave a wolfish grin.

'First off, our severance pay.'

'Your ... you want money? This is a shakedown?' I was trembling now, with genuine outrage. I even flexed against the strap, which I knew was a waste of effort, although given time I reckoned I could work it up or down and free my arms. I suspected I didn't have that much time, though.

'Just the money Asparov gave you,' said Mitval.

'Gave me. Not you.'

Mitval frowned at this. 'Nevertheless, we would like it back.'

Back? It didn't belong to them in the first place. But then, I didn't feel it was rightfully mine, either.

'I no longer have it,' I said. 'It was too much cash to leave lying around.' Especially with a daughter with Indonesia on her mind.

'So where is it?' Mitval asked.

'In a strongroom. In a secure location. I wasn't going to leave it with the cornflakes, was I? But I can get it. There was no need for this charade. I don't care if you have it. To be honest, I'd rather have a dose of chlamydia than keep it.'

Ain't that the truth.

Bojan and Mitval exchanged glances. Something seemed to pass between them, because both men nodded in agreement

The Serb prodded me with an iron bar of a finger. 'Tell us how to get it.'

'You see, we have to start new ventures now you have lost us our livelihood. We need capital,' said Mitval, as if he were making a pitch on *Dragons' Den*. 'And that is our money, really.'

'The man I have given it to won't just hand it over to anyone who pitches up. I'll have to be there.' And preferably alive. 'Take this off me and I'll come along with you. Then I'll hand the money over. I'll just have to make some calls first.'

'No calls,' said Bojan. It broached no argument.

'OK,' I said. I could worry about Mrs Sharif later. I just hoped Ben wouldn't ask too many questions when I turned up at his office with this circus of chimps in tow and told him I needed to make a withdrawal. 'The sooner we get started, the better.'

'I agree,' said Bojan, looking questioningly at Mitval. Again, a non-verbal exchange passed between the two men. Some decision was made. Mitval nodded. 'OK. Leave her able to walk and speak. I'll be in the van.'

TWENTY-FOUR

After the front entrance of the church had creaked shut and slammed with an ominous thud, there was a moment of silence when nobody moved. Least of all me. I was holding my breath, trying to anticipate what was coming next. It didn't need too much imagination. Then Bojan and Roman disappeared from my sight. I heard a sound like reluctant nails squeaking out of wood and the scraping of furniture. Bojan began speaking and I wished he hadn't.

'Vuk and I were in the Drina. You know how the people in The Hague are always saying rape is a war crime? They are right. A terrible war crime. What they always forget is it's pretty good fun, too.' He giggled at that. 'Vuk here was our go-to guy for that sort of thing. Jesus, the man has a dick like a . . . what's that snake?'

'An anaconda,' said Roman/Vuk helpfully.

'Yeah, like an anaconda. It could fuck you or squeeze you to death. Ain't that right, Vuk?'

I heard a soft 'oh shucks, this old thing' chuckle which, under other circumstances, might have been self-deprecating. It sent a ripple of cold fear down my spine. Paul, who had served in the Balkans, had told me about the Drina and the systematic rape of Bosniak women.

'But, you know, Vuk misses those days. Don't you, Vuk? So we thought, yeah, let's try some of his greatest hits.'

They reappeared carrying a large, once highly polished table that was now scuffed and stained. They set it to one side and between them plucked me out of the chair and pushed me face down onto the surface. They swung my legs up. My heart was banging against my ribs with enough force to resonate through the wood. I kept running down my options to suppress the panic I knew was building. It didn't take long. It was a short list.

I seemed to have run out of snappy comments, which is just as well as I'd run out of saliva, too.

Vuk crouched down so his face was level with mine. As he spoke I got a waft of sewer-like periodontal disease. Once smelled, never forgotten. My father had it in spades. It was just one of the many, many things I disliked about him. 'So, what we thought was, we start with a fuck in the arse. Eh?'

I felt Bojan gather my skirt either side of the vent in the back and tug. The seam split open.

'But you are probably used to that. I thought maybe we could try rimming. You know that?' He gave a little smile. 'Don't worry, I perfumed my ring for you specially.'

When he laughed it was like the smell from a garbage chute wafting over me. I was torn between hawking the liquid surging up from my stomach into his face and suggesting that he probably says that to all his girls. In the end, I said nothing. I had to modify my response. Non-compliance but non-resistant too. And I had to forget the smart-assed comments. I had to let all the tension go from my muscles, hope they'd grow bored. This was going to hurt and humiliate in equal measure. Of course it could all be hot air, a particularly foetid sort, coming from that mouth. Just a bit of psychological torture. Maybe he had no intention of shoving his spotty arse in my face. Maybe.

'Now, missie, we are going to cut the strap. Better if you can move your hands. I like my balls squeezed. And a little tromboning, always good for me. But if you fight . . .' He held something in front of my eyes. It took a moment for me to focus. Two six-inch nails. The sound that had reminded me of nails being pulled from wood was just that. He showed me the claw hammer he had used to extract them. 'We shall nail your hands to the table. Understand?' When I didn't reply he touched my cheekbone with the cold face of the hammer. 'Understand, missie?'

I nodded and he straightened and his mouth began to distort into a grin, before he twisted away with a scream, leaving a miasma of blood and bone behind.

Only then did I hear the sound of the gunshot.

I didn't hesitate, I rolled off the table, bracing myself as I slammed into the floor, raising a cloud of dust and grit that filled my nose and eyes. I blindly shuffled myself so I was beneath the table. Another gunshot, booming high up into the once-holy roof space.

I blinked and snorted to try and get my senses back. When I could keep my eyes open I saw Vuk, slumped down to his knees and swaying. The bottom of his face was unspeakably grisly and glistening, like a freshly painted war-wound by Francis Bacon. His mandible made a clacking sound as the ruined jaw moved up and down.

Vuk's eyes were filled with fluid, weeping down his cheeks and he was staring at me with ... what? It looked like he was pleading for something. I managed to swivel on my hip, bring my left leg up and I kicked him as hard as I could in his chest. An animal-like noise came from deep in his throat as he careered back into the chair I had recently vacated and lay still, blood pooling around his head.

There came the rolling burp of a weapon on automatic fire and the whine of a ricochet and a tinkle of broken glass. The boom of a large calibre pistol followed, close enough to hurt my ears, and then a silence – if you could call the humming in my head silence – descended on the church.

I watched the legs of a newcomer take unhurried strides towards me, the sneakers on his feet making almost no noise. The face that appeared was etched with concern. 'You hurt?'

'Bruised,' was all I could manage. I didn't trust my voice. In truth, I didn't trust myself not to burst into tears.

'Good.' He produced a pocket knife and sliced through the restraining strap. Immediately a bloom of pins and needles began to play over my arms. The binding had been tighter than I thought.

'Just hold on, we'll get you out of here. My guv'nor wants a word.'

As he leaned in to help me out, I thought that maybe I'd been a bit too cruel about his haircut. It didn't look at all like he had a turd on his head.

I'm not a brave person. Not particularly. It's just that the army and my training taught me a few tricks to keep things together under pressure. Sure, all that stuff about compartmentalising the panic, about not allowing the fug of terror to cloud your senses, I can do that. But it was always like going into a metabolic overdraft. Sooner or later there was a reckoning. That was why I didn't mind having to hold the coffee cup with two hands to stop it shaking.

We were outside a Costa coffee shop, not far from the church. I had on a borrowed coat, to cover the rip in my skirt. Opposite me was the 'guv'nor' who had introduced himself as Russell Swincoe. He was early- to mid-forties I guessed, with a rather bland, forgettable face that would run to jowly soon. He had on what looked like brand-new dark denim jeans and a waxed cotton jacket of some vintage. He didn't look – or speak, given his public-school accent – like the man who had just ordered one of his people to blow the face off a Serb. But I was glad he had.

'Who the hell are you guys?' I asked. 'And why have you been following me?'

He stirred a sugar into his black coffee. 'First things first. Do you need to be checked out by a doctor?'

I shook my head. 'No, the cavalry got there just in time.' All I had, apart from the shakes, was a wasp buzzing in one ear thanks to my proximity to the weapons discharging, but that would pass. 'Thank you.'

'Our pleasure.'

'Except you're not the cavalry, are you? Who are you exactly?' I repeated.

He looked at his watch. 'You still have time to keep your appointment with Mrs Sharif and her daughter.'

'Hold on. How did—?'

He rode roughshod over my question. 'You'll need to clean up a little. We have your handbag, by the way.

But I can get you some replacement clothes down here within ... fifteen minutes. Or run you home.'

'Home would be good.' I had never spoken four truer words.

'Finish your coffee. Lawrence will drive you.'

Lawrence was the polite young man, one of those who had rescued me. The driver with that turd-like hairstyle I found myself quite liking now.

'How are you going to explain the gunfire in the church?' I asked.

'Oh, it's a film production,' he said. 'Don't worry about that.'

He was right. That was not my concern. I had other questions.

'Will Vuk live?' I asked.

'Do you care?'

'Not especially. Just curious.'

'He will, but from the look of him, he'll not be chewing many steaks. I think he has a life of soft fruits in front of him.'

'With what he has behind him, that's no bad thing.'

'True. But they aren't the sort of people you should upset, you know.'

I didn't know how to respond to that. I had had no intention of upsetting them. I didn't even want their poxy money.

'And Bojan?' I asked.

'The other Serbian? We lost him, I'm afraid, but he

has one of Lawrence's nine-millimetre bullets in him somewhere and probably a lot of glass. We have the man from the van.'

'Mitval. What'll happen to him?' I asked. 'He wasn't the worst of them, you know.'

'Yes, well, it's all a matter of degree. As he has been implicated in importation of Afghani heroin before now, I do believe he will be shipped back to Mother Russia.'

'You believe?'

'I think I can guarantee it.' There was a self-satisfied twinkle in his eye as he said it.

'OK, so you guys are authorised to use firearms. And you can whistle up ambulances and ship out people with serious gunshot wounds without bringing out choppers and SCO19. And phony film crews appear to be on speed dial. But you're not cops.'

A raise of the eyebrows was all I got and a little dimple in one of his slightly over-fleshy cheeks.

'And you seem to know a lot about me. And the people who took me. And you are keen to get me back to the Sharifs.'

'Very keen. It is imperative to us you get back to work.'

'That's very touching.'

'We have our reasons. Mainly because we had our own person ready to go and work for the Sharifs.'

I remember the conversation with Mr Sharif, about a nice Muslim girl who almost got the job. 'Miss Gill.'

A smile. 'The same.'

'Own person? What does that mean?'

'We wanted someone inside that house we could trust.'

'We' was beginning to annoy me now. 'I think she overplayed the Muslim card. Mr Sharif might not have liked anyone too judgemental.'

His nose wrinkled a little, as if a fly had just flown up his nostril. 'Perhaps.'

I could feel my insides slowly giving up their quivering. 'Look, are you going to tell me who you are and what is going on or are you going to play the enigmatic Englishman?'

'Oh, I rather like that role.'

'I've never cared for it, Mr Swincoe, if that's your real name.'

'It is. For reasons I will explain, we need to get a person inside the Sharif household. One of our own. To be our eyes and ears. We thought we had it covered with this PPO lark, making sure there were no other applicants, but then you breezed in from left field ...'

'Why do you need someone in there?'

That bounced right off him. 'Then we realised we had a stroke of good fortune with you.'

'How's that?'

Another twinkle in the eyes as he smiled. 'Well, you're family, near as damn it.'

I drained my coffee. I would have to be leaving if I

was going to make it to Highgate and act as if a kidnapping and a near-rape hadn't happened. Oh, and get a grovelling apology to Nina. 'I don't like cryptic crosswords, either. Can you just say what you mean?'

He sighed, almost petulantly, as if I wasn't playing the game properly. 'We are the Security Service.' He took out his wallet and showed me an impressive set of credentials, and then slid a much plainer business card – name and number only – across the table. I palmed it. 'Or MI5 if you prefer.'

It didn't come as a massive shock, given what I had just witnessed. It had to be the Security Service or the Met's SO15 or SCO19 to run around with all that firepower. 'If I'm your family, you are a very distant relative to me.'

He rattled his spoon in his cup, put it in the saucer and knocked back the coffee. 'Well, not really. I know you think that your husband worked for the British Nuclear Constabulary. That's not entirely true. For the past three years he had been seconded to us. The Security Service. You see, your Paul was what you might call a spook.'

TWENTY-FIVE

I killed a man once.

Well, half a man, strictly speaking. Zero point five of a human life. Oh, I probably killed more than that. In a firefight you loose off high-velocity rounds at unseen assailants and you hope that one of them might have hit home and silenced the gunmen and gunwomen.

But this one guy, he was up close and, as they say, very personal.

He was on base, one of the local interpreters, the ones who were meant to be anonymous. I knew him as Latif, but I doubt that was his real name. Because, of course, his own countrymen might blow his head off or worse if they knew he was helping us.

Latif was around twenty-five, maybe a little older, good-looking, tall and aristocratic, with very good English. We had conversed on no more than half a dozen occasions, but I found him charming and easy-going, with a nice line in cynical, black humour that fitted in well with the squaddies' own.

I had just left my billet and was strolling towards the Medical Supply Stores – this was shortly after my encounter with Freddie and the Rupert and I still needed to top up my field medi-pack, which was running low on some items – when I saw him coming towards me, his gait slightly off.

That's all it was. He usually walked like he was Omar Sharif or Yul Brynner or one of those old movie stars – proud and a touch arrogant, with an almost feline grace. But this time he was on jelly legs.

It was hot and dusty in the compound as always. Another low-flying helicopter, a Lynx this time, had kicked up a grit storm, causing shouts of abuse from the soldiers in the open. I was beginning to think it was a game those chopper boys liked to play.

There was the usual racket, of bored conversation, heated arguments, a bit of jokey banter and the hiss of power washes and air lines as vehicles were cleaned off. I heard the familiar laugh of Captain Charles, as dry as the desert air. As I passed Latif, under the relentless glare of the sun, our eyes locked. I can't say what I saw there. Maybe there was nothing to see. But just as our shoulders almost brushed, he pulled down the cloth covering his face and said one word.

Run.

I slowed and turned. I could feel the sun burning my neck and the sweat forming under my breasts and arms. Yet here he was wearing a heavy chapan – basically a loose kaftan – over his salwar kameez tunic and trousers. He had to be roasting in all those layers.

Run? Why?

I watched as he threw off the chapan and for a moment it seemed to stand on its own, as if the invisible man were inside, but as it collapsed I saw the light glint off the battered magazine of the AK-47 Short he was carrying.

Ahead of him, a group of six or seven men, sitting in the shade, were writing letters or reading books. They hadn't looked up. Nobody had noticed him, not yet. All you need is a 'not yet' for an AK to do its work.

'Latif!' I shouted.

He didn't seem to hear.

The gun came up so slowly, I wondered if Latif was willing what happened next to come about. Hoping he didn't have to carry out this atrocity. That someone would stop him …

Look, when you have a man in front of you, part of his body torn open, blood soaking into the jaundiced earth, you don't have time to fumble or hesitate. Your fingers can undo buckles and straps of a medi-pack pretty damned quickly if you just concentrate. When they need to, my fingers can fly. Right then, they needed to move faster than they ever had.

So I wasn't surprised I had the scalpel in my hand even as he was pulling back the bolt on the automatic rifle. And it made no sense not to plunge it as hard and as deep into his neck as I could manage.

The blood sprayed onto the sandy floor, pitter-pattering in spurts rather than an even gush.

I stepped back as he turned, the handle of the scalpel still stuck into the flesh, the smaller crimson droplets seeming to dance away in the sunlight.

I had the good sense to move to one side as he raised the rifle because I knew what was coming next – the bullet that would really take him out, fired from the Browning of a quick-thinking young lieutenant. So I didn't actually kill Latif. But I started the process.

'Are you feeling all right?'

I glanced in the mirror, suddenly back in the BMW, back in the moment. Behind me was Mrs Sharif. She was leaning forward.

'I'm fine, Mrs Sharif. I was concentrating on the traffic. Sorry, did you ask me something?'

'Only that you pick me up at four p.m.'

'Of course.'

Shit. I had been thinking back on the last time I had gone to pieces. After I had stabbed Latif I had suffered from nightmares, especially when I found out that insurgents had taken his mother and sister and forced him to carry out a close-quarter shooting or they would be ...

Well, they were, and they probably would have been

anyway. Their mutilated bodies were left outside the camp one moonless night. I suspected Latif knew how it would play out. *Run*, he had said. Why? We had no special bond. Maybe because I was a woman and he was thinking of what would happen to his own female relatives.

I took a deep breath. Back in the army I had the luxury of being able to wallow for a few days. Now, I didn't. Now I had a spy telling me that I was duty bound to work for them.

As I took the roundabout at the top of Muswell Hill and down Dukes Avenue, I looked again at Mrs Sharif. She had her head down, thumbing through a copy of *Vogue*, and I wondered if what Swincoe had said was true. That somewhere inside their lovely home was a cancer. That her husband, for all the whisky and conviviality, had some link to Blade of Islam. The outfit that had murdered Paul.

He said he would tell me more that evening, at a venue to be decided. In the meantime, I had to proceed exactly as normal and certainly not offer the Sharifs any clue about what he had said.

The Blade of Islam.

What on earth could the beautiful fashion-mag-reading, Victoria Beckham-wearing woman in the rear of the BMW have to do with a misogynist bunch of ISIS-loving fanatics? She was as secular as me, and doing a better job of bringing her daughter up in this world. After all, it was hard to imagine the level-headed, quietly ambitious Nuzha cutting herself in secret.

I pulled over outside the health club and reversed, careful to make sure I couldn't be blocked in. I wasn't that distracted that I had forgotten every last precaution. You always park facing outwards, never nose-in. Gives a cleaner, faster exit. I looked down the line of cars before I said: 'You're clear to go. Four o'clock then, ma'am,' I added, checking the dashboard clock. A little over two hours.

'And we'll pick up Nuzha on the way back and you'll have the rest of the day free. Thank you.'

She slid out, grabbed her nappa leather gym bag and walked off towards the entrance. I watched her go, the physical manifestation of a poise and style that, right then, seemed to come from an alien place.

I exited the car park and, out of habit, started a slightly different route back. The emotional punch that hit me within a few metres drove the breath from my body. I pulled over and pressed a hand to my chest. I thought for a moment I might vomit as the iron-tinged stench of blood on sand in the bright morning sun came back to me and then another smell, that of sawn wood and beeswax.

I knew what it was and I had to ride it out. The hammer blows would come thick and fast – Paul, Jess, Matt, Bojan, boom, boom, boom – but like a tsunami victim, I just had to hold on. I put my head on the steering wheel for a second and let the tears come.

And as I did so, I missed something really, really important.

'I thought you spies liked to meet on bridges.'

Swincoe looked up at me and rose, indicating I should sit opposite him. I hesitated. We were in a side alcove in the public space of The Dorchester on Park Lane, and sitting in the high-backed chairs would block my view of much of the room. I gave the immediate area a quick once-over. I recognised a male member of the Kuwaiti royal family, dressed in Persil-bright *gutra* and *dishdasha*. Freddie had PPO'd for them in the days when she was still on The Circuit. She used to tell a story about taking the teenage girls to a cinema event, when the father had hired the Odeon Leicester Square for one of their birthdays. Only when they arrived did it become clear that, thanks to the preponderance of traditional head-to-toe burkas, all the guests looked identical to her charges. It took precious minutes when the lights went up to establish which were their princesses, as much seat-swapping had taken place. From then on Freddie had taken to spraying an IR marker on the burkas of her girls, so, with appropriate eyewear, she could spot them in a crowd.

'Here.'

He handed me a folded piece of paper. I flipped

it open. It was a series of squiggles and it took me a second to work out what it was.

'Three possible exits from the room. One more than you get on a bridge, unless you plan on flinging yourself off. Plus Lawrence is floating, just in case.' He again indicated I should sit. 'That was what you were worried about?'

I took my place opposite him and smoothed down my skirt. Jil Sander, from Net-a-Porter. I was wearing my best labels – and highest heels – the sort of clothes I would never wheel out for clients. But The Dorchester and MI5? A different matter.

Swincoe pointed at his glass as a waiter appeared. 'G and T?'

Yes, please, my brain said. 'Mint tea,' my mouth decided.

'Everything OK this afternoon?' Swincoe asked when the man had left.

'How do you mean?'

'With the Sharifs? You managed to act as if nothing was amiss?'

'Put it this way, I was fairly sure I wasn't being followed.' I hadn't checked the rear camera USB yet, but I hadn't spotted anything suspicious. 'Which made me a little more relaxed.'

'If we hadn't been following you and seen your Russian and Serbian friends snatch you ...'

'I know. You've made that point. And I'm very

grateful. Am I now in for the "The-least-you-can-do-in-return" speech?'

He managed to feign looking a little crushed at that. 'I'd like to think we would have stepped in even if we didn't have an, um, interest in you staying in one piece. We are meant to be the good guys, you know.' His eyebrows did a little dance, as if courting sympathy. It was comical enough to make me warm to him, just a little.

'OK, give me the BBP.' I assumed he knew that meant Basic Briefing Protocol.

Swincoe leaned forward, as if to get his drink, and allowed his voice to drop a little. 'We first became aware of the Sharif name around the time of the Mumbai massacre. You remember?'

I nodded. In 2008 a group of Pakistani extremists had stormed the Taj Hotel, among other targets, causing more than 160 deaths and 300 injuries across the city. The response of the Indian police and elite forces was still used in colleges and on courses all over the world to teach how *not* to react to terrorist attacks. 'You're not telling me he had something to do with that?'

'The raid was organised and funded from Pakistan. There was a figure mentioned several times by the name The Tailor. He was apparently the source of money to recruit and train the Fedayeen lads in the Chelabandi Hills and the Af-Pak border. The lads – that's what most were, boys – had been recruited in

Faridkot. It was where the Sharif family first settled after Partition.'

'That's as maybe. But there's quite a lot of tailors in Pakistan.'

'True. But we know of at least one instance where a Sharif was mentioned in plain language in the same sentence as The Tailor. Plus Sharif had paid a considerable sum of money into a bank called Karachi Consolidated. It went bust. An angry mob burned its offices to the ground. The money was never recovered.'

It seemed an elaborate way to launder terrorist funds, but I had no experience of the Pakistani banking system. However, there was one thing I was aware of. 'Sharif is not an uncommon name. And even Ultras make bad investments.'

'Plus Sharif travelled to Paris twice in the weeks before the massacre at the Bataclan.'

'He's in the fashion game. It's all pretty circumstantial.'

'We know.'

'And he drinks like a fish and hates all religion.'

Swincoe raised one eyebrow, as if surprised I would fall for that old trick. 'You know about righteous sinners? Those given dispensation to walk among infidels, to act like them, if the cause is holy. But you are right. It's not watertight by any means. Which is why we can't spare the manpower to put a whole surveillance team on him. Not with another sixty-odd ongoing serious and confirmed threats in London, Birmingham and Bradford. That's sixty we know are some way along to lethal action against British citizens. The trick is knowing when to scoop them up, making sure you have enough to put them away for a long time. Get that wrong, and we'll be hung out to dry. It means we are so stretched, we'll take whatever we can get.'

'And that will be me, will it?'

'Mint tea, madam?'

'Thank you.'

'Shall I pour?'

'Please.'

We both sat back and appraised each other while the delicate china was filled with tea.

'No,' he said, once we were alone again. 'That's not you. You have a military background, much like my own. I know you are security conscious ... yes, letting yourself be snatched was a, um, slip-up. But we know you are usually up to snuff. And as I said, you are family. No, "Take what we can get" means we infiltrate however we can. Look, at best MI5 can manage perhaps six hundred field officers at any one time. And bear in mind, it takes more than one-on-one to execute a worthwhile surveillance. And that we have close to ten thousand on our primary watch list.'

He let that number sink in. 'What about GCHQ, phone taps, all that? I thought you chaps could read every email we send.'

He tugged at an earlobe, irritated now. 'You think the enemy don't know that too? Look at the way the newspapers spilled the beans on how attacks in France, Belgium and Germany were thwarted by phone intercepts. I think we are beyond assuming our enemies can't or won't read the Western press.'

I wasn't ready to reclassify the Sharifs as 'enemy' just yet, so I kept quiet.

He took a breath and modulated his tone. 'Besides, the American internet companies are less willing to play ball with us since that silly bastard Snowden blew the whistle. To cut a long story short, the Indian Intelligence Bureau picked up traffic about The Tailor again. Thinking that another Mumbai was on the cards, they made some arrests and, using techniques we would probably frown upon, established that The Tailor is in the UK. Planning something similar to Mumbai or Paris. Possibly another luxury hotel or shopping street.'

Ah, that explained The Dorchester. I'd thought it was an odd choice for a spy. He was trying to demonstrate how vulnerable London would be to a group of armed fanatics. I instinctively sat up straight, transferring my weight so I could stand in one smooth movement. I felt a desire to check out those exits he had scribbled down, just in case. 'Even a Muslim-owned one like this?'

'There were plenty of Muslims who died in Mumbai

and at the sites in Paris. Once you start the process, you can't control who lives or dies. But London has no shortage of other choices not owned by financial arms of Brunei, Saudi Arabia, Kuwait or Qatar. The Ritz, perhaps. Claridge's. The Lanesborough. Perhaps they would hit Bond Street or Sloane Street or an arcade. Perhaps there would be multiple targets, like Paris.'

Despite myself I shuddered at the thought of AKs being deployed on the streets of my city. 'So you need to establish if Sharif and The Tailor are one and the same?'

'Yes, but our options are limited. As I say, financial and manpower constraints mean a full surveillance is out of the question. We can't plant bugs because, like most businessmen, Sharif has his house swept on a regular basis. There is a new one that turns itself off when it detects a sweep, but it's the size of a paperback book at the moment. There are ways around this, however. For example, if you would agree to be miked up—'

'Tell me about Paul.'

The interruption threw him off his pace. 'What?'

'Paul. I'm family, apparently. Tell me what Paul was doing when he was killed. And don't give me all that national security bollocks.'

The face seemed to shut down a little and he stiffened. 'I can't reveal—'

I was on my feet before he had finished, the mint tea untouched.

'Where are you going?'

'Where does it look like? Home to my daughter. My au pair is already on triple time. You are costing me a fortune and wasting my time.'

I could feel eyes on me as other hotel guests wondered what was occurring, but I stood my ground.

'Very well, I'll tell you about Paul. Now will you please sit down?'

I did so, and sipped my tea.

'The Blade of Islam is not a single group, but a loose umbrella of cells, each acting independently. Think of it as an evil version of the Spar shop chain.'

I hadn't heard that analogy employed before, but I got his point. It was a branded franchise of extremism. 'So there is no single leader as such?'

'That's right, no one figurehead we could go after. It's more of a multi-headed hydra. But there is a guiding council, and, after plenty of effort and not a little luck, we got an asset into that.'

'Where does Paul come in?'

'The council had a series of meetings to discuss a proposal from one of the cells about a scheme to blow up a nuclear plant.'

'Which one?'

'Does it matter?'

'Humour me.'

'Dungeness B.'

That nuclear reactor, I knew, had had its operating

life extended to 2028. It was close enough to London for any incident to create serious panic in the city, not to mention the coastal towns of Kent. But as Paul used to tell me, creating a nuclear accident from outside was easier said than done. Bad engineering and nature could do it, a man with a bomb in a suitcase or an RPG missile, not so much.

'The cell was appealing for manpower and funding. The council had asked for a feasibility study. On the day when this was presented, we . . .' His words tailed off as a waiter checked if he was in need of a refill. Swincoe waved him away.

'Yes?' I prompted.

'We wired our man so that Paul could listen in on the discussion and assess whether it was a viable risk or simply some jihadist fantasy.'

'And?'

'The latter, he had concluded. But on the day of the presentation . . . our chap was rumbled, you see. As the meeting ended, they grabbed him and found the wire. He'd already turned the transmitter off, so the listening team, which included Paul, had no idea. But the council knew that there had to be ears nearby. The Blade of Islam sent out three hit squads into the surrounding streets, searching nearby flats and checking any suspicious vans. One of them found Paul, as he came out of the Transit. He'd . . .' Swincoe swallowed. 'It's an easy mistake and someone should have spotted him, but he left his headphones around his neck.' I groaned. 'So it didn't take even an evil genius to guess what he'd been up to. They followed him. Waited till he came out of the shop with his hands full so he couldn't draw his weapon. You know the rest.'

I didn't say anything for a while. Then I managed, 'Thank you.'

'He died doing a good job. A bloody important job.'

I wiped away a tear and sipped some more of the lukewarm mint tea. 'And the asset in the council?'

A small shake of the head. 'He died doing a good job, too.'

I let out a long slow breath. 'But let me get this clear. You want me to wear a wire in the Sharifs', just like that asset? If he is part of a Blade of Islam cell and I am, what did you call it, rumbled?'

I let the question hang, but he didn't let it stay there for too long. He quickly polished off his G and T and signalled for another. 'They'll probably kill you, yes.'

TWENTY-SIX

'What's the name on the cup?'

'Starbucks?' I offered.

The girl behind the counter answered as if she were talking to a particularly disobedient pet. 'No, what name do you want me to put on the cup? When it's ready to collect.'

'Why do you need to put my name on it?'

'So you know it's your order.'

I looked over my shoulder. Jess was outside the coffee shop, concentrating on her phone, as usual. There was nobody else in sight.

'But I'm the only customer.'

The young lady sighed. Her accent – Spanish? – became more pronounced. 'We have to put a name on the cup. It is the rules.'

'Jess.'

'Jess. Excellent.'

Outside, Jess looked at my double espresso and said: 'I didn't want one.'

'You haven't got one.'

'It's got my name on it.'

'Yeah.' I pointed up the road. 'Shall we?'

I was taking her to Islington for brunch. In my bag was the long-awaited letter from the school about the Indonesia trip, although Jess didn't know it had arrived and that I had read it. Three times. She thought brunch was just a treat. Not a device for delivering news in a public place.

She'd wanted to go to Jamie's, but that's not my idea of a good time so I swayed her with the promise of banana French toast. I needed a coffee beforehand because of the little behind-the-eyes throb I had developed thanks to staying up half the night with a bottle of pinot going over and over what Swincoe was asking me to do. Spy on my Principal. Well, on my Principal's father. Either way it was like breaking a fundamental PPO commandment and it left me feeling queasy, even factoring out the wine.

Initially at least, it was something simple – they would replace my iPhone with one of their own, with a high-gain microphone. I would simply leave it lying around with the car keys. They would do the rest remotely. They would turn it off during any sweep, but even if it did register – who didn't have a smartphone these days?

Do I look that stupid? I wondered. That was just a test, a toe in the water, to see if I could be trusted with such a straightforward task. You don't toss minnows like me in with the sharks straight away. If I agreed to go along with them, then it was a slippery slope to ... where? That was the question. Would I end up compromising Mrs Sharif and Nuzha? Well, getting their husband and father arrested on terrorism charges was at least an inconvenience.

Think of it as carrying on Paul's work, Swincoe had said as I was leaving The Dorchester, having told him I would think about it. I couldn't help, after the second glass of red, remembering where Paul's work had got him. I looked down at Jess, walking and texting, and thought how that, should I go the same way, I would be handing her over to Matt by default.

She glanced up, just for a second before the screen dragged her back. Normally I wouldn't tolerate this, and still wouldn't while we were eating, but since Laura's revelation about Jess's condition I was using my best kid gloves. As we turned north towards Camden Passage, she asked: 'You OK, Mum?'

'Yes. Why?'

'You're acting a bit moist.'

Not my favourite word at the best of times and one whose meaning seems to mutate like a virus, just to keep we parents off balance. I was fairly certain 'moist' had meant 'lame' the previous week, but it had clearly evolved. At least I hoped it had.

'Meaning?'

'Weird. Distracted.'

The lights changed and we walked across. 'Since when?'

'Since you went back to work, mostly.'

'Jess, can you just put that down for a second.'

I couldn't see them, but I could almost hear her eyes rolling in their sockets. But she pocketed the phone.

'Is it a problem, me being back at work?'

She shook her head. 'No. It's ... better than before. It's just that when you get home, you're not always at home, if you know what I mean.' She waved a hand. 'It's like you're still out there.'

'I'm sorry. It's been—'

'It's not a problem, Mum. I'm just saying. And Laura is safe.'

Safe. Another one. It could be a greeting, a farewell, an adverb, an adjective or a noun but not all at the same time, apparently.

Jess pulled out her phone again. 'Don't worry about it. Can I have pancakes instead of banana French toast?'

Indeed she could.

I went for eggs Benedict, promising myself a lengthy run that afternoon to pay off the debt to my body. While we were waiting I managed to snatch the phone off Jess and put it in my pocket. There was a squeal of outrage before she realised she was drawing attention to herself. I knew I had the tiniest of windows before she powered down into arms-folded sulk mode.

'I need to talk to you.'

'Mum, not now.'

'Not now what?'

'Not now with the is-everything-all-right-at-school questions. Is anyone bullying me? Am I being made to feel like I should have sex? Am I Snapchatting pictures of my tits?' She blushed on that one.

'Are you?' I asked, despite myself.

'No! But they're the questions all mums ask. We keep a list of them. Top Ten Most Embarrassing Questions.'

'That wasn't what I wanted to talk about. None of that stuff.'

She relaxed, just a little.

'I've decided you can go to Indonesia, and I will pay towards it—'

The rest of my sentence was muffled as she leaned across and threw her arms around me, knocking over a glass of water as she did so. I had to say my piece. She would have to earn some of the money herself, possibly by babysitting or a part-time job. And she would have to agree to come with me to a family counsellor, to talk about Matt, although it would really be a cover to try and get to the bottom of the self-harming. Therapy by stealth.

I managed to untangle her arms, mop up the spillage

and was about to launch into my caveats, when a face I recognised only too well came past the table.

They had dumped him in Edmonton Cemetery. It was becoming quite the villains' playground. Some of the proceeds from the Hatton Garden safety deposit box heist had been hidden there. And the dismembered hands and feet of an unknown female had been left sitting on top of a selection of gravestones after that. And now, Vuk.

His image had been on the front of the *Observer* that had been carried past us, just as the food arrived. I no doubt confirmed Jess's diagnosis of weirdness by rushing out and buying my own copy. I managed to have a half-decent stab at the eggs Benedict, but my appetite had gone. What I really wanted was a cigarette and another espresso.

I did manage to get my conditions across to Jess, who said she would leaflet locally for babysitting jobs and would 'think about' counselling, but that it would be highly embarrassing. Couldn't she do it by herself? Maybe with Laura, someone closer to her own age to metaphorically hold her hand?

Indeed she could.

In fact, the whole therapy ploy had been Laura's idea. Make it seem like Jess is in control of the situation, she suggested. Maybe even let her suggest she come along, which she would happily do. Now that was all over and done with, I calmed down enough to have a second go at my brunch.

When we got home I spotted Lawrence sitting in a white Vauxhall, reading the *Sunday Times*. Did it have the Vuk story too? Is this what he had come to tell me? 'Wanted War Criminal Executed in Gangland Feud' is how the *Observer* had put it. I had only scanned the story, but Vuk had indeed been responsible for mass rape and executions. He had also moved into the drugs trade in London and, according to the report, had been shot in a turf war.

Yet Swincoe had said he was expected to survive. Had they decided he would be too much of a burden on the NHS? Or that the world was better off without him? Or had the gunshot wound to the face been more lethal than they had first thought? I remembered that sewer-breath of his and the menu of what he planned to do to me and, you know what? I didn't give a shit which it was.

I ignored Lawrence until I had taken Jess inside and given the flat a once-over. Nothing was out of the ordinary, so I went back down, locking the new reinforced door behind me.

I slid into the passenger seat of the car. He was dressed in tight skinny jeans, Converse slip-ons and a checked shirt. There was a diamond stud in one ear I hadn't noticed before and the hint of a tattoo poking over the right side of his shirt collar.

He couldn't look less like a spy if he tried. Which, I suppose, was the idea. 'You been sent to keep an eye on me?'

Lawrence smiled. 'I don't think you need keeping an eye on. Seen the papers?' He rustled his *Sunday Times*.

'About Vuk? Yes. But that still leaves Bojan out there, wounded or not.'

'The guv'nor wants to know if you've made up your mind.'

'It's a Sunday,' I said, reaching up and turning the rear-view mirror towards me. 'Day of rest.'

'He said you said you'd sleep on it.'

'I didn't say how many nights.'

His fingers drummed on the steering wheel. 'Why did you join the army?'

'What's that got to do with anything?'

'I was reading your jacket.' He meant my MI5 file. As Paul's wife I was bound to have one. 'Not an army family. Not the usual demographic. What was it? Patriotism? The desire to serve your country?'

So he was going to play the Defend-The-British-Way-Of-Life card? If I was patriotic enough to join the army, maybe I'd become an unofficial foot soldier for MI5. For once I told the truth about why I enlisted. 'I think I had the idea that they would teach me how to kill my father.'

No surprise registered on his smooth features. 'And did they?'

I nodded. 'Yes.'

'And did you?'

'You know the answer to that.' I glanced up at the mirror once more as someone passed behind the car. Dog walker.

'You can stop that now.'

'Stop what?'

'The scanning. The checking the rear-view mirror. The Orange alert status. Day of rest, remember.'

'PPOs have days of rest. I'm not sure parents do.'

'Bojan was picked up at St Pancras last night, checking in for the Eurostar to Brussels. I don't think he was off to The Hague to turn himself in. But we have him. We thought you'd like to know.'

I felt like a punctured gas envelope as some of the tension left my muscles. It had been nagging at me constantly. Bojan was out there. He knew where I lived. Knew I had a little girl. Had threatened her when he snatched me. And he would be more pissed off than ever now. But Lawrence was telling me he was out of the picture. Yet again, I owed them.

'Is he heading for Edmonton as well?'

He shook his head. 'That was just a convenient disposal of a man who had inconveniently died on us. No, there are plenty of people who want to get their hands on Bojan. Here, America, Holland, Belgium, Croatia and Serbia. Whoever gets him, he won't be troubling anyone except lawyers for a long time.'

It must have been the relief that made me form the next sentence. 'Tell Swincoe I'm in.'

I regretted it as soon as I said it. But then, that night, I remembered to play back the reversing-camera footage from Saturday. And I knew I'd done the right thing.

PART THREE

TWENTY-SEVEN

The Sharifs were in Dubai for the Whitsun break. Not because it was Pentecost, but because Nuzha had two weeks off school – poor Jess had to make do with just the one, but then the more you pay for education, the shorter the terms – so a holiday abroad would not interfere with her studies. I was not invited. It involved some sort of extended family get-together and, although they didn't say as much, I'd stand out like the sorest of thumbs. Mrs Sharif told me it would be a pretty conservative affair, as it coincided with Shab-e-barat, the night of forgiveness, which some of the clan still celebrated. That night, God would look back on the deeds of each person during the previous year and decide the fate of the coming twelve months. So her husband would have to metaphorically cork his Talisker and she and Nuzha would hide their hair and lower their eyes into modesty. You were expected to feel shame and guilt for your transgressions and ask forgiveness.

In fact, she explained, on that night Allah forgave all sins, apart from soothsayers, magicians, people who are full of hatred – *mushahins* – alcoholics, people who harm their parents and those who insist on committing fornication. I guess she thought Mr Sharif didn't count as an alcoholic. I didn't think so either, but one man's social drinker is another's raving dipsomaniac.

And fornication? I wanted to ask Mrs Sharif what she thought should be done with fornicators, but I bit my tongue.

Shab-e-barat didn't sound like too much fun but then again, there are those who find Christmas an extended form of abuse – but with the English spring still stubbornly chilly, there would be sun and there'd be shopping and they were putting up at the Burj-al-Arab, so there'd be plenty of gilt to go with the guilt.

And security? Ali, who was also staying behind, had sent his deputy ahead of the family and he had contracted AirShield for the job. It was a good choice. Its operatives had local knowledge that it would take Ali and me weeks to acquire and they used females where appropriate.

It all meant I had some free time, which I desperately needed. Free time with Jess and the opportunity to have a good read of the letters that had come from Matt's solicitors, asking if I had considered his 'contact time' with Jess. I needed a sounding board for that, so, before my meeting with Ben Harris at Hippolyte, I met Nina in a restaurant on Farringdon Road, where I slipped into a wooden booth and realised I had to play origami to get my limbs in.

'Don't moan,' she warned me. 'At least they have cushions on the benches now. Time was you left here unable to feel your arse it was so numb.'

I gave the menu a quick glance. It was mostly offal and cuts of meat I had never heard of. But it all looked and smelled good. The truth was, I wasn't hungry. There was too much ahead of me that day to risk a post-lunch slump. Nor a drink. The latter news left Nina looking like I had not so much rained on her parade as taken a dump on it from a great height.

'You go ahead,' I said. 'This one is on me for standing you up the other week.'

It was, in fact, three weeks since my kidnap and my agreeing to work for Swincoe. Disappointingly, they had not been in touch apart from one brief meet with Lawrence, who assured me they were just making sure the phone/bug was foolproof. Which was fine by me – I didn't want some lashed-together bit of kit that would mark me out as a snoop.

'Right.' She looked up at the waitress. 'I'll have a glass of the ... no, I'll have a half-bottle of the Abadia de San Campio. And the offal on toast to start, followed by the Fosse Meadows Chicken. And the chips.' She fixed me with a stare. 'The chips are the best in London.'

'And for you?' the waitress asked.

'The red mullet. A side salad. And tap water.'

Nina pouted a little. 'Jesus, it's like being out with Gwyneth Paltrow. I know I told you to watch your diet, but not when you're with me, please. So, what's so important you'll come over and watch me have a good feed while you pick fish bones out of your teeth?'

I took the latest letter from Anthony Hazlitt & Co and slid it over.

'Supervised contact?' she asked. 'With social workers? Christ, he's not a pervert.'

'Come on, Nina, start by being on my side.'

What Matt, through the solicitor, was asking for seemed reasonable enough. He wanted some time at one of the teenage-focused National Association of Child Contact Centres where, for a couple of hours every other Saturday afternoon, he could 're-acquaint himself with Jess and vice-versa' as it said.

'They cost money, those things. Couldn't he just come round to the flat?' suggested Nina.

'Could he fuck. I'm not buggering off because of him. It's a foot in the door.'

'What does Jess say?'

I let my eyebrows do the talking.

'You haven't told her?'

'We've got a lot on our plate at the moment.' Laura and I were still inching towards the therapy session. The good news was, Laura said she thought Jess

244

hadn't cut herself since the day I had agreed she could go to Indonesia. She was too busy. Laura claimed her browsing history mainly consisted of checking what vaccinations she needed and if you could wear bikinis on remote Indonesian islands (an armful, and no, respectively). 'I mean, we've broached the subject, but not these exact details.'

'I think you have to tell her,' said Nina. She tasted the wine and nodded her approval, eyes widening in anticipation as the Galician was glugged into her glass. 'Look, it's this simple. If you say no, he can go to a family court and the judge will make you do this. The thing is, once you get dragged kicking and screaming down that route, everything is out of control. You might think being a bodyguard is a decent profession for a mother – no, I know you're GPOs or whatever you like to call yourselves – but who knows what the court will think? Lousy hours hanging out with lousy people who are lousy with money.'

She never did see the appeal of being a PPO, did Nina.

'What you think is benign or normal, you might find Matt's solicitor will consider evidence of neglect or indifference.'

My throat dried as I thought of the marks on Jess's arms. I hadn't told Nina about that. Now probably wasn't the time.

'So co-operate, is what you'd say?'

Nina drank. 'Yes, it is. You have a solicitor?'

'Yes.'

'Use him. Keep everything polite, business-like. If it goes all Jeremy Kyle, you'll end up losing Jess, emotionally if not physically. And for fuck's sake, get her input before you decide anything. She might not want to give up Saturdays for Dad. You have to be able to trust her.'

Luckily the offal on toast arrived at that point, because I was about to blurt out how Jess was on the fringes of a world where parental trust came second to parental deceit. One thing at a time.

Nina spoke between hearty mouthfuls. 'Do you know what Matt is up to? How he's making a living?'

I shook my head. I could only run one surveillance at a time, and my head was full of the Sharifs and Swincoe.

Nina began to smack her lips in pleasure. A tiny trickle of red-brown juice escaped from the corner of her mouth.

'Oh, my phone just buzzed,' I lied, tapping my jacket pocket. 'You carry on, won't be a sec.'

I managed to extricate myself from the wooden booth with some degree of elegance. Outside, I took in a lungful of what passed for fresh air on the Farringdon Road and checked my phone. There was a missed call, from what would appear to the casual listener to be an automated machine trying to get me to sue someone or other. In reality it was a request for a meeting with

Swincoe or Lawrence. The last word would tell me which of six possible locations. Sometimes you wonder if spies know just how predictable they are.

I ignored that call for the moment and made my own. If Nina had done one thing so far, apart from demonstrate that offal-eating is not a spectator sport, it was convince me that I needed back-up. I was spreading myself thinner than Marmite on toast.

So I called Freddie, my old army mucker. I didn't know it then, but that was the moment when it all started to unravel for me.

Not every ex-soldier joins The Circuit. The percentage among the hard guys – the SAS, the SBS, the Royal Marines and the Paras – is high. They work for the outfits, mostly British, American and South African, that specialise in Hostile Environments. One day they could be escorting a convoy in Afghanistan for HM Government, the next doing it on ten times as much pay for Frontline Services or Stemler Solutions. Quite a few work for the likes of Nicholls Steyn & Associates, which provides security for the Oscars in LA and the Indian Cricket Board, or for Matrix A, another South African firm which covers the Pakistan CB (neither of them easy accounts, as cricket really is war by other means out there).

Most officers leaving for Civvy Street, though, gravitate towards the City, and not usually in security roles but in management and personnel. And the enlisted men and women? Well, I was lucky, lucky that people on The Circuit were just beginning to recognise that a woman with medical training and a basic grasp of the game could be of some use.

But every day I saw others without that good fortune. Sure, they were outnumbered by those who came out of the forces and got on with life. You don't notice those, the reintegrated. But the streets of London and other cities are littered with the others, and not just the obviously homeless, although ex-military make up a disproportionate percentage of rough sleepers.

No, there is another category of the war-damaged, almost invisible to regular people, those who cross the road when they come to a petrol station, because even the slightest whiff of fumes sends them back to the day when they pulled body parts from a downed Chinook, the ones who crouch behind a wall when a car backfires or reach for an SA80 they are no longer allowed to carry. Then there are those that walk with their heads in the air. Not out of any sense of superiority. They are scanning for half-opened sash windows or roof tiles that had mysteriously lifted despite there being no recent gales. Sniper patrol.

I found myself wondering what the story was with Tom Buchan, the canal boatman. A continuous cruiser, he'd said. Someone who wouldn't stay more than a few days in one place. Bad things must have happened around him. To people he liked. And he keeps moving on in case it happens again, keeping contacts to a minimum, not risking making friends. The canals would suit that. And, apart from the chug of the engine, it's quiet down there. For many who succumb to PTSD – and I think that is all of us who served, albeit to varying degrees – it is the sounds that are the commonest trigger for an episode.

I wondered which conflict or conflicts he would have seen. He was about Paul's age, so perhaps Northern Ireland or Bosnia. I would put him at too young for the Falklands, too old for Iraq and Afghanistan. It didn't matter, combat stress had certain repeatable and pre-dictable parameters whichever conflict you served in. Why was I thinking of Tom Buchan suddenly? I switched to thinking about something else, before one of Freddie's lewd comments popped into my head unbidden. I began to consider how I would tackle the Russian, now he had agreed to see me.

There were no stupid drones buzzing overhead this time. I pressed the intercom at the gate, said I was there to see Mr Asparov and it swung open. No robot, RSCA car was offering to save my legs by whisking me up the drive. The cameras still followed me, though, and there was one black-suited security monkey next to a Range Rover, arms folded across his chest, face impas-sive, eyes invisible behind sunglasses. It was overcast so the Persols were unnecessary. He was probably the sort that wore them indoors. Never a good look for a PPO – you might as well wear a Bodyguards'R'Us T-shirt. There was a uniformed chauffeur polishing the Range Rover's bonnet. Another bad choice by Mr Asparov. The chauffeur, not the Range Rover.

The butler opened the door as I approached and stepped aside with a slight inclination of his head and something – pity? – I couldn't quite place in his eyes. The Slavic cheekbones-on-heels was there too, more solicitous this time. 'I'd just like to apologise for the manner of your last visit.'

The manner? As if someone had used the wrong fork in my presence. 'Let's get this over with. I have things to do.' *People to see, crimes to commit.*

She showed me into the same office as before, the one where Mitval had interviewed me and I'd witnessed the dance of the revolving artworks. It was empty.

'Mr Asparov will see you shortly. Please take a seat.'

I did so and placed the aluminium flight case I had been carrying on the desk in front of me. The house seemed to settle into quiet. The tick of a clock, the hum and growl of a vacuum cleaner on an upper floor, the faintest tinkle of piano music.

I looked at my phone. I had to be back in north London within two hours. I wasn't in the mood for games. I stood, put the attaché case on my vacated chair and turned to leave.

'I do love my wife, you know.'

The voice coincided with the whirr of electric motors and the thunk of magnetic bolts being thrown. A crack had appeared in one corner of the panelled wall behind the desk, and it grew as I watched, bleeding a bright, modern light into the gloomy office.

As the wall retreated, so Asparov was revealed, rather melodramatically, I thought. The room behind him was mostly shades of white and grey, and it reduced him to a mere silhouette.

'Come through, please.'

'Said the spider to the fly.' I was well aware of what that space behind him was – a panic room. Windowless, secure, soundproof. I'm not a fan. In a panic room, nobody can hear you scream. And there's usually only one way out.

'I shall leave this section open, if it would make you more comfortable.'

I picked up both the flight case and the chair it had been resting on. The chair, I left straddling the groove the hidden door travelled on. I doubted the electric motors were powerful enough to crush even a repro Chippendale.

'That's rather an expensive door stop,' Asparov said with amusement in his voice. So maybe it wasn't a repro after all.

'You'll be less likely to close it, then.'

I looked around the room. There was no desk in

here. It was contemporary compared to outside, with pieces that suggested Danish design. At one end there was a small kitchen. I checked the walls and spotted a faint outline in the paintwork. 'Pull-down bed?'

A nod. 'Electrically controlled.' Of course it was. No oligarch would do anything as vulgar as operating something manually.

'Very nice.'

He pointed to one of two couches. 'Please, sit.'

I did so, in the centre, so that he was forced to sit elsewhere. As he selected an armchair, I got a good look at him. His blue suit was beautifully cut – Brioni or similar – to hide a little paunch. He was smaller than I expected, probably misled by the swimming pool mural, at around five-seven or eight. His hair was thinning, swept back and probably dyed. The face was long, slightly lugubrious, and I suspected he'd had work done. He certainly had on the teeth, because they outshone everything else in the room.

'Why the change of style in here?' I asked. 'Boodles out there, Bauhaus in here.'

'Oh, this is what I prefer. Eames, Baughman, Aarnio.'

I pointed to one of the pictures on the wall. It was mostly matt white, with a single glossy stripe down the centre. 'And does this rotate?'

'The Ryman? Hardly. That out there? I inherited it. The whole place. But you know, it's how people expect we Russians to be, so why change it? More money than taste. And if we show our taste, well, we are simply phoneys playing at having a good eye. A Russian can't really like Ryman or Richter. You would be surprised how easy it is to lull people into a false sense of security when they think they are dealing with someone who has just popped out of a yurt in the Urals.'

Did they have yurts in the Urals? Well, he was in a better position to know. I pushed the case towards him with the toe of my ankle boot. 'Yours, I believe.'

He looked down at it with something like distaste. 'It's a bomb.'

I saw the flash of panic cross his face, the body tense so that he all but levitated, his eyes swivel towards the open wall panel.

'At least, it could have been.' I reached down and flicked it open, letting one side fall to reveal the neat stacks of cash within. 'I walked past one guy in the grounds, was eyed up by half a dozen cameras, so at least one CCTV operative is on duty, let in by Jeeves up there.' Yes, I knew Jeeves wasn't a butler in the books, but it was a convenient shorthand. 'And escorted by Svetlana or whatever her name is. Nobody asked to look inside the case.'

'Sloppy,' he said.

'Not as sloppy as you'd be if a couple of pounds of Semtex had gone off at your feet. Where do you get your people from?'

'Mitval I brought from Russia. The others I got from the best. At least, I was told it was the best. UBG.'

Universal Body Guards.

'But they only have male security operatives, which is why I went to Hippolyte for you.' I was guessing Svetlana didn't count as muscle.

What UBG has is the best website, the most gushing testimonials, and Colonel Forbes-ffrench, late of the SAS.

I told him what I thought. 'The people they employ are bumped-up bouncers who have done a five-day course and got themselves a bit of paper that says "qualified bodyguard". Look closely at Forbes-ffrench's medals and you'll see they are a mix of eBay buys and decorations from pre-WW2. I mean, he's not a young man, but I don't think he served at the Somme.'

Asparov looked pained. 'He's a fraud?'

'He is.' Although not all his people are rogues, some just took everything at face value and wondered why they were looked down upon on The Circuit when they produced their UBG certificate.

'But the SAS?'

'Slovenian Air Security. Which, incidentally, Colin Brown, that's his real name, incorporated in Ljubljana so he could use the initials.' There were plenty of guys who have served in The Regiment who would love to give him a good kicking for that. They don't take kindly to their name being taken in vain.

'I see I shall have to reconsider my staffing.'

'Did the chauffeur come from UBG?'

'No. Why?'

I don't like chauffeurs. Not personally, but as a concept. They are usually very good people individually, capable and droll, and perfect if their role is to be a posh cab driver. The problems start when they try and combine chauffeuring with a PPO role. They do love their cars, you see. They spend more time with them than their employers. Or wives and husbands come to that. So when there is that split-second situation where they might have to ram another car to force their way out of a jam, they often hesitate. Just for a vital half-second. You can see it in their eyes: *But I'll scratch the car if I do that*. They love their vehicles too much, and it can become a liability.

'No reason,' I said, not feeling like giving away too many trade secrets. 'I assume you had Hippolyte's computer hacked just to get my address? So you could deliver the money?'

He gave an enigmatic smile. 'You'll take a coffee?'

'Only if you make it.' Three would be a crowd in that room. Plus I didn't want him to invite a third party in who might not really be there to act as a *barista*.

'Of course.' He rose and walked over to the kitchen area.

'And regular, please. Not something that has been crapped out of a rodent's arse.'

He looked upset at my choice of language, which pleased me. Childish, but rewarding all the same. 'I don't think civets are rodents,' he said evenly. 'How is Jamaican?'

'Perfect.'

As he set about grinding the beans, I picked up the flight case and placed it on his seat. 'So what was this payment? Blood money? Yet another problem that could be solved by throwing cash at it?'

'Not at all. But I thought you deserved compensation.'

'I won.'

'Prize money, then,' he said with a smile.

'How did you find out about it so quickly?'

'Elliott was outraged, or as outraged as a butler can be. He sent a CCTV file to me in Moscow of the, er, incident in the gym.' Good old Jeeves. 'That was totally unacceptable. The men had been dismissed immediately. I hoped the money would go some way to an apology.' The coffee machine began to make its gurgling sounds. 'I still do. You don't have to return it.'

'But I do. Otherwise you'll just go on thinking money fixes everything.'

'Doesn't it?' Asparov raised his eyebrows in mock surprise. He thought for a moment, rubbing his chin as he did so, as if expecting to find stubble. 'It was meant as a genuine *mea culpa*, not a ... a sticking plaster. You think we oligarchs, as you like to call us, are all immoral robber barons. Isn't that right?'

I had no opinion on that. But if pressed, I'd come down on the side of yes.

'But all I did to make my money, initially at least, was what your government does all the time when it sells off the Post Office or Lloyds Bank to its friends in the City. Is that immoral?'

I'd probably go with yes again. But I said nothing.

'Such things happen all the time, all over the world. I simply offered to buy up shares from the public at a fair price to give me control of a fertiliser company. And most did sell, making a thousand per cent profit along the way.'

I bet there are not that many of the public that now had chauffeurs and wannabe pop-star wives, I thought, but again kept quiet. He came over with two cups of black coffee, moved the case and sat.

'Look, Mr Asparov, I'm sure you're a regular Robin Hood compared to most, but it's immaterial to me. I appreciate the gesture of the money, even if I deplore your choice in staff, but I can't take it. It feels . . .'

'Wrong?' he suggested.

'Toxic.'

He flinched at that. I had upset him – again. But then that's partly what I was there for. I'd been very upset in that house myself.

'You said you loved your wife, when you first did the trick with the wall. What was that all about?'

'Something else other people find hard to believe.

You obviously didn't hear the beginning of the sentence. I said: I wanted to hire you, or someone like you, because I love my wife. I value her. I know what people think. She is a gold-digger, I am a fool who wants a trophy wife. And I have seen *Citizen Kane*.'

'I haven't.' It was true. Paul went on and on about it until in the end I was frightened to watch it, because nothing could possibly live up to that billing.

'Well, Kane creates a career for his wife as an opera singer, even though she can't sing. I can see the parallels.'

I drank some of my coffee.

'And because she is wife number three, they expect her not to last long. I think they underestimate her. But they are right – it is very difficult to find a woman who is not blinded by money.'

He made a gesture that suggested I was one of these few. Well, I won't be blinded by ten grand. You'd have to bid me up a little.

'How is the coffee?'

'Lovely. Forgive me, but I must be going.' I took a larger hit of the coffee and put the cup and saucer on a low fibreglass table.

'Coincidentally we are off to Jamaica soon, Katya and I. Geejam. You know it?' I shook my head. 'A hotel and recording studio. Katya is doing some work with Max Martin. Then New York, Los Angeles, Moscow, Paris. I'll be away for ten days, two weeks. So, while I have you here, I'd like to ask you a question. Perhaps two.'

I stood, just to show him my time was precious and I really did need to be going. 'Ask away.'

'Who would you go to for better security people?'

'Someone specialising in your niche. Not doing a jack-of-all-trades or doors or mainly serving governments in hostile environments. Domestic close-protection specialist. Maybe draw some from Hippolyte, because ideally you need a mix of men and women, and then maybe go to someone like FrontFirst. But really, anyone who knows The Circuit could put you a half-decent team together.'

'That's what I thought.' He drained his own coffee and also stood. 'Next question.'

'Yes?'

'Would you like the job?'

TWENTY-EIGHT

An hour later I watched an RAC van pull into the courtyard outside the health club. I raised a hand and the vehicle turned towards me. With a deft spin of the wheel, the driver positioned it diagonally, behind the BMW X1, blocking it from the view of anyone else using the car park. The van's hazard lights flicked on to show it was attending an emergency. The door opened and One-Eyed Jack stepped stiffly from the cab with a chorus of groans and grunts.

'My God, are you OK?' I hissed.

'Never better.' He opened a compartment in the side panel of the truck and extracted a Snap-On toolbox. 'I decided to play in a dads' football match last night. Bloody hell, most of them have forty years on me. Look, I'm walking like Boris Karloff. I don't think me knees can bend any more. All that and driving in London, I forget how horrible it is ...'

'Jack, when a man is tired of London ...'

'He's tired of strife, I know. Now, what do you want to do here?'

We both looked at Mrs Sharif's X1. It was parked in a numbered bay outside the health club at Alexandra Palace where she allegedly did Pilates. Lord knew what it cost her to have it there permanently. I had seen it leaving shortly after I had dropped her off that first afternoon, in the wake of my kidnap by Bojan and Mitval. I hadn't looked at the reversing camera footage immediately and I almost missed the fact it was her, except she was fussing with a hijab as she drove. And that movement caught my eye. Still, it could have been mistaken identity, so I got Jack to run the plates. It was her car. And on each subsequent occasion when I took her to 'Pilates', I had watched the bronze-coloured X1 leave within five or ten minutes of me pulling away.

She was up to something, all right. But what? In any other family I might have thought – *a secret lover*. In fact, I hoped it was. Because with the Blade of Islam hanging over the household, it was possible that she had even less pure motives. Could it be that Mrs Sharif was the link to BOI? I didn't want to make that accusation until I could be sure.

'Can you get me in?' I asked Jack.

'Last year, no problem. This year, they've changed the software. Best I can do is drill out the key barrel. Make sure I don't set off the trembler, mind.'

261

'Even Mrs Sharif might notice her car hasn't got a lock.'

'I can replace it. Thing is, her key won't work. But how many people use keys these days? How many people even know there is an emergency key in their electronic fob?'

It was a good point. 'OK, let's do it.'

'How long have I got?'

'Till Friday. That's when they get home.'

'I think I'll have it cracked before then,' he said, kneeling down with much huffing.

I walked out from behind the van, trying to look like the distressed woman whose BMW had stranded her. A steady stream of other cars, mostly high-end, came and went from the car park, nearly all carrying women dressed for the gym, most of them too preoccupied to even notice an RAC van. Quite where Jack had sourced that particular cover, I had no idea. I knew it was better not to ask, because the reply would always be gnomic, involving some 'mate' somewhere. I heard the drill begin to whine.

I hadn't taken the job with Asparov. I had told him that when I had more time, I would consider advising, especially on the female aspect. He had seemed satisfied with that. He had apologised once more for Bojan and Mitval and their vile behaviour. And he had said that, now I had returned the money, he was very much in my debt. If I needed any help, any time,

I was to ask him and he was duty-bound to offer his services.

I felt like I was in a scene from *The Godfather*. Yes, Paul did persuade me to watch that one.

'Excuse me, are you from around here?'

The expectant mother with the double buggy holding two toddlers looked like she'd been dipped in bleach she was so pale. Her blonde hair was hanging in rats' tails and she had the dark smudges under her eyes of sleepless nights.

'No. But can I help?' While I said it my instincts made me look over her shoulder and then do a casual 360 of the area. Harassed pregnant mums make for good cover.

'I'm looking for the deer.'

'Bambis!' one of the boys shouted.

'Bambi,' echoed the other.

I hated to disappoint them, so I whispered it. 'They've gone,' I said. 'Re-located. Apparently the herd wasn't doing too well in such an urban environment.'

I only knew this because I'd read the notices pinned to the park railings while I was spying on Mrs Sharif.

'Oh what a shame. Anything serious?' she asked.

'With the deer?'

She indicated the RAC van. 'Your car.'

The whining of the drill had stopped. 'Nothing they can't fix.'

I watched her head for the park and the empty deer

enclosure, looking for any sign that this wasn't just a casual encounter. But the boys' squeals of dismay when she told them the Bambis had departed seemed genuine enough. I went back to where Jack was kneeling, having plugged a laptop into a diagnostics socket on the BMW's doorframe.

'What are you doing? I just need to switch on the bloody sat nav,' I admonished him.

'Nah, quicker doing it this way. I'm downloading the driver profile. It'll tell you how she drives, if she's got a heavy foot on the brake, if she regularly busts the speed limit, her mix of urban and non-urban driving. When she last had a drive-through ...'

'Can you code me a key from that download if need be?'

'Yup. Jordan'll do it.'

'And tell me where she goes most Saturday afternoons?'

Satisfied, Jack pulled the plug from the housing.

'Yeah, that too.'

Afterwards we went for coffee at a place in Friern Barnet, opposite the grand sweep of what was once a massive mental hospital. It was now flats, complete with a Virgin Active gym, which sold for a million or more each. Who's crazy now?

I stuck with the coffee plan, but Jack went for something called a brandizo, with eggs, avocado, chorizo and chillies. It was on me, so he ordered a large portion. Next to him he had the laptop open and was scrolling through what looked like machine code to me.

'Here we are. Every time she goes, she punches up "favourite destinations" and the same postcode.' He tapped it into his phone and sent it to me. 'N4. You know where that is?'

'Not far from here, I think. What's the rest?'

I put the entire postcode into Google maps on my phone and the familiar blob of a pointer came up with a name next to it. My face must have betrayed something, because Jack asked: 'What is it?'

'The Bounds Green Fatih Mosque.'

'Fatih? What's that?'

I knew, because I had been to the site of the same name in Istanbul, which I suspected was rather grander than its namesake just off the North Circular. 'It means, "The Conqueror's Mosque".'

What I really needed that night was some downtime to try and assimilate everything that had happened, or was about to happen. But Jess decided she was going to play the dutiful daughter and instead of retreating to her room, she insisted we sit down together and watch some TV. So we did, but my mind wasn't really on the antics of a bunch of genetically deficient West Londoners, although she seemed to find the whole thing riveting. She gushed about some of the girls' clothes, telling me where you could get affordable copies of the designer labels. She also explained the interpersonal relationships between the characters, but it would have needed a particularly complicated flowchart for me to sort out who was straight, confused, gender fluid and who was in transition. Or just a twat.

In the ad breaks I broached the idea of spending a few hours with Matt every other week or so 'just to get to know him again', as if she'd ever known him in the first place, to see if she would like him back in her life. I stressed it was all up to her. If at any time she thought it was a bad idea, we would go back to zero access.

'If you like,' she said, thus kind of agreeing but shifting the responsibility back to me. I took it as a maybe.

That was enough for one evening. There was still the question of therapy, but I would leave that to Laura for the time being.

At about eight the doorbell rang. I checked the built-in camera in the door on my phone. It was Freddie.

I acted surprised, as if I hadn't texted her and told her to come over if she could. I needn't have worried. Jess was pleased to see her, because she had a legitimate excuse to abandon playing happy family and scurry off to her room to continue watching the programme. I was happy because I could now stop feeling like I wanted to put my foot through the television (although I suspected you could no longer put your foot 'through' a modern flatscreen).

Freddie always reminded me of an impish version of Audrey Hepburn, with her pointed chin and short, bobbed hair. Freddie wasn't actually her real name. Her surname was Flint, so it was inevitable what the army would do with that – 'Flintoff', which evolved into 'Freddie'. She claimed she preferred it to Judith, her given name, and, in truth, she didn't look like a Judith.

While I fetched the glasses, she shrugged off a very expensive biker jacket – worn over a floral dress I recognised from Jigsaw – and sat on the sofa in the spot recently vacated by Jess. I took up position next to her and we made polite conversation for a while. I asked her about her love life.

'Love life? That's very Mills and Boon, isn't it? No more love life for me. Just sex. I have a gaggle of young men who like the idea they can fuck an older woman. No strings attached. And you know, they're great. Twenty-year-olds, I mean. Their dicks stay hard forever and they've got six-packs and they shave all over. I mean all over. Very smooth.'

'Must be like having sex with a dolphin,' I offered.

'You're just jealous. What about you? Anyone?'

'Yes. He's skinny, bronzed, beautifully put together.' She looked interested until I held my hands six inches apart. 'And about this long.'

'Ah. Well, what else?'

'Some interesting developments in the work department.'

'Out with it then, I haven't got all night.'

I must have babbled, because by the time I drew breath, she had drained her glass and mine was still full. 'Fuckin' hell.'

'Yes. Fucking hell.'

Freddie laughed. 'You still put a "g" on the end, you posh bitch. Come on, I'm empty.'

I topped her up. 'So can you help me?'

'What with? The secret squirrel bit? The mad Muslims? I'm not sure I'm up to speed for all that.'

'No, not the mad Muslims.' Although that remained to be seen. If they were mad, bad or dangerous, that is.

'Is that mosque in Bounds Green one of the bad apples? Like Finsbury Park was?' Freddie asked.

'I don't know. I couldn't find anything on the web. There's no Abu Hamza figure if that's what you mean. I'll ask Nina to do some digging.'

Freddie made a sour face. She and Nina had met a couple of times. It wasn't a meeting of minds. 'This mosque thing on Saturdays. Isn't Friday the day of worship?'

'Maybe she's not going to worship.'

Freddie put a hand on my knee. 'You have to be careful. I mean, what happened to Paul when he took up with that shit.'

'Don't worry about me. I'm going to hand everything over to the spooks and stand back. It's Matt I need your help with. I think I am going to agree in principle to the idea of him meeting Jess at a Contact Centre.'

'Really?' She didn't like Matt much, either, which was ideal for my purposes.

'It's no good hiding my head in the sand. This isn't going to go away. The next step is he goes to the Family Court. I don't want that to happen.'

'Nope, stay out of court if you can.' Freddie had endured a long legal battle with her 80 per cent gay ex, who had managed to hide most of his assets. She did OK in the end – I could see from the label that the biker jacket was a Roland Mouret – but not as well as she might have done. Still, she had a nice house in Dartmouth Park and, apparently, a pack of fuck-dolphins, so I didn't feel too much pity for her.

'He says he is clean and out of the drugs game. But he either owns or is renting a fancy place on City Road. Has he got a job? A wife? I need whatever ammunition you can get me, so that if it all goes tits up I can blow him out of the water. And I'll pay, of course.'

She wrinkled her nose. 'Nah. Don't really need the money. Be fun.'

'I'll pay,' I insisted. 'Give it to the Save The Dolphin fund.'

'Meow. Don't be catty. It doesn't become you.' She drank some more wine and her forehead furrowed in thought. 'Can you give me some basic details? Like his old National Insurance number. Maybe his passport number if he still has the same one?'

'They might be on some old paperwork somewhere, I suppose. Why? What are you planning?'

'Nothing illegal. Well, nothing too illegal ...'

'*Freddie* ...'

'Don't *Freddie* me. Look, the thing is,' she said forcefully, 'what little I know of Matt ...'

I didn't like that tone. 'Yes?'

'If you're going to go down and dirty on this.'

'Uh-huh?'

'Then so's he.'

'I know.'

'And he might be ahead of the game.'

I felt a jitter of fear dance around my abdomen. 'That's also true.'

I didn't realise at that point just how far Matt was in front of me: on the home straight, while I was barely out of the starting blocks.

TWENTY-NINE

I needed to run the next day to clear my head. One bottle with Freddie had become two and neither of them were the best vintages. In fact, I'm not sure either of them actually had a year on the label.

The Sharifs had one more day away, so I didn't have to be over there at the usual seven, so I waited till Laura came before setting off. She arrived with a slightly more listless attitude than usual. While Jess packed her bag I took her aside.

'You OK?'

'Yes, of course.' The smile looked forced.

'Really?'

'Really. Well, a little boyfriend trouble.'

'From Queenstown? Has he met someone else?' Long-distance love affairs were tricky within the UK. I would imagine they were fraught with difficulties when it involved the other side of the world.

'No, he's just being ... it's all right. We did some FaceTime and, what with the time difference, he was drunk, I was sober, my period had started, my sister is getting a divorce. Not a great time.'

Having said all that she seemed to visibly lift. 'You mind if I have some Weetabix?'

'No, go ahead. Did you get any further along with Jess about, you know . . .' I drew a finger across at my upper arm, unable to speak the words.

'I think it's still under control.' She paused. 'You know, if you are worried, you could always get a doctor to put her on some medication.'

'No.' I hoped that was firm enough.

'It's not the stigma it once was, you know. Most of my friends have been on it. I was, for a while.'

'Last resort,' I said. 'And I don't think we're there yet.'

'Nowhere near.' She opened the cupboard that held the cereals and took out three biscuits of the cereal, then doused them with milk. I felt a pang of hunger, but suppressed it. Women burn more calories on an empty stomach, apparently.

'I'll see you later,' I said.

'Have a good run,' Laura offered through hamster-like cheeks.

I did my usual loop down to Broadway Market and on the way back I saw an electric-blue narrow boat reversing into a space, the frenzied churning of the water loud against the morning quiet. As I came level, Tom Buchan looked up and raised a hand, as if he'd just gone to get a newspaper rather than disappearing for days on end.

'You in a hurry?' he shouted over the engine.

I bent over, grasped my knees and panted till I could speak without a wobble in the voice. 'Not particularly.'

'Come on. I got something for you.'

Twice. Twice I've met him and both times I've had scarlet cheeks and ...

I catch myself. As if he cares what I look like. He's only got me a replacement sweatshirt. Calm yourself, girl.

I climb on board the Slim Pickens. *He ducks inside so I follow. 'Hot?' he asks.*

I really must be glowing. 'Warm,' I admit.

'Hold on.'

He fills and then hands me a glass of water and I take the opportunity to get my breath back. His hand touches mine as I take the drink. His skin is warm and a little scratchy from the calluses but I experience a small fizz in the pit of my stomach. I quickly look away, as if I am really interested in his bloody coffee machine.

'Want one?' he asks.

'Maybe later.'

I slide past him and walk into the living area, examining the pile of books he has on his coffee table. They are a strange mix of pulp thrillers and classics. Jane

Austen? What sort of man reads Jane Austen? Maybe there is a woman in his life after all.

I am about to turn and ask him about Northanger Abbey *when I'm aware that he's standing behind me, close enough that I can feel the mass of his body. I stiffen slightly, a professional instinct when a man moves into my personal space. I force myself to relax, pretending to be absorbed in his Henning Mankell hardbacks and after a moment I feel a hand on the small of my back. When I turn, his hand remains there and he spins me in a half-circle so that we're facing. I start to speak but a finger brushes my lips. I'm not sure he could hear my voice over my booming heart anyway.*

I take a deep breath, feeling more in control now. He has made the first move. It is mine to reject or accept.

I reach behind me and pull off my hairband to release my hair, still damp from the morning shower. The fresh shampoo smell drifts between us. His hands are resting lightly on my hips now and we are at the tipping point. The point at which I either jump or freeze. I am aware I don't own this space, it's on his turf, his terms, his boat. On the other hand, it's refreshingly neutral for me – I'm not a mum, not a PPO, just ...

I slant my face to his, waiting for his lips. He moves in but drops his head to make contact with my neck, a feather-light brush of skin on skin. It's my turn to smell his hair, surprisingly clean and fresh.

The flutters start now, moving down from my chest, through my abdomen, settling between my legs. God, I've missed this.

'You OK?' he asks softly.

It's the final option to step back from the brink. I don't take the cue. I just nod. He takes my hand and leads me down the corridor. There's a compact, wood-lined room containing a bed at the end. It's small, but neat and white, with surely too many pillows for one man. My head sinks into them as I roll onto the mattress and feel a base that is hard and unforgiving.

Deftly, he sits astride me without putting any weight on me. A slight sideways dip of his head, another 'are you sure?' question with his eyes. Jesus, how many green signals does this man need? I lift up a little to remove my T-shirt, revealing my oldest sports bra. But at least it is front fastening. As if I'd been planning on easy access. I see his eyes flick to the clasp. He dips his head again to kiss my clavicle, my throat and my breasts through the bra.

I unsnap the clasp, all shyness forgotten. I barely recognise myself. I start humming a tune in my head, because I feel certain that any minute I will hear Freddie's voice in there telling me exactly what I am behaving like. She has the good sense to keep it zipped.

He kisses me on the lips now and I press back. I

wriggle out of the Lycra leggings. No pants, mainly because I didn't want a VPL, but now ... well, that's easy access, too.

He sits up straight to observe me fully. My back is arching upwards in an attempt to keep contact. He rolls off me and onto the floor, takes his shirt off, unbuckles the belt and undoes the button-fly on his jeans. I put my hand out to stop him taking the jeans off. Half-dressed sex always did have a certain frisson for me.

He scoops me up with a hand under my waist and manoeuvres me to the edge of the bed and gently pushes his way into me. There is a pause, where I enjoy the feeling of him inside me. Been a while. He begins to move slowly but easily. I want it fast but I force myself to look at a spot on the wall to stop me from coming too quickly. I'm frightened to breathe.

Tom grabs my waist and slides me further onto the bed. He's on top of me now and fully in me, holding his body above me, light but strong. But I want to feel the weight of him, so I push to unlock his elbows and pull him down, reaching behind to grab the loops of the jeans that are now slung under his buttocks. I yank him closer so that our hips lock together and I whisper: 'Now.'

Afterwards, I lay on the bed, splayed out like a starfish, while Tom went to work on his coffee machine. I felt as if I had been filleted, that if I sat up – tricky with no spine – my limbs would flop like rubber. There were aftershocks playing over my lower belly. I swore if I looked I would be able to see the skin rippling. 'How did that happen?' I gasped.

'I think the man gets an erection and then puts it in the lady's—'

'Tom, stop it. You know what I mean.'

He offered me my coffee and as he did so his eye went down my body. An unexpected wave of embarrassment hit me. I set about gathering up the sheets and pulled the covers around me. 'What are you doing?'

'Don't look at me.'

'Don't look at you? We've just … well, I think we might have moved beyond that sort of coyness.'

I took the coffee but kept the covering in place. Little flashes of what we had just done came back to me.

'What are you feeling?'

'Joy and pain,' I replied glibly.

'Like sunshine and rain.'

'Yes. That song was one of …'

Ouch. I felt a sourness in my mouth as Paul's shade shimmered between us and then faded.

'And I thought you were only going to give me a new sweatshirt.'

He banged his palm on his forehead. 'Doh. I'll …' He indicated going to fetch something.

'No. It'll wait.'

Tom sat next to me and ran his fingers through my hair. It was bizarre, to be touched like that, with a tenderness. I couldn't tell if I liked it or not. I wasn't used to contact with a stranger.

Well you'd never have guessed that from what you just did. Twice.

Thanks, Freddie.

Tom cleared his throat. 'I really didn't mean this to happen. I mean not straight away. Not today.'

'Did you want to book an appointment?' I asked. 'My diary is really not that full.'

'Nor mine.' I was strangely glad to hear it. 'Look, I'm not a "girl in every canal basin" kind of guy. It was just as much a surprise to me.' The beat was just perfect. 'A nice surprise.'

He pulled on some tracksuit bottoms and a T-shirt. 'You off now?' I asked.

'No, I just can't say what I have to say naked. Doesn't feel right. Or respectful.'

It was a bit sudden for a proposal, so it couldn't be that. And how respectful you can be while wearing a Robert Crumb T-shirt was a moot point.

He composed his face into something serious. 'The last time we met, I wasn't entirely straight with you.'

'About?'

'About who I am. My name isn't Tom Buchan. Well, it is now, but it wasn't when I served with Paul.'

278

I really did feel as if the centre of the bed had turned to marshmallow and I was sinking into it.

He touched my wrist and I pulled away, the warm glow I had felt inside doused by icy water. 'Let go. What the fuck are you talking about? Served with Paul where?'

'In the army. Look, as I said, I didn't want it to happen like this. In this order.' I made to speak, but he shushed me. 'Please ... just listen. When you told me about Paul dying, I knew that something wasn't quite right. You see, a couple of months ago I heard that Gary Shepherd, a Scouser, had been the victim of a hit-and-run accident about a year back. Only it was a bizarre hit-and-run, because they took the trouble to reverse over him, making sure to squash his head. Then, a week later, I read that Norrie Newton, another one in our squad, he'd been found floating in the sea off Cornwall. Two of them, you see. Out of seven. Then, you told me about Paul.'

'One is possible, two is probable, three is definite,' I said softly.

'Yes. Someone murdered Paul, but I doubt it was this Blade of Islam you keep going on about.'

'Do you know who it was?'

He shrugged, as if not wanting to commit.

I found I was shouting. 'Do you know who killed my husband?'

He swallowed hard. 'Yes.' And then his voice became cracked and small. 'I did.'

THIRTY

'After Bosnia, we were sent in next door as part of K-FOR. You know what that is? Paul must have talked about it. A United Nations peacekeeping force in Kosovo, trying to stop the Serbian-Albanian conflict tearing the country apart. Jesus, it was a mess. The UN Mandate was a piece of toothless shit. We couldn't fire our weapons, except in self-defence. The protocols of engagement meant we couldn't intervene in any situation unless we were ourselves in danger. We watched the KLA ethnically cleanse a village of Roma. No, not watched. Heard it. We saw the bastards go in, knew they were up to something, and we just stayed where we were, outside, next to our Warriors and personnel carriers and Land Rovers, engines running, weapons cocked, and listened to the pop of small arms and the screams of women and children. Two hours, while our captain tried to get permission from UNMIK to go in. Not a bad bloke, Charlie Clarkson, but he was a stickler for procedure.

'But you know, we soon became part of the problem. The United Nations Mission, I mean. Just like in Bosnia '95. Christ, it's happening now in the Central African Republic. Right now. The peacekeepers, the aid workers, the NGOs, well, they're men, mostly. So, in Kosovo as elsewhere, the locals, very enterprisingly, opened up brothels to offer the usual services to the men. But brothels need prostitutes to service the clients. Clients they had by the thousand. And so they filled those whorehouses with girls they'd kidnapped, duped or bought. They gathered them from across the region – Moldova, Bosnia, Romania, Bulgaria, Ukraine. Two grand would get you a beautiful fifteen- or sixteen-year-old. Selling her cherry covers most of that, then you get two years of clear profit, maybe three, before she's a worn-out husk of a woman. Or girl. And then she's shot in the head and dumped in a river or in landfill. Nobody cares. Who was doing this? *Every-fucking-one.* Every side. Jesus, there were even some UN troops involved in the trafficking, running girls and women from mountain villages down to near the bases for a fee or a few shags on the tab.

'So, you have to understand we were pretty hacked off with the situation, right? Same old shit – we're soldiers but we aren't allowed to fight. Which makes us police, except we can't arrest anyone. So this day, we are heading towards a village where we have had reports of a house set on fire. Three vehicles, a Land

Rover, a Bulldog PC, and a Warrior armoured infantry carrier. We were in the latter, seven of us. Me, Paul, who was a first lieutenant at the time, Norrie Newton, Captain Clarkson, Harry Transom, a medical support officer, Gazza – Gary – Shepherd and Alan Findlay, big Scottish lad. Good boys, all of them. So we are about halfway to this village and the bloody Warrior throws a link on the track. Not a disaster, but time-consuming to fix. And one thing we learned is that when you get notice of something going down, unless you are on it straight away, you tend to get there when there's nothing but ash and cinders left.

'So we have a quick conflab, and the captain decides he'll go ahead with the Bulldog, which is where our translators were, and the Land Rover, which is the most vulnerable vehicle. He gives us a corporal, Rog Lloyd, in his place and that leaves the seven of us and the Warrior crew to replace the damaged section of track. The right decision. That puts Paul in charge. We get out and stretch a bit, have a fag or two while the crew get the right part ready. And we realise it's a beautiful day. This section of the road snaked through a lovely valley, with wooded hillsides and a stream running next to the road. And it was quiet, apart from the crickets. We'd got so used to shouting and screaming and gunfire and arguments and burning buildings, we didn't know what real quiet was. So nobody said much. We took off our helmets and either sat there at the roadside or leaned against the Warrior.

'About five minutes in we hear these bells. A tinkling. And about halfway up a slope, comes this little herd of goats. We guess they're heading down to the stream, 'cause the sun is well up and it's getting hot. Ten, eleven, then maybe twenty of the buggers. And behind them, a girl, goading them on with a switch, a long thin stick. I don't know how old she was. Sixteen at a guess, if that. As she gets nearer, we notice she's got a shotgun slung over her shoulder. Now, back then and there, nothing surprised us. Who could blame her for wanting to protect herself?

'But as she comes down the hill we can see other figures in the trees. On both sides of her. Paul stands up and shouts at her to go back, but she just waves, thinking it's a greeting. We have no translator with us, they're both in the Bulldog. So then the men emerge into the open and there's about eight of them, ranging from fourteen to fifty. To this day I can't be sure, but I thought they looked like the guys who did the Romas. They've all got a weapon of some description – pistols, shotguns, old hunting rifles, one AK.

'And they start heading towards her. You know, straight for her. It takes a while for her to notice. When she does, she unslings the shotgun. But I don't have to tell you, it's one thing having a weapon, another having the guts to use to it. Plus, they've spread out.

You know that technique, right? It makes it difficult to choose a target, when you've got a crescent of them on either side.

'So now we're all on our feet, waving her down. You know, come to us, we'll look after you, leave the fuckin' goats, but she's frozen, unsure of what to do, who to shoot. The men get closer to her. Paul lets rip with a burst in the air. Birds break from the trees. The men stop, look at us, and then one of them, fast as a snake, steps in and rips the shotgun out of the girl's hands.

'Now she realises exactly what they want, and you can feel her fear even from that distance. It's sickening.

'One of the men, an older one, starts to jeer at us. They make all sorts of gestures, which looked pretty obscene. Goading us. They knew we couldn't touch them. Some of the younger ones had begun to paw and prod at the girl. She was lashing out at them, which only made them laugh more. It was like a vile game of "It".

'Then another guy, I'd say about thirty, the one with the AK, he walked down the hill, ten, fifteen metres down, so he is closer to us. He unbuttons his pants and flips out one of the biggest cocks I've ever seen. I mean, there's always one, isn't there? In a group like that, always one hung like a donkey who takes every opportunity to whip it out. His looked like you should have a licence to take it for a walk. The others cheer.

He waves it about a bit at us, points at it, then at the girl. Just in case we were particularly slow.

'So he starts working at it while we watch, running his hand up and down the shaft, pulling back the foreskin, until he has this great stonker on. Two of the men have the girl by the wrists at this point, so she can't go anywhere. The rest are clapping, this sort of rhythmic, almost flamenco-like dance clapping. As if this is some kind of cabaret.

'The man with the hard-on raises his hands above his head, standing there like a three-legged stool gone wrong, when Norrie puts a bullet through him.

'Bang.

'The sound echoes down the valley, seems to take an age to die away. Nobody moves, except the guy who falls forward, jamming that erection into the ground like a tent pole.

'Paul yells at Norrie. "What the fuck did you do that for?" Norrie shrugs. And then we all realise something at exactly the same time as the men do. We've started, so we'll finish.

'You see if word got out that K-FOR troops had exceeded the mandate, had interfered ... well, the whole place would go up. Political chaos. Court martials. Glasshouse. Disgrace. We didn't have a choice. Even Paul saw that, even though he tried to stop us at first. We advanced up the hill, firing. They scattered, but we got most of them. One of the little bastards was quick, though. He zigzagged like a good 'un. You could see rounds hitting the ground around him, but he was like bloody Billy Elliot, dancing his way through the gunfire. So I took Paul's Browning pistol off him and went after this kid.

'He bolted into the trees and he knew the terrain but he had a desperate man after him, and after about hundred, hundred and fifty metres, he had to cross a clearing. I knelt down, took aim, and blew his left calf muscle out. He went down heavy.

'I could hear the Warrior starting up. The crew had got a move on when they realised what had happened. A hillside full of bodies was no news once we hit the road. A hillside full of bodies with British soldiers with red-hot smoking barrels nearby . . . no thanks. So they wanted to get out of there. I heard someone call my name.

'So I reach the kid, who has turned over onto his back, and I can see he's even younger than I thought. Twelve, maybe. Probably not capable of doing any-thing to the girl at his age. He says something to me in between gasps – he's in a lot of pain. A nine mil to the leg is no laughing matter. Might have shattered the bone for all I know. There's a lot of blood. I have no idea what he's jabbering about, but he's obviously pleading for his life. Just like that little girl would have done.

'I heard a burst of gunfire. I'm being summoned back.

'I raised the pistol, pointed it at his head, closed my eyes and squeezed the trigger.'

I felt like I hadn't drawn breath for fifteen minutes while he'd been talking. My chest ached. Finally I sucked in a good lungful. He hadn't looked at me once while he had been speaking, just stared at the floor or the ceiling, anywhere but me.

I waited until he had run out of words and asked, 'The girl?'

'Elona? She was OK. Bit shook up. We took her with us and got the translators to convince her that silence was the best option. She wasn't stupid. She knew what had happened. We had saved her life. We'd broken the mandate, but saved her life. As far as I know, she never spoke of it. And if it is any consolation at all, Paul didn't begin it. He held back, until it was all too far gone. Then he had a choice, stick with his mates, his comrades, or get them sent down as criminals. He chose his squad.'

'I'm not going to judge you, or him, on that,' I said quietly. I knew that what happened out in a combat zone can seem starkly black and white in hindsight. A war crime is a war crime, no excuses. In reality, the truth gets very blurred out there. Was it the right thing to do? Ask the girl. 'But what about you being responsible for Paul's death? You said ...'

'I didn't kill the kid. I couldn't. I shot the ground beside his head. Went back and told them he was done.'

'Won't blame you for that, either,' I said.

Now he looked directly at me, his eyes blazing with an intensity that made me feel very vulnerable wrapped just in a few scraps of sheets. 'While I was away from here, when I left that morning, I went to do some digging. About the boy I let live. His name is Leka. They call him the equivalent of "Hoppy", because of his limp. He's a warlord of sorts. The nastiest kind of warlord. Drugs, women, extortion, violence for the sake of it. I think he grew up wanting to find the men who killed his father, his uncle, his brothers. I think he's got people here hunting that squad down. I think by letting him live, I killed Paul.'

THIRTY-ONE

I am not a detective. Not Sherlock Holmes, Inspector
Morse or even Hetty Wainthropp. I am a PPO,
a bodyguard. I live in the moment, most of the
time. What will happen in the next thirty seconds
concerns me, not what happened yesterday or a
week ago, not unless it has a direct bearing on the
security situation. Anticipation, that is the key on
The Circuit. Mind reader, crystal-ball gazer, that
helps. But I can't do crosswords and I am useless at
sifting clues and evidence. So what to make of Tom
Buchan's claims?

I was sitting in my car, opposite the Bounds Green
Fatih Mosque, churning his story over in my mind. I
was right about the mosque. It didn't quite match up
in grandeur to its Istanbul cousin. It looked as if it
had been converted from a double garage, opened up
and built upon. It was sandwiched between a multi-
occupancy house and a 24-hour greengrocer's. And it
was busy. But then it was Friday morning. It was also

the day the Sharifs were due back, although Ali was doing the airport run, which was fine by me.

There was a constant stream of men of all stripes coming and going from the place of worship, from those who looked like photo-fits of swivel-eyed extremist clerics (although I was well aware that looks can be deceiving in that department) to the smartly dressed who were popping in on the way to work. The owner of the grocery store had set up a little street stall where a young lad with a mop of black curly hair was selling soft drinks as well as access to 'washing facilities' out back.

There was a separate door through which women entered. All who did so were heavily covered, not in full niqab, but with just the oval of their faces showing. They would also be devoid of perfume. Yet Mrs Sharif left the health club car park wearing a casually draped headscarf and, most days, a dab of Éclat d'Arpège. Not good enough to pass muster for entrance to Friday prayers.

But Mrs Sharif didn't come here on a Friday anyway. Saturday. What for? Private prayer? Instruction? Perhaps she didn't want the secular Mr Sharif to know she retained an adherence to her faith, despite the Western trappings of her existence.

So, that was one Puzzle of the Day.

The second one was to try and determine who was telling the truth about Paul's death. According to

Swincoe he was murdered by the Blade of Islam. No doubt in his mind. It was tied in with Paul's work for MI5. It made sense.

Buchan's scenario required more of a stretch. I had no doubt the incident he described in Kosovo happened, or something close to it. But the idea that this child grew up to be so hellbent on revenge that he tracked down a British squad, long scattered to the four winds, almost beggared belief. Buchan himself might well have some form of PTSD. He certainly had paranoid tendencies. He had spoken about 'Trouble' as if it were a real character that was on his tail, constantly tracking him down to disrupt his life, to hurt people close to him. 'You have to understand, Trouble will always find me,' he had said.

So, do you believe a government secret agent or a slightly wonky-in-the-head ex-soldier with combat stress?

I had no idea. Like I said, I'm no Sherlock Holmes.

And yet, there were those two other bodies besides Paul's. What, statistically, were the odds of three out of a squad of seven men dying? Well, let's be generous, let's include the three-man Warrior crew as being complicit, although Buchan had said that they had played no part in the massacre. Thirty per cent fatality rate, all the deceased in their forties? It didn't sound probable.

My phone on the seat next to me flashed its little

light show. Two messages. One was from Mrs Sharif, who must have landed: *Nuzha would like to go shopping this afternoon. Can you take her?*

I wasn't meant to be on call, but as we always said, flexibility is everything in the job. Jess was going to the V&A with Laura, as part of an after-school art project, and I had nothing to do but brood. And pry into Mrs Sharif's secret life. And perhaps, I realised at that moment, I had it all wrong. Perhaps she was just having a common-or-garden love affair with a married man or a handsome young lover.

It made me think of Buchan and the feel of his body pressing me into that hard bed and what happened to my insides when he first slid into me. A few neural fireworks went off at the memory and those damned flutters started again. He might be wonky in the head, but everything else was fully functioning.

And Paul? I could hear Nina's voice, that no-nonsense Scottish accent stronger than ever. *Ach, Paul's dead. He's past caring.*

Yes, but I'm not. It still felt like a betrayal. But one I could probably live with. One, if I was honest with myself, I'd like to make again.

Of course, I messaged back to Mrs Sharif. *Pick her up at two?*

Yes, fine, pinged back straight away. The battery-life symbol in the corner of the screen turned red as the message went. This MI5-issue phone might be all-singing and all-dancing but the damn thing needed re-charging daily.

The second text was from Swincoe, in the guise of someone offering, thanks to a 'new government initiative', to give me a half-priced kitchen: *We need to talk*, is what it really said.

We did need to talk. I needed to run Buchan's tale about Paul's death by him, so a meet was fine by me. I checked the time on the dashboard, then sent the message accepting. Another came back, apparently making an appointment for a salesman to visit me. But it translated as: *Midday, at Kenwood House*. That would give me plenty of time before I had to take Nuzha shopping. I took one last look at the Bounds Green Fatih Mosque, but clearly it wasn't going to help me solve anything, and I started the engine.

If you stand at the southwest corner of Kenwood House and look across over London, the view, apart from the crane towering over Witanhurst, the enormous private residence on Highgate Hill, owned by the Guryevs, is much the same as would have been enjoyed by generations of the Mansfields who once owned the mansion. There are no mobile masts, no steel and concrete towers. All I could see was a lawn rolling down to a lake, with a rather lovely white bridge reflected in limpid waters and, behind that, a wall of trees. It was like stepping out of the twenty-first century, back three hundred years ago when Kenwood's most famous inhabitant, the mixed-race Dido Elizabeth Belle, lived there. Except in her day, cattle grazed the lawn and the dairy on my right was operational.

You might fancy a stroll down the lawn to stand on that fetching white bridge with the Palladian balustrade that crosses the body of water known, for no clear reason, as Thousand Pound Pond. If so, you'll be disappointed. It is in fact a fake, known as the Sham Bridge, a flat Hollywood-style 'front' standing on the water's edge, designed (by Robert Adam, no less) to please the eye but not to traverse the lake.

In truth, I knew little of all this before that day. I had found Swincoe staring out over trees that hadn't quite come into full leaf, and he had decided to give me a brief history of the view and, I feared, a tour of the house's various artworks – there was a 'rather good' Gainsborough, he said – before I blurted out: 'Can we get a coffee?'

'Of course. Sorry for prattling on. This was a famous dead-letter drop for spies and their handlers back in the 1970s. The Russian Trade Delegation is just across there.' He waved a hand towards the east. 'Forgive me. We used to practise fieldcraft training round here.'

We bought our drinks at the counter in the Steward's Room and took them into the courtyard. It was overcast and both of us were wrapped up warm. I wondered how the Sharifs would feel coming back to a gloomy English spring after the light and sun of Dubai. Maybe that was why Nuzha wanted to go shopping, to cheer herself up.

'So, have you got anything on him? Sharif?'

He shook his head. 'No. Your phone picked up only boring stuff,' he admitted. He was hangdog, his jowls looked like sun-melted butter. 'We almost got a man in, a proper bug-planter, by creating an electrical fault, but I think the security guy got suspicious. He didn't let him out of his sight.'

Ali was too good to fall for that. 'Nor would I have. Oldest trick in the book, the TV repairman, the phone engineer, the dangerous gas leak.'

He smiled at that. 'We do have a rather limited repertoire.'

'So what's next?'

'You haven't noticed anything out of the ordinary?' he asked, fixing me with a wide-eyed stare.

Did I want to sick him onto Mrs Sharif just yet? What if it was an innocent liaison, and I was responsible for blowing her cover or ruining her marriage? I just needed to be sure. Perhaps I would follow her to the mosque the next day. Then perhaps I could tell him for certain. 'Not really.' I sipped my Americano. 'I do have something to ask you, though. About Paul.'

'Really?' He unwrapped a sugar cube, dropped it

into his coffee and gave it a vigorous stir. 'I thought I'd covered everything.'

I gave him the short version of what Tom had told me, without mentioning Tom. He said nothing for a while, sipping his coffee while the fingers of his left hand drummed on the table. It was an irritated little tattoo.

'You know of this how?'

'Someone who served with Paul.'

'So you said. Do you have a name?'

'Only his first one.' *Well, that's not true.* I ignored my inner scold.

'Which is?'

Something made me lie a second time. 'Neil. I just bumped into him.'

Swincoe gave a small huffing sound. 'Did you? Isn't that something of a coincidence? "Bumping" into an old chum of Paul's? Not something I really believe in.'

I agreed but I said: 'That doesn't mean they don't happen.'

He gave another small grunt, as if accepting the point. 'Well, given our resources, I can easily check out the details.'

And get him to confirm that your husband was a murderer? a little voice in my head chided. *Good call.*

'I mean, have three people from Paul's unit really died?' He leaned in, his voice taking on a harsh edge. 'Did it not occur to you that if there is some sort of foreign hit squad targeting our ex-servicemen, well – that it is a job for MI5? For me and my colleagues?'

He had a point. 'I suppose it is.'

'And that by keeping quiet you are putting other men's lives at risk?'

'Possibly,' I conceded. 'On the other hand, we are talking a potential murder charge, a war crime—'

'In some people's eyes, maybe,' Swincoe scoffed. 'I was in the service, you know. I know what it's like to be at the sharp end, to have to make those sort of decisions. My interest is purely in getting to the truth of who killed Paul, not raking over some cold coals.' He hesitated. 'Sounds to me like the lads deserved medals. Now, what is his name?'

I had to push the next few words out. 'He goes by Tom Buchan.'

'Not Neil?'

'No. I . . . as I said, he has admitted to a war crime and I thought it best—'

'As I said, that is no concern of mine. I am sure nobody wants to bring this up officially after all this time. Where is he now, this Tom Buchan?'

'I think that's an alias. Well, I'm sure of it. And he's on his boat. On the Regent's Canal.'

'What you have told me, about a lad seeking revenge . . .'

'Sounds crazy, I know.'

'It does.' He gave his cheek a thoughtful scratch.

'Let us say for a moment it's true, that Paul was murdered because of something he, and others, did while serving in K-FOR. That's something we can investigate. Without raising red flags in The Hague or at the MOD, believe you me. But meanwhile, the Blade of Islam still exists, and it is possible that the Sharifs are funding them. What you have told me does not alter the basic facts. We are fighting a slippery, implacable enemy that wants to harm the UK. The country your husband was dedicated to protecting. You have my word I will look into this Tom Buchan's story. Meanwhile, I have something you need to do for us.'

'Which is?'

He leaned back, glanced either side, and came back in. 'There is a laptop Sharif carries with him everywhere. A gold MacBook. You've seen it?'

I nodded. 'It's always on his desk.'

'It's not connected to the internet. It's off the grid entirely. No emails, no browsing history.'

'So how does he communicate from that?' I asked.

'Encrypted USB sticks, we think. Easily hidden, disguised, transported, destroyed. The game has wound back fifty years, thanks to the amount of electronic surveillance we put out there, what with GCHQ and the NSA. It'll be back to invisible ink soon.'

I had a sudden sinking feeling. 'You want me to steal the computer?'

He shook his head. 'No, it would probably have some sort of remote wipe facility. All our laptops do. Had to, as junior agents seem to have a habit of leaving them in the back of taxicabs. These days, rather than panic about national security, we can send a message that orders the machine to, well, self-destruct. Or at least delete all its files.'

'Until the other side learns how to block that signal.'

He gave a rueful grin. 'How true. But we don't know how to do that with Sharif's laptop. What we want you to do is upload the hard drive.'

'Won't that be protected?'

'From copying? We doubt it. It will have various encryptions in place on the material. But let the boys at GCHQ worry about that.'

'And if there is nothing there? About Blade of Islam?'

'We'll destroy it, of course. We aren't interested in his personal life or his business dealings. Just the other company he keeps.'

'Might keep,' I reminded him.

'Might keep,' he agreed.

'I don't know . . .'

'Are you frightened you'll be caught?'

I hadn't even thought of that. 'I was thinking more of the moral dimension.'

'Moral? Let's talk about the morality of beheading British soldiers on the streets of London or massacring a lobbyful of hotel guests. And I think you crossed into a different moral dimension when you agreed about the phone.'

'It seems like a much bigger step. I'm not comfortable with theft.'

He closed his eyes as if in irritation. 'What if I find out about your Tom Buchan by, say, Monday.'

'Find out how?'

'What's his barge called?'

'The *Slim Pickens*.' I spelled it out.

'Really?'

'Belonged to some old actor, apparently. Wasn't Tom's choice. Bad luck to change a boat's name when you buy it. So he said.'

'He seems to think about bad luck a lot.'

Swincoe had a point there.

'Well, the British Waterways Board will have a record of who has the licence for the *Slim Pickens*. One phone call and we can go on from there. Get an idea if he is telling the truth about Paul. See if you are dealing with a war-damaged fantasist. Would that offer change your mind?'

I checked my phone. I had to be going. 'I'll sleep on it.'

He gave a solemn nod. 'Very well. But we'd like to get the files as soon as possible. The threat level is moving towards Critical. GCHQ say there is the sort of nervous chatter around BOI that suggests something is going to happen.' He gripped my wrist for emphasis. 'And happen very soon.'

Brent Cross was one of the situations where I needed the disabled sticker that One-Eyed Jack had scored for me. Unless you have one of the Blue Badge mobility badges – or a baby and pushchair to legally park in the other designated bays – you can't park close enough to the exits for comfort. At least, not for me. If you want to evacuate, then you don't want to be running over hundreds of metres of exposed tarmac. Maybe, I thought, there were times when those self-driving RSCA cars that Jack hated so much would come in handy.

When I picked Nuzha up, there was a palpable tension in the house, an atmosphere that felt like a thunderstorm was developing indoors – heavy and unstable. Mr Sharif was stamping round in his office or, at least, that was what it sounded like from the other side of the closed door. Now and then he could be heard yelling on the telephone.

I raised my eyebrows at Ali, the security man, who shrugged his broad shoulders and told me Nuzha would be down soon.

'What's happened?'

'Family disagreements in Dubai,' he whispered, coaxing one end of his moustache into a needle point. 'We were lucky we weren't there by all accounts. I think they want Nuzha out of the house so they can have a good go at each other.'

Mrs Sharif had appeared, thanked me curtly for agreeing to take her daughter shopping and disappeared. The storm clouds felt more oppressive than ever and I was glad to scoop up phone and keys and leave.

As we parked up in the disabled bay near to the entrance to the John Lewis store, I turned to Nuzha. 'Everything all right at home?'

I was fully aware I had taken a step over an invisible line. The politics of home life was not my concern. She gave a knowing smile, as if she could read my mind. 'Yes. Why shouldn't it be?'

'No reason.' I went to get out.

'Oh, you mean all the shouting? That's something to do with Father's business. Nothing to worry about, so Ammi said.'

I got out and opened her door, checking the surrounding area for threats. It's a shopping mall. The main danger was to credit card balances. Still, you have to do it.

I stood aside. 'How was the holiday?'

'It was fun. Mostly. Abbu, Father, went off to Qatar for two days for meetings.'

Qatar. It rang a bell. As we walked to the entrance I Googled the country alongside the phrase 'sponsors terrorism'.

302

According to the *Daily Telegraph*, money from that Gulf state's business community had flowed to the vicious Libyan Dawn group and to Ahrar al-Sham in Syria. It drew the line at claiming money went to either ISIS or BOI, but the implication was there.

I made a mental note to tell Swincoe to check out any Qatar/Sharif links.

'I'm glad you had a good time.'

'It was too hot, really,' she admitted. 'I stayed inside, at the villa, and read. You know Philip Pullman?'

I knew enough about him to know that he wasn't big on religion. Not Richard Dawkins, perhaps, but someone who asks questions of organised worship and finds it wanting. 'I think Jess read *Northern Lights*. She didn't like the film, though.'

'*The Golden Compass*? No. I read all three, though,' Nuzha said proudly.

'And what did you think?'

She whispered the reply. 'It wasn't the sort of God my relatives talked about in Dubai.'

It was just as we reached the double doors that the hairs on the back of my neck stood up.

'What is it?'

I didn't know. Something. Condition: Orange.

'Let's go back to the car.'

'Why? We haven't even been in yet.' For the first time, Nuzha sounded like Jess had at her age. Like she still could be now. Whiny.

'I'm not sure. I'm not happy. Come. Please. We'll go somewhere else.'

'Where?'

'Oxford Street. Bicester if you like. Anywhere.'

What had caused that? Think. Not visual. I had been staring into the store at that point, checking what was beyond the two sets of doors and making sure we could move between the pair – so as not to be trapped in the little vestibule space – as quickly as possible.

Yet a sudden desire for E&E – Escape and Evasion – had gripped me. I did a quick 360 and registered everyone in the vicinity. Old guy in a mobility scooter, two teenage girls, fists full of Hollister and MAC bags, a guy in a windcheater, looking for where he had parked his car, numerous mothers with kids of various ages and a couple of wash-your-car-while-you-shop operatives, wheeling their carts up and down, touting for business. I gave each of the latter a good stare even as we were walking, but they appeared to be the real deal.

I held on to Nuzha's hand as we crossed back to the BMW, my head turning like I was on Wimbledon's Centre Court. A Polo reversed out of a space nearby and I swerved us away, but it was coming out of the parent and child bay. I looked at the driver. Minimal threat.

I blipped the 7 series open with the key fob and pushed Nuzha, still muttering complaints, into the rear. Thank God for the Blue Badge disability sticker, because within a minute of me flipping out, we were heading for the exit.

'Camden!' Nuzha shouted. It wasn't a request.

'Yes, ma'am. Camden it is.'

I watched in the mirror for any pursuit, but none was apparent. Nor did anything ahead of me look like anything other than shoppers. Still, I stayed there in the Orange zone as we headed for the North Circular.

Not only am I not a detective, I'm not psychic. None of us are. Not even Freddie. There was no female intuition at work telling me there was trouble. No hunch. No Spidey sense. An event had triggered the E&E response; it's just that it was subliminal. Either I had spotted something that my brain registered at a deep level, or I had heard something.

I closed my eyes for a split second and I saw it. There had been a reflection in the window. The guy walking away, hands in his windcheater, when I grabbed Nuzha.

But it hadn't been the image of him in that glass, not in isolation. There was an aural component too. A sound. That of a camera or a camera phone. Almost too quiet to hear.

He'd been snapping our photos, had probably taken a sequence, and I hadn't noticed until the last moment because I had been too busy searching the internet on the phone. Careless.

Fuck you, Tom Buchan and Russell Swincoe, you've filled my head with shit and I've lost sight of the fundamentals of PPO – protect the Principal.

I glanced at Nuzha in the mirror and she smiled. Camden was obviously a decent substitute for Brent Cross.

No matter what Swincoe's suspicions about the Sharifs, I had to tell them some of my own. That Nuzha was being watched, by person or persons unknown, whose motives were for the moment unclear.

But they soon would be.

THIRTY-TWO

Friday night and the fridge looked like a crime scene – everything of value had been stolen and only the sad and the worthless remained. Some floppy carrots, half an iceberg lettuce and an out-of-date round of goat's cheese were all that was on offer. And a third of a bottle of wine. I ran through all the *Ready Steady Cook* options with those and came up blank.

I was still worried about the photo-taking incident. I had asked for a face-to-face with the Sharifs when I dropped Nuzha off, but Ali warned me the dark clouds had turned into a full *Sturm und Drang*. So I told him my concerns and he promised to make sure Nuzha was on the property for the rest of the night. There was nothing else I could do, so I came home to examine my fridge.

I was beginning to think of going the takeaway route when I sensed Jess behind me.

'Mum, there's a sleep-over tonight. Do you think I could go if I finish all my homework?' It was a relatively soft, tentative approach, but with plenty left in the tank if something more forthright was needed.

I cut to the chase. 'What kind of sleep-over?'

'Pizza and a movie.' Sounded good. I wondered if they'd let me join in.

'Whose house?'

It was often at this stage that some character, a new friend I had never heard of, was wheeled out. I knew all the dodges. I'd done them myself. Claiming to be sleeping over at one friend's – a girl my mother knew and trusted, or at least trusted the parents – when in reality it was an all-night party at a far more racy alternative. If Mum had only bothered to search the bag that held my 'pyjamas' the game would have been up.

'Whose house?' Stalling, not a good sign. Cue alarm bells.

'It's at Chrissie's.'

The bells faded. I knew Chrissie, liked her parents and her older sister – whom I'd used for babysitting – and they didn't live too far away. But was Chrissie the 'beard' for something other than pizza and a movie?

'The thing is, I thought we might stay in and have a, you know, have a chat, maybe watch some TV again.'

'*Chat?*' She pronounced it the way one might 'leprosy' or 'nits'.

'But if you want to go, then that's fine.' A beam of a smile began to form. 'But only if I can pick you up in the morning. By ten.'

I couldn't decide whether the expression that invaded her face was disappointed or puzzled. 'Why?'

'It's a surprise.'

It'd be a surprise to me, too. Because I had no idea what excuse I'd use for pitching up at ten in the morning. But I'd think of one.

'OK, thanks, Mum.'

'I'll give you a lift over.'

That way I could stop at the theatre for wine on the way back. After all, a third of a bottle for a Friday night? Behave.

It would still be light when I got back. Maybe I could fit in a run along the canal, pick up something at the vegetarian place near Broadway Market. That would be the healthier option than the Indian takeaway.

And nothing to do with the *Slim Pickens*. Nothing at all, despite those fluttering butterflies in my stomach. I am not doing that again. Not with him. Cheap lust and easy passions are too dangerous for a professional like me. Too much vulnerability. I couldn't afford that.

Ah, the lies you tell yourself.

Before he became a nuclear cop, Paul tried his hand on The Circuit. He struggled at first. He didn't have the sense he was contributing anything to society by looking after what he called 'pampered yobs'. But he was approached by the British Council to work as a PPO for some of the cultural tours it was organising to more hostile environments – Shakespeare to Iraq, Ayckbourn to Haiti, YBAs to Kabul, that kind of thing.

His first assignment was chaperoning a group of jazz musicians to Saudi Arabia. True, Saudi Arabia is hardly the New Orleans of the Middle East. In fact, jazz is frowned upon, not least because of its louche connotations of booze and brothels. The British Council got round this by deeming it a 'musical education' tour for expats and their children, with the music to be played in school gymnasiums during the day, rather than at night, when the more sinful side of jazz might appear.

The tour went well, so he told me, thanks to local fixer Tony and his wife Sarah, who knew how to navigate Saudi sensibilities. But then, unlike me, Paul liked jazz, or at least the Miles Davis stuff the lads were adept at reproducing, and the Muttawa religious police gave them little hassle about playing the devil's best tunes.

Heading back to the airport from the secure compound where they had been staying with the promoter, Paul heard the crump of an explosion. He looked in the wing mirror and saw the coil of black smoke rising from the gated compound. His mind went into rewind. The laundry truck that had passed them as they left. Something, maybe just the look in the driver's eye, had flipped an alarm in his head, but, as they were leaving the country within the next two hours, he had ignored it.

'Stop,' he shouted at the driver who, having seen the smoke for himself, did no such thing.

Paul's phone trilled. He answered. There was sobbing on the other end. Then a supreme effort to speak. It was Sarah. 'No matter what you see, keep on going. Don't come back. Tony's dead. He was still in the lobby when the bomb went off. Get out of this fucking country, now.' Then came a wail of anguish and the line went dead. Sarah knew that a second device might well have been planted to take out first responders and anxious relatives. As well as any concerned jazzmen returning to see if they could be of assistance.

Paul sat chewing the inside of his cheek until he could taste blood, as a stream of urgently flashing lights roared past them on that desert highway.

Once he had got the band airside, Paul turned around and went back to see the carnage. The bomb had only killed three people, four counting the bomber, which nobody did, a small miracle judging by the size of the crater. There was this smell in the air, he said, concrete dust, scorched metal, burning fuel, the stench of human flesh, a cocktail he would never forget.

As I lay, half-asleep, I thought I could almost taste it. And then I realised I could. I sat up and shook the sleep from my head, remembering the evening and my stopping off – despite every protestation I had made – at the *Slim Pickens*.

I sniffed. An acrid, rubbery smell was coming from nearby. Something was burning.

As I moved from the bedroom down the hall and into the living room, pulling a dressing gown around me, I could see flames licking up the wall. Or the reflection of them, bouncing off the water. The fluid, dancing pattern was overlaid with the more regular streaks thrown by the rotating blue and orange lights. In all, it looked like a very poor psychedelic light show.

I opened the doors and stepped onto the balcony and blinked as particles attacked my eyes. The stench was stronger out here, the sound of crackling and spitting amplified by the limpid water in the canal basin and the brick and concrete edifices that lined it.

Some way to the east, beyond the bridge, I could see the burning boat, now launching little Roman candles of sparks into the sky, and the barges on either side being frantically backed away, in case the blaze should spread. Shadowy figures moved on the quayside, some playing streams of water onto the vessels, others further back running Do Not Cross tape and keeping the gaggle of onlookers at a safe distance, doubtless in case a gas bottle went up.

I could feel the panic rising in me, a prelude to the guttural shock that would floor me, my heart quivering like a bird trapped in a room, flinging itself against my ribcage, the first shivers of horror invading my brain, but I killed all the sensations dead. This was no time for a raw, incapacitating burst of emotion. I had to deal with this. My other self, that is, the detached professional, not the one who had had sex with Tom Buchan a few hours before. She had to shine a cold, clinical light on what this meant. And she had to act on it.

As I stepped back into the living room and imagined I could feel the heat of the inferno on my back, I allowed one thought to register.

Trouble had found the Slim Pickens *at last.*

PART FOUR

THIRTY-THREE

'Yeah?' I could hear the thickness of sleep and maybe the desiccation of alcohol in Freddie's voice.

'It's me,' I said.

She made a noise that was an acknowledgement, although it barely qualified as language.

''S up?' A beat. 'Jesus, what time is it?'

I was sitting on my sofa, now fully dressed in jeans and sweatshirt, watching the first tentative light of dawn bleach the residual glow of the fire from my wall. 'Early.'

I heard the muffled cadences of another, huskier voice coming down the line, then Freddie again. 'Go back to sleep.'

I imagined a hairless boy-man rolling over and pulling the covers across his head.

'Sorry, Freddie, I didn't mean to disturb you.'

'Probably shouldn't have rung my telephone at this hour then, eh? No, fuck off.'

For a second I thought she meant me. But then

the Dolphin raised his voice – disappointingly using words rather than clicking sounds – and there was an answering bark from Freddie. 'Jesus, can you give me a minute, I have to put the hamster back in his cage.'

I held the phone away from my ear for a while, only half-listening to the snarling and spitting at the other end. She came back on loud and clear at the tail end of the spat. 'Because she's family, and you're just a cock and two balls on legs. Close the door on your way out.' She let out a long sigh and spoke to me. 'Quite a nice cock and two balls, and not bad legs either,' she said wistfully.

'Family, am I?' I asked. The last time anyone claimed me as a relative it was MI5.

'Close enough. Rather you than my tight-fisted sister and her retard of a husband. I'm going to walk through to the kitchen and make coffee. Just talk, I'll listen.'

So, I told her everything, from the feeling I'd had that my picture had been taken with Nuzha at Brent Cross, through sex with Tom Buchan – she managed to bite her tongue there – right up to the mysterious explosion on his boat.

'Christ, and you're talking like you are reporting a cat up a tree. Blown up? The fuckin' thing was blown up?'

I watched a grim-faced Tom pad across the living room in bare feet. We had had a flaming row because he had wanted to go down to his boat. I told him that was the last thing he needed to do. If it was an accident, the fire brigade would find out what caused it. If it wasn't ... well, there might be people watching. People who might well assume he was dead. Which gave him a breathing space. It was a long slog, but he finally accepted that. Tom made the symbol for a drink – and possibly a peace offering – and I gave a thumbs up and made a T sign. 'If I hadn't decided I wanted sex in my own bed, he'd have been on board.'

'Does he know how lucky he is?'

'What, having sex with me or not being burned to a crisp?'

'Oh, ha-ha. I don't know how you are so calm.'

'Nor me. But I am. For the moment.' I wasn't sure how long this would last. I had to get Tom to some sort of safety – I would imagine that would cause an argument, even though I was equally certain he had nowhere to go other than the now-defunct barge – and the same applied to Jess. If the shit that was happening was even peripherally connected to me, I wanted to know my daughter was safe from harm.

'What do you want me to do?' Freddie asked.

'I need someone to talk this through with, to try and make sense.'

'Not this Tom?'

I watched him take out a jar of instant coffee and peer at it in distaste, as if it contained human remains. 'I think he's about to go into mourning for his coffee machine. Also, I have plans for him. No, I need you to walk with me through the last twenty-four hours. Try to make sense of it.'

I didn't mention that I wasn't sure how much I could trust him.

'OK.'

'And ...' I didn't quite know how to phrase this. I was feeling alone and outnumbered. There was something I needed, if I was going to get to the bottom of this.

'And what?'

'I need to know you've got my back.'

Which, of course, meant I was expecting trouble. There was an intake of breath that morphed into a small, ironic laugh as she exhaled. I felt a warm glow of relief flush through me. 'OK, Buster. It'll be just like old times.'

I hoped not. Old times meant blood and death. But, of course, I hoped in vain.

THIRTY-FOUR

I had to wait for a less antisocial hour before I made my other calls. Meanwhile, I checked the contents of my RTG bag. I dressed in a ProTex bra, T-shirt, sweatshirt and jeans chosen not for the label but for the amount of Lycra in them, which imparted more freedom of movement. Over the top I put on a lightweight KOTOL SF combat jacket, as used by the Army Ranger Wing of the Irish Defence Forces, the Republic's equivalent of the SAS. It was the usual multi-pocket number, but with slots for cellphone and a metal and Kevlar reinforced sheath that took the Eickhorn knife. There was also a built-in pistol holster. How I wished I had a pistol to go in it.

Meanwhile, I swapped the SIM card from my MI5 iPhone to the mobile from my RTG bag. It was a distinctly dumb phone – an old Nokia – with no singing and no dancing allowed but it had a battery life measured in months not minutes. Plus, I no longer trusted that smartphone. Hackable, as Jack might say, very hackable.

Shortly after seven the message I had been waiting

for pinged through and I left Tom in the flat while I went to bring my car closer to the exit. I felt naked as I walked across the courtyard to it, the corrosive smell of the *Slim Pickens* still hanging in the air. I wasn't sure there were eyes on me, but it felt like it and I strained to keep the walk fluid and natural. Don't run. Don't let them know you are on to them.

Of course, it could just be another dose of paranoia. Whoever torched the boat – and the smart money had to be on the kid from Kosovo, all grown-up and seething – there was no guarantee they had seen me take Tom back to my place. It had only been because I knew Jess would be out for the evening and I had red wine in the flat and he didn't have any on board that I insisted. A craving for something other than corner-shop sauvignon blanc – and, I had to admit, a somewhat softer bed than the spine-bruiser on the boat – had saved both our lives. For now.

There was one other consideration. I had told Swincoe about Tom. Perhaps that was stupid. Was it possible MI5 was out to get him, too? But if I applied that old Sherlock Holmes maxim about eliminating possibilities – even if I couldn't remember the exact wording – it was more likely to be an Albanian bandit than Her Majesty's Secret Servants.

I spent ten minutes checking my Golf for a tracker. Nothing. I then sprayed the number plates with liquid glass, a totally illegal way of making sure that London's camera recognition systems wouldn't clock the registration. Another speciality of One-Eyed Jack. Thing is, it tends to raise alarms among operators, who don't like being blind. They then usually put out a stop-and-detain message, so it is a one-short-trip option only.

I reversed as close as I could to the door of my block and waited. Tom had no phone, of course. He was down within a few minutes and slid in next to me. He looked pale and shaken. But then, he had lost everything he owned.

'I've got to warn the others in the squad,' he said.

'I thought you had?'

'It was only a theory before this. Should we tell the police?'

I had a better idea. 'We will, in a roundabout sort of way. But I don't want them taking you in for questioning or anything like that. Not for a few days.'

'Look, I know you said to stay away, but can we drive by, take a look at my boat?'

'No.' I said it with all the firmness I could.

'There's a road opposite the mooring we could go down.'

I turned and fixed him with what I hoped was a piercing stare but were probably just the red-rimmed eyes of a madwoman. 'Tom, listen to me. No. Not a good idea. If there are eyes-on hereabouts, they'll be there. You know that. Don't you?' He ought to, if he'd been listening to a word I had said.

Tom scratched above his ear in a way that looked like a nervous tic. Some of the stuffing had certainly been knocked out of him. 'Yeah.'

'You know how to contact the others at risk from the Albanian?'

'I have phone numbers here.' He tapped his chest. 'In my wallet.'

'I'm going the long way round now. Sit up, keep your eyes open and tell me if you see anything suspicious. Right?'

He licked his lips like a scolded dog. 'Right. Where are we going again?'

'Somewhere safe.'

It was closer to eight by the time I was satisfied there was no tail and, for the third time, I found myself travelling up to a grand house on The Bishops Avenue.

I pulled up in front of the door and there he was, my favourite butler, complete with little bow of recognition.

'Jesus. That's some fucking safe house,' Tom said.

'Isn't it?'

The Asparovs were on their yacht down in Monaco, but when I told him I needed that favour he had promised me, the boss had made sure Elliott knew to expect me. There was only Elliott, a housekeeper and three security guards in residence. The latter took turns looking at multiple CCTV screens, finger on the buzzer connected to an instant-response private security company. That was what made it a safe house.

Elliott walked down the steps and opened the door for Tom, who had apparently been welded to his seat. 'Do you have any luggage, sir?'

I was already out. 'Elliott, you can drop the formalities. Someone set fire to all his clothes.'

An arch of an eyebrow at the impertinence.

'Can you show him the ropes. And the panic room?'

Elliott nodded and stood aside as Tom stepped out.

'Elliott, Mr Asparov said I could take another car. This one might be compromised.' I didn't want to be pulled for having liquid glass on my number plate. But it meant I got to the Asparovs with minimal chance of anyone recording my progress.

'Of course. He requested the least conspicuous model.'

Actually that was me. 'Good.'

'And he asked me to give you this.' I held out my hand and he tossed the phone across the top of the VW. 'It is keyed to his private cellphone. Plus it is Bluetoothed to all the vehicles and it will operate the outer gates here as well as any garage doors.'

'And the car?'

He pointed to a concrete block at the far side of the house with a steel door. 'Take the car elevator down to level three. Garage level. You can leave your ...' He gave a look that suggested I had turned up with a shopping trolley full of all my worldly possessions '... Volkswagen around the back.'

'Car elevator?' asked Tom.

I got in and started the engine. 'You're not in Kansas now, Tom. Shut the door. Oh, and Elliott?'

Elliott bent at the waist so he could see me. 'Ma'am?'

'I know it was you who tipped off Mr Asparov about Bojan and his little games. Thanks.'

'It was a pleasure, ma'am,' he said, and it sounded like he meant it.

Oligarchs tend not to buy understated cars, it defeats the purpose. Asparov's vehicle collection – the usual Lambos, Ferraris and Bentleys – was housed in a circular Ferris Wheel-type system, a rotating garage that seemed not much smaller than the London Eye to me. A button spun the entire periphery until the car you desired was on the ground and you drove it off the steel pan it sat on. Then you simply edged straight into the car elevator. The lift had sensors that detected when there was a vehicle inside and automatically closed the doors and started its ascent.

My new car had already been driven off its metal platform and was sitting in front of the elevator, keyless fob on the dashboard. So it was that, fifteen minutes after arriving, I was driving out through the gates in the most anonymous car in the collection, a Porsche Cayman. If it hadn't been the colour of a startled tangerine, I might even have blended in with the local traffic. Still, it meant that Freddie had no trouble picking me up and swinging out onto my tail.

I put her number into the Asparov phone and tried the Bluetooth on the Porsche. It worked perfectly. 'Hiya. Can you hang back and see if anyone is playing silly buggers?' I asked. 'Try not to lose me, though.'

'If I do, I'll just look for the glow in the sky. You think he negotiated a discount for that colour?'

'Money is colour-blind,' I said. 'I'm going along the A1 for a while, see what happens.'

'Everything else OK?'

I put my foot down and the Cayman displayed an admirable keenness as it accelerated away. 'With a bit of luck.'

And the kindness of strangers.

The Sharif household still had the atmosphere of a powder keg, but I ignored it. Whatever was going down had nothing to do with what I told them over coffee in the conservatory.

Sharif softened his bear-with-a-sore-head approach long enough to quiz me.

'So you think this man was taking photographs of Nuzha?'

'I suspect, that's all. I said he was taking photographs. It might not have been of her.'

'Then who?' Mrs Sharif asked.

'Me.'

'You?' Mr Sharif made it sound offensive; as if it was inconceivable anyone would want to catch me on film. Looking as I did that morning, he might have had a point.

'Look, a friend of mine has run into some trouble. It is possible they were trying to ID me. Some East Europeans. There is also ... well, my ex-husband might be behind it. I just don't know. But what I am saying is that a PPO must never become part of the problem. There is a chance I am. Then again, it might be Nuzha they are interested in.'

'So what are you suggesting?'

I took a deep breath. I hadn't discussed this with Ben Harris, but he had his finder's fee and he'd get a percentage of my wages no matter what happened. 'I should stay away, temporarily at least. I can get you someone else to look after Nuzha from Monday onwards. Perhaps a friend of mine called ...' I gulped back her nickname. 'Judith Flint. But meantime, put Ali and the team on Orange status. He'll know what that means.'

'So you won't drive me to Pilates?'

'Oh, fuck your Pilates,' interjected Sharif. 'I want you here. With Nuzha, till we sort this and your bloody family out.' He stood, leaned over me and wagged a finger in my face. 'What kind of trouble are you in with these East Europeans, young lady?'

'I'm not sure I am in trouble, not yet. As I said, a friend might be. I just want to play it safe.'

'Safe? You were employed to keep us safe. Not bring threat to this household. If you have put my family in danger with whatever is going on with you, you will rue the day you ever heard the name Sharif!'

He left with much slamming of doors and I heard him shout for Ali.

A silence settled over the room, broken only by the calls of the green parrots outside. For the second time that day I wished I had a pistol. I hate those birds.

'Mrs Sharif, can I ask you a question?'

'If you wish,' she said haughtily.

I watched her pick up her cup and sip her coffee. With the spring sun slanting through the windows onto her face she looked older than usual. I could see how she might be looking down a gun barrel at forty.

'What happened in Dubai?'

'How do you mean?'

'Well, either something happened or someone has swapped your husband for an alien.'

'Business, that's all.'

I stood and walked over to the glass doors of the conservatory. A white cat prowling across the lawn froze and looked at me defiantly, padded off and shat in the middle of the lawn. Another critic. I turned back. 'What sort of business?'

'Family business. Nobody ever believes this, but

having money, lots of money, is a burden. It sets you apart forever, creates jealousy and a sense of ... entitlement in others. We have a very large family, between us. Here there is just Nuzha. We can pretend we are a compact unit. Over there ... it's like trying to ... What's the expression? Herd cats.'

'I'm sorry about Pilates. Perhaps you could drive yourself.'

She gave a thin smile. 'I wouldn't do that. Not because of the driving, I am perfectly capable.' Don't I know it. 'But Mr Sharif has spoken. Oh, I know you think he is a liberal, Western man. But scratch the surface.' She mimed running a thumb down skin. 'Tradition runs deep. And after losing his son, the thought of anything happening to his daughter ...'

'I understand.'

'So I won't be disobeying him. At least not on this occasion.'

There was a twinkle in her eye when she said it and this was probably the window to ask her who it was she met when she went off in that BMW X1, but I let it drift by. I had a way of finding out that wouldn't involve accusations of spying and betrayal.

'What will you do now?' she asked.

I spoke with a confidence I didn't feel. 'Get to the bottom of this. And whoever is doing whatever it is they are doing, stop them.'

THIRTY-FIVE

By early afternoon I had relaxed a little. Tom was secure at the Asparovs'. Nobody could track him there. Jess was safe. She had been picked up by Laura from Chrissie's with a hundred pounds to go shopping for new clothes. That was the surprise, or so I claimed on the phone. She didn't question it. I didn't want her going back to the flat. So after a spree in Top Shop and River Island, Laura had deposited her with Nina, who had promised to keep her close.

After I had briefed her, Nina wrote a story to post on the NewsX anonymous blog about the possible link between several deaths and an arson attack on a boat in London. Tom would kill me, but Nina was able to tip off the police about the post she had 'stumbled' across – and let them think they had joined the dots – without us coming out into the open. It meant they would track down and possibly protect the remaining members of the unit who, even if they didn't take Tom seriously, might well believe the police. Would

Tom see the story? I doubted that he had ever used the *Guardian* website. One thing Nina had discovered in her trawling was Tom's real name, but I let it pass. Names aren't that important.

My phone peeped and I checked it and added some more time to the BMW X1's parking. I didn't want it towed away. We were sitting a good hundred metres from it, in our own parking bay. Using the key One-Eyed Jack had cut me from the diagnostics theft, I had driven the X1 and left it outside the mosque as bait. Freddie had followed in the Cayman with me, alert for any hangers-on. Now we were in the Porsche watching our lure. She used the time to bring me up to speed on Matt.

'No visible means of support, granted, but he eats at places like Kitty Fisher's and the Typing Room.'

'Who with?' I wondered if he had looked up any of our old friends.

'A variety of people. Men, women, his girlfriend.'

'Girlfriend?' Despite myself I sounded like an aggrieved wife.

'Well, I assume so. She's popped up a couple of times.'

'You have pictures?'

'Not great, mostly phone ones.' She held up the screen to show me a fuzzy image of Matt, taken across a street. 'I'll send you a couple off the Canon taken with a decent zoom.'

'What's your instinct? Is he straight?'

She let out a long breath. 'That's a nice place he's got. Rented. But three thousand a month they go for.'

I whistled.

'What aren't you telling me?' I asked Freddie.

She looked disappointed. 'What makes you think I'm holding something back?'

'The way you're squirming. Either you've left your vibrating butt plug in or you have more to tell on Matt.'

'Damn. You know everything.' She began to put her hand down the rear of her jeans. 'If I can just reach the switch . . .'

'Freddie!'

'OK.' She settled back down in the seat. 'He's had a vasectomy.'

I think she enjoyed the way my jaw hinged open. 'What? When?'

'I don't know.'

'Then how'd you find out?'

'The National Insurance number you gave me. Access to health records. He's tried to have it reversed. Went private for the vasectomy, but NHS to have his dangly tubes stitched back up.'

'Jesus.'

'Didn't work, though. Still a seedless orange.'

'How did you get all this?'

'Cost me three hundred quid.'

'I said I'd pay.'

'I know. But the sad thing is, time was I could have got all that and more for the price of a blowjob.'

'The bottom's dropped out of the blowjob market, so I heard. Ten a penny these days.'

'So it's not just that I am losing my allure.' She pouted her lips.

'Well, that too.'

The punch on the arm was harder than really necessary.

A vasectomy? Well, I could see how that might appeal in the days when he was busy screwing his way around the clubs of the Balearics. And then the reversal attempt? A sudden realisation that there would be no more kids. Jess would be his last shot at genetic continuity. I supposed that explained why – after facing up to mortality with the death of his father – he had bowled back into our lives. I almost felt sorry for the little prick.

'Now, tell me again why we are sitting staring at this BMW.'

So I did, everything I knew about the Sharifs. From Partition, through the brickfields of Pakistan, the clothing empire, the dead son, their talented daughter, and the problems they were having now. Freddie brought up pictures of the family, agreeing about how attractive the mother was, and even locating one of the dead boy, a fiercely handsome yet delicately featured lad, who had inherited his ammi's eyes. It was taken on a snow-flecked mountainside, the day before the earthquake struck. Just as I had finished the background briefing Nina called me. 'The package has arrived safely,' she said conspiratorially.

'Stop it, you sound like a drug dealer.' Whatever could have made that pop into my mind?

'Jess is here,' she corrected. 'You want a word?'

'Sure. Hello, darling.'

'Hello, Mum. You should see what I got . . .' I didn't really listen to the details, just relished the girlish excitement in her voice. It was only towards the end she thought to ask: 'Mum, when can I go back home?'

'Soon. Not just yet.'

'But why can't I? What's happened?'

'I'll explain later. Help Nina around the house. Love you lots.'

I hung up before she could say anything else. It was only a matter of time before she realised her favourite shoes were back at the flat and we simply had to go and get them. I'd cross that bridge later.

'We're up,' said Freddie, snapping my attention back to the job in hand. 'POI.'

Person of Interest. I watched as a figure wandered across the street, bent down and peered inside the BMW, cupping their hand against the glass to cut the reflection. The POI then stood up straight and scanned the street, the face set in an expression of puzzlement.

'Mrs Sharif didn't phone to cancel then,' I said, puzzled.

'Maybe she doesn't like to use them. These days phones have a way of biting you in the arse. Call history, itemised billing. Hold on ...' Freddie had a monocular to her eye and was watching the POI pad back across towards the mosque. 'Not going in the mosque. Heading next door.'

'I can see that.'

'You got the address from the sat nav, yes?'

'Yes.'

'You know postcodes aren't unique to one building.'

'Of course I do,' I snapped.

'And anyway, if that mosque was originally a garage, it would share the code with the house next door. Which, by the look of those doorbells, are flats.'

I let that implication sink in. No mosque visits might mean there were no Muslim terrorists involved with Mrs Sharif, or vice versa. And by the look of it ...

But Freddie was ahead of me by leaps and bounds. 'You check out the eyes?' She gave my arm a gentler punch and smiled. 'At least we know what happened to the son.'

Just to the east of the bandstand on Parliament Hill Fields is a white obelisk. Not very tall, it has no inscription on it whatsoever. Yet there it stands, a monument to ... something. I had heard it called The Pillar of

Free Speech and it was mooted to be a gathering place for modern-day pagans. There were none of those about that I could see, but it made for a convenient landmark for a meeting with a spy. After all, aren't they supposed to be protecting free speech and the British way of life? Which included the right to call yourself a pagan without having a limb chopped off. Or your head.

I saw Swincoe as I entered the park. Or at least I saw his tomato-coloured trousers, the sort that only posh men can get away with, mainly because they don't give a shit what anybody else thinks. He also had on a Barbour jacket and a tweedy trilby. He looked like he'd been scooped up from the races by flying saucer and dropped in London. Then it struck me. It was Saturday. This was his idea of weekend clothes.

There was a fresh wind whipping at me as I reached the stone, and I pulled the hair off my face. 'When do we get to do Waterloo Bridge?'

'That's for the big boys and girls. Are you OK? You look—'

'Like shit. I know.'

'A little tired was the only observation I was going to make.'

I was closer to the truth. I looked like someone had been practising Japanese calligraphy under my eyes and my skin had taken on a dry, granular quality. Furthermore, I was well aware that my energy levels were low. I could feel my concentration drifting. As Paul used to say after a double shift, I was like a V-12 running on ten cylinders.

'Aren't we conspicuous up here?'

'I don't think so.'

'I think those trousers are.' I did a 360. I spotted young Lawrence and his famous haircut, walking a dog near the bandstand. I wondered if it was his or if it was an MI5 employee. There were joggers, mothers with buggies, tennis players and several men with trousers almost as vivid as Swincoe's. Maybe he was right. Nobody gave us a second glance.

'We can have a coffee over there.' He pointed to the single-storey café between the bandstand and tennis courts.

'Not coffee,' I said, listening to my body for once. 'But I haven't eaten in a while. A sandwich, maybe.'

'Of course.'

I waited a few moments before I asked my next question. 'Swincoe, have you been photographing me? Or Nuzha?'

He shook his head. 'No? Why would we do that?'

I explained about Brent Cross.

'Not us. You have my word. It is a little alarming. If you read the situation correctly.'

'Yes,' I admitted. 'There is that.'

As we set off down the slope he handed me a small, opaque plastic package. 'The external hard drive.

Don't worry, you don't have to do anything. The moment you plug it in it'll search and download. And it's remarkably fast. There's none of that clock ticking down nonsense you see in the movies. A few seconds is all it will take. A minute tops if there are a lot of images and video files.'

I slipped it into one of my many jacket pockets. 'And you were meant to give me the truth about Tom Buchan. Someone put a torch under his boat. Luckily he wasn't on it at the time.'

He flinched a little. 'Really? Which someone?'

'I reckon either the Albanians or you.'

'Me?' He looked genuinely taken aback. 'What on earth do you say that for?'

'Because I tell you about him and the next thing I know his barge burns out. Or is that one of those coincidences you don't believe in?'

'It must be,' he admitted, 'because MI5 is not in the arson business. You have to believe that.'

'Did you check him out? You were going to see if his story hangs together.'

'I'll know on Monday,' he said. 'Even the security services slow down at the weekend.'

I tapped my jacket pocket. 'Are you sure about this?'

'About what?'

'About the Sharifs. I was wondering if we've ... you've ... just started seeing bombers under the bed.'

He narrowed his eyes and cocked his head, as if I

had suddenly broken into speaking Urdu. 'Why do you say that?'

'Because not every Muslim is a terrorist.' I was thinking how wrong I had got Mrs Sharif.

He stopped, well short of the café. 'That's true. But almost every terrorist is a Muslim. These days at least. And if he has nothing to hide, there will be nothing on that drive when you get it back to us. Nothing that would interest us, anyway. We delete, you go back to work, we carry on looking for The Tailor.'

Swincoe turned on his heel and it took me three lengthy strides to catch up with him. 'What's brought this on?' he asked without looking at me.

'I thought you were barking up the wrong tree,' I confessed. 'I thought I'd discovered that Mrs Sharif was the bad apple.'

That stopped him. He halted and spun to face me. 'How so?'

I told him about the phoney Pilates lesson, the secret drives, about the mosque and about what we eventually surmised was going on. 'So you see, we ascribed base motives to everything. But it was a mother's love for her son.'

'This mosque is where?'

'Bounds Green.'

He took out his phone and tapped it. 'It's not on any watch list.'

'I told you. It's not about the mosque.'

'So Mrs Sharif has a secret. Perhaps Mr Sharif has one too. A nastier one. You'll copy the hard drive on the computer?'

'I have said I am staying away. Until I figure out what is going on.'

A ripple of irritation crossed his features. 'You said what?'

'That it's best if I keep my distance from the Sharifs until I find out if I am the object of the curiosity.'

'Really! I thought I had impressed upon you the urgency of this matter.'

We had reached the café. We went inside and bought coffee and a KitKat for Swincoe and tea with a cheese and ham sandwich for me. The papers had again been arguing about whether processed meat was carcinogenic. Right then, it seemed like a chance worth taking.

We sat outside, even though the temperature was dropping and a wind was keening through the tennis courts' fencing. It had driven everybody else except a couple of hardened smokers inside. That was fine by us. I told him about the photographs, my ex-husband and the canal boat.

'Where is Buchan now?'

'Safe,' I said.

He nodded, recognising a need-to-know when he heard one.

'This woman you'll send in as a replacement. Freddie?'

'Freddie. It's not her real name. She's called Judith Flint.'

'Will she do it? Download the hard drive for us?' He couldn't hide the harsh, irritated edge to his voice.

'For Queen and Country?'

'Something like that. For the lives and limbs of people she has never met is another.'

'I'll ask.' But I had a feeling Freddie wouldn't be quite the soft touch I was. After all, she didn't have a murdered husband to avenge.

'Good girl.'

'Don't call me that.'

'Sorry. Let's just go back to Mrs Sharif. You are sure that this person she is meeting on a regular basis is her son?'

'Well, despite everything, yes, that's one thing I am certain of. They look just like sisters.'

I slumped down next to Freddie in the Cayman. Her own car was parked in Swain's Lane. But she showed no sign of going to fetch it.

'Where you sleeping tonight?'

'Good question,' I said. 'Probably at Asparov's.'

'With Tom?'

'In the same house, yes,' I replied tartly. 'I don't think I'm up for anything else. What's wrong? You've got a face like a slapped arse.'

'Something's off.'

'I could do with a shower maybe, but—'

'No, shut up. Something is way off beam here.' I hadn't seen or heard Freddie like this outside a combat situation. She held up the monocular. 'I got a good look at the pair of you through this. Your Mr Swincoe. You didn't recognise him?'

I felt ice pool in my stomach. 'No. Should I have?'

'You probably didn't see him at his best last time.'

'Last time?'

'When he was fucking me in the medical stores that day you barged in.'

'No.' I almost shouted in my disbelief. 'The Rupert?'

'Yes. And his name's not Swincoe. And as my dear old dad used to say, if he's MI5 my prick's a kipper.'

THIRTY-SIX

'You caught the sun? You're very red.'

I was standing in the doorway of one of Jack's hangars. I'd been there a couple of minutes before he noticed me. He had been under the bonnet of a Rolls-Royce of a certain age.

'Water pump's gone,' he explained. 'Thing is, they don't make them except to order. You have to wait for five other people's water pumps to break before they can be arsed to do a run of them. So could be a week, could be six months. I've a mind to go about sabotaging people's water pumps to speed the process up.' He wiped his hands on a paper towel and then ran a palm over his bald pate, as if checking whether some of his long-departed hair had decided to return.

'You sure you're all right?'

'It's my blood pressure, Jack.'

I went outside and lit a cigarette. I'd picked them up on the way out to the airfield. As I lit up I had a what's-wrong-with-this-picture moment. 'The planes have gone.'

'I got tired of them all moaning and the council coming round saying they was a health hazard,' said Jack from behind me. 'Cut 'em up, sold them to Lenny Crane for a hundred sovs. I must admit, it looks less cluttered. What's giving you blood pressure?'

I turned around and before I could formulate words, I began to cry. The cigarette slipped from my fingers onto the tarmac. His sinewy arms snaked round me like fat steel cables and for a brief second I felt safe in there.

'Take your time. I'll get you a drink in a minute.' He squeezed me tentatively, in that way men do when they are sending a clear signal that the sexual content of a hug was zero.

My chest stopped heaving and I sniffed.

'What kind of drink?'

He gave a little laugh. 'You was always a fussy cow. How about a beer?'

I nodded. He returned with a couple of Kronenbourgs, both opened. 'Nothin' fancy,' he said.

It was cold and I gulped half of it down. Then I lit a second cigarette, unable to hide the tremor in my hands. 'I think I'm being played,' I said.

'Who by?'

'That is the question. Freddie Flint is trying to find out.'

'Freddie? I thought she'd packed it in.'

'She's come out of retirement for me.' I gave a cough-laugh that sounded like I was a forty-a-day barmaid. 'Christ.' I looked accusingly at the cigarette.

'What can I do?'

I took out the hard drive Swincoe had given me. 'Check this out.'

'For what?'

'I don't know. You're the computer geek.'

'Jordan! Jordan, get out here.'

He took a while coming, but eventually a lanky boy with a thick, bushy beard emerged from one of the other hangars. He was wearing long shorts and a skater T-shirt. His left arm was crooked across his chest, his left leg dragged as he walked and when he spoke his face contorted. 'Yeah?'

'My eldest, Jordan.' Jack introduced us and we shook hands. Jack passed the hard drive across. 'See what you make of that. And quick.' The young man nodded and slouched off at what to him was probably top speed.

'Cerebral palsy, before you ask. Difficult birth. Don't let this fool you.' He mimicked Jordan's bad arm. 'Sharp as a tack.'

He walked over and sat in one of the scruffy plastic chairs that were scattered about the place. He invited me to do the same. I did so, stiffly. I was seizing up. Lack of sleep was catching up on me.

'It's not me who does all the advanced computer shit, you know. I can do the on-board diagnostics stuff, but beyond that most of it is double Dutch to me. But you know, doesn't do to admit weakness in this game. I used to outsource all the tech, but then I discovered why Jordan hadn't left his room for five years. I just assumed he was having a particularly long wank, but it turns out he was busy turning himself into a bit of a genius.'

We sat in silence for a moment watching the sun break free of the clouds as it approached the horizon. An orange glow crept over the hangars. I shivered, thinking of the flames on my living-room wall.

'Want to tell me?' Jack asked.

'I haven't got it in me. Nothing personal, Jack. And besides, I haven't made sense of it myself. I just think I'm being taken for a fool by the man who gave me that box of tricks.'

I had just finished my beer and was contemplating asking for a second when Jordan reappeared. He looked even paler than before, his beard a solid black against the pallor of his skin. 'Dad. Will you come here?'

I rose as well, but Jordan's voice squeaked up an octave. 'No, Dad. Just you.'

I exchanged glances with Jack. I hoped I got across what I was thinking. *Don't let the tears fool you. It happens now and then. But it's just an overflow*

*system. It relieves the pressure on the internal dam.
Standard operating procedure. Back to normal now.*

'She's good, son. Stand on me.'

Jordan gave an on-your-head-be-it shrug and limped
back into the hangar.

I took up the rear as we trooped solemnly inside.
The front section of the space was the usual chaos
of cars, some of which looked like they had been the
victim of an automotive Jack the Ripper; others were
sitting dusted with a layer of powder and grime that
could be measured in centimetres. I noticed an old
Lancia, a marque I hadn't seen in a while, a beautiful
Alfa Spider from the 1960s and various Fiats.

'Welcome to the Michael Caine shed,' said Jack.

I looked at him, puzzled.

'The Italian Job.'

Jordan's domain was in the latter third of the
hangar, delineated by a stud partition wall and a half-
glazed door marked Private. There was a sticker that
said: 'You Know Nothing, Jon Snow' on the glass. I
knew how Jon Snow felt.

We followed Jordan inside into a work area domi-
nated by screens, from tiny six inches to massive Mac
monitors. There were computers and drives of every
vintage, some looking as if they were old enough to
be props in *2001: A Space Odyssey* (another film
Paul insisted was a masterpiece; I quite liked the
furnishings).

Jordan sat down in a leather chair that had seen better days and stabbed at a keyboard. I could see that Swincoe's little hard drive was plugged into the side of it. The screen came alive as Jordan's good hand danced over the keys.

'This is what's on the drive,' he said.

It was blank.

Nothing but white. It was the sort of image Asparov would probably pay a million dollars for if you told him it was Robert Ryman.

'It's empty?' I asked, disappointment in my voice.

'What were you expecting?' Jordan asked.

'I don't know. Some sort of virus?'

Jordan glanced at his dad. 'It's a multi-layered hypodrive.'

'Like in *Star Trek*?' I asked, still gliding on Paul's coat tails. I was wishing I'd paid more attention to his fanboy ramblings.

'That's hyperdrive,' Jordan corrected.

'Jordan,' admonished Jack. 'We can't all be Kevin Mitnick, can we?'

I nodded sagely, as if I knew what that meant.

'A hypodrive will act like a normal drive. This, for instance, has enough memory to copy a hefty hard drive. Which will show up on this screen.' He tapped the monitor with a knuckle. 'If you let it, that is. But as it copies, it injects data into the computer at a deep level. Like a hypodermic syringe.'

So it was like a virus, I thought, at least as I understood it, but I kept quiet. 'Such as?'

'What we are seeing here is only the ground floor of the drive. There is a basement level. At least one, maybe two, but I've only got one.'

'What's on that?' I asked.

'You sure you want to see?'

'I'm sure,' I lied.

'There is no visible way to access this layer, but usually there are ghost buttons. Ones you can't see, but if you drag the cursor over them, it changes shape. Like here. And here.' He moved the cursor to the bottom left- and bottom right-hand corners. 'You have to click them in a sequence of three – left, right, left. Like ...' He looked at me. 'Are you ready?'

I took a breath. 'Go ahead.'

'Like this. It starts the slide show.'

I might have lasted thirty seconds. I'm not sure it was that long. But it felt like an eternity before I walked quickly outside and threw up that old sandwich all over Jack's tarmac.

Jess asks if she and Laura can go out for Wagamama and a movie.

I looked at the text on the tiny Nokia screen for an age before the words made sense. It was like my cognitive skills had come free from their mooring and were spinning down some river wild towards a massive waterfall. I was partially looking forward to the oblivion when I went over the edge. Anything to stop those computer images flashing into my mind. No matter how high and how tough I built the barricades, they found a way through.

No, I replied to Nina. *Please keep her in the house.*

There was a long pause before the reply came. *Too late. Sorry. It's only down the road.*

Jack came out with a second beer. It was getting dark now and tiny flies and the odd moth were clustering around the external lights. I could see at least one bat dancing through the beam out of the dusk, gorging on insects. I rinsed my mouth with the beer and spat. Then took a proper hit.

'They're fake,' I said.

'Of course they're fake,' he said. 'Jordan reckons he can prove it pretty quickly.'

'My own daughter. Fuck's sake, Jack, do you really think—?'

I was getting screechy and he grabbed my bicep and squeezed. It was like his fingers were iron in my flesh. 'Hold it together.'

I thought about lighting up again, felt the familiar snake writhe in my stomach, but I killed it stone dead.

'Someone is setting you up. You, Jess and that other little girl. Who is the man in the photos?'

'Mr Sharif. If I'm a patsy, so is he. But it's not about who is the patsy, is it? The question is: why? Why do *that*?'

Jack nodded. 'When I was a copper—'

'Hold the phone,' I said in genuine surprise. 'When you were a what?'

'A copper. Plod, you know. This was a long time ago, mind. More *Dixon of Dock Green* than *The Sweeney*.'

I didn't think it was polite to ask who *Dixon of Dock Green* was or to point out that *The Sweeney* was hardly contemporary. Jess pulled that sort of when-dinosaurs-roamed-the-earth stunt on me all the time. Just the thought of her name caused a spasm in my stomach. I'd call her, soon, but first I had to get everything straight in my head.

'So what happened?'

'Look, back then, the police was more bent than the crims. Straight up. We took backhanders off pimps and thieves, you went to Soho, free shag if you showed your warrant card. The Flying Squad, most of them was on retainers from the likes of the Adamses and the Richardsons. Real villains, not clowns like the Krays. So I resigned. Went in and told my Super. He asked: "Why are you resigning, exactly?" I said I was appalled by the endemic corruption. Except I didn't know what the word endemic meant then. I might have said total. The bloke looked at me and said: "We'll put down dissatisfied with pay and conditions." After that, I thought, well, whatever I do on this side of the thin blue line is no worse than what they're doing over on that side. Why am I telling you this?'

'You said, and I quote: "When I was a copper" dot, dot, dot.'

'Oh yeah. We always used to say, take it from the top. Go back to the very beginning. Because somewhere along the way, you took a fork in the road you didn't mean to. Know what I mean? Come inside, cup of tea, hot toddy, whatever, and tell me and Jordan everything.'

I nodded. 'Just don't interrupt.'

'Quiet as the grave.'

It took close to an hour, give or take, and while I drank coffee with a splash of whisky and Jack did another beer, I went through everything from the day when I first heard of Asparov and Sharif. It was difficult to remain dispassionate, but I think I did well enough weaving the threads together, even if I did feel like punching a wall. Jess? Why involve Jess in this scheme? I pulled out the mobile and dialled, desperate to speak to her. Voicemail. I remembered she was most likely at the movies or in the concrete shell of a noodle place. I left a message that probably sounded like I'd gone slightly insane. I tried Nina. Same thing. Shit. Mobile phones are fabulous, clever inventions.

When they do what they are meant to do. Which is everything except phone calls, it seems.

'Do you still have that phone they gave you?' Jordan asked when I had finished.

'No.'

'Good. Because chances are it has been recording every email, text and phone call.'

'Jesus. I can't keep up with this.'

Jordan gave a knowing smile. 'Nobody over twenty-five can. Two more years, I'll be struggling. You have another phone?'

I handed over the Nokia and Asparov's phone, the one that Elliott had given me. Jordan plugged it into his computer and spent five minutes peering at the screen.

'The Nokia is an antique, nothing to worry about. This one is just a regular phone with some fancy Bluetooth stuff on it. I've disabled the remote switching – nobody can hijack it or trace it.'

'Thanks.' I took a shaky breath. 'OK, let's talk about the elephant in the room,' I said when he handed the phone back. 'They have photographs of ... stuff they want to load into Sharif's computer. Pictures of Nuzha with her dad. And her dad with me. All manipulated. But why?'

I considered my own question for a moment.

'Perhaps—' began Jack.

'Shut up,' I snapped. 'Sorry. Almost there. I think.'

He managed to keep quiet for the best part of a

minute. 'Who is this Swincoe really? If he's not a spook?'

'Freddie is on that. Took her a while to remember his surname. Coates. Simon Coates.'

'Working for?'

I could only shrug at that. 'There was nothing on any search engine we could find.'

'It's pretty vile,' said Jack. 'What they have done.'

I didn't need reminding.

'And consider this. With a clear head. Could any of them be real? Not the ones with you in, obviously. The others.'

I forced myself to think back. There were images of me, apparently delivering Nuzha and Jess to Mr Sharif. Images of me watching while ...

'No. Fuck, no.' I hoped that wasn't optimism speaking, just logic and instinct.

'So, deep breath, here you go. You have already posed the question. It is the only one that matters right now: why? Why the fuck take photos of you and this little girl—'

'Nuzha. And Jess.' I felt a fury rising and managed to park it. It would be useful, perhaps, later. But such anger really does cloud your vision. And I needed 20/20 right now.

'And create *these* kind of images from them?' The distaste in his voice was riper than sloppy Camembert. I knew how he felt.

However, fearing that my base nature will one day shine through, they have a proviso that I can be removed if I ever bring disgrace on the family.

'Jesus,' I muttered.

'What?'

'It's a coup,' I said. 'An attempt to stain Sharif's character so deeply he'll lose his company.'

'With fake photos?'

'But some people will always think there's no smoke without fire.'

'But your daughter? And you? Why?'

I found it difficult to speak for a second, to voice what I was thinking. I waited until some saliva came back into my parched mouth, and tried not to shout. 'A white girl. Muslim men abusing white girls. It's a brilliant way to get it splashed all over the *Mail* and the *Express*. All Swincoe has to do is tip off child protection. They find those images. Nuzha is taken into care. Sharif arrested ... hysteria in the press. *Newsnight. Question Time.* Radio Four. It wouldn't wait until there was a trial. He'd never come back from it. Not over there in Pakistan. It's all about honour and disgrace and shame.' I clicked my fingers. 'That's why ... Oh, Jesus.'

I was on my feet. 'They might not need those images. I've handed them the best weapon yet.'

'Where you going?'

'Back to the mosque.'

I was halfway out of the hangar before I turned. 'Jack. One last favour.'

'What?'

'You haven't got a gun lying around, have you?'

THIRTY-SEVEN

I was ten minutes down the road when I figured out I was being followed. I glanced at the sat nav on the Cayman's dashboard and deviated, taking a sharp left onto a country lane. If I wasn't trying to shake them, I would have carried straight on for the A40. There wasn't a whole lot down Marker's Way. Nevertheless, those headlights swung after me. I hadn't clocked a tail up on the way to Jack's, but that didn't mean much. The storm raging in my brain meant my capabilities were blunted. Now I had to forget what I had seen on that hard drive and address the current situation.

I punched in the Sharifs' number. It was Ali who picked up. 'Ali, it's me. I am going to give you some instructions, I want you to take them seriously. I wouldn't do this unless there was a credible Red Level threat.'

'A threat? Who to?'

'All of you. You have to get your Principal and family off the radar and lay low.'

The Cayman drifted, coming out of the bend a little ragged. I corrected with a snatch at the wheel and it responded beautifully. I looked at the map again. The lane was going into a series of sinuous curves. I peered at the lights glaring in my mirror, wondered what the guy behind was driving. Could I push him into a mistake?

'Get them out of there, somewhere safe. They'll be coming for Nuzha and Mr Sharif.'

'Who will?'

'The police. He's being set up. Mr Sharif.'

'You're certain?'

'On my daughter's life.' That seemed to convince him. 'And Ali, get everyone's phone and computers professionally scanned for hidden files. Just in case. You got somewhere you can go for now?' Of course he had. As if someone like the Sharifs only had one home.

'Yes.'

He probably wouldn't blurt out anything anyway, but just in case I reminded him. 'Don't tell me where. If the police come for me, I want to be able to say hand on heart, I don't know where you are.'

'What's going on?'

'It's just business, Ali. Someone wants the business.'

I heard a growling noise down the line. It was more beast than man.

'Put Mrs Sharif on, can you?'

It was a few moments before she picked up the handset. 'Hello?'

'Mrs Sharif, it's me. Ali is going to ask you to do something, no questions asked. I'd be grateful if you could do exactly what he says. Now, answer me this. Does he know?'

'Who?'

'Your husband. Does he know who is in Bounds Green? Don't ask me how or why I know, just tell me.'

'That he is alive, yes. That I visit? That he is in this country? No.'

'Can you call him? Your son?'

A pause.

'It's an emergency. Life and death.'

'Then, yes, of course.'

'Tell him to wait there, indoors, until I get there. Which flat is it?'

'Three. Is Asma in danger?'

It wasn't the time to mince words. I was hoping a little profanity rather than politeness might hammer home the point. 'You all are. Someone, maybe your family, maybe Mr Sharif's family, are out to fuck you all. Do what Ali says. Now. Without question. There is a shit-storm heading your way.'

I must have sounded convincing. 'Very well.'

'And Mrs Sharif?'

'Yes?'

'What did you just say your son's name was?'

'She's called Asma.'

*

I tried Freddie, to see if she could get over to Asma's any faster than I could, but the number was engaged. I hoped she wasn't busy fucking Flipper. And she was meant to have sent me some image files over of Matt. I felt a flash of irritation at that, but let it go. Matt could wait. So could calling Nina. Jess was safe there. Only I knew where she was. Right now I had a pair of head-lights in the rear-view mirror I had to lose. I tossed the phone onto the passenger seat and concentrated.

I was way off course now. The voice guidance was telling me to make a U-turn, I think. He was telling me in Russian, so I ignored it. I used the paddles to drop a gear and pressed the pedal. I felt a pressure in my back as the Porsche accelerated into the bend. A jab on the brakes. Correct. Back on the gas. On another occasion I might have laughed out loud at how she barely twitched. Bugger the back-endy 911, give me a Cayman GTS any time, even if it does look like a hairdresser's car.

Above the unmistakable low growl of my boxer engine I could hear another noise, that of a bigger, heavier engine behind. I couldn't quite make out what it was – there were no street lamps – but it was a saloon-y type car, but with some poke. A Jag or an Audi maybe. I was sure I had the legs of him, but all he had to do was stay close.

I banged the wheel in frustration. I had given them Asma. I had told Swincoe I thought Mrs Sharif was visiting a mosque, when she was secretly meeting her transgender son. There was no doubt they were related – they looked almost identical. They had told the family he had died in a climbing accident rather than reveal the truth, that the one son Sharif had had turned out to be 'special'. That was enough to bring disgrace on the family. Enough for him to lose his company. They didn't need those images on the computer drive now.

The lights behind flashed me a quick semaphore, asking me to pull over. Yeah, right.

I was coming up to an A-road that would take me onto a dual carriageway. I ran my fingers over the buttons on the fascia and found the traction control. I turned it off. I instantly felt the Cayman start to dance a little more, as if the tempo of the music had changed. Now I needed both hands on the wheel as I negotiated the turns, correcting with a series of tiny jerks. It felt like the original car's wicked sister.

As we came out onto the A-road I prayed this sleepy part of Bucks was mostly watching Saturday-night TV. I reached inside my jacket and pulled out the Eickhorn knife and jammed it between seat and console. I then placed one hand on top of the wheel, one on the bottom. It allows a big 'bite' – maximum turn – in one swift movement.

As I came onto the main road I accelerated into it, stomped the brake, spun the wheel and hoped the fact that the engine is at the rear in a Cayman would do most of the work. Freed from the computer nannying, the back broke away and I heard the tyres squeal as they scrubbed on the asphalt. My head jerked and banged the side window as I came round, but I had done enough to be facing the pursuer. Back on the throttle, right into him, favouring the left side.

Hidden gas cartridges triggered the front air bags as the front end of the Jag bent and splintered with a sickening noise. The one from the steering wheel exploded over me. I stabbed it with the knife even as it tried to swallow my face – you relax into the impact, not brace yourself – and it collapsed like overblown gum. I poked at the passenger-side bag and it too deflated with a sigh of disappointment.

Steam from the other car's radiator clouded the night air between us. I hoped mine hadn't gone too. In the Cayman it is offset on the right-hand side. Even if it had gone, most of my important mechanicals were at the rear, so they were probably OK. Time to find out. I cut away the remnants of the airbag, selected reverse and pulled back none too gently. Debris flew up, body panels screeched, but I felt myself come free.

Warning lights flashed at me, telling me the airbag had been deployed. Thanks for that, as if I hadn't noticed. I spun the wheel and floored it. The Cayman tramped a little, then the back tyres gripped, the power went to the road and I was away. I put traction control back on. I wiggled the wheel back and forth, checking no steering rods had been bent. Another warning light came on. I ignored it. I still had two headlamps, but one of them appeared to be scanning the sky for enemy aircraft. I'd pull over soon and try and make the front more presentable, or at least less nickable by any traffic cop. Cosmetics weren't really my worry. She just had to get me back to London and then one day soon I'd be calling Mr Asparov to explain that he had a gap in his rotating car cassette.

One glance in the mirror as the road swept to the left, towards the soft glow in the sky that marked the capital, and what was left of my tail was lost to the night. Was the other driver OK? Like I gave a fuck.

THIRTY-EIGHT

When, a million years ago, I had been doing a security check on Martyn, Gemma's transvestite advisor, I had discovered that the whole gender issue subject was incredibly complex. Martyn was a straightforward – if one could use that phrase – transvestite. He liked wearing women's clothes, hair, make-up and shoes. What he didn't want was a male partner. He was happily heterosexual in most ways. But beyond that, things got a little confusing for me. There were those who felt like they had been imprisoned in a body moulded to the wrong sex. They took more extreme steps than Martyn – growth hormones to produce breasts, for example – but initially I could never quite figure out if they wanted sex with a man. Then I was given a defin-itive answer: 'It varies.' And that was what I learned by dipping a toe in those murky waters. It varies, in every combination you can possibly think of.

Exactly where Asma fitted into the continuum, I had no idea. He – she, she, I reminded myself – was very slight, smaller than her mother, and just as striking looking. But whether it was all superficial exterior work or if she had gone for more substantial re-engineering it had been impossible to tell from the glimpse Freddie and I had had of her.

I pondered all this as I emerged from the Uber at Bounds Green. The Cayman had given up the ghost on the North Circular and I had left it in a self-storage unit's car park. It was just as well, it was far too conspicuous now, orange and totally buggered up. I got the driver to drop me at the far end of the road from the mosque and Asma's flat.

I tried Freddie again as I walked along the street. This time she picked up.

'Where've you been?' I asked.

'Here,' she said. 'I texted you. And sent you those photo files.'

'I had to ditch my phone,' I confessed. 'Compromised. And the Nokia can't handle photos. I'll text you a new number.'

'Where are you now?'

'Picking up ...' I paused mid-stride when I saw the car, then remembered myself and carried on. Don't look surprised. It was a white Range Rover Evoque that crawled by, a diamond in the rough in this part of the world. I watched it cruise past the mosque and make a left.

'You there?'

'Yes,' I said. 'I'll call you later and fill you in on everything.'

'Do you need me?'

'I don't know. Can you keep your phone with you?'

'Where are you now?' she asked once more.

'I'm taking Asma, that's the son ... er, daughter we saw. I'm taking him, her, to the Russian safe house. I'll get a cab. I'll figure out what to do from there. If I need you, I'll whistle.'

'OK.'

'And Freddie, do you know where you can get a BB?' Back in our army days a BB was a bang-bang, a gun. Jack hadn't been able to help apart from an unwieldy shotgun they used for shooting rabbits.

I heard her blow out her cheeks. I was clearly asking for the moon. 'Dunno. I'll make some calls.'

'Thanks.'

'You think you'll need one?'

I was level with the flat now, and I pressed the bell. 'Honestly? I have no idea.'

The battered silver box on the wall made a buzzing sound. 'Yes?'

'Asma. I'm a friend of your mother's. And your father's.'

The buzzing stopped.

'Hello? Asma.'

I heard a sweet car engine purring behind me and I glanced over my shoulder. The Evoque, still prowling.

I checked for the knife in my jacket, stood back, and kicked the door lock, splintering the jamb. I didn't have time to argue with some paranoid trannie over an Entryphone.

I was hit by the rancid smell of multiple-occupancy housing, the aroma of dope mixing with cabbage, curry and damp. Flat three was on the second floor, and I stabbed the blade where the Yale lock met the woodwork, and felt the catch go. My shoulder did the rest.

'Asma, I am here to help.'

Asma thanked me by stepping out from the kitchen into the hall, raising a Colt .45 and shooting me in the face at point-blank range.

THIRTY-NINE

Christ, it hurt. You know how in the movies someone gets shot, they roll behind a crate, light a cigarette and say, 'It's just a flesh wound'? There's no such thing as a flesh wound from a .45 bullet. It burrows into muscle and cartilage, bursts veins, capillaries, arteries, and when it hits bone, the whole shaft becomes crazy paving. Then there is the shock, fast and debilitating. You get shot by a big round like that, you generally just wait for the next one to finish you off, rather than make some quip through the cigarette smoke.

I know this because I caught a bullet. In Iraq. I still have the scar, just above my right hip. Freddie dragged me to safety, saved my life. So in the second I realised what had happened in that hallway I felt a burst of relief that masked the pain in my cheek. Asma was holding a Colt .45 all right, but one of the .177 gas air pistols made in Germany under licence from Colt. Same size, same shape, same weight, just lacking the original's firepower. Thankfully.

I was on her in a second and wrestled it from her grip. I had half a mind to backhand her with it, but she was whimpering already. 'You could've had my eye out,' I yelled. 'Now, listen, you are blown. Blown. You understand?' I gripped her shoulders and shook. 'I need to get you to safety. Otherwise you'll be used to hurt your mother and father. She must have told you I was coming.'

'But she also said that some men might come to get me.'

I touched my damaged cheek. 'Do I look like a man?' Maybe this was what they meant by gender confusion.

'I'm sorry. I was frightened.'

I heard footsteps on the stairs, a sharp rat-a-tat. 'Is there another way out?'

She indicated one of the bedrooms behind her. 'Fire escape.'

'Get onto it.'

I walked back down the hallway, forcing myself not to touch my face until I had a mirror and tweezers, but I could feel blood running down my cheek. The left side of my face was throbbing, too. Those air pistols pack enough punch to crack bone.

I saw his shadow from the feeble landing light, judged the distance, stepped out and grabbed his throat. I had him back inside in a second, the Colt shoved up under his chin. You have to know guns to know the fake. I was guessing this young man didn't.

'Who the fuck are you?'

The noise he made was horrible. But then I realised I had forced the barrel almost into his buccal cavity. I backed off a little and asked again.

'I came to see if Asma was all right. Someone ... someone broke down the front door.'

'That was me,' I confessed. I took a step away to look at him. Black curly hair, beard, dark skin, more than twenty, less than twenty-five. 'Name?' I demanded.

I still had the gun pointed at him, so he said: 'Okan. We own the shop ...' His eyes moved in the direction of the all-night grocery store next to the mosque. In fact, I'd seen him serving drinks outside the shop at Friday prayers. I figured he was on the level. 'Is she all right?'

'She will be.' I wondered if he knew that she was originally a he. It wasn't important. 'You want to help, Okan? To help Asma?'

He nodded.

'You have a car?'

He nodded again. 'At the back of the shop.'

'Keys?'

He tapped the pocket of his jacket and I dug in there. 'What is it?'

'Toyota Corolla.' Good – anonymous, boring. 'Will I get it back?'

'Of course,' I said, not knowing the truth of that. My track record that day wasn't promising. 'Now go back downstairs. There's a white Range Rover Evoque hanging around. If anyone from it asks, you saw Asma leave in a yellow Porsche Cayman. OK?'

The kid nodded, his curls shaking as he did so, but his eyes told me that it hadn't gone in. I gave his face a light slap. 'Look, pay attention. Yellow Porsche Cayman, heading north. Bit banged up, but driveable. Got that?'

'Yes.'

'Thank you. And Asma will thank you.'

I dropped the gun in one of the outer pockets of my jacket. The bulk against my hip felt oddly reassuring, even though it was a phoney. 'Call the police if you want.' I'd probably have to deal with them sooner or later. 'But give us a head start, OK? She'll be safer where I'm taking her.'

I ran to the rear of the flat, into the bedroom. A sash window was open, curtains billowing, and, as promised, when I stuck my head out in the night breeze there was a metal staircase. There was just no sign of Asma.

And then someone else voiced my thought.

'Where the fuck is she?'

You'd think, being in the army, you'd get used to having guns pointing at you. But ours wasn't a particularly close-up war. There were no stand-offs. You heard, rather than saw, guns. The distinctive thud of an AK or the chatter of a Type 8 machine gun. Then there were the sniper rifles, the ones where, thanks to some supersonic distortion, you heard the whine of the bullet passing you before you heard the thump of it leaving the barrel. They said, if you heard that latter noise, they'd missed. If you didn't ...

So, very rarely have I been in a situation where someone had a pistol levelled at me, and here I was, twice in one day. Except this time, it was Lawrence, Swincoe's coiffured sidekick, who was threatening me. And his pistol was the genuine article.

Glock 17, I noted. The Generation 4. Nice. Except when it's heading your way.

The thing is, no matter how much you tell yourself you'll be brave, that they'll never pull the trigger, that you can handle it, talk your way out of the situation, staring down that little 9mm hole and knowing what one bullet – let alone the seventeen the mag holds – can do has a way of scaring the shit out of you.

So my mouth was dry when I spoke. 'I have no idea.'

'What happened to your face?'

He asked with what sounded like genuine concern.

'I cut myself shaving.' I wish I could stop that.

Lawrence thought that was funny, in the context. 'Is she out there?'

'Asma? No.'

'Pity. Because if we don't go with Asma, we'll go ahead and publish the pictures. Give her up and you'll

373

save yourself, and your little girl, an awful lot of embarrassment.'

'You are a sick fuck.' I was understating the case, but I couldn't afford to let the red mist I could see building in front of my eyes cloud my judgement.

'Jesus, why didn't you just do what you were meant to? Not up to speed on tech, we were told. Didn't know a hard drive from a hard-on. Just wind her up and off she'll go, for Queen and Country.'

'But you're not, are you? Queen and Country. You aren't MI5. Not you, not Swincoe.'

He ignored that. He waved the pistol a little to indicate the flat. 'You aren't hiding her in here then?'

'Nope,' I said. 'She's gone.'

He tutted. 'I'm going to have to take you to Swincoe. See what we can salvage. Jesus. You know, we hadn't clocked this she-male freak. No idea. If we'd known, we could have just gone with that. Sure you don't know where she is heading?'

I shook my head. 'Not a clue.'

Lawrence put his head to one side and some stray hairs flopped over his forehead. 'You know, I thought, that day in the church, I thought I could quite fancy you. Bit of older cunt. I reckon I could have had you. The gallant knight rescuing the damsel in distress. I'd still do you.'

'Shoot me now. It'd probably be more fun.' I cursed my big mouth again, but he chortled once more.

'Come on, we're going downstairs.'

'Nope. Not going anywhere.'

'I will shoot you. In the arm if I have to. In the leg, although you'll have trouble on the stairs. Come on, why are you acting like a bloody martyr? It's just a bunch of Pakis fighting among themselves. What do you care? It's *business*. Not ISIS or ISIL or Blade of buggery Islam. One part of the family want to fuck the other part without getting their hands dirty. As they said to us, ten years ago they'd have just assassinated him.'

'I'm sure he's very relieved.'

'Mind you, they'll probably kill the freak when they get hold of it.'

'Her name is Asma.'

'Whatever. Why are you being so stubborn?'

Protect the Principal, I thought. If Swincoe was on The Circuit, he was on the other one, the one they usually classify as mercenaries. Guns for hire. Moral compunction not required.

'It's the job,' I said.

His eyes flicked down to my jacket pocket. I saw a shadow of concern cross his face. 'You carrying?'

I made a little noncommittal tightening of my lips.

'You are. Fuckin' hell.'

'Now would be a good time.'

'For what?' Lawrence asked.

'I wasn't talking to you.'

The blade sliced through the muscle of the upper arm, emerging streaked with Lawrence's blood. It was a smart choice of impact point. It wasn't going to kill him – that was too much to ask – but the bicep automatically contracted, the gun pointed to the ceiling and went off. The boom was like a punch to my skull but the bullet buried itself in the ceiling, sending down a flurry of plaster.

Lawrence screamed as the knife was yanked out. I knocked his gun hand aside, then pulled my own pistol out. 'Yup, I'm carrying.' And I slammed it across his young, unmarked face as hard as I could.

'Fuck.' Okan had gone quite pale. He still had the wicked boning knife in his hand. Blood was dripping off the tip onto the carpet, but it was so stained, a few more blotches wouldn't matter. 'That must have hurt.'

'Let's hope so.' But he wasn't feeling it now. He was a heap on the floor. And now I had a Glock 17. Ho, ho, ho. God moves in mysterious ways.

'Do you know where she is?'

'In the shop. Hiding in the meat store.'

'I am on her side,' I said.

'Yeah, I heard.'

I took the knife and wiped it on Lawrence's hoodie. As I handed it back I asked: 'How did you know you'd need that for him?'

'I didn't. It was meant for you.'

My turn to laugh. I had to admire his spunk,

because he didn't know the Colt was a replica. Yet he was willing to come and tackle me with that blade snatched from the kitchen next door. 'Okan, I am a professional bodyguard.'

He looked down at the crumpled form of Lawrence. I'd have to tie him up before we left. 'No shit.'

'And I will take Asma to somewhere safe from those who would harm her.'

More nodding ensued. 'I believe you. I do.'

'Good. One more thing.'

'What?'

'Does your shop sell matches?' Not for a cigarette. I was done with them for the moment. They can tie up your hands at inconvenient moments. And I wanted to be as hands-free as possible.

He nodded and pointed to my cheek. 'And plasters.'

FORTY

'He doesn't know, does he?'

'My father?'

'Okan.'

'About me?' Asma shook her head – I was beginning to get the right pronoun fixed in my head – as she slowed for traffic on the North Circular. We were taking a roundabout route to The Bishops Avenue. I had found the Evoque parked up with someone in it. Fortunately they were playing some godawful EDM shit, and it was easy to sneak up and jam broken matchsticks into the air valves of the two rear tyres – thank God they weren't run-flats – to bleed out the air, an old trick Jack had taught me. I could have stabbed a blade into them, but there are sensors for rapid decompression – such as a blowout – that trigger dashboard alarms. There are too many bloody computers in cars these days.

I reckoned the Evoque would be out of action for a while, but still, I wanted to keep my eyes peeled in case there had been back-up. That was why Asma was driving. Not particularly well, but it meant I could get in the occasional 360.

'Stay left, we are coming off here.'

'His family are Turkish. They have similar attitudes to my family. Better dead than trans.'

'But he's sweet on you?'

She turned those big doe-eyes on me and, unconsciously I'm sure, batted her eyelids. 'He's just a friend.'

'That's some friend who stabs a guy holding a gun for you. Greater love has no man that he should put a knife through someone. He's sweet on you.'

Asma let out a little giggle, that was almost feminine, just pitched slightly too high.

My phone pinged. Freddie, reminding me to give her a new number to send the images to. I texted her the one for the Sharif handset and I asked her to make sure they were compressed. *Look at me*, I thought. *A dodgy hard drive, some hacked phones and suddenly I'm a regular Steve Jobs.*

'Want to tell me about it?' I asked.

'About what?'

'Everything. How we got here. How you got here. Just get past this van here.' It wasn't promising any trouble, but it was obscuring too much of the road.

The Corolla clanked forward. Mechanically it was a piece of junk, but Okan had had it resprayed in a metallic gold, with red flames emblazoned along the side. I was hoping for inconspicuous. I was saddled with a prop from *The Fast and the Furious*. Still, the upside was, it was so ridiculous nobody would think a PPO worth her SIA accreditation would be in it. Hiding in plain sight, I think it's called.

'It started when I was twelve. I began stealing clothing from my mother, my aunties. I had a hoard of them under my bed. Sometimes, late at night, I would experiment with make-up. By the time I was fourteen, I was beginning to sneak out when I was dressed.'

'Dressed?'

'You know. Looking like this. Only not as good.' She smiled at the memory. 'My idea of make-up then made me look like an Andy Warhol painting.'

'Right at the lights.' Home run. No sign of anyone with an interest in a rocket-logo'd Toyota. It was beginning to rain, which would make us even more invisible. People concentrated on their driving more when it rained at night. 'Keep your speed down and your distance from the car in front.' Not that a sudden stop was likely with that car's brakes. I could tell they were spongier than Square Bob's pants.

'I've only been driving a few months.'

Like I couldn't tell. 'You're doing fine.' I checked my phone. Still downloading. And it was down to 15 per cent charge. I'd have to see if I could pick up a charger at the Asparovs'. I also had to think how to thank a man with more money than I could imagine. He had said I could use the house to put up a friend while they were away. He didn't know I was turning it into the Alamo.

I put the phone on the centre console and moved the Glock to my lap. 'So who discovered you?'

'School. I boarded. I had a friend who ... we gravitated to each other. We both went out one night, dressed and underage. We went to a hotel bar. Some man tried to pick us up, bought us drinks so we didn't have to go up to be served. But the barman saw us and called the police.'

'Shit.'

'I moved schools. Came here, to England. Had therapy. Didn't help. I got into trouble at a place called Dick's Dive. Soho.'

'When was this?'

'I was fifteen.' That explained it. You'd be hard put to find anywhere as colourfully named as Dick's Dive in Soho these days, not now Crossrail and chain restaurants have reduced it to a beleaguered little compound.

'When I was sixteen I came into some money. Not much. But I told them I was going to live as a woman. All the time. No more hiding. This is me from now on, I said. My father ...' She let out a sigh.

'I can imagine.'

'You'd think in this day and age, a man like him would understand. But no. He said if I did that, his

381

son was dead to him. I said he had never had a son in the first place. My mother persuaded me that there was a way forward. We would kill off Davood Sharif and invent Asma Abbas. Such things are easier in Pakistan.'

'But why Bounds Green?'

'The imam at the mosque. He offers prayers for people like me. He believes we can remain in the faith. Plus there is a clinic, nearby. For the electrolysis and injections. It is, was, only a temporary place to stay. But in Bounds Green I am unlikely to run into any of the family. Once I am fully a woman, then nobody will be any the wiser. I can be introduced as a distant relative, perhaps. But while I'm half and half, I am an embarrassment . . . as it says in the song, there's always something there to remind me.'

I laughed. I was beginning to like this . . . person.

I wasn't sure how to phrase the next question. 'So you'll go all the way?'

'Next year. I can't wait.' She looked at me. 'And before you ask, I'm not gay. It's more complicated than that.'

'I know,' I said, thinking of Martyn. *No politics, no religion and now, no gender judgements.* 'Right, turn here and we are there.'

The lights on the A1 changed to red and I looked at the phone. Freddie's pictures had downloaded. I gave a quick swipe through them. It wasn't until we were turning into the Asparovs' that I began to scream.

FORTY-ONE

'You going to keep it?'

'Shut up and pass the SwiftKlot.'

Ewan 'Tom' Jones has gone into shock, not through blood loss, although Christ knows there is enough of that, but sheer surprise at being alive. They are called 'legacy' mines, which make them sound like they come from Fortnum & Mason or Harrods, but all it means is that they were left behind by the Russians.

Around us is a group of WMIKs, the Land Rover 'Wolf' vehicles, equipped with .50 calibres. This was meant to be a simple resupp convoy to a Forward Operating Base. But before we reached the FOB we came under sustained mortar attack just outside Marjah. The air is full of the ear-bruising punch of high-calibre weapons and the whump of mortar rounds detonating.

We have dragged the wounded lad down to a ditch, and are now cleaning up the damage. He was lucky. One of his oppos took the full blast. There is nothing *we can do for that one, other than scoop up the body parts.*

I duck as rounds zip over our heads. Theirs or ours, I can't be sure. They don't discriminate when it comes to lifting the top of your skull off. I am feeling terrible. I have the squits and I hate what I have seen of Afghanistan, it's just another dust-choked country with a political situation even more confused than Iraq. After what happened with Latif, I no longer trust the locals, especially not the kandak of the Afghan National Army we are working with. Six hundred men, every one a potential Taliban sympathiser or infiltrator. My nerves were shredding.

But then again, being pregnant didn't help.

Our .50 calibres started up again. 'Where's the fuckin' CAS?' Freddie says to herself as she gets a drip into the young man's arm. He is going to live. If we can get him out of the ditch.

In a situation like this Close Air Support is essential, otherwise we could be stuck for hours.

'Man down!'

I look at the radio, then Freddie. 'My turn.'

'You can't go in your condition,' she says.

'Fuck off.' I ask for a confirmation of position and got a LOCSTAT in reply. I stick my head up. I don't need the coordinates to spot my destination. A low blockhouse about four hundred metres away. I could see the muzzle flashes from within and little puffs of

cement where the incoming rounds buried themselves in the walls.

I strap the medi-pack back on. A shower of grit breaks over us from a mortar shell. Freddie grabs her rifle. We are governed by the LOAC, the internationally accepted (apart from insurgents such as the Taliban) Law of Armed Conflict. We are medics, it says, not combat troops. We can fire in self-defence. We can engage if we think our casualties are in danger. Freddie has a broad interpretation of this – you can lay down covering and suppressing fire for a colleague and if you hit an enemy, then tough titty. I fully endorse this attitude.

As I grab the top of the trench, I can hear engines over the residual hum in my ears. I look up. Three Apache helicopters. Flame bursts from the sides of the lead one, the reassuring whoosh of the solid-fuel rocket engine reaches us later. He has let his Hellfires go. The ground shakes as the thermobaric warheads create fireballs and the ground ripples beneath my feet with the rolling detonations. Part of the ditch wall collapses. The other choppers unleash the air-to-surface missiles and the air feels alive and squirming, like it is made of invisible snakes. Spirals of black smoke climb to sully the blue sky. I suspect the atomised enemy mortars and their crews are in there somewhere.

Our casualty groans. Freddie pours some water on his lips. His eyes flicker open. 'OK, Jones. The party is over, the Apaches just toasted them. We can get you out of here now.' Freddie lifts the radio handset to order a casevac, now the chopper won't be flying into a mortar zone.

'I'll let you know what Cat the other casualty is.'

I pull myself out of the ditch, feeling suddenly naked, even though the gunfire has ceased. I begin my jog over to the bunkhouse. The pack almost unbalances me, but I hump it higher onto my shoulders. I've gone five or six steps when the bullet finds me. It really is like being hit by a truck. I am spun around almost a hundred and eighty degrees and I go down hard. I wait for the pain. It's on time. I feel like I am being branded.

Freddie drags me back into the ditch and cuts the straps of my pack. I can feel her fingers probing and I scream.

'Lucky bitch. In and out. Lie still.' She puts a clean dressing round the back so the bacteria-laden dirt can't get into the exit wound.

'Is it near ...?'

'No,' she says. 'Not unless you were planning to give birth through your waist. You're going to keep the baby.'

And I did.

FORTY-TWO

Neither phone was working. Not the Nokia, not Sharif's. Again, brilliant technology until you really, really need it, and then it decides to fuck up. I tried Nina on speed dial, then punching in the numbers manually, but I had zero coverage.

'Fuck,' I snarled. I was a hair's breadth away from smashing the damn phone on the dashboard.

'What is wrong?' asked Asma as we jerked to a halt outside the Asparovs' front door. It opened and there was the reassuring figure of Elliott, framed by a silvery light.

'Look, I've got to go. You'll be OK here.'

'What? Go where?' There was panic in her eyes at the thought of being abandoned.

Elliott gave his habitual bend at the waist. 'Welcome back, ma'am.'

'Can I use a landline?' I asked him. 'I can't get a signal.'

'There is one in the main reception room, ma'am.'

'Where's Tom? Mr Buchan?'

'Also in the main reception room.'

I shoved the Glock in my waistband – the 'Safe Action' system to prevent accidental discharge really does work – and if the sight of the gun gave Elliott pause for thought he didn't show it.

'Aren't we close to Highgate?' Asma asked as she got out of the car.

'Yeah, your parents' place is not much more than a mile away. But don't worry, nobody knows we're here. And Elliott will lock it down tight once I go. Won't you, Elliott?'

'Indeed, ma'am,' he said with just a touch of glumness. I guess he didn't sign up for hosting a ragbag of fugitives.

The house felt oddly sepulchral as we walked down the hallway, past the office where I had first been interviewed a lifetime ago, and the lift down to the gym, our footsteps echoing about the lofty ceilings. The only sign of habitation was a faint grace note of smoke, either pipe or cigar, in the air.

'Elliott, can you get Ms Sha . . .' Then I remembered myself. 'Ms Abbas something to eat?'

My own stomach rumbled – when did I last eat? A sandwich, but I tossed that onto Jack's tarmac. But more importantly I was desperate for the lavatory. Buster was back – I had to have a pee. 'Is there a loo down here?' I asked Elliott.

He pointed to a door we had just passed. 'Great. I'll catch you up.'

It was mock-Victorian, full of cutesy Pears soap ads and Dickensian drawings and came complete with a high-level cistern with a chain pull. The lighting, though, was ultra-modern bright and the mirror unforgiving. I peeled the round of plaster off my cheek and looked at the crater from which I had removed the pellet. It was going to look like I had one hell of a smallpox scar. I replaced it with another from the Elastoplast pack I had got from Okan, then, carefully placing the gun on the sink edge, sat and emptied my bladder.

When I had finished and wiped, I hitched up my jeans and put the Glock back in my waistband. I splashed water on my face and pulled my hair back. I needed something to hold it in place, but the various wall cabinets contained nothing so useful as a hairband, so I let it fall again. Still, the reflection in the mirror was marginally better now. I looked at my phone again. Still no coverage. I thought of the way I had been betrayed and, harder than intended, punched the glass. A jagged crack appeared, distorting my face. I looked like a Mr Hyde version of myself.

'Put it on the tab,' I said to my fractured face.

I bustled out of the lavatory, determined to be on my way as quickly as possible while the anger still burned within me. I could hear voices and I followed them down the hall.

I stepped into a large room clearly partly inspired by the Palace at Versailles, what with its Christmas-tree of a chandelier, elaborate plaster wall panels, enormous portraits of people you wished were your ancestors, gilded mirrors and white, embroidered sofas and padded seats. It was the sort of room that demanded you wear a periwig. As advertised, Tom Buchan was there.

I just didn't expect to find him hog-tied to one of those fancy chairs.

I scanned the room from right to left as usual, but you didn't need any formal PPO training to know what was wrong with this particular picture. Tom was strapped to the chair with gaffer tape. Asma was on a sofa, shaking. Next to her, smoking a small cheroot, was a relaxed-looking Swincoe. Not MI5, of course, but working on The Circuit. I wondered who was paying his wages. Whatever was happening, this was what we called an OTT-plot, a long-play scenario named, not for being over-the-top, although they often were, but the founder of the International Bodyguard Association, famous for his elaborate ploys. Major Lucien Victor Ott was long dead, but his penchant for deception and mischief playing lived on.

Elliott was standing to my left, as stiff as a cigar-store Indian, and I gave him a look that should have seared a hole in his forehead. He returned a small, apologetic shrug.

But it was the two men standing by the grand piano who really took the wind out of my sails, although it probably shouldn't have. After all, an OTT-plot some-times required grand deception and misdirection. And I had been misdirected all right. The pair I hoped never to see again were both smiling at my obvious shock and dismay. One Russian, one Serbian.

'Welcome back,' said Bojan.

'Please, sit down,' said Swincoe.

I looked at the phone in my hand. I needed to make that call.

'Don't bother,' said Mitval. 'The house has been numbrella'd.'

Even I knew that a numbrella was a blanketing device invented by the Israelis to prevent calls from mobile phones. The idea was to stop anyone setting off an IED by phone when its troops raided a house. I could see a regular, old-fashioned telephone on a small table close to the piano. I looked at it greedily.

'I need to call my daughter,' I said to Swincoe. 'It's not about . . . about this. It's personal. You have my word.'

'No calls,' he replied, sucking on his cheroot. 'Not now at any rate. If you will put the gun down at your feet before you sit down. Thank you.'

I did as I was told. Now Bojan came over and patted me down. He found the knife and the air pistol. He relieved me of my phones, too. He carried on with the search, paying particular attention to my breasts.

'Careful, they're programmed to explode if handled incorrectly.'

'I look forward to seeing them without all the armour on them.'

If I had been in possession of exploding tits I would happily have detonated them right there and then. 'I thought you were under arrest.'

He laughed in my face. I could smell the sweetness of alcohol. ''Fraid not.'

'And Vuk? That was a ploy?'

'No, Vuk is dead,' said Bojan with some satisfaction. 'Vuk was an arsehole. Vuk was talking about doing a deal with the ICC. He had to be got rid of. Two birds with one stone ...' The ICC was the International Criminal Court in The Hague. So Bojan needed to shut him up and Swincoe needed a way to convince me he was the real deal, an MI5 operative. What better way than to kill a man before my very eyes?

Bojan picked up the Glock and walked back, placing my entire arsenal on the closed mirror-finished lid of the piano.

'Sit,' repeated Swincoe.

I did so, trying to keep as calm as possible. I looked at Tom, but he was wise enough to keep quiet. I didn't want a man promising me it would be all right, we'd get out of here somehow. We were outnumbered, out-gunned, out-manoeuvred.

'How did you know I'd come here?'

It was Mitval who answered. 'We recognised the Porsche.'

'Very distinctive colour,' added Bojan.

'So you were tailing me from the airfield?'

'In two cars,' said Mitval. 'So your little stunt didn't inconvenience us too much. How is the Porsche?'

'A wreck,' I confessed.

'The Jaguar too,' admitted Mitval, without much irritation. I wondered if that was Asparov's too. That was quite a bill we were racking up.

'So what's the plan now?' I asked Swincoe.

'Where's Lawrence?'

'In Asma's flat.'

'Alive?'

'With what we technically call a flesh wound. I dressed it before I left. I doubt he would have done the same for me.'

'You know, you really have been so very trouble-some. Not what we were led to believe at all.'

'So Lawrence said. He seemed to think I should just walk away.'

'But you won't, will you?'

'That's not the point. The point is you can't be sure what I'd do if you let me go. Would I keep my mouth shut? Who knows?'

'She would. We both would,' said Tom, looking at me as if I had taken leave of my senses. 'You'd have my word.'

I shook my head at him. The amused look on Swincoe's face at the thought of Tom's 'word' being worth anything told me I was thinking along the right lines. Any promises we made or guarantees we tried to make were just hot air. They weren't going to let us go. Not at this stage.

'So, you're not MI5,' I said to Swincoe. 'You've been hired to disgrace the Sharif family by an outfit back in Pakistan. Right?'

'Close enough.'

'Matrix A?'

It was his turn to look surprised and possibly impressed. 'Very good.'

'Matrix A has the Pakistani Cricket Board contract,' I said to Tom. 'Cricket is a pretty corrupt game over there. Who is to say the PPOs don't get infected.' I turned back to Swincoe. 'So, the whole business with those two clowns over here was set up to make me think you were MI5.'

'It was a bit of late improvisation. When we found out someone was following you, we made it our business to find out who and why. We found Mitval and Bojan. Bojan there gave us Vuk to dispose of, you were then convinced we were after Blade of Islam.'

'And Asparov? In on it too?'

'No,' said Swincoe. 'Asparov is a man blinded by love.'

'There must be simpler ways to dislodge Sharif.'

'There is. Kill him. But we dismissed that. In the event of his death, Mrs Sharif gets control. And after that, Nuzha. The family balked at mass murder.' He sounded disappointed. 'The thing is, we can still release the computer files that you discovered. We have already recovered the drive from your friend at the airfield. It wasn't the only one, but it was inconvenient to have a duplicate in other hands.'

'Jack? And his son? Did you hurt them?'

'They saw reason,' Swincoe said softly, in a tone I found chilling.

'I need to call my daughter.'

'So you keep saying. The answer is still no.' He turned to Elliott. 'When is Asparov due back?'

'Ten days, sir.'

'That's plenty of time to bring the Sharif empire tumbling down. Especially now we have the lovely Asma.'

The girl let out a frightened sob.

'Oh, don't worry, all we need is some, shall we say, candid shots of you naked. Showing the world what a freak Sharif has for a son. Or should I say daughter? Perhaps he is Sharif's very own ladyboy.'

'I am not a ladyboy,' Asma hissed.

Swincoe gave a bemused smile. 'Have it your way.

But anyone who looks to see if *those* photos are doctored will be unpleasantly surprised.'

'And what about us?' I asked.

'Well, I've been thinking about that. Mitval here has been showing me the panic room. You two might be quite cosy in there for a week or so. Get to know each other a little better. I'm afraid we will have to disable the switch that opens the door, and the one that summons help from an outside security force, but once we've done the job … Elliott tells me there are plenty of provisions.'

There was something in the leering way he said 'get to know each other a little better' which suggested he already knew that we were more than friends. 'Did you torch the boat?' I asked. 'Tom's boat?'

'Why would I do that?'

'Because he knew the truth about how Paul died. And therefore that you were bullshitting me. And I was stupid enough to tell you about him.'

'Neverthless, it wasn't me.'

Swincoe looked over at Bojan and Mitval. They both shook their heads.

'Not us.'

I closed my eyes. If I was locked away for a week, God knows what might happen to Jess. Especially if they did release those computer files. If the authorities could find her to put her into care, that is … I needed to speak to Nina.

'Look, I really do need to call my daughter.'

'Change the bloody record, will you?' Swincoe snarled. Then he took a breath and spoke more evenly. 'I'll tell you what. We are not monsters. Write a note saying you have been called away on business for a few days and we'll make sure—'

'No!' My voice was unnaturally loud in the room and the single word seemed to hang around for an age. 'You don't understand. She'll be gone.' The thought detonated a pipe bomb going off in my chest and when I closed my eyes I felt tears squeeze out onto my cheeks. 'He'll take her.'

'Your domestic problems are no concern of ours. If you had just done your job for MI5, like you thought, none of this would have happened.'

'Fuck you,' I said, with all the feeling I could muster. 'Fuck you.'

A shrug. 'Mitval, perhaps you and Bojan can take these two to the panic room. I'll set up for the photographs of our little hermaphrodite friend here.'

'Hold on. You promised.' It was Bojan, stepping forward from his place at the piano to stand in front of Swincoe. 'Remember?'

'Promised what exactly?' But I could tell Swincoe was teasing. He knew perfectly well what the Serb meant.

Bojan looked at me. 'A return match.'

FORTY-THREE

'What sort of return match?'

'Shush.'

We had been deposited in the panic/safe room, the all-white, tasteful one that Asparov had shown me, while Bojan 'got a few things ready', whatever that meant. I was in no mood to admire the décor, the modern art or indeed listen to Tom. Only one thing was going through my mind: Jess. Jess. Jess. Jess.

And to get to Jess I had to get out of this house.

'I want to know what he is talking about,' Tom insisted.

'Don't speak to me,' I snapped. 'I have to think.'

I began at the beginning, the call summoning me back to the PPO world, through Bojan and Mitval's novel interview technique, the Sharifs, Swincoe's rescue at the church, the 'chance' meeting with Tom at the canal.

Tom.

I looked at him, opening cupboards and pulling

out drawers, trying to keep busy. Who are you, Tom Buchan, with your cock and bull stories about Albanians and why my husband was murdered? What were the odds of you pitching up along *my* canal? But I was beginning to think everyone I thought I could trust had betrayed me. All it needed was for Freddie, Nina and Jack to be hookey and I had a full set.

'What do you think happens if there is a fire in here?' he asked, rapping a knuckle on the wall.

'Those circles on the ceiling blow off as sprinklers descend. Might be foam, too. There's steel cladding, too, probably. Fireproofed. You're wasting your time thinking we can burn our way out.'

He pulled out some tinned food from a cupboard. 'We could live here for ten days, easily.'

I meant to laugh at the ludicrousness of that, but it came out as a strange honking noise. 'Look, what's happening?' he asked, coming over.

'In a few minutes a man is going to take me downstairs and beat me to a pulp. This time, he'll win. Then he is going to bring me back here. Sometime during the night the air supply to this room will be cut off. Or carbon monoxide pumped in. Then they'll arrange it like we crept in here for some kinky sex games and suffocated.'

Another thought occurred to me.

'Oh, and they'll probably throw in Asma, just to

make it kinkier. A transgender threesome. Oh dear. Ten days? We'll be lucky to have ten hours.'

Pennies dropped with a clatter. 'That's not going to happen.' He doubled up his search, rifling through the desk. 'Phone!' he said, tossing it to me.

I switched it on. Twenty per cent battery. Signal: nil. Wi-fi: not available. I pocketed it anyway. If I did get out, the first thing I'd do would be to call Nina and Jess.

'Anything else useful? Like a gun?'

Tom shook his head. He picked up a paperweight shaped like a globe and weighed it in his hand. 'I'm not going to let them take you.'

There was something about the set of his jaw that was comical. 'I think the phrase is: over your dead body. Bojan wants to do this. The last time we fought—'

'Whoa. The last time?'

'That's generally what a return bout means. A rematch.' I gave him a quick rundown on what had happened in the gym last time. 'I hurt him and I hurt his Serbian pride. Obviously part of his price for helping Swincoe in his OTT-plot was another go at me.'

'Bastard.'

'He won't kill me there and then. At least I don't think so. He just wants me to beg for mercy.'

There was something else that had slowly dawned on me. I knew exactly what they were getting ready.

Somewhere they could tie up Tom in the gym. Bojan wanted him to watch while he took me apart. I really didn't want that to happen.

Tom let rip with some fruity swear words and banged the wall. I put my head in my hands. I couldn't afford to lose it now. There might be a window, a little opportunity, and if I wasn't fully alert it might just flash by. I had to stay as sharp as I could, even with a broiling sea of panic threatening to swamp me.

I felt Tom's hand on my shoulder and looked up. 'This is all my fault,' he said.

'I don't think my naivety and stupidity are down to you.' He went to speak and I cut him short. 'Don't give me that "Trouble will find me" bollocks. Shit happens. People like Bojan and Swincoe happen and whoever wants to screw over the Sharifs happen. There's nothing you can do, not right now. Don't think of trying to jump them when they come for me. They will shoot, I am sure.' I could see a small tic working by his eye. I had to convince him not to be foolish, to quash the male pride that would spur him into action. And maybe get him killed. 'I have to get through this. For Jess's sake if nothing else.'

'What do you mean?'

I took a breath. It hurt just to say it, to visualise what I had done. 'I told you I put Freddie on to Matt, my ex?'

'To check he was bona fide, yes.'

'She finally sent through some decent pictures of his girlfriend. Matt and her kissing, walking hand in hand, arm in arm.'

'So?'

'The girlfriend in the pictures, Matt's girlfriend, is Laura. My au pair. Jess's new best friend.'

'Shit.' He let the implications of that sink in. 'Look, we have to fight back. Being passive isn't an option.'

'OK,' I said eventually, standing back up. 'Fill a jug with scalding water from the coffee machine. Put in as much sugar as you can.'

'Why?'

'The sugar sticks to the skin. Makes the scalding much worse.'

He winced, whether at the thought of the resulting burn or that I knew such horrible things I couldn't tell.

'OK.'

'Give me the paperweight.' He handed it over. 'Come on, we haven't much time.'

As Tom turned to go, I hit him as hard as I could.

FORTY-FOUR

I sometimes tell people, usually after a few drinks or when I am feeling snarky, that I joined the army so I could learn how to kill my father in unarmed combat. It's a joke. Mostly. People always assume he must have 'interfered' with me in some way. But he was no Fred West. Just a miserable little shit. The man could suck all the life out of a room just by stepping into it. Disapproval was his default mode. He made the *Daily Mail* look like the *Good News Times*. His idea of a foreign holiday was the Isle of Man, although he thought the locals a bit too progressive in their politics. Fancy giving up the birch.

It was the effect he had on my mother that I resented most. Just as he could poison the ambience of any gathering, so he siphoned every bit of joy from my mother's existence. He was a champion practitioner of negging – using negative comments to undermine women – way before the term was invented.

What he did want was a child at Oxford. This, it

seemed, was prime boasting material down at the quantity surveyors where he worked. I don't think either me or my friends were Oxbridge material. Russell Group, maybe. And he fancied a daughter who did English literature, history or philosophy. I was always more science based. I favoured medicine. He told me bluntly I had a better chance of being prime minister than a doctor.

But the more he banged on about my glorious future academic career, the more I was determined to find my own course. I was worried he might like the idea of me joining the army – after all, I'd be helping kill foreigners. But, gratifyingly, it caused a peak in his blood pressure and he went so red I swear he was in danger of stopping traffic. Not while he had breath in his body, he said.

So the army it was.

My mother died just before my wedding to Matt. It was only then, looking at her old videos, that I fully realised what he had done to her. Not so much a husband, more a parasite, like ambulatory, anthropomorphic mistletoe, living vicariously on another human being. On the earliest videos, dating back to her teen years, there were family holidays to Spain, surfing in Cornwall, music festivals – music? Who knew? – and plenty of alcohol. Then, in the later ones, when my father had appeared on the scene, even the colours seemed to darken. Within a few years of her marriage there were no more videos. What did she die of? It had said ovarian cancer on the death certificate. I reckon it was an overdose of him, poisoning her slowly, like decaying nuclear waste.

I told my father not to bother coming to the wedding.

We honeymooned in Devon. Matt got a deal on a cottage in a small village called Newton Ferrers. It was on an estuary and you could watch the tide ebb and flow, uncovering a little concrete walkway that connected Newton Ferrers to its sibling at Noss Mayo. It meant that at low water you could do a little pub crawl. Not that I was drinking.

Matt was a considerate lover. Sometimes too considerate. It was as if he had read a manual on 'How To Satisfy Your Partner In Bed'. He was forever making sure I was going to climax, and sometimes I felt like the organ at the Royal Albert Hall, his hands were all over the place, pulling out all the stops. I had him searching for the G spot, wriggling up my arse, squeezing my tits. Sometimes I tried to count just how many limbs Matt actually had. I reckon he had skipped the chapter headed 'Sometimes Women Just Want To Be Fucked'.

It was different later on in the pregnancy. Some libidinous hormone had me in its grip and when Matt said he was worried about putting his weight on my ballooning stomach, I would turn over and present, like a horny baboon. Then he found his Instant

Orgasm mode. For himself, that is. That was when I first invested in a vibrator. Not something they sell in Mothercare, but maybe they should.

And then his best friend Leo organised a week-long stag party in Ibiza. In my mind it happened almost as soon as Jessica squeezed her way out of me (although technically it was me doing the squeezing) into the birthing pool at the maternity suite. In reality, it was a couple of years later, just as we were going into the terrible twos with Jess. Parenthood and domesticity had drained us, I couldn't deny it, but there was plenty of light at the end of the tunnel. Except his light turned out to be a big flashing strobe with a four-to-the-floor soundtrack. Balearic beats and smiley faces were passé, but I couldn't get through to Matt on that score. I was a killjoy, he said. *Like father, like daughter?* I wondered. And so, frightened of turning into my dad, I cut him some slack and he ran off and broke the rope.

And now there was Laura, the cuckoo in my nest. Laura with her excellent references (possibly genuine, of course) and her empathy with Jess. And the boyfriend she met travelling. Who wasn't in New Zealand at all, but just down the road, planning to win back his daughter. Perhaps she did meet him travelling, that much might be true. Yet she was far too young for him, surely?

But then, perhaps she just played that up, with her

scrubbed face and scrunched-back hair. She could be thirty for all I knew, not even close to Jess's age.

Had Jess even self-harmed or was that just a mindfuck for me, created by Laura? Or had Laura encouraged her to do it, so that when social services came into the picture, I would be made to look like an ignorant, bad mother?

All this and more went through my mind as I trussed up Tom. It is a very thin line between knocking a man unconscious and fracturing his skull. I hoped I hadn't crossed it. But I knew the alternative was Tom playing Rambo and getting himself wounded or worse. I'd seen macho save-the-little-lady behaviour like that on the battlefield. It never ended well.

I could hear voices outside in the main office. They were here to take me downstairs. Last time, I had been able to use my anger to fuel my fight. This time, there was too much of it to harness effectively, a cacophony in my head that had to quieten down. I didn't need to be thinking about my mum, Jess, Matt, Paul, Laura, my dad or Tom, all of whom were demanding my attention.

No, I had to do this on my own.

FORTY-FIVE

'The rules are simple. Just like before. You get past me, you can go.'

Not just like before. Same location – we were back in the gym. But this time there was no audience. Mitval had brought me down at gunpoint and then asked me exactly where Lawrence and his driver were. I told him – there was no point in holding out that information – and he left to call them. The numbrella phone-masking device would probably only reach as far as the perimeter fence.

He had asked Bojan if he would be all right with me alone and Bojan had laughed, a strange, scary sound. Looking at his pupils, I wondered if he was high. Maybe that was what the short interval had been about, time for the Serb to take something that gave him an edge. That and prepare the straps that had been intended to hold Tom. They hadn't been too happy that I had cheated them of that. But it was better for me this way. Better for Tom, too. A headache – maybe even concussion – was a small price to pay for missing out on this.

'So, just you and me this time,' Bojan said.

'I don't think they'll let me go, even if I got past you. Would they?'

Bojan shrugged. 'Possibly not. But put me down and I won't try to stop you. That's one less to worry about.' He held up his hands. 'Look, no guns. That would make this meaningless. Like I said, it was round one to you. Round two . . .'

I looked beyond him to where the lift was located, tucked just out of sight. It seemed so straightforward. He followed my gaze and went into a defensive crouch. I shrugged off my jacket as quickly and as smoothly as I could, not wanting to provoke an attack while I was entangled in my sleeves. I tossed it to one side and it landed on the back of the rack of free weights.

I pulled my sweater away from my body, a move he misinterpreted.

'The titty trick won't work this time, so don't bother. They aren't that good anyway.'

Negging, even here.

He began to circle clockwise, keeping the crouch as if ready to spring forward. If we did the full half-circle, my back would be to the lift. But, as before, I'd have to turn to sprint to it. I had the feeling he wanted me to do that. The circle continued. I let the opportunity pass.

'You can make the first move, you know,' he said.

'Ladies first? How old-fashioned.'

He answered that with four fast paces forward and there was a flurry of arms in front of my face. I blocked one, two, three and then a finger hit my eye. Pain exploded around the socket and that side of the room was lost in a squall of tears. Then he had hold of my left hand and, with a squeal of glee, he bent two fingers back.

I yelled in pain but I managed a wild fist to his cheek and then he backed off.

He didn't have to tell me that the eye was for what I did to him last time. But Jesus, it hurt. I had to ignore it, because now he had switched to pacing left and then right, like a caged panther. His glare never left me.

While I blinked some use back into my left eye, I tried to analyse what he had done. I had previously recognised some of the moves from Krav Maga and they were still there. But he hadn't shown too much finesse with them last time. Bojan was a street thug and it was likely his repertoire was a grab bag of tricks, which he adapted for the situation.

I heard Colonel d'Arcy's voice in my head. 'Krav Maga is all very well, but there is a key element you should remember. The art of serendipity.'

I glanced down at my hand. It was swelling along the back, puffing up. The fingers were probably broken.

It was certainly throbbing like a big bass drum. I had to work around it. Was that serendipity? Or a fucking nuisance?

It was the kicks next, and he came in with a balletic grace that belied his body shape. There was a spin, a feint, and then a kick to my upper thigh. That leg immediately collapsed on me and I staggered to one side. A deep thumping ache spread over it. I looked at his boots. Steel toecaps. He could break my arm if he aimed properly and kicked hard enough.

One eye, one leg down. Not going well.

I wiped the sweat off my upper lip with the back of my sleeve. That was some sort of signal because he came at me with a flurry of kicks and blows to the upper body. As a toecap caught my hip with a bony crack, I leaned in as close as I dared and, ignoring the thumps to the kidneys, I slid a palm under his chin and punched with as much force as I could muster. His head snapped back and he spun away.

I'd hurt him. Just a little. I could see it in his eyes. He was breathing hard, but it was deep and controlled. Mine was panting, shallow and ragged. I filled my lungs. Normally I would have done a mental status report on my body, but it was just one big ache, with hotspots of extra intensity.

I moved around the mat, positioning myself as best I could. The next move relied on my going down. The trick would be not to stay down.

I positioned myself with my back to where my coat had landed. I feinted, bluffed, and managed a smack to his ear, just enough to make him smile at my audacity. He came at me, in close, one-two to the chest, targeting my breasts, knocking the wind out of me. I let myself fall, grabbing his head as I went back, not trying to do anything fancy, just pulling him on top of me. Despite the cushioning mat, I knew this was going to hurt and sure enough I felt as if my ribs had been squeezed in a nutcracker as I hit the ground with Bojan's full weight on top of me and his face in my tits.

I just hoped I had judged the distance correctly.

One of the doctrines of Krav Maga, so the Colonel told us, is to use anything to hand as a weapon – bottle, broom or baseball bat. None of those were available in the room, but there was a rack of free weights and my right hand scrabbled for one of those before Bojan could break entirely free.

My instinct told me to go for the heaviest I could lift, but that would be counterproductive. The angle wasn't good and there wasn't enough room for me to swing something in the eight, ten or twelve-kilo range. Instead, I chose the smallest and lightest, and brought that round with all the explosive energy I could put into it. The dumbbell was a substitute for what was known as a *yawara* stick in Japanese martial arts, where they are used to break bones, crack skulls and damage pressure points, depending on their size. I was aiming behind Bojan's ear, but a shrug of his shoulder knocked me off target and dissipated some of the force. Even so, I felt a change in the tension in his body and I pushed him to one side. As I rolled free I felt a little tug in my left side.

I got to my feet and my head swam. He arose more cautiously, a malevolent look in his eye. He rubbed his neck with his left hand. But it was what was in his right that worried me. A knife. My knife. The Eickhorn. Last seen on top of the piano.

I felt as if I had a stitch in my side and I cautiously reached around to touch the spot. I knew then that he'd stabbed me during the tussle. Not very deeply, but it had penetrated through my sweater and snagged through the ProTex bra. My fingers came away tipped with blood. The reinforced sides of the underwear had saved me from too much damage.

'That's cheating,' I said.

'You have a weapon,' he replied, pointing to the weight in my own right hand.

'Not quite the same.'

He backed away and I knew what he was expecting me to do. I could think of no alternative, so I moved to my left and scooped up my jacket. As I wrapped it around my left forearm, I tried to position it as carefully as I could. There were two things in there that might deflect a blow. One was the reinforced mesh pocket designed to hold an unsheathed knife, the other the otherwise useless telephone I had picked up in the office. I tried to make sure they were along my forearm, but with limited success. I felt like one of those fiddler crabs with asymmetrical claws as I waved the padding at Bojan. He didn't seem especially alarmed. The knife changed everything. Advantage: Bojan.

The first lunge parted the material with a shushing sound. I knew how sharp that bloody knife was. The second was clever, bypassing the jacket and coming within a centimetre of slicing open my face. I felt the wind from the blade brush my skin.

'You know the Cuckold's Grin?' Bojan asked.

'No, but I have a horrible feeling you are going to tell me.' I sounded breathless. I couldn't inflate my lungs fully without a lightning bolt running down the intercostal muscles. Maybe he'd penetrated deeper than I had initially thought. I decided not to speak any more. It would tell him far too much.

'In some countries, like Serbia, if a woman was unfaithful, the husband was allowed by village elders to make two cuts in her. Cuts that the public could see, you understand. Most men opted for here. And here.' He used the index finger of his left hand to show lines running from each corner of the mouth. 'Some made the strokes up, so the wife would always seem as if she was grinning. Hence the name of the punishment. Others went down, for the sadder option. The Cuckold's Frown. Perhaps we will go for both options.

One side up, one side down. Then you can decide which will be your best profile.'

The strike came on the final word, an old, tired trick that almost worked. I sidestepped and the knife flashed by. I pushed it away with my padding and brought down the dumbbell, but it seemed to bounce off his wrist. No knife clattered to the floor.

I heard the lift behind him whine into action. He read my mind. 'Mitval. Time to wrap this up.'

As he readied himself to spring on me, I put the jacket across my chest and charged, swinging the weight at his head. As I careered into him, the Eickhorn swept into the jacket and I felt it snag on something. The mesh, I hoped. I pulled the dumbbell across my left shoulder and brought it across his face, making lucky contact with his nose. But then I heard and felt the knife rip free. I tried to back away, but knew I simply wasn't fast enough. I was still in easy range for a thrust up into the abdomen, the lungs. I had been wrong when I said to Tom he wouldn't kill me. That was exactly what he wanted to do.

I allowed myself to lean back into the run, teetering on the edge of losing balance, almost stumbling as I came to the end of the mat. In the end, it was my height that once more saved me. I was aware of a shadow over my head and I dropped the dumbbell, reached and grabbed the pull-up bars that I had used when Mitval put me through my paces. Gripping with the left wasn't easy, but I was tall enough to hook my wrist over it, without using those damaged fingers. It wouldn't last long, but I didn't need long. I felt something tear in the gash in my side as I pulled myself off the ground, brought my legs up to my chest and straightened them as explosively as I could.

I wasn't lucky this time. Luck had nothing to do with it. I saw him twist his head away and corrected, getting him under the jawline with a satisfying crack of neck vertebrae. He caught his heels on the mat perimeter and he went down.

I let myself drop into a crouch and scooped up the weight again, waiting for the inevitable spring back up. I knew I was pretty far gone. Like that phone in my jacket, I was probably down to about 20 per cent. Little flares of pain were firing off all the way down my left side and my throat and lungs felt as if they had been blowtorched. My left hand looked as if it had been inflated with helium.

The lift pinged its arrival at the gym/pool floor. I pulled myself up to my full height, ready for one last push. But, as I had already discovered that day, everything changes when a man with a pistol comes into play.

FORTY-SIX

The Eickhorn had gone in right up to the hilt. Blood, thick and claret-coloured, welled around what was left showing of the blade. As well as the sharp tang of the blood I could smell something else, sharp and faecal. I reckoned some part of the intestine had been punctured. I fetched some of the towels and put them under Bojan's head. He was a pallid shade of grey and it was his turn for shallow and painful breathing. He looked down at the knife in his gut and said the only possible thing in the circumstances. 'Fuck.'

I glanced up at Elliott, the new arrival with the gun. He had lost his jacket and had rolled up his shirtsleeves as if he meant business. Perhaps he did, but I could tell he wasn't used to firearms. 'What happened to Swincoe?' I asked.

'He has a bump on the head.' I didn't ask the question but he answered it anyway. 'I always hated these bastards,' he muttered, indicating the wounded – possibly dying – man. 'Right from day one.'

Of course, it had been Elliott who had told Asparov what they had been up to in the gym the first time I had taken on Bojan. Perhaps he was one of the good guys.

'They had Greta locked up,' he said. Greta? He must mean Svetlana with the cheekbones. 'To keep me in line. I managed to free her . . . and here I am.'

'Good job,' I said. Although not that good. He had picked up the air pistol, not the Glock. How was he to know? The Colt looked real enough. But it was a toy, really.

'Listen, Bojan, that is a bad, bad wound. You are going to die unless I get help. I can only do that by making a call. Is there an outside line here?'

He shook his head.

'Where's the numbrella?'

'Fuck you.'

I crouched and grabbed the handle of the knife with my good hand. 'I don't have to twist this and torture you. All I have to do is pull it out. You noticed the serrated edge? Designed to cause maximum damage as you extract. I'd guess you'd bleed out in two, three minutes. If we can get a proper medical team here, you might live. But otherwise . . .'

I applied the tiniest force on the handle, moving it maybe a millimetre. He saw sense. Or maybe he saw a big black hole waiting for him. 'By the car garage, outside. Master there, two slaves either side of house. Turn off the master, you'll get a signal. Jesus.' He grimaced and said something in his native language. 'Hurry up.'

I wanted that knife, wanted it very badly, but what I was telling him was more or less the truth. There was a lot of blood now. I searched and found a pressure point that seemed to stem some of the flow. 'Elliott, you are going to have to press here. I am going to go and get my daughter. I'll make the call on the way.'

'What about the . . . what about the girl you brought? Asha, was it?'

I closed my eyes for a second. Protect the Principal. And their family.

What about my own fucking family?

'Asma,' I corrected. 'Where is she?'

'Round the corner. Holding the lift door open.'

'Isn't there a fire escape? I mean, stairs? The manual option?'

'There was, but they were bricked up when they did the mural. Mr Asparov asked who ever heard of a swimming pool catching fire?'

Fucking idiot.

'She's not in a good way,' Elliott said. 'Swincoe was rough.'

But Asma would slow me down. Get me embroiled. I needed to get to Jess. 'You'll have to look after her.'

Elliott groaned.

'Come on, she won't be any trouble.'

'Not that. That.' He nodded towards the computer

419

desk. Above it, the monitors showing the outside of the house were displaying a Range Rover Evoque parking up, and men getting out. Lawrence. Christ, and *two* other men. Reinforcements.

'If you take the lift down to the garage level, the large car elevator comes up outside the house. Then maybe you can outflank them and disable this numbrella.'

He offered me the gun. I went to reach for it, but he pulled it away. 'Take the girl with you. Don't leave her here.'

'What about you?'

'Who notices the butler? I'll take my chances. And it wasn't me who stabbed him.'

It wasn't me either. He'd stabbed himself as he fell – but I let that pass. I fetched more towels and Elliott mopped up some of the blood.

'I'll take the girl with me.'

Sorry, Jess, I promise it won't cost me too much time. I'm coming, darling. I felt a sickly stab of guilt. But, I reminded myself, I had no idea if Jess was in any immediate danger. But right here, right now, men were going to come for us.

Elliott handed the Colt over. It might just buy me some time later. Besides, it felt good. I pulled on my slashed jacket, winced as the material brushed my damaged fingers, and slipped it in the pocket. I checked the phone again, just in case. Nothing, of course. Fifteen per cent.

'You'd better hope I get through,' I said to Bojan.

He tried a smile, but it didn't quite come off. 'I'll say a little prayer.' Elliott accepted another clean towel from me. 'The code to open the panic room is 5879, hash.'

'Thanks.' I'd almost forgotten about Tom. He must have come to by now. It was probably a different kind of anguish he was going through up there. But I had enough extra bodies to fret about and I put him to the back of my mind.

I was almost turning the corner to the lift when Bojan shouted. 'Hey.'

'What?'

'You were good.'

'Yeah. I was, wasn't I?'

Asma was wearing Elliott's jacket, which came down to her knees. She looked to be naked underneath. 'You OK?' I asked.

'Why did you bring me here?' Asma half-sobbed. 'Why?'

'I thought it was safe,' I said, entering the lift.

'I hate you,' she hissed. 'I hate all of you.'

'I know. I don't blame you.' I put an arm round her. 'Let go of the doors.'

She stepped away from them and they slid shut. I hoped nobody had called the lift upstairs. I pressed G for garage, one floor down. It seemed like a lot of heartbeats before the button illuminated and the machinery began to turn.

I had only been in the garage once, when I drove the Porsche Cayman out. When we stepped into it, nothing had changed. Still the carousel of cars, the workshop area, the flashy bicycles. I ignored it all, apart from one of the bikes, which I used to make sure the lift door wouldn't close. I didn't want anyone coming down after us.

I guided Asma through the garage to the other elevator, the industrial-sized one large enough to take a car up to the ground-floor garage – located outside the house – and pressed the 'call' button.

Nothing happened.

It occurred to me after punching it three more times that I'd got us trapped.

Then the power went out.

FORTY-SEVEN

There is a man coming to hurt us. Probably more than one man. Two or three, perhaps. Not four. They won't need four to deal with us. After all, we are trapped. There is no way out from this cold, concrete shell. We are crouched in the dark, dozens of feet below ground. The power to this level has been cut. There is no phone signal. Which is mostly irrelevant because my phone is almost out of battery. What I do have is two broken fingers on my left hand and the pain is making me sweat.

I slide my good hand into my T-shirt and find the knife wound I have picked up. It is long and shallow and oozing along its length. The blade cut through the fabric and has almost severed my bra. I think that was the idea. I give it a tug. The remaining nylon and Kevlar webbing seems to be holding. It should do, it's a ProTex, standard issue for female Secret Service agents in the US who also don't want their tits falling out at inconvenient times. They cost a small fortune. Right now, it feels like money well spent.

It can't be long now. I reach out with my right arm and touch warm skin, trying to reassure, but she recoils at my touch. Asma blames me for all this. She's right. I was meant to keep her safe from harm. It's my fault we ended up down here.

In the army they told me about controlling the battle space. That firefights had to be undertaken on your own terms, not the enemy's. I had to admit, I'd lost control of the battle space. I'd lost control of everything.

SIT-REP, as we used to say, AGTOS. Situation Report: All Gone To Shit.

I can hear voices now, echoing down the enormous lift shaft that will bring the men to us. Then the whoosh of air, the ding of a bell, a muffled warning ('Doors closing'), the soft whirr of very expensive, very well-maintained machinery, with its own power supply, as the industrial-sized lift descends.

The whining of the lift has stopped. I hear a distant, disembodied woman say that the doors are opening. But it isn't on our floor. There is an intermediate one, a full-sized automatic car wash. More voices creep down the shaft, all male. A laugh. Not a very nice laugh, either, more one of disbelief at how easy this was going to be for them. And how hard it would go with me.

'Are they going to kill us?' *Asma asks from the darkness, a crack in her voice.*

'Not if I have anything to do with it.'

That, apparently, is not too reassuring, because she begins to sob, great heart-breaking catches in the throat. I pull her close. 'It'll be OK. They're only angry with me.'

I step away into the blackness.

'Don't go.' Brittle and afraid.

'I have to.'

'Where are you going?'

'To get something to fight with.'

It sounds as pathetic as it felt. My left arm is burning up now, as if someone had held a lighted candle to the fingertips and was now playing it up over my arm and forearm. It hurts enough to make my breathing dangerously shallow. I make the effort to fill my lungs, wincing as it stretched the knife wound open. I check it again. There is more blood than the last time. I need the SwiftKlot in my RTG bag. It will have to wait.

A bell pings.

'I won't be a second.'

The machinery whirrs, the cables take up the slack.

Colour: beyond Red.

I use the torch in the phone to scan the garage for car keys. Maybe one of the vehicles could be a weapon. I find the safe on the wall and guess it is probably crammed with electronic key fobs. It has a numeric keypad. My heart leaps as I remember that everyone uses the same codes, over and over again. I *punch in the numbers Elliott had given me and press hash. Nothing.*

I hammer at the safe with the butt of the Colt, but it is made of stronger stuff than the gun. The side panels on the butt splinter. The safe stares at me, imperiously. I drop the useless weapon to the floor.

I walk back towards Asma, stopping off at a work-bench. A hammer. A hammer and a long screwdriver. That is the sum total of what I have managed to find to save us. I struggle to raise the screwdriver with my left hand. Trying to make a fist, even with the good fingers, causes me to gasp. Fire shoots up my arm. I had to face it: I was single-handed in every sense of the word.

How long do I have? Seconds.

I place the hammer under my left armpit and try the phone one last time. Still useless.

The doors of the elevator part to bleed out a vertical bar of white-hot light. Within a second, the whole garage is flooded with it, and I see the blurred outline of the men within, standing in the glow like aliens in a spaceship from a sci-fi movie. Then another, unmistakable, noise.

That of a round being chambered into the barrel of a gun.

I look at the mute vehicles. Bloody technology. If only cars could be hotwired like in the old days. One-Eyed Jack taught me how to do that ... and he had told me something else ...

426

'It's like a phone app. Remote Security and Control App. You key in a code, then you can lock the car, open it, immobilise it, start it up, put the bleedin' radio on, some of them even have a "come to Daddy" feature. Or Mummy in your case.'

I scan the carousel of cars, now illuminated by the light from the elevator. There is a Ferrari on the lower tier, facing the garage doors. I scroll the phone's display until I find a car symbol. Three per cent now, please, please hold on, battery.

I see it on the second swipe. RSCA. The remote activation for cars that Jack was so disparaging about. Keyed to Bluetooth. Great, playing to my strengths. For once, I had to put my inner Luddite on hold.

I press the button and the screen gives me a log-in option.

Enter Pin. Shit. I try the 5879, hash. Nothing.

I hear Jack's voice chiding me in my head. The owner's name is the default code. I try Asparov. Nothing. The figures are moving from the garage now, cautiously in case I have a trick up my sleeve. Do I? Asma snakes her arms around me, her body rippling with fear.

Asparov 5879, hash.

Still nothing.

'I love my wife.'

He loves his wife? I try Katya 5879 and press hash. I am in.

Now a real voice, not one inside my cranium. 'Just bring us the girl. Nobody need get hurt.' Swincoe. Good.

I scroll down the list of cars on the phone display, find the Ferrari and select it. It gives me yet more bloody options. Start car, turn on radio, put on heater . . .

There it is: E-Evac. Emergency evacuation. I stab at it, twice, and for a moment I think nothing has happened. Then a click and I hear the car roar into life, a deep, primal growl.

I crouch, as if bowling, and then throw the phone underarm, so that it skids along the ground and into the lift.

Come to Mummy.

It is at that point I remember that I can't tell one Ferrari from another.

It was a Ferrari on the upper level of the spinning-wheel storage system that responded, not the one on the ground floor. Of course Asparov had more than one Ferrari. The Xenon lights flashed on to full dazzling beam, that beautiful engine screamed, and it leaped forward. I watched it in horror as it wheel-spun off its base into thin air. There seemed to be a *Loony Tunes* eternity before it crashed to the concrete with a brittle explosion of metal, glass and exotic carbon-fibre compounds. Then, those fat rear tyres gripped and it accelerated towards the elevator, fishtailing as it went.

I knew what should happen next. The auto-stop beams would detect people ahead and apply the brakes. It would buy me a little time, not much more. Except that the leap from a great height must have jarred something loose or smashed the sensors located in the front spoiler, because the Ferrari kept going, until it rammed into the rear of the elevator with another shriek of bodywork and glass, and I heard the screams over the still-revving engine.

Before I could react, the lift's sensors detected the weight of a car and it began to rise.

'*Doors closing.*'

Asma and I said nothing for a second as darkness returned, just breathed in air full of rubber and exhaust fumes. I wondered how many of the men were dead or injured in that lift. Lots, I hoped. I had to take a chance that most of the opposition had been in there and it would take time for them to recover. I had just the one way out now – the way we came in, the smaller elevator.

'Have we won?' Asma asked, as I led her back to that other lift, removed the bicycle and pressed for the ground floor. I weighed the hammer in my right hand.

'Not yet,' I said. 'But we're getting there.'

FORTY-EIGHT

'Holy fuck!'

I didn't blame Nina. If she'd turned up on my doorstep looking as I did, with a luridly damaged cheek, a bloodshot eye, broken fingers, a weeping knife wound and wearing a jacket that looked like a crazed Samurai had attacked it, I'd have said the same.

'What the hell happened?'

All I had managed to say on the phone before it finally died on me was for Nina to make sure Jess was safe. I'd left behind me chaos. I'd managed to get a perfect strike with my bowling Ferrari, breaking bones and causing massive haemorrhaging among four of the five men who were coming to take on a wounded woman and a frightened cross-gender girl. Swincoe had been among the worst injured.

I had released Tom, called police and ambulance and then helped myself to the Range Rover Evoque which had been left with keys in it. They'd be coming for me soon. The coppers. So many questions to answer. So many questions I would like answered. But I was so drained, I couldn't even formulate them.

'Can I see her?' I asked.

'Of course.'

I followed her eyes up the stairs. It looked like a mountain to climb. Nina saw my expression. 'Go and sit through there. I'll bring her down.'

'Can I have a drink?'

'There's one open on the table. Help yourself. It's the good stuff.'

It might be the good stuff, but I treated it rough, glugging out a large glass and taking an unlady-like gulp. I almost coughed half of it back up as I slumped on the squishy sofa. Nina had never gone for the modern minimalist look and she had taken advantage of the fall in the price of eighteenth- and nineteenth-century furniture to pick up some classic pieces. Not my taste, but it suited the house, which was a Victorian terrace which had avoided attention from the 'knocker-throughers' who seemed to prefer one vast impersonal room to the cosier warrens the original builders intended.

As I took my second hit of the Pomerol, I wondered how poor Tom was getting on. He was certainly furious when I finally freed him.

Would he stick around after this? I'd like him to, I realised. If he ever got around to forgiving me for slugging him with the paperweight. Perhaps he'd eventually come to the correct conclusion – that I had done it to save his life. We still had to get to the bottom of the torching of the *Slim Pickens*. If Swincoe didn't do it, maybe there really were mad-dog Albanians on his tail. My feeling was that Tom would decide that trouble had not only found him, it had pissed down his leg, drunk his booze and shagged his wife. Maybe I was the trouble in question. I certainly felt like it.

Only much later would I discover that, probably at that precise moment, Tom was staring at the body of Elliott. The butler's throat had been cut. There was no sign of Bojan, just Bojan's blood. He had lost enough to fell any other man. God alone knew what extricating the Eickhorn to murder Elliott had done to his insides. As I would later say, I should probably have used a sharpened stake through the heart on him. Next time.

The room gave a little lurch. I checked my knife wound. The bleeding had, if not stopped, then slowed. But I needed a hospital. Or a decent medic. I looked at the dead phone again. I'd use Nina's landline to call Freddie. She would come running. Best battlefield medic I ever knew. And Christ I'd been in a battlefield. And she wouldn't ask awkward questions like A&E about knife wounds. Even so, I still had a lot of explaining to the police to do. I had to get the story straight in my mind. The room did its merry-go-round trick again. I was on the edge of fainting, but I took a large breath. I just had to keep it together until I had held Jess in my arms.

The door opened and I turned to look at my daughter.

There was only Nina, her face devoid of colour, her mouth a perfect 'O' of horror. The two words she spoke were my very own sharpened stake through the heart.

'She's gone.'

EPILOGUE

I am waiting to hurt a man. I am not sure how, yet, but my RTG bag has everything in it I need to restrain him and inflict pain. Mask, tape, handcuffs, soldering iron, blowtorch, Taser, sedatives, both oral and IV, retaining straps, Sig-Sauer pistol, as supplied by One-Eyed Jack, who feels he owes me one after handing over that hard drive. But they had threatened to hurt Jordan. I understood that.

Water under the bridge.

I'll stop hurting this man when he tells me the truth, but part of me hopes he will hold out for a little while. I want him to sense just a tiny portion of the agony I have been living with for weeks now. It's not cancer, but it feels like cancer, eating me hollow. I am a husk. There's no heart, no emotion left. Just a sort of ill-focused low-level hum of anger, as if there is a hate generator somewhere within me, bleeding bile into my system.

Never mind. Hatred can be useful.

I am sitting in my car, less than a hundred metres from his home. He'll be back soon, back from his plush offices. I'll move forward as he pulls into the drive. I'll take him as he gets out of the car. I'm not worried if he sees me. I'm beyond that now.

It is two weeks since the events at the Asparovs'. A version of what happened has appeared in the newspaper. Nina would have written the most accurate one. But she couldn't bring herself to, not after what she considers her failure to protect Jess.

More water under more bridges.

I don't blame Nina. Laura and Matt would have got to Jess somehow, sometime. They had prepared the ground well and clearly decided to strike while I was otherwise engaged. Willingly or not, Jess had gone with them. That's one of many things we don't know. Did Jess jump or was she pushed? The police asked me that over and over again. No matter what happened, I always contended, it was kidnapping. Close the ports, the airports, the roads, SHUT THE FUCKING TUBE.

We didn't see eye to eye, me and the police. Not after all the other stuff I had landed on their doorsteps.

The Sharifs were grateful, though. Asma was kept out of it all, the images on the hard drive were pronounced fake. Back in Pakistan, rogue family members were purged. I was offered money, cars, my old job back at an increased salary.

There's only one thing I want in this life and it isn't in their gift.

And Tom? He's talking about buying a new boat when the insurance money on the *Slim Pickens* comes through. He hasn't said as much, but maybe he agrees that I am too much like the trouble he has been trying to avoid. I'm certainly going to be trouble for someone this evening.

Dusk has turned to a deep azure twilight, but the night is still warm. Summer is here, at last. I roll my window down and flick my cigarette butt far away from the car. Force of habit. I don't really care if anyone knows someone has been sitting in the same spot for three cigarettes'-worth. I look in the mirror at headlamps approaching from my rear, but I can tell by their height it is an SUV. The car I am waiting for is a Maserati. It belongs to Ben Harris.

I don't know yet where the bastard fits into all this. For the past week or so, from the moment the tumblers clicked into place about his initial involvement, my brain has been spitting out ideas, theories, connections, as well as random snatches of conversation I half remembered. Like, they were told I was a technical klutz. That I wouldn't ask questions.

As Lawrence had said: *'Jesus, why didn't you just do what you were meant to? Not up to speed on tech, we were told. Didn't know a hard drive from a hardon. Just wind her up and off she'll go, for Queen and Country.'*

My suspicion – no, more than that, it is a whisker away from a certainty – is that they approached Ben Harris asking for someone they could manipulate. Fragile, bereaved maybe, who was also a couple of pulses behind the beat on the latest technology. And there I am, vulnerable, wrong-footed, finding my way back again.

Just how much of it was pre-planned, I couldn't be sure. Probably some kind of sham MI5 intervention to convince me there was an Islamist element to the Sharifs, to appeal to my sense of revenge for Paul, was at the core of the plan. Did Harris have anything to do with Matt? Or was that coincidence? My money was on the latter, that my ex-husband appearing was just a random event. But I had to be sure.

And where was Bojan? Did he survive or did he bleed to death, slowly and painfully like he deserved?

I'll find out the truth soon enough. But not too soon, I hope. Dark thoughts live with me now. All my skies are cloudy, oppressive. I am not the same person I was five, six weeks ago. Good. That person couldn't do what I am about to do.

At last the Quattroporte growls by. He has it in sport mode, which gives the exhaust a more gravelly note, but does little for the performance. I've been brushing up on my supercars since the garage fiasco. I'll never confuse a California with a Testarossa ever again. I start the engine of my Golf and pull out after him. He won't notice. There'll be Verdi or Rossini in the CD player. If he looks in the rear-view mirror, it'll be to check his hair. But it's time to fess up, Mr Harris.

Tonight won't give me all the answers to my questions. Only some. Real life is too confused, too untidy to deliver me neat, bow-tied solutions, like the whereabouts of my daughter. It'll be a start, the first step on the trail. But in the long run, I know there is only one person can bring Jess back home where she belongs.

Samantha Rae Wylde.

Me.

THE HURTING KIND

a SAM WYLDE thriller coming in 2018

We are looking for a PPO to accompany our client on an extended business trip abroad.

- The successful applicant will be fully qualified in defensive driving and escape and evasion techniques (with a refresher course completed within the past two years).
- SIA accreditation and Firearms Authorised for Continental Europe essential. A licence will be issued once in France.
- The final destination will also be revealed once there, due to security considerations.
- Passport should not include any recent visits to Middle Eastern countries.
- Applicant must be available for one to two weeks of continuous travel.
- Client stipulation is for transport by land only (due to a fear of flying).
- Hours flexible, pay competitive.
- Must be ready to begin at short notice.
- Female preferred, for operational reasons.

One year on, the hate still burns in Sam Wylde. But a woman has to make a living. Even if it involves killing.